SECRETS OF THE WHOLLY GRILL

SECRETS OF THE WHOLLY GRILL

A NOVEL ABOUT CRAVINGS, BARBECUE, AND SOFTWARE

LAWRENCE G. TOWNSEND

CARROLL & GRAF PUBLISHERS
NEW YORK

SECRETS OF THE WHOLLY GRILL
A Novel about Cravings, Barbecue, and Software

Carroll & Graf Publishers
An Imprint of Avalon Publishing Group Inc.
161 William St., 16th Floor
New York, NY 10038

First Carroll & Graf edition 2002

Library of Congress Cataloging-in-Publication Data is available.

ISBN: 0-7867-0965-0

Printed in the United States of America
Distributed by Publishers Group West

To my dear friend, Lynn Duryee,
who urged me to fire this up, who tended it along the way,
and whom I could not have done without,

and

To my wife, Laura,
who feeds the flame within.

Lenny Milton trundled out to the mailbox in his quiet suburban neighborhood in San Jose. The four-foot-wide walkway to the sidewalk from the front door of his little rental house seemed to have narrowed gradually since he had moved his office into his home. Knowing it would only depress him, Lenny weighed in this morning anyway, tipping the scales at 342 pounds a new high. If he'd been a six-foot-six monster lineman for the 49ers, he might be able to justify it. Instead, at five-foot-seven, he was a monster, all right, but more of the cookie variety. The sunlight, his first of the day, bounced awkwardly off his shiny nylon drawstring pants and silky blue Hawaiian shirt—*triple* XL. Once again, he started to feel like a great big buffoon. For the thousandth time he resolved to do something about it.

Inside the mailbox, to his surprise and bewilderment, along with the usual dunning notices from credit card companies, was a large package marked PERISHABLE, bound in thickly padded white freezer wrap. Above Lenny's name and address in large red print it exclaimed:

FREE SIRLOIN TIP INSIDE!

Tantalizing strands of wispy smoke were rising up from the words *sirloin tip*. Lenny couldn't believe that somebody would be dropping a free steak in *his* mailbox. This was manna from heaven. He flipped the large package over and read on:

> FREE INTRODUCTION! As a Loyal ThinkSoft Customer, You Are
> Invited to Become a Charter User of THE WHOLLY GRILL OUTDOOR
> COOKING INFORMATION SYSTEM. A Whole New Way to Enjoy
> Everything You Love About Barbecue. FREE Flash Frozen Sirloin Tip
> Pre-Marinated in Wholly Grill Barbecue Sauce! The Only Sauce with
> Smoke Crystals . . . for a Burst of Hickory Flavor!

Instantly he was famished. He couldn't wait to fire up his trusty old Weber grill and try this newest taste sensation. He hurried into the house and tore off the outer package. A brochure in dazzling colors, featuring a state-of-the-art grill, fell out onto the kitchen table. The sirloin tip was surrounded by dry ice, bound in more white freezer wrap, and encased in clear plastic shrink-wrap. Beneath the shrink-wrap he read the notice:

> WARNING!
> BY BREAKING THE SEAL AND ACCESSING THE WHOLLY GRILL
> MARINATED MEAT, YOU AGREE THAT THE AFORESAID MEAT WILL
> BE PROMPTLY COOKED ON THE WHOLLY GRILL OUTDOOR
> COOKING INFORMATION SYSTEM ("THE SYSTEM") AND ONLY ON
> THE SYSTEM. SEE DETAILS TO LEARN HOW TO PURCHASE THE
> SYSTEM.

Lenny quickly read the brochure. The gift he received and the system he would have to purchase were from ThinkSoft's brand-new Wholly Grill division. Lenny had heard the company was making a new product announcement today. Could this be it? The latest thing from ThinkSoft! Lenny's home-office shelves were crammed with boxes of software from ThinkSoft, most of which he had received free in the mail. Having received them for free, he'd felt obliged to register as a user. Since he was registered, they sent him discount offers for software upgrades that, even if he wasn't using them, he'd ended up buying out of force of habit.

But this freebie wasn't going to require a mere software upgrade. It required the purchase of a grill with a whopping suggested retail price of $1299, and on top of that it cost another $3.95 per hour to connect the modem to a main computer that controlled its operation. He loved the idea of combining his passions for new technology and taste sensations under one hood. And he couldn't help but notice it was one helluva new gizmo. Unlike his Weber—which, now that he thought about it, produced uneven results—the black barbecue grill in the brochure, which resembled any large gas barbecue grill in size and shape, cooked with laser flames! And it was crammed with electronics—a small screen, a keyboard that pulled out from under the grill, and various ports and slots for plugging in yet-to-be-explained accessories.

"Wow!" Lenny said to himself. The glossy photos made it look tasty, too—with close-up shots of Wholly Grill Smoke Crystals, glistening on the barbecued meat, waiting to be crunched into. "For a burst of hickory flavor," it promised. That wasn't all. There was more:

Purchase the System and Get 6 Consecutive Weeks of Assorted Wholly Grill Marinated BBQ Selections Delivered to Your Door *at No Extra Charge,* Just for Registering Now as a Wholly Grill Charter Member. A $200 Value!

The brochure went on to explain that in order to make fulfillment possible on the scale of the Wholly Grill North American Launch, the infotech giant had formed a "strategic alliance" with Axco Systems, an innovating meatpacker out of Lubbock, Texas, that was "fully committed to this initiative, results-oriented, and intently focused on technology's cutting edge in the same way as ThinkSoft." That sounded like smart business to Lenny, and the steady supply of meat sure added to a great buy.

Or was it? Lenny took a deep breath and put the brochure down. He could feel himself getting caught up in the moment again. Get real, he thought to himself. His finances were in ruins. He had been forced to cut costs by moving his small insurance sales business into his home. But he'd been a big failure in controlling expenses, too, having just purchased a third computer for the business when told he needed only one, and he had bought more software than he could possibly use.

And then there were the escalating food bills. Any money saved on rent for an office had been invested in snacks. The stress of his financial pressures was certainly one of the reasons he'd been looking for solace in his refrigerator.

Maybe he should store the free sirloin tip in his freezer until all his options were fully explored. He opened the door to his upright freezer and looked in.

The businessman inside Lenny could see that the outlook for tenants in search of freezer space was disheartening. Ben & Jerry held the choice lease on the top two levels, with an option on two more. Ice cream, sherbets, and frozen yogurts, all crammed in, made them an ideal anchor tenant. The other tenants were crowded into the remaining floors: Tater Tots, Tombstone Frozen Pizza, Aunt Jemima Waffles, Sara Lee Coffee Cake, Cool Whip, a box of frozen Snickers, and a tall stack of Lean Cuisine stuffed between Farmer John Sausages and Mrs. Paul's Fish Sticks. All loyal tenants. He didn't have the heart to send even one of them packing.

He scanned the freezer one more time; there just wasn't any way to

4

scooch anything a little more to the side to make room for the free package of meat. If he broke the seal of the shrink-wrap, cut the sirloin tip in half, and put the halves in smaller, separate plastic bags, he might manage to squeeze them in somewhere. But the terms on the package said he could only break the seal if he was going to cook the meat "promptly" with a Wholly Grill System purchased from ThinkSoft. That's what it said. That was the deal. Lenny was a man who could be counted on to hold up his end of a bargain.

He heard his dog, Lady J, wander into the kitchen and stand in front of his feet, although he couldn't see her below his shirt and stomach. She was a three-year-old Chihuahua with bat ears, Dumbo-sized in proportion to the rest of her. Her snout, like a big black olive at the end of a small pointy nose, formed such a strikingly perfect triangle, she appeared to have a third eye. He swore she was an "old soul," possessing an extra sense, difficult to explain, which he loved.

Picking her up and holding her in front of the freezer, he showed Lady J the freezer predicament. "What am I going to do, girl? See anything?"

Her little nose sniffed away at the freezer; then she squirmed to be put down. He set her down on the kitchen table—a favorite spot—up high and close to the action. Whenever she'd had enough of this perch, she would jump down to the chair and then to the floor.

He was beginning to unravel, alternating between anger at ThinkSoft for putting him in this quandary and despair at his own inability to come up with a solution. The idea of tossing directly into the Dumpster some gorgeous sirloin tip, pre-marinated in the latest taste sensation, disturbed him deeply—to the very pit of his stomach. He hated to see food wasted.

He noticed Lady J on the kitchen table pushing something around with her nose, determined to make it sit still so she could lick it. He quickly figured out what it was, recalling that he had torn off some

5

leftover pork butt and eaten it on the way out to the mailbox. Lady J had found an envelope with just enough food smudges from Lenny's greasy fingers to tease her senses.

"Whatcha got there, Lady?" he asked her.

The target envelope, not surprisingly, hailed from a credit card company. Unlike the others, however, it was not a dunning notice. It was an offer of a new credit card from OmniCredit Bank of New York. He already had an OmniCredit VISA card that was delinquent over ninety days. Perhaps the OmniCredit computer had forgotten. Perhaps OmniCredit thought he would be so grateful to be issued more credit, he would want to transfer the old balance onto a new card. Regardless of the thinking of OmniCredit, an idea was taking hold in Lenny's mind: Maybe it was his destiny to purchase a Wholly Grill Outdoor Cooking Information System after all.

The envelope, auspiciously pre-smeared in Lenny's favorite pork butt sauce, heralded the good news:

PRE-APPROVED OMNICREDIT MASTERCARD!
LOW 5.9% INTRODUCTORY RATE.
SEE DETAILS INSIDE.

Flushed with excitement, he tore it open and found that he'd been pre-approved up to $2800! He read on. To activate the credit card, all he had to do was charge something.

Pre-marinated and pre-approved, all in the same day! It was a sign from the Big Kitchen in the Sky! He knew exactly what to do with the windfall that had dropped in his lap.

He picked up the brochure again to make sure he knew exactly what he was getting. It was a terrific buy, all things considered. Charter membership also entitled him to 50 HOURS FREE on-line grilling time, which could amount to months at an hour or less per day. Plus, by registering on-line with a valid credit card (to cover the eventual expiration of his free time), he would receive FREE the commemorative Wholly Grill Inaugural Collection barbecue set ($150 value), comprised of tongs, grippers, skewers, spatulas, meat forks, and kebob racks. Tilting the photo slightly to one side under his kitchen light, Lenny observed that the gleaming tongs, skewers, and meat forks, in particular, seemed to be gazing straight ahead— supremely pitiless, ready to pounce on those weekly deliveries to his mailbox. They all had been "specially engineered to interface with the powerful System software to ensure deployment of optimal taste intensity."

As if that weren't enough, a sheaf of 32 coupons—four sheets, eight apiece—dropped out of the brochure, offering up to $750 in savings toward future upgrades, add-ons, and sundry "tech-cessories" or toward the purchase of a backup System. How could he go wrong? Given the whole package—with the free meat subscription, the comped grilling time, the Inaugural Collection, and the coupons all thrown in—his decision turned out to be a no-brainer. The System was a real bargain by any measure.

Lenny felt great, too, that he had solved his dilemma. He'd found a way to lay his hands on the pre-marinated meat and still honor his end of the ThinkSoft deal. Later, when he talked to a lawyer, he learned he had also agreed to "assume all risks"—hazards to body and mind he knew nothing about, risks the company denied even existed. Much later, after his small case somehow ballooned into a monster class action affecting millions, his lawyers described what ThinkSoft did as a way to draw riches, like blood, from the weaknesses of people like Lenny. It turned out to be a horribly *raw* deal. But that was not clear until much later.

Right now the barbecue gods were smiling down on him.

"Good girl!" he said, scratching Lady J under the chin.

Lenny's many years as a loyal ThinkSoft user were paying off. He was getting the treatment he deserved. Not just any piece of meat, this was premium-select sirloin tip. By tonight, and with a creatively financed $1299, that sirloin tip would be laser-flame roasting on his own Wholly Grill Outdoor Cooking Information System—*free*, at no personal cost to him.

Lenny rubbed his hands. Oh, boy, a high-tech burner for charring, searing, and sizzling! Just the way he liked. He was so sure of that.

< 2 >

Earlier The Same Day

"Ladies and gentlemen, this is your captain again. Until we get clearance from San Jose International, we'll be in a holding pattern here, fifteen miles southeast of the air terminal. Meanwhile, if you look out the left side of the cabin, you'll see we are right above Santa Tostada, which is the southernmost . . . the very edge of Silicon Valley."

Persi Valentino looked up from the Windows on her notebook computer and peered out the real one to her left. This view of the old Mission Santa Tostada was better than the most spectacular postcard shot she had ever seen. What lay beyond—the bright morning light playing on the crystalline structures of high-tech startups—seemed to be bursting out of the earth below in real time. Every week for the last two years she had made this commuter flight from Los Angeles to San Jose, covering Silicon Valley for the *GoldenWest Business Journal*.

"Well, if it isn't Persi Valentino!" a male voice greeted her from the aisle. She was sitting at the back of a half-full plane with empty seats all around, four to five empty rows on either side.

"Hi," she said, looking up. She knew his name was Jake MacAully but decided it was best not to give him the satisfaction of recognition. Like her, Jake MacAully was a technology writer—he for the *San Jose Mercury News*. Strikingly tall, at about six-four, Jake had the tanned athletic good looks of a tennis pro and the reputation among female reporters of never doubting his appeal. Persi's friend Lisa Tom, at the *San Francisco Chronicle*, had nicknamed him "Jake-on-the-Make" MacAully. At least ten years older than Persi, he especially had a thing for petite women—what Lisa had wryly observed were to him perfect "micro devices."

"So, are you covering the product launch today at ThinkSoft?" he asked. With her seat comfortably reclined, Persi was looking up at Jake MacAully hovering directly over her, supporting himself with one hand on the aisle seat and the other on the seat in front—as if there were no other vantage point from which he could carry on this conversation.

"I'll be there," she said. "I can't wait to have Art Newman sell me on something I can't live without, like maybe the long-awaited upgrade to nineteenth-century snake oil." She knew that would put Jake off a little, since he considered Art Newman a personal friend. Art Newman was the spokesperson, chairman, and founder of ThinkSoft.

Jake winced at the remark, nearly standing up straight again. "Just because he has a lot of money and a lot of clout doesn't make him a bad person. Art's vision represents the future of this industry. He's a true entrepreneur. It's a privilege to know him." Jake couldn't resist implying that he was on a first-name basis with one of the richest men in the world.

"Frankly, I'm more interested in seeing Joon Newman than dear old dad," Persi jibed, referring to the co-founder of ThinkSoft, Arthur Newman, Jr. In trumpeting the product launch event, ThinkSoft had also announced that Joon was going to be there—the reclusive wunderkind who, seven years ago at age fifteen, had invented reasonware, the new and revolutionary form of artificial intelligence software used by everyone.

Art Newman had taken what was a simple invention and turned it into something else—a multibillion-dollar monopoly on the reasonware operating system. The word *reasonware* was coined by Art Newman but never claimed as a trademark, a rarity for ThinkSoft. By dedicating the term to the public domain—purposely letting it be a lowercase *thing* like its precursors *software* and *artificial intelligence*—Art Newman had shrewdly and instantly defined a whole industry for his company to control.

"Say, listen," Jake said, opting to change the subject, "I've got my car at the airport. I have to go downtown. Can I give you a ride to your hotel?"

"Thanks, but I've got my own car. I drove it up last week," Persi said. "Starting tonight, I live here now. No more commute. They've made me resident correspondent for Silicon Valley." At age twenty-four she was the youngest resident correspondent in the history of the *Golden West Business Journal.*

Jake's eyes lit up, suggesting even he might be impressed with something other than himself. Having succeeded thus far in keeping him at bay, perhaps she shouldn't have mentioned her promotion, she thought. Sure enough, as if he had given himself clearance, Jake suddenly swooped down and made a tail-hook landing in the empty seat next to Persi.

"Congratulations!" he gushed. "The least I can do is introduce you to the night life here." He pulled an electronic organizer out of his jacket pocket.

"Speak of the devil," she said, as if his organizer were possessed, programmed as it was by the latest version of ThinkSoft's reasonware operating system.

"Check it out. For a CE version, it does amazing things," Jake said, referring to the Compact Edition. "If I punch in one appointment that conflicts with another, it gives priority to one and automatically kicks out an e-mail to the other with a personalized explanation of why I won't be there. So how does next Saturday look?"

"You want to enter my name and e-mail address and leave me to hope that the little bouncer in there likes me enough to let me stay in? Gosh, I don't think I have a chance," she mocked. She wiggled her finger at the small device in his hands. "Problem is, your little man takes orders from Art Newman, and I'm afraid Art doesn't like me. You know that. I always ask him too many pointed questions. I'm doomed to get the dreaded e-mail."

"Come on, you know that's not the way it works. It's been prepro-grammed with *my* preferences," he said, with a fulsome smile.

Before she could break the bad news to him about *her* preferences, they were interrupted again by the captain's voice.

"For our visitors to Silicon Valley, nearest us and out the left side of the cabin, the big white church is the historic Mission Santa Tostada." The captain seemed to relish his role as aerial docent. "Next to that, on what used to be seven hundred and fifty acres of mission orchards, is the world headquarters of ThinkSoft."

Jake leaned over to look out the window, brushing her shoulder and bringing his head too close to hers, as if getting his first glimpse of the panorama below.

"And beyond that you can see all the new high-tech startups that wouldn't be there but for the growth of ThinkSoft over the last few years. As you may know from reading the papers, the new area of Santa Tostada—with ThinkSoft and its related startups—has come to be known as Saint Chip, not necessarily the guacamole and salsa kind." The captain chuckled to himself.

At the same moment Jake beamed smugly. He had been the first reporter to dub the area "Saint Chip" six years ago. It might have been his lone fifteen minutes of fame.

"Now if you'll sit back and relax, we'll get you on the ground as soon as we can."

"We'll start with the action in Saint Chip," Jake pressed on. "Who better to do that than yours truly?"

Persi looked down at the screen on her computer. She must have inadvertently hit the HELP button when he leaned over. An unwanted pop-up menu was obliterating her view of the article she had up on the screen. She punched ESC to escape.

"That's really nice of you—thanks—but right now is impossible. I'm working seven days a week." She shrugged. "I'll take you up on that when things start to settle down."

"Then I'll get back to you," he said. He stood and started to make his way back to the front of the aircraft. Her line about working seven days a week had come off as polite and sincere. It should have, since it was true.

After saving her article, putting the notebook in its case, and stowing it away, she looked out the window again. The layout of Old Town Santa Tostada—with the Spanish mission-style buildings, gardens, orchards, and open space—was in stark contrast to ThinkSoft and upstart Santa Tostada to the east. The streets, buildings, and infrastructures of Saint Chip were stamped into the ground in a tight grid pattern. They resembled a printed circuit board of giant microchips, electronic components, and mysterious bumps and ridges—mysterious at least to the nonengineer. She recognized the internal architecture of a personal computer and considered the universal quest that led to its development: a design whose sole object was to consume, contain, process, and manipulate an ever-expanding glut of information. And no company was more suited to that task than the one whose motherboard was just below, ThinkSoft.

Security was tight for all the high tech firms throughout the Valley as a firewall against espionage and theft of trade secrets. ThinkSoft, however, went beyond the norm. There were federal prisons with less security. Upon arriving at the main auditorium, all members of the media had to submit to an identification and picture-taking process for each and every visit to ThinkSoft.

Clipping her badge to her coat, Persi looked at the photo. Due to the delayed flight she was running late, and her short brown hair was wildly tousled. Her bright hazel eyes glared straight ahead as if in a stare-down to the death with the ThinkSoft camera. It would not have surprised her if, at that instant and based on the visual data, a mainframe computer at ThinkSoft was profiling her, concluding that a loaded AK-47 must be hidden in her purse.

Once inside the auditorium, her ears were assaulted by the driving recorded sound of the most popular rock group in the known universe, Severe Tire Damage. The boys in the band were humping and thumping the cavernous interior, as promotional images of their highly touted Irreversible World Tour, sponsored by ThinkSoft, flickered on the giant video screen atop the stage. Mixed into the sequence of live performance shots were pictures of the notoriously crazed band members booting up and thoughtfully interacting with ThinkSoft reasonware products.

Persi found a seat amid the crowd of reporters as the music stopped. She watched Jake MacAully make his way into the lone empty seat in front of her just as Art Newman strode out onto the stage. He was fitted with a cordless mike. The forty-eight-year-old CEO and chairman was decked out in white tails—a far cry from the usual dress at ThinkSoft, where the young workforce wore jeans, T-shirts, and less elegant attire morning, noon, and night.

Art Newman was handsome in an insipid sort of way, pleasant enough to the eye on first impression but difficult to read further. Not surprisingly, before Grace Telemarketing, his previous business venture, nobody seemed to know what Art Newman had done, where he had been, or who he was. It was known that Grace Telemarketing sold everything from toilet fresheners to long distance services. Other than information about Grace, all that was public knowledge about Art Newman was that he had raised Joon alone, although rumors abounded that Joon's mother had been institutionalized when her son was very young. But to look at Art Newman, there was no evidence of any skeletons. His black hair was flawlessly slicked back, nothing out of place.

"Welcome, my fellow pilgrims, to the Information Age." The crowd hushed. It was never clear when Art Newman was being tongue-in-cheek and when he was perfectly serious. "We at ThinkSoft are always proud to be on the cutting edge in the quest for innovations." A video collage of ThinkSoft software products and logos for its information services streamed across the giant screen. "Today we announce the coming of a new era, converging previously diverse technologies. We do so, as always, with awe-inspiring innovation. The newest from ThinkSoft is, simultaneously and in real time, being announced as forthcoming, launched as a new product, shipped *to* and actually landing *in* stores . . . all on the same day!"

A thunderous ovation followed. Persi clapped halfheartedly. This was Art Newman's way of deflecting the criticism leveled against his company in the past for announcing vaporware—software neither designed nor actually developed yet, but making for great press releases and often followed by coverage in the business columns.

The crowd hushed again. Dramatic classical music flowed gently, then more forcefully, from the sound system. "Without further ado, allow me to present to you—the next generation of ThinkSoft information products!"

With a loud splash the music ramped into high volume: Severe Tire Damage's biggest hit, the band's most lyrical melody in its entire Irreversible repertoire, "Cravin' You Bad, Baby."

Cravin' you bad, baby,
Losin' all controh-oh-ol.
T'get one taste o' you
Gonna sell my soh-oh-oul . . . .

Two young women in black spandex shorts wheeled onto the stage a boxy-shaped object draped in black velvet: about four feet high, four feet wide, and two feet deep, possibly a large computer. Art nodded to the two women to pull the cover off while he added the flourish.

"Ladies and gentlemen! Behold . . . the Wholly Grill!"

The music stopped. The crowd stood up from their seats and stared in stunned silence. Persi's eyes panned over the new product on stage and the close-ups on the big screen, hearing some murmurings and a few "oohs!"

"This is it!" Art pressed on. "The next big thing! Marrying high technology and outdoor cooking. Another first from ThinkSoft!"

From the wings, dozens more young women in spandex shorts suddenly emerged to pass around platters of barbecued chicken drumsticks. Several reporters took one bite and then lunged after the platter to grab more. Taking a pass on this techno send-up, Persi was caused to lament how far away she was from her personal favorite: her grandmother's old-fashioned charcoal-broiled *pollo alla diavola*.

Marrying high technology and outdoor cooking? The thought of Art Newman, the high priest of high tech, presiding over the surreal marriage of a computer and a plucked chicken was making Persi a little nauseated.

"This is what technology is all about," Art Newman crowed, "making people's lives easier and more enjoyable."

Persi recalled he had used the same line when he introduced the latest version of the reasonware operating system.

"Let me tell you a little about how this state-of-the-art system works." He was using a laser pointer to highlight features on the overhead screen. "First off, it comes bundled with a proprietary sauce, Wholly Grill Barbecue Sauce with Smoke Crystals." He licked his lips suggestively. "You can't use any other sauce with the system, and you wouldn't want to. You can get rid of that odd assortment of bottles in your refrigerator." Only Art Newman could make an antitrust violation sound like a consumer's best friend.

"I have a question about that!" Persi shouted, waving her hand.

Art Newman must have recognized the voice. Without looking at her directly, he told the crowd, "Let me finish giving you the operational features, and then I'll welcome any questions. In order to activate the grill, you need merely connect the modem here and dial up the main server at ThinkSoft, which will turn on the grill and, specifically, the grill's series of laser flames. The lasers scan and digitize the chicken and transmit the digitized information to the control server at ThinkSoft, which performs calculations, automatically calibrates the flames, taking the cut of meat into account, and produces the juiciest barbecue the world has ever known. You'll never have to check the grill again. It's all done for you."

Another scattering of *oohs* and *ahs* followed, particularly from those who were still licking their fingers from the barbecued chicken. At the same time, thirty or forty reporters jumped up and began shouting to get Art Newman's attention. As was customary at a ThinkSoft product launch, no one would dare sit down from this point forward.

"Question here!" Persi shouted, waving her hand. Also standing was Jake MacAully, minimizing any view Art Newman might have of Persi, who was more than a foot shorter than the *Mercury News* reporter.

A reporter from *The Wall Street Journal* reeled in Art's attention. "Do you expect to be able to use your market muscle in software to gain a dominant share in the barbecue grill sector?"

"Barbecue grill?" Art Newman repeated with polite indignation. "What you see before you, together with the Wholly Grill sauce and the on-line access to the main server at ThinkSoft, is not a barbecue grill. I promise you, we're not even competing with makers of barbecue grills—or makers of pots and pans, for that matter. What you see is . . . an outdoor cooking information system. It's all about information. This is completely different. What's so exciting is that we've created a new business paradigm in the food preparation industry."

Paradigm, whether "new" or "shifting," was one of Art Newman's favorite words. Persi had come to interpret it at ThinkSoft product launches as not just hackneyed MBA-speak but rather as an unwitting euphemism for *sharp practices* and *predatory intent* in whatever market Art Newman was describing.

"Question here!" Persi began, having timed it perfectly to be the first voice at the end of the last answer. But Art Newman called on another reporter closer to the stage, whose question was garbled through a mouth stuffed with chicken. "If a remo' compooter shumwhere a' ThinkShoft,"—he gulped a chunk of chicken and struggled on—"ish deshiding when a meat ish cooked"—he swallowed again hard—"how you sure iz done a way you like it?" The word *you* launched particulates of poultry that struck the hair of the woman directly in front of him, also facing the stage and unaware that she'd been bombarded.

For this he was probably paid twice Persi's salary.

"Not to worry," Art said. "In SETUP you punch in your preferences. Wholly Grill is fully scalable—anything between blood rare to crispy well done. We can really deliver when *we* say, 'Have it your way!'" Art got some laughs for that line. They were starting to warm up to his pitch.

"What does the name Wholly Grill mean?" a woman asked right in front. "Is there something mysterious going on?"

Art deadpanned. "Verily, it's a mystery how Wholly Grill delivers such a divine taste." He got some more laughs. "But seriously, let me tell you how the name came about. Sure, there are a number of grills out there with electronic components. But this is the first one that's a 'whole e-grill,' wholly electronic. Voilà! The name Wholly Grill. It was my humble offering, and it stuck."

Persi could see that Art Newman again noticed her efforts to get his attention but averted his eyes, nodding to Jake MacAully instead. It was becoming clear that if she wanted her questions answered, she too would have to create a new paradigm—for reporters starving for the truth.

"So what exactly does the modem hook up to? Is there something special about the central computer that controls the cooking process?" Jake was tossing out a softball question, designed to endear himself to Art Newman and land him more exclusive interviews with the CEO of ThinkSoft.

"It gratifies me deeply that you would ask that," Art said piously. "You all know that the soul of ThinkSoft is its intellectual property— patented technologies, know-how, and trade secrets we alone have developed. The main Wholly Grill server, with its closely guarded proprietary database, aggregates data from grills all over the world via our network and uses it to optimize the content—taste-wise—of each piece of barbecue. This is our ultimate intellectual property. We call it the Wholly WORD—another humble suggestion I made. WORD is an acronym for 'WAN Optimization of Research and Development.'"

"Did you say 'wand,' as in magician's wand?" a reporter asked. Persi did not recognize him. Because of word out that Joon Newman would appear, a number of nontechnology reporters had turned up.

"No." Art chuckled respectfully. "But it works like magic. I said WAN. W-A-N. It's an acronym for Wide Area Network. Our network is composed of our Wholly WORD server connecting with what will soon be millions of barbecue grills around the world."

"Any more acronyms in there I should know about?" the same reporter asked in a weary voice, already suffering a mild onset of information overload.

"Those are the only ones my engineers have told me about." Art smiled sympathetically.

The young women came from the sides of the stage and rolled the Wholly Grill away from the center of the stage, where it was blocking part of the screen.

"Thank you, ladies," Art said as he too stood back from the screen. "Although Joon Newman could not be with us in person today, we will beam him in *live*. Do we have that?"

Immediately, Joon Newman's face filled the giant screen. The camera drew back; he was sitting by himself on a stool in an empty sound stage. Although his expression was uncharacteristically blasé compared to the last time Persi had seen him, at age twenty-two he still had a very boyish face, with a trademark tuft of red hair sprouting on top of his head. He was as thin as a silicon wafer, causing his tortoiseshell glasses to seem thicker than they were.

Persi remembered seven years ago when Joon had been a champion computer-game player. A number of stories were written about the boy with the stratospheric IQ who loved and had an awesome talent for computer games. The photographs invariably were of him grinning hugely and holding a trophy. Then he disappeared for a long spell before reemerging as the inventor of reasonware. Persi had heard that Joon's retirement from the computer-game competition circuit had not been voluntary.

"Joon? Are you with us?" Art asked.

"I hear you," Joon responded. Both the sound and the tone of his voice seemed remote.

"What do you want to tell everyone about Wholly Grill?" Art asked.

Persi detected a curious flat affect in Joon's speech. Not quite looking directly into the camera, he seemed to be reading from a Tele-Promp-Ter. "This is a great day for ThinkSoft. I congratulate the members of the Wholly Grill development team on their success. Although I was not on that team, busy as I was with my own development projects, I am very excited about this new technology." His seemingly prepared remarks concluded, he looked around, then added earnestly, "Now can I have some?"

"You sure can!" Art beamed.

The sound stage filled with a reprise of "Cravin' You Bad, Baby." To the delight of Jake MacAully and others, a scantily clad beauty sashayed from behind the camera toward Joon with a platter of drumsticks. Joon attacked the platter to the cheers of the viewers in the ThinkSoft Auditorium.

"Thank you, Joon," Art responded from stage left. "I know I speak for everyone here when I say thanks for taking the time to share your enthusiasm about Wholly Grill with us."

Joon spoke again, now looking directly into the camera. "I want to say something else. I have a strategy to bring us to a new level." Persi recognized the language—*strategy* and *new level*—borrowed from his computer games.

Art Newman was now looking back at the screen, apparently caught off guard. While everyone was looking up at the screen at Joon, Persi noticed that Art Newman was rubbing his hand on the front of his neck.

Joon continued. "We can win a crucial battle in our quest to find and eradicate the Source of Darkness and save the Universe. We now have powers to rescue injured and mistreated inhabitants of the Realm of Creatures. Let's seize the opportunity to help those who've been abused—" Suddenly the screen went blank; Joon was cut off.

"Thanks, Joon! More on that later," Art said. "Meanwhile, why don't we move on? I'll take more questions."

A number of reporters were shaking their heads, as if they had now witnessed for themselves what they had long suspected about Joon Newman's mental state. At the same time, from the left side of the auditorium, there were snickers and isolated bursts of laughter, but nothing more from the throng of usually inquisitive journalists. Art Newman was casting about for the next question on the right side of the auditorium, pretending to ignore Persi Valentino, towering above the crowd on the other side. She had kicked her shoes off and was straddling her seat by planting her bare feet on the armrests on either side. With the CEO of ThinkSoft finally in her sights, the intensity of her expression bore an uncanny resemblance to the picture on her ThinkSoft security ID. With her arms akimbo, and balanced as firmly as an Olympic gymnast, she was poised to vault into Art Newman's face.

"Yes, there's a question," he finally said, with a good-natured smile, still acting as if he had not been avoiding her. Appearing at ease with Persi's stance, he added, "This is an example of the democracy that ThinkSoft technology can bring. It levels the playing field. The small can be big." His supporters chuckled in appreciation of the charm he was using to neutralize the barbed questions that were undoubtedly coming.

Persi attacked. "Did I hear you say that the Wholly Grill barbecue sauce comes *bundled* with the grill? Does that mean you are going to force consumers to purchase only Wholly Grill barbecue sauce once they use up the first bottle?"

"In fact, the shrink-wrap license requires that only Wholly Grill barbecue sauce be purchased and used." Art paused and explained in an aside to the nontech reporters, "The shrink-wrap license is just like the ones we use, as does everyone else in the industry, on software products. Under the shrink-wrap, purchasers are plainly notified that by breaking the seal they agree to our terms of use. This is necessary to protect the intellectual property and prevent misuse of the product, be it software or an outdoor cooking information system."

Persi was not done. Jake MacAully was looking up at her in astonishment. The men on either side of her were in a readiness mode, should she fall from her perch, but she was not about to give Art Newman that satisfaction.

"This is not the first time your company has required, as a condition of purchasing one of your products, the purchase of another. Can you justify that legally?" When she stretched to her tiptoes to deliver the question, her "safety net" team lunged for her with open hands at the ready.

"Wholly Grill utilizes a closed architecture. Other sauces or grills are simply incompatible. Beside,"—he scoffed—"this cutting-edge grill isn't some fire-based throwback to the Stone Age. These are lasers. You need to use the compatible sauce or you might be exposed to injury."

Persi was not in a position to challenge these claims—yet—but she was determined to finish the investigation she had started, whatever it took. For the moment she wasn't quite ready to yield the floor without one more shot. Actually, she was feeling quite comfortable a shade over eight feet tall.

"Your company is famous for flooding consumer mailboxes with free software. After you get them hooked, you have lifetime customers buying your upgrades. How are you going to market to the backyard brigade? Aren't you a little out of your element?"

"Everything about this technology is a natural extension of our core business of getting information into the hands of our customers to make their lives easy." Art Newman smiled at her, supremely confident. "You'll see."

‹ 3 ›

Lenny couldn't believe it was now 10:30 P.M. It had been a thoroughly exhausting day ever since he opened his mailbox a few minutes after noon. Having borrowed a truck from a friend across town to haul his grill home from Costco, it was 3 P.M. by the time he rolled it onto his back patio.

"Some assembly required," the literature had understated. He read about a third of the 412-page Wholly Grill Outdoor Cooking Information System Owner's Manual before abandoning it for the 42-page Wholly Grill: Your Quick Reference Guide. It was 5:30 before he realized he was just getting the assembly going. At 6 he made another trip to the store because he needed a much longer telephone line to reach from the jack in the house to the modem-equipped grill on the patio. Not ideally, the closest telephone jack was his main business line.

By 7:30 in the evening when it was assembled, he dialed up ThinkSoft to register as a Wholly Grill user. He answered a detailed questionnaire about all his likes and dislikes that affected the calibration of the laser flames to his personal taste. Then he punched in his new credit card number and clicked a box on-screen agreeing that he would be charged $3.95 per hour for on-line grilling time. He tried to take LENNYM as his screen name but twenty-six Lenny M's had already signed up; he settled on LENNYM27. Finally, he selected LADYJ as his password. That would connect him to the private network—in effect, the mother of all starter chimneys, because only it would turn on his grill.

By 8:30 he was starving, but heroically he resisted all snacks that would only dull the taste sensation. Tearing away the shrink-wrap and the freezer wrap, he placed the gorgeous pre-marinated sirloin tip onto a barbecue platter. Fully primed for the gratification he had so painstakingly orchestrated, he dialed up the password-protected network that would turn the grill on.

That's when his dark night of the soul set in. Each time he dialed up, the modem would whine and wail, itching to make the electronic handshake. But each time it quit, the screen flashing SORRY, YOUR CONNECTION HAS BEEN CUT OFF DUE TO HEAVY NETWORK TRAFFIC. TRY AGAIN LATER.

An hour later, at 9:30, he was still getting the same frustrating screen display: SORRY, YOUR CONNECTION HAS BEEN CUT OFF and TRY AGAIN LATER. Evidently, more telephone capacity had been dedicated to registration than to letting users connect. He began to panic. He did a double take on the torn freezer wrap on his kitchen table; it gave him a chilling reminder of what was PERISHABLE. Lenny had determined how he might save the sirloin tip, but he was less certain that he could save himself. As a final resort, at 9:45 he had fired up a mound of charcoal briquettes on the old Weber.

And so, against all odds, he had made it to 10:30. He was so weak with hunger for Wholly Grill, he began drifting aimlessly around the house, occasionally stopping to lean up against walls and doors. Should he perish, Lenny thought, there was no body bag that he would fit into. The eleven o'clock news live-cam would zoom in on him being unceremoniously hauled out on a stretcher borrowed from Marine World. There was nothing he could do about his untamed size at this juncture, but the Hawaiian shirt and black sweats would make him look like he just washed up on the beach from the Big Island. He mustered enough strength to change into a pair of slacks and a nice-looking sport shirt—tailless so he wouldn't have to tuck it in.

The briquettes were now ready. Lady J knew it too. She came running out to the patio as he spread the coals and laid the grill over them. He lifted her up to the small table next to the Weber, where she liked to act as barbecue sentry dog. He plopped the meat on the grill and felt himself relax for the first time since he had visited his mailbox earlier that day. It felt good. He needed to relax more. His doctor told him that, for a thirty-eight-year-old male, his cholesterol was off the chart, and stress only made it worse.

In his daylong travails he'd made mighty efforts to honor the terms on the package that the sirloin tip be cooked ON THE SYSTEM AND ONLY THE SYSTEM. But that didn't seem fair when he actually went out and bought the System, only to find it wouldn't let him connect and turn on. He later had to ask himself if he would have done differently if he'd stopped and actually read the complete set of all the "terms and conditions" handed down by ThinkSoft, like, for example, this one:

> *You will only use the Information System when connected by the Information System modem to the proprietary outdoor cooking information and control server hosted by the Company . . . In no event shall the Company be responsible for your inability to connect with the Wholly WORD or for any interruption of service you may experience, including loss or spoliation of meats, fish, and other perishables.*

The meat hadn't even begun to sizzle yet. He left the lid off for a moment and went to the back hall to get a Budweiser out of the beverage refrigerator. He unscrewed the top of the quart bottle and drained a third of it. That, too, made him feel better. By tomorrow he surely would be able to get through and get his Wholly Grill fired up, he thought. Meanwhile he would cook the pre-marinated sirloin in Wholly Grill sauce and at least get an idea of what this new taste was all about.

Just then he heard a crash and an unearthly squeal from the patio. He lumbered quickly to the living room and looked out through the sliding glass. To his horror the grill had turned into a flamethrower; a conflagration of sirloin tip was shooting spicules of fire in all directions. One such flame had hit Lady J squarely in the face; the hairs around her eyes were still on fire.

He ran outside to where she had jumped down from the table. He was able to doused the flames by emptying the bottle of beer over her head. Then, quickly tossing the lid on the grill to contain the fire, he grabbed the garden hose and sprayed the half-dozen balls of flames around the patio.

Only after putting the hose down could he collapse into a patio chair, still reeling. "Poor girl!" he said. "Come here and let's have a look at you."

Lady J was whimpering. She started to run toward him but collided with a table leg. She fell back on her haunches and took off again, this time running smack into the leg of a chair. Finally she reached Lenny, who, in terror and disbelief, stared into her eyes. They were black and covered with a milky gray film, encircled with blood. They were not looking back at him.

"Oh my God, Lady J! You're blind!" He petted her feverishly. "My poor little baby! Gotta get you to the doctor right away. You got burned real bad." The two of them whimpered quietly together. Then, composing himself as best he could, he stood up to go inside and call the vet.

He stopped briefly in front of the gleaming new Wholly Grill system. Still frozen on the screen was the manufacturer's empty apology: SORRY, YOUR CONNECTION HAS BEEN CUT OFF.

‹ 4 ›

Edwin G. Ostermyer exploded through the front door into his office reception area as if he were a star football player leading the charge onto the field for the Super Bowl, bursting triumphantly through the giant paper banner to the crowd's roar.

"Hold all my calls," the lawyer bellowed at the receptionist—his third in the last three months. Edwin never bothered to learn their names, referring to each of them as the "New Receptionist."

The phone rang three times and stopped; the call rolled into voice mail.

"Nobody's called," she said, absorbed in a game of solitaire on her computer screen, oblivious to the call she had just missed. Her hair resembled spikes of cotton candy, in three rigid rows of bright pink. Edwin's stride came to a sudden and unscheduled stop; he turned his head and glowered at the New Receptionist with his sharp green eyes.

Arriving a few paces behind his boss this Monday morning was the new associate, Will Swanson. Although he could only see Edwin's backside in an intense stare-down with the New Receptionist, he knew well the apparition she faced. Encountering Edwin eye to eye was like an aerial view of Cape Canaveral: a giant nose chiseled to a point that would, if deployed, surely reach the heavens. Right now the nose was trained on the New Receptionist like a heat-seeking missile poised for launch, the surrounding face reddened with readily ignited indignation. Edwin's fervor—and his large, mostly bald head, balanced on a five-and-a-half-foot stout frame—made him seem taller than he was.

"You are to answer the phone on the first ring!" Edwin fumed. "If I ask you to hold my calls, you are to take the information and tell them I will call back as soon as I can."

"Uh, I guess I missed that one," she said. "But I'm doing a lot of things at once." She shuffled an envelope from one side of her station to another and straightened the telephone console. Fresh out of make-work, her right hand automatically settled on the mouse and resumed play.

Edwin fixed his glare upon her for one more moment before releasing it. Even when Edwin was not angry, he possessed a striking, if by no means handsome, demeanor. Reinforced by television ads and vigorously orchestrated publicity over many years, Edwin's unforgettable looks drew clients as surely as a famous company logo. It had occurred to Will, whose practice was but three months in the making, that he might have to wait decades before he had Edwin's drawing power. To the young lawyer's way of thinking, his own plain vanilla good looks—average build, brown hair, and friendly blue eyes behind a subdued pair of glasses—were a liability when it came to developing a reputation in the legal field.

Will had been offered a job at McKenna Covington, a big, old, and highly respected firm in San Francisco's legal aristocracy. He was invited to be the newest member of the firm's "estate planning and probate practice group," which meant probating wills, an arduously slow and dull court process, or meeting with blue-haired widows in dire need of giving away money to avoid death taxes. Teasingly known as having a practice in "gifts and stiffs," it was indeed deadly dry stuff. He had no regrets about taking a pass on that offer, choosing instead to inject himself into the lively milieu of trial lawyers.

However, taking the job with Ostermyer, a maverick plaintiff's lawyer in San Jose, was not without complications of a personal nature: his parents. He'd grown up in the heart of San Francisco society in well-heeled Pacific Heights. Although by the map only forty miles south, San Jose and the Law Offices of Edwin G. Ostermyer were a world apart from his roots in the city. Until he surprised everyone and made the decision six months ago to turn down the job at McKenna Covington and join Edwin, Will had been following a blueprint of his life handed down to him by his father: college, majoring in business; law school, focusing on taxes and trusts; and a career at an old and prestigious San Francisco firm, practicing estate planning and probate.

But instead of heeding his father's direction, he'd taken someone else's: that of his ex-girlfriend, Dagmar Brittman. Before she'd broken off, she persuaded him to go after a job with her Uncle Edwin, who had recently won a highly publicized class-action lawsuit.

In truth, before Dagmar held out this lure, he was already primed to abandon his "painted footsteps" career path for an off-road adventure in trial practice. For fun, and merely to earn a few easy units, in the spring of his last year in law school he volunteered as an intern at Health's Fury, a private foundation that waged legal battles against environmental lawbreakers when the state or the EPA failed to act. Giving far more time than asked of him, he was caught up and swept away by the excitement of a big trial. An East Bay oil refinery was accused of leaching poisons into the community's groundwater, though it denied any wrongdoing. As a Health's Fury intern, he worked with the team of lawyers who succeeded in convincing the jury that the defendant did the dirty deed and, worse, tried to cover up the health threat. Enamored with the courtroom drama and the thrill of helping real people, Will was hooked. All he needed was a nudge.

The name Edwin G. Ostermyer was familiar to Will because of his frequent appearances on TV and the high-profile product defect and criminal defense cases he handled. The name also figured prominently on the Health's Fury letterhead, joining other distinguished trial lawyers and community leaders volunteering on the nonprofit's board of trustees. That held a further allure to Will Swanson, future lawyer: Edwin believed in worthy causes while at the same time he managed a thrilling practice. After the Health's Fury trial, destiny itself was in play; Will Swanson would never be the newest member of the estate planning and probate practice group at McKenna Covington.

"You should try to get in with Uncle Edwin," Dagmar urged him, in her velveteen voice. "The pay might be low to start, but over time you'd make more. It would be great experience. Before long, you'll be a crackerjack trial lawyer." When her pale blue eyes lit up as she painted the picture for him, it was impossible not to see himself as a potent force rising in the ranks of trial lawyers. He also envisioned himself, from time to time and with Edwin's blessing, handling cases for Health's Fury or taking on victims who'd been cheated by overreaching corporations   an unthinkable scenario if he were at McKenna Covington. Then Dagmar gave him the sign he was waiting for: "I've set up an interview for you with Uncle Edwin." Everything she said seemed an utterance from the oracle. He shined in the interview, and Edwin offered him the job.

On this Monday morning, as Will caught up with Edwin striding down the hall, his boss was still stewing over the scene at the front desk. "That's where our clients come in, through the front door and my toll-free lines! New business is the lifeblood of the successful practice I've spent twenty-seven years building. But try to explain that to the New Receptionist!"

They reached the door to Edwin's office. He stopped and turned to Will. "Now that you're on board and settled in, I was thinking it's time *you* started developing some business of your own."

Will raised his eyebrows to show he was listening. At the same time he was thinking what his father had said: "You're going to work for that *pariah* of the business community? He sues legitimate tax-paying job-producing companies! You're turning down the brass ring at McKenna Covington for what, to be a low-paid lackey in that . . . lawsuit mill?"

"I have one word for you." Edwin paused at his office door as if he were about to impart the secret of the universe. "*Manufacturers.* I've sued thousands of them: manufacturers of automobiles, lawn mowers, airplanes, toaster ovens, you name it." He swept his hand at the various exhibits from his trials that surrounded them and decorated the walls. "Of course, this is Silicon Valley where they make things like *soft*ware! Ha! They would have you believe they're making downy pillows and frilly linens, I suppose. Make no mistake! They too are manufacturers, just like the rest of them. A banquet is spread before you. I say, Eat 'em up!"

On the wall behind Edwin hung a mounted toaster oven, so thoroughly blackened and burned it looked like a large mutant bug. It had caused an apartment building in downtown San Jose to go up in flames. The wall that framed the New Receptionist's station featured the entire underside of a defective Ford pickup truck that had squashed a Geo Metro.

"Yeah, I'd like that. To start bringing in clients of my own," Will said, as if he were thinking out loud. Then he looked at Edwin. "But is this a good time? I've got plenty of work—"

"If you're going to be a real trial lawyer, you need to handle cases on your own. You need to get into court." Edwin gave the knot of his Hugo Boss tie a reassuring pinch and smoothed the silk, top to bottom. "Learn how to present a case."

"Believe me, I want to learn," Will said, in an eager voice. Then he tempered it to convey he was not unhappy with the work he was doing. "I've learned more in these first few months doing the case analysis and papers than I did in the first two *years* of law school."

"That's where you start, case studies. Then you step up to the plate and take on a malfeasant yourself." His own words must have triggered a memory. The elder lawyer began to speak wistfully, as if summoning up a long-cherished love affair. "I'll never forget my first manufacturer. The results of the bar exam were published in the paper, but due to a defective printing press my name and eighty-five others were wrongfully omitted in the morning edition of *The Legal Institution*, resulting in incalculable lost income for all of us. Two days after I was sworn in, I sued the manufacturer of the printing press: a class action—also my first!—on behalf of all the victims." Edwin gleamed. "Nicely settled, I might mention. So, what say you? You on board or not?"

"Count me in," Will said, suppressing his actual excitement. This was as fast a start as he had hoped for when he took the job. "I'll put together a business development plan," he added.

"Good. But don't cut back on your billable hours," his boss reminded him. "I've got some new clients who need your research right away. I've got important matters to attend to this morning. Why don't you see me after lunch for those files?" And Edwin directed another go-get-'em nod at the young lawyer before disappearing into his office.

Will felt a spring in his step but managed to stand still for one more moment. These first few months he had done nothing but work on Edwin's caseload, yet already he was encouraged to bring in his own clients—not hand-me-downs from his father, or dead people in needed of probating, but real flesh-and-blood clients who had sought *him* out because of *his* legal savvy. It was a giddy sensation, that of a great adventure about to begin. On his own at last, he was eager to take the first crack at carving out his identity in what seemed like an endless frieze of lawyers.

As Will started down the hall toward his office, where he would draft a plan, he overheard Edwin barking instructions to his personal secretary. "Stop the legal work you're doing! I need to fax out a press release ASAP!"

‹ 5 ›

Phil Torres, chief of Real Estate Operations for ThinkSoft's far-reaching network of shiny black buildings, stopped on the walkway between Admin 2 and RD 1. Hearing his name paged, the Chief grappled with the walkie-talkie on his belt and wrested it free. Instinctively his eyes settled on the electronic scoreboard overlooking the volleyball courts below, there to provide recreation for the teams of young coders ceaselessly grinding away at the unlimited reasonware programming. In idle mode, the scoreboard flashed the company's media-saturating slogan over and over:

ThinkSoft.
What Do You Want to Get Out of Today? ®

"Yeah, what is it?" the Chief barked, hitching up his pants.

"I need you to clean a Level One Security lab," the static voice ordered him. It was Carl Blanchard, a security guard from the eighth floor of RD 1.

The Chief bit his lip: *Here we go again.* This wasn't the first time some self-satisfied imbecile from Security tried to tell him what to do. After all, the Chief commanded a militia of building engineers, plumbers, electricians, groundskeepers, and custodians. He couldn't resist toying with the pesky caller. "Do you want me to hike up to the eighth floor myself and sweep up for you, or would it be OK with you if I send someone else?"

"Can clear you to send substitute," Blanchard replied, in law enforcement staccato. "But only if you can vouch they are . . . "—he hesitated—"like you: totally harmless . . . security-wise, that is. You copy?"

His baiting had backfired. He, the Chief, was totally harmless? The mere suggestion caused his jaw and throat to twitch uncontrollably, as if gagging on his own venom. "Listen, you police academy dropout," he snapped, his voice rising. "You little shopping mall rent-a-cop reject! Who the hell do you think you're talking to? You think I'm going to drop everything and come running when you call?"

Blanchard remained unruffled. "Noncompliance. Will report as breach and request Enforcement. Repeat," he underscored, "the lab is Level One Security."

But for the hiss of the radio in his hand and under his breath, there was silence. The Chief hated it, but he knew his marching orders. Ever since he began working in Silicon Valley eight months ago, he'd been learning to put up with the upside-down pecking order. At ThinkSoft the crown jewels looked nothing like the Plexiglas buildings over which he was steward. Here it was all about *intellectual* property: invisible, intangible, almost unreal, but treasured more than veins of gold or gushing oil in times gone by. That's why Security, the Chief learned, trumped the usual corporate hierarchies, with all the gentility of martial law. But duty didn't mean he had to go out of his way, and certainly not for this highly trained twit.

"Why, whaddaya know!" the Chief shouted into his radio. "We're in luck! Hold on here a minute."

Down below, a young female custodian was picking up litter from a Friday night volleyball tournament between rival company divisions. He called down to her. "Say, you! Yeah, come on up here."

She abandoned the large rolling trash container and walked up to him. He recognized her vaguely. The petite brunette was indeed *bonita* but looked only faintly Latina, probably a mix. Though she'd been on staff only three weeks, she would have to do.

"You're an REO/PTE, right?" he asked, meaning Real Estate Operations/Part-Time Employee.

She gave him a quizzical look.

"You work weekends *solamente. ¿Verdad?*"

She nodded. He had become adept at the hybrid language for those on his crew who spoke little English.

"*¿Como se llama?*"

"*María*," she said, touching the picture ID on her shirt. He squinted a little to look at the photo and read her full name: MARIA VALENTINO.

"Listen, Maria. I'm going to need you to stop what you're doing now and go clean up a lab in RD One." He pointed to the building. "Go to the top floor. See Mr. Blanchard of security. *¿Comprende?*"

Another affirmative nod.

The Chief picked up his walkie-talkie again. "I'm sending up Maria Valentino." He examined the badge again. "That's ID number AD Eight-five-seven. And listen, I'm giving you one of my best people. Don't ever say I didn't cover Security's ass—bigtime! Over and out."

Persi Valentino, the technology reporter, was careful to stay in character as "Maria." Turning from the Chief, she moved toward RD 1 methodically, perfunctorily, as if to convince anyone watching that she was nothing more than the tiniest *bit* of information—among billions of other zeroes and ones of computer code—about to execute the most trivial instruction in the entire enterprise of the company. But the truth was she had to restrain herself from running. She was going to penetrate ThinkSoft's main research and development building at last!

Persistenza Maria Valentino was actually her full name. It could help her squeak by as Hispanic, but in fact she was Italian through and through. Two days after the product launch—five weeks earlier—she had showed up at a back office at ThinkSoft. Dressed incognito and with her middle name, fluent Spanish, and feigned broken English, she was able to land this dead-end weekend job.

Since then, as janitor-on-a-mission, she had been busy cleaning inside office buildings—all the while picking something out of a wastebasket here, peeking at a desktop memo there. But even if she uncovered the evidence she was looking for, she knew she couldn't write about anything learned through clandestine channels. She called it research. ThinkSoft would call it industrial espionage.

The *Business Journal* didn't know about her moonlighting and for good reason. Because of lawsuits, news journalists had become cautious about using such information-gathering techniques. Employers faced lawsuits. Reporters were fired in a heartbeat. She had to be careful.

Riding up the elevator of Building RD 1, she glanced around for security cameras. Seeing none did not mean she was not being watched. She looked straight ahead at her reflection in the polished stainless steel doors to double-check her appearance. At five-foot-two she was certainly not an obvious threat to ThinkSoft, especially in her gray janitor pants and baggy shirt, upon which hung the unusually large employee identification badge.

When the elevator doors opened, she came face-to-face with Carl Blanchard sitting behind the security desk. Wearing a cheap maroon blazer with a bright silver ThinkSoft Security badge and a polyester white shirt, Blanchard neither smiled nor greeted her. Indeterminately between fifty and sixty years old, short and wiry, he had fleshy Ping-Pong ball protrusions for cheeks, with wrinkling all around his eyes and forehead. She couldn't decide if he looked more like a half-dried plum or an unrealized prune. He squinted at the name and photograph on her badge and pursed his lips as if she were a potentially virus-laden diskette he was forced to insert into his pristine system.

At his core, she decided, he was all prune.

"Follow me," Blanchard said. "You're to do a once-over of RD Eight-oh-seven. Technicians were in there all day Saturday. It needs to be cleaned up for Monday morning."

A heavy set of keys jangled and bounced off his hip as he walked in front of her. He opened the janitorial supply closet and began handing her items without looking up. "You'll need a broom, dustpan, mop, rag, spray disinfectant cleaner, and a sponge." As he recited each item, he checked it off on a clipboard.

She followed Blanchard down the hall, passing a number of empty "clean rooms," where a single speck of dust could spell disaster. Although primarily a software company, ThinkSoft conducted research into chips and related technology. In these clean rooms, workers wore shiny "bunny suits" to preserve the contaminant-free environment. Both the reporter and the janitor in her had wondered who actually cleaned these rooms and with what. She filed it in the back of her mind as an idea for a future story.

They finally arrived at lab RD 807. He opened the door and swung it open. "All right. It should take you no more than twelve minutes to clean in here." A precision nut, he no doubt had NASA in his future. "Don't touch the cases in the center. Do floors and counters only." He turned and walked back toward his station around the corner and a hundred feet away.

She immediately began mopping the floor in case he decided to double back and surveil her before returning to his station. While cleaning, she could not keep her eyes off the three large glass cases in the center of the lab. Rats were living in them—just the kind of R&D she was looking for. This was not ThinkSoft business-as-usual. It was unlikely that these rats were writing code. These were Wholly Grill rats!

She quickly surveyed the scene in each glass module. In one, the rats were being subjected to some kind of smoke. Barbecue? The glass pre- vented her from smelling it. Hurriedly she scanned the action in the next case. Rats were shaking uncontrollably, evidently suffering, but there was no smoke. She glanced down the hall to see if the watchman was coming. Still clear, she peeked into the last one. There, fat rats—getting fatter—were feverishly gorging themselves on food smothered with what had to be barbecue sauce. One thing was clear about this last group—and the minds that spawned them. They were out of control.

She returned to her rapid cleanup of the floor and counters. It seemed there was a fourth group of laboratory rats, two-legged and not as civilized, who had left pizza boxes, soda cans, crumbs, and crust all over the counter and on the floor. After she disposed of the last box, she opened a button on the shirt of her gray uniform and pulled out her feather duster—one she had custom-ordered. Built into its top was a discreet button that activated a camera whose lens was at the other end hanging on a snake cord buried in the duster. With her thumb on the button silently clicking away, she made a few gratuitous dusting sweeps at each of the glass cases as she shot the entirety of the first two rat communities, sometimes holding the duster at most undusterlike angles to get it all.

She glanced at her watch, her heart pounding. She snapped a few more anyway. Just then she noticed that a file drawer built into the third case near the floor had been left unlocked and slightly ajar. Looking through the windows into the hallway to make sure Blanchard was nowhere near, she bent down and pulled the drawer open. One file name grabbed her attention: STATUS OF BETA TESTING from ThinkSoft's Neuro Group, marked LEVEL ONE CONFIDENTIAL. She pulled it out and skimmed over it quickly, a few phrases jumping off the page:

Two Neuro Group products in beta testing: Wholly Grill and Electronic Truth Serum . . . . E-Serum human subjects will broadcast their own security breaches . . . .

Not two seconds passed when suddenly, and somehow by merely

holding the file, an irrational but uncontrollable electric charge surged into her skull.

"Hey! I'm taking this file!" she shouted in the direction of the hallway and Blanchard's station. The words gushed from her mouth. "Hiding it under my shirt! Check me when I leave! Employee theft in progress!"

With the spellbinding current sweeping through her, she was about to take the file and her monologue out into the hallway—perhaps even in search of Blanchard—when one more fragment of the report managed to reach inside and pierce her consciousness:

Initial test group, unaware and involuntary, composed of part-time company custodians.

The last line stung like a slap across the face. Her voice was silenced as instantly as if someone had hit the MUTE button. The sheer rush of awareness that *she too was an experimental rat*—in a much larger glass case—shot through her head, enough to override whatever had triggered the compulsive speech of the moment before.

She stuffed the file back in, slammed the drawer shut, and drew a deep breath. The thought of something bigger and more powerful than she had imagined—something frighteningly unknown—made her tremble. Still reeling, she started dusting aimlessly around the floor.

"What the hell are you doing?" Blanchard, who was standing at the door, demanded. "I told you not to touch the glass cases! And where did you get that duster? I didn't give you a duster!"

"*Señor*, I have this when I come." Her hands still shaking, she mustered a barely calm voice and an accent she counted on would register with him as not-smart-enough-for-subterfuge. "I hold like this." She showed him by placing the duster in her back pocket and out of his reach before he could grab it from her.

"Pick up the items you brought in here and follow me," he scolded, looking at his clipboard. "That was a breach of security procedure. Compren-day?" he added with a sneer.

‹ 6 ›

Since moving to San Jose and starting his new job a few months ago, Will was only making the traditional Sunday night dinner at his parents' about once a month. Tonight was the first time in five weeks. When he had been living in the San Francisco area and attending law school, he visited almost every week. When he and Dagmar were still together, he would occasionally bring her home with him.

His parents had never approved of Dagmar. They never said anything to him one way or another about her; that's how he knew. That too had angered and fueled him all the more to prove he could make it on his own terms. After all, Dagmar had credentials that couldn't be overlooked: beauty, style, and elegance. But that wasn't enough for his parents; it stung when he overheard his mother on the telephone refer to Dagmar as "Naugahyde," her shorthand for people, particularly women, she was fond of describing as "not the genuine article" or "with everything adorning her hide yet nothing real inside." That was another thing that burned him about his parents' attitude—as if there was something wrong with having new money. Dagmar's father, an engineer and German immigrant, had made a fortune in Silicon Valley. She had grown up in "San Jose society," something Mary Beth Swanson considered an oxymoron. As far as Will was concerned, Dagmar— now an ex-girlfriend and out of the picture—was the scapegoat for what his parents considered his ill-conceived career choice.

The three of them were seated in the oak-paneled great room in the family home where Will grew up, facing a custom-built cabinet holding the television and surrounded by a wall of books. A few empty shelves displayed photographs of Will and his younger sister, Bridget, an undergrad at USC. To their backs was a window that framed a spectacular panorama of the North Bay where—from left to right, north to south—Will never tired of gazing out at the Golden Gate, the Marin Headlands, the Marina, Angel Island, and Alcatraz.

"How's it going, dear?" his mother asked politely, as she flipped through a copy of *Architectural Digest*. She followed the unspoken protocol they had evolved: Ask a broad question that made no reference to his job. Will was supposed to answer with something equally nondescript, and then they could talk about a variety of neutral subjects, unless, of course, his father started in on him. He knew it embarrassed his mother; she was simply incapable of explaining to her friends that her son with the sterling future at McKenna Covington had gone to work for a no recovery/no fee lawyer in San Jose.

"Everything's fine," Will answered obligingly.

"Let's get some scores," his father said, picking up the remote and punching on the TV. Roderick Swanson liked to turn on ESPN *Sportscenter* on Sunday nights to pick up the weekend highlights. The TV came on to cable Channel 58, where an announcer was charging through the News in Brief. Will prayed his father would quickly move on to ESPN. A certain commercial was scheduled to air regularly on Channel 58—one his parents had never seen—and he didn't want to be there when and if they ever did. Without saying a word Will fixed his eyes on his father's right thumb, idly scratching the side of the remote. Before flipping to ESPN, Will's father paused to listen:

"The stock in Silicon Valley–based ThinkSoft Corporation shot up another ten points today, fueled by the wildly successful launch of Wholly Grill. . . ."

Will shuddered. Predictably, stock talk and market news would take priority over ESPN. Roderick Swanson was president of a successful financial services firm in downtown San Francisco: Swanson Breckenridge, specializing in life insurance, employee benefits, and management of 401(k) plans. It was hammered into Will that frequently those clients made ripe candidates for estate planning lawyers. If he had taken the job with McKenna Covington, as his father had urged him to do, he would have been set up for life, guaranteed— right out of the gates—to bring more new business into the firm than many of the partners who had been there for years. New clients would be served to him on a silver platter, discreetly, quietly, and without tasteless self-promotion. His father couldn't believe he had turned down the golden opportunity at McKenna Covington for the law offices of Edwin G. Ostermyer.

"Now, there's a company you should have a piece of," his father said.

"Huh?" Will managed.

"If you were at McKenna Covington, you'd have some money and a stock portfolio by now. I'd get you in on ThinkSoft. That stock will touch the sky and keep right on climbing."

Will said nothing. His anxiety was growing. Perhaps he should have readily agreed simply as a device to deploy the right thumb. If he had any money, he thought to himself, he'd invest it right now in a company developing telepathic remote controls. Instead, Roderick Swanson put the remote down and removed his glasses to rub his eyes. That was his way of wordlessly signaling his frustration with his son.

"We'll have more News in Brief next hour and a full report at eleven." The announcer signed off.

Without warning—without Will's having a chance to take a deep breath—the commercial burst onto the tube. It filled the room, demanded their attention, and startled them as much as a home invasion. The entire screen was consumed by Edwin G. Ostermyer, suddenly all talking head and bellowing voice. The Nose was trained on its TV audience:

"I'm Edwin G. Ostermyer, trial lawyer. You may have read about the millions I recovered recently on behalf of cheated consumers. . . . "

Will glanced sheepishly sideways, left and right. Both his parents seemed to have been shot with a stun gun, instantly rendered mute and motionless. The ad made reference to a highly publicized class action Edwin had brought against a group of doughnut manufacturers who sold "donut holes" that were—Edwin convinced a jury—"not begotten of real doughnuts." They were merely dollops of dough squirted by a dough-squirting machine. He had successfully recovered millions on behalf of a large class of defrauded consumers.

It was not the worst fraud ever perpetrated on the public, but it had served its purpose well in garnering Edwin plenty of media attention. Since then, he'd been able to gain leverage from the publicity the "donut hole" litigation had earned him.

"If you are hurt by a defective product, I promise that I will expose the ugly truth about the manufacturer. I'll prove that the company's case is just like a doughnut: The truth is all glazed over, but when I finish with cross-examination we'll see there is nothing inside. I'll expose those holes."

Solemnly he held up for the camera an unusually large doughnut with an unusually large hole in the middle. He looked through the hole, taking care to hold it far enough away from his nose to avoid any resemblance to a game of hoop toss. Simultaneously and involuntarily, Mary Beth and Roderick Swanson dropped their jaws as if they were about to be force-fed what they were seeing.

"Put a fighter in your corner. Let me punch holes for you."

At the end of the thirty-second spot, Edwin's hands dove into a bucket of doughnut holes and popped them in his mouth two at a time. At the very end he sustained for the camera the look of a killer, of a hired assassin. Will had been in Edwin's office during a brief telephone conference with the director of the ad. Edwin had said, "It has to be a look that bespeaks relishment of the spoils of victory . . . a predator . . . of *anything* or *anybody* that stands in my way. Edwin G. Ostermyer, Predator of Doughnut Manufacturers. That's what people want. Make me look ravenous to go after their oppressors!" That was the look the Swansons and other TV viewers saw as the toll-free number flashed on the screen in large print.

And then it was over.

Mary Beth Swanson's expression suggested she had seen her son's employer pitching the Law Offices of Muammar Khadafy. She was dumbstruck, horrified. Roderick Swanson stared grimly ahead, equally in shock. Finally, he turned and glared at Will for several painfully long seconds. Then he stood and walked out of the room; his steps were heard ascending the stairs toward the bedroom. He would not return.

"It's just a way of bringing in business." Will finally broke the silence, speaking loudly in the direction of the receding footsteps. "Product defect lawyers perform a valuable service to society, and successful ones make good money doing it. Face it, people get hurt by products and need help. TV ads are a way to reach them."

Indeed, the ads were hugely successful. Will Swanson, however, was talking into dead air. This jury wasn't listening to him. He'd have to do a lot better to make his case. And it was going to be a long time before he was welcomed back on Sunday night.

<h1>‹ 7 ›</h1>

Landing his first-ever client, courtesy of the Santa Clara County Bar Association Lawyer Referral Service, was easier than he thought. He tried not to seem too anxious, but it was downright exciting. If cleared, this would mean he would have a client he could call his own—for whom he alone was responsible—even if it *was* pro bono.

"I'd really like to help you," Will said, leaning forward in earnest at his desk. "Of course, I'll need to clear it with Mr. Ostermyer, but looking at your income and the debts you've told me about, you're eligible for pro bono representation."

"What's pro bono mean?" Lenny Milton asked, tilting at Will—spilling over, out of, and otherwise threatening the continued structural integrity of Will's only client chair. The small space was furnished exclusively by Office Barn. Books and client files were stacked everywhere.

"*Pro bono publico*, for the public good," the young lawyer explained. "That's where lawyers take clients for no charge as a public service, particularly where there is a financial hardship. It sounds like you qualify, based on your income situation." Will studied the yellow pad he had been filling with notes, then furrowed his brow. "I'm sorry, what kind of insurance did you say you sell?"

"I sell malpractice insurance for brokers."

"For what kind of brokers?" Will asked, taking more notes. "Real estate? Insurance?"

"No. Strictly mattress brokers." Lenny leaned back; the chair groaned. "It's a new company—Mattress Mutual—the first to specialize in this market. Mattress brokers have special needs, you know. But so far it's been difficult to sell them on the idea." Lenny shook his head dejectedly. "It's a—"

"Sleeper in the insurance trade?" Will couldn't resist. They both laughed in a way that solidified the bond between them. Lenny's big round face lit up. Will liked Lenny. "Here's what I'd like to do," he continued. It felt good to know what to do—to be able to help another human being with legal problems. He glanced down where he had written the word PLAN at the top of the yellow pad and some notes below it. "First, let me see if I can negotiate with your creditors so you can avoid filing bankruptcy. Second, we need to do something about the barbecue grill accident and all the vet bills you're facing. I'll write a letter to ThinkSoft and demand reimbursement of your money and payment of your bills. However, in order to prove you should get your money back, you should try to connect a couple more times and document that you can't get through."

"Because of what happened to Lady J, I don't want the Wholly Grill anymore," Lenny said, pain in his voice.

"I know you don't," Will said. "But we need to make a record of more than one night you've been unable to connect with the Wholly WORD. If ThinkSoft refuses your claim, I think a small claims judge would be more likely to agree with you. Of course, you can't have a lawyer in small claims, but I can help you put together the presentation of your case."

"I just want to make sure I can take care of Lady J," Lenny said, the sadness rising again in his voice. "And if you can get the bill collectors to back off a little until I get my business going . . . ?"

"Good. Then we've agreed on a plan," Will said. "Let me get the OK on this."

Will excused himself and headed down the hall toward Edwin's office. He felt good about his first solo client intake. He liked Lenny, and he had come up with what seemed like a simple and straightforward plan, the right combination of lawyer help and client self-help to set Lenny right. It was a heady experience to reflect that a client had sought him out for professional advice—calling for real legal analysis and judgment—and would even have paid for it if he were able.

Will had learned his first week on the job that nothing Edwin touched was simple and straightforward. It seemed as if every legal dispute Edwin handled required that special weapons and tactics be summoned to the scene—"SWATtorneys" leaping out of the backs of trucks and charging into courtrooms with bayonets and briefcases. That was Edwin's MO, at least for his clients, but this time it was *Will's* client. He had a sensible plan that Edwin need only approve.

Finding Edwin in his office, Will briefly explained Lenny Milton's situation. "So, if it's OK, I'd like to take him on and help him out pro bono. I think I can get it wrapped up quickly."

Edwin pondered. "You say he bought this grill from ThinkSoft? I don't believe I've ever sued them before. Hmm, I've got an idea . . . *Pro bono publico* is noble and worthy; don't get me wrong. But *pro bono promo* is even better; everybody wins. Bring Lenny Milton into my office."

Will had no idea what Edwin was thinking—he rarely did—but he returned to his office to retrieve his client and his yellow pad.

When Will and Lenny arrived back in Edwin's office, it was obvious that Lenny was in awe of the well-known trial lawyer. The walls in Edwin's spacious office were covered with framed news clippings of his cases and photographs of Edwin with politicians and public figures. "Wow! I get to meet Edwin G. Ostermyer?" Lenny had said, when Will told him of Edwin's request.

"Will has told me a little about your case," Edwin said to Lenny, now seated in the office. "Although we could take your case pro bono, it occurs to me that you have a case here for damages over and above the vet bills. We could take this case on a contingency. Will, of course, would handle it. You still pay nothing, but I think you should end up with more than just the vet bills. You've been wronged terribly."

Lenny looked quizzically at Will. "Well, I'm not sure. In the license I agreed to be responsible for using the meat on the wrong grill. That was the deal."

"What?" Edwin was incredulous. "A license to grill?"

"ThinkSoft put shrink-wrap licenses around the barbecue *and* the free sirloin tip," Will explained to Edwin. "The sirloin license says the purchaser agrees to cook the pre-marinated meat only on the Wholly Grill system and not on his Weber."

"Let me get this straight," Edwin said, staring up at the ceiling as if contemplating a world gone mad. He pulled out a pad of white legal paper and sketched a boxlike barbecue grill.

"What color is the offending device?" Edwin asked Lenny.

"Black," Lenny answered, glancing at Will for a clue as to what Edwin was doing.

"I should have guessed." Edwin snorted. "These merchants of death, dismemberment and—in the tragic case of Lady J—eternal darkness." Edwin put down his blue pen and picked up a black one. He quickly colored the grill black, going well outside the lines. He then wrote the words *shrink-wrap license* and circled it; he drew a line between the grill and the circled words.

"And so what, pray tell, does this *license to grill* have to say?" Edwin asked, contempt for manufacturers seeping from his voice.

"Various things," Will replied. "It says that Lenny agrees to use the Wholly Grill only when connected to ThinkSoft's Wholly WORD." Edwin didn't seem to have any interest in what it actually said; Will continued anyway. "That they are not responsible for interruption of service—"

"And that I can only use Wholly Grill barbecue sauce," Lenny interjected, grieving. "They won't let me cook meat with my own marinade."

Edwin threw down the pen he was holding and bolted to his feet. "This is fraught with abuse!" He began pacing the room, working himself up to a crescendo. "This is an illegal restraint of trade! Worse, it usurps rights guaranteed to you under the First Amendment of the United States Constitution." Edwin walked over to the window and looked out. He seemed to be looking not just at the gray street below or the parking structure across the way but somehow beyond, as though he were seeing all of America. "The right to free speech, the right to worship where you please, and—yes!—even the right to baste with the barbecue sauce of your own choosing. You had every right to ignore the illegal agreement!"

Will waited a moment before begging to differ. "Actually, courts have upheld those licenses. That's why I thought Lenny should try to rescind the agreement." He turned to Lenny to explain. "Rescission. That's where you exercise your right to cancel a contract because you didn't get what you paid for . . . like being able to dial in and turn on your grill."

"I'm not sure it's a good idea to ignore it," Lenny added, speaking to Edwin. "The company enforces these agreements."

Edwin scoffed. "How can they do that? People using barbecue sauce in their own homes? Talk about a contract with no teeth!"

Lenny glanced at Will, smiling sheepishly. "Oh, I think they have *teeth* all right. I read some stuff on the Internet last night. They have a group called the Society of Manufacturers for the Enforcement of Licenses, K-Nine Division. This group, which goes by the initials, SMEL, is kinda like the music police. You know, the ones that go after the Girl Scouts for using their music at summer camps."

"ASCAP," Edwin said. "The American Society of Composers, Authors and Publishers. And there is BMI, too. They enforce the rights of copyright owners for public performances of music belonging to their members. If it isn't Girl Scout camps, it's in bars and restaurants where music is played." Will had noticed how Edwin loved opportunities to show a prospective client how knowledgeable he was, be it a technical issue in an automobile accident reconstruction, a fine point of criminal procedure, or even the rarefied world of copyright enforcement.

Edwin focused again on his pad of paper. He sketched a dog with a conelike nose—possibly a German shepherd—and drew a line between the circled words *shrink-wrap license* and the dog. On the line he wrote the word *enforcement.*

"So you think there's something illegal about this?" Lenny asked.

"To say the least!" Edwin replied, without looking up. He was now drawing a picture of a file cabinet. He drew lines with arrows at both ends between the file cabinet and both the German shepherd and the barbecue grill. "I can't wait to subpoena the documents that show they knew there was a danger in using Wholly Grill barbecue sauce on another grill. It's a classic failure-to-warn case! I can't wait to expose them!" Edwin was getting that ravenous look, as seen on TV.

"I don't think you can sue them and ignore the license," Will repeated politely. "If you sue only for negligence and product defect, don't you think they'll—"

"Of course we can!" Edwin pronounced. "We won't sue on the contract. We'll go after their failure to warn. Strictly negligence and product defect claims." He turned to the young lawyer. "Will, prepare a contingent fee agreement and file a lawsuit immediately in Municipal Court."

Edwin leaned forward, stretching his arms out enough to display the monogrammed initials on his shirt cuffs.

"And I know how we can promote an early settlement." The white Egyptian cotton of his French cuffs protruded, retracted, and now fully protruded from his suit jacket. "We'll issue a press release, letting them know we mean business. When they see I'm involved, they'll want to settle quickly."

Will tore out the yellow sheet of paper with his plan on it. He crumpled it up and threw it in the wastebasket in frustration. Neither Edwin nor Lenny seemed to notice. The young associate bit his lip and didn't say a word. He couldn't protest—not in front of his client—as much as he wanted to grouse about Edwin's imposition on *his* client. Besides, Lenny appeared overwhelmed by Edwin's self-confidence and sense of injustice.

"I just want to be able to take care of Lady J. You're right. If they had only warned me." Lenny almost broke into tears.

Edwin rose and walked over to Lenny. He stood behind his chair and put his hands on Lenny's shoulders. Both men looked into the mirror behind Edwin's desk: Lenny looked at the reflected image of Edwin; Edwin looked at Edwin. "I was so sorry to hear about Lady J. Obviously she's a best friend in the truest sense. But let me assure you that the case you have is a lot juicier than that sirloin tip ever would have been. We shall not rest until we all—not just you and I but Lady J herself—see justice done."

‹ 8 ›

It was still early on a Saturday morning. Persi rolled her cleaning supplies to a row of cubicles on the sixth floor of Admin 1. Dusting from
station to station, she couldn't help but notice that one computer had
not been shut down or logged off the company's network.

On the screen were several program icons she recognized—for
launching word processing, calendar, and spreadsheet applications—
but one stood out as temptingly unfamiliar: a bright red graphic in the
lower right corner inviting her to open SECRETS & SOLUTIONS. The
name held her imagination hostage. *Solution* was another hackneyed
conceit from the tech lexicon; companies didn't sell software *products*
but rather *solutions*. Knowing ThinkSoft, SECRETS & SOLUTIONS was an
infotech product whose implied logic ran like this with its unsuspecting customers: We can't tell you the solution to your problem
until you pay us; even then, we'll have to deliver the solution under a
shroud of secrecy and confidentiality to which not even you, the customer, can be privy. That way you can't be sure whether you've bought
a solution or a bigger problem.

Persi's right hand reached out to the keyboard, but she had to be
careful. What if it had something to do with the remaining skeleton
in the Neuro Group closet: namely, Electronic Truth Serum? This
much she had concluded: Just by firmly holding the file last week, the

stunning E-Serum—whatever it was—had been activated, causing her to rat on herself.

She dusted around another minute, her eyes never wandering far from the beckoning icon. Finally, she yielded to temptation, laying the duster aside. Listening for any approaching sound, and careful not to grasp anything or leave fingerprints, she placed a cleaning rag over the mouse and double-clicked it.

She was taken by surprise when the screen filled with color and motion, accompanied by a drumbeat and electronic music. A knight, mounted and taking off, dominated the screen; an aged wizard with hand held high bade him farewell. The title, SECRETS & SOLUTIONS, splashed across the top half of the screen and announced, "The Quest Continues."

Instead of the secret memos and data she expected to see, a computer game loaded on screen, one she had never heard of. She clicked on HELP, then ABOUT, and learned it was created internally and anonymously at the company. Questions and requests for tech support were directed to gamemaster@thinksoft.com. Available only on the company network, the game seemed purely for the amusement of overworked coders in need of occasional diversion. Clicking on FILE, she found that this cubicle dweller had been playing the game for six months and had advanced three levels, but with an endless number of levels to the game she could play on indefinitely.

Persi was familiar with the different types of computer games— role-playing games, real-time strategy games, adventure games, and virtual reality games—having written articles about this segment of the tech industry. Game designers took care to build in an all-consuming goal, or sometimes a set of goals, for players, everything from scoring points to defeating the aliens and saving the world. Reading a brief overview in FILE, Persi learned the object was to gather clues and survive obstacles along the way in order to obtain "ultimate know-how," but what that was or what it would do was not explained. A surviving player, according to what Persi read, would eventually come upon the "Holder," whereupon "all would be revealed." This game appeared to be a combination of adventure and virtual reality.

She clicked START, bringing on the alternate world. A knight popped up, ready to take direction. This was no ordinary knight; it was the cubicle dweller's custom-designed "avatar," an animated graphical representation assumed by a real person for venturing into cyberspace. Avatars were the alter egos for visitors to virtual worlds and often, at least symbolically, told something about their flesh-and-blood sponsors who dwelt off-line. Persi expected this cubicle was occupied by a woman, based on the few personal effects: a hairbrush, a photo of a boyfriend, and sticky notes with feminine handwriting. Her knightly avatar was clad in iron everywhere except on the head, hands, and feet—the standard issue for this game—but was accessorized with a plumed hat, long nails, and ludicrous high heels.

Entering the game in progress, Persi found herself—through her borrowed avatar—in a medieval village, a mysterious castle in the distance. A beggar, crouched against a wall, jumped up. Dropping his cloak, he turned into a soldier of the Dark Kingdom and advanced toward her in attack mode. He was joined by a vicious dog that leaped out from a nearby door. Spike heels notwithstanding, she ran swiftly down a cobblestone street to a white door leading into the Temple of the Realm. Temporarily safe, she found twenty objects there to select from, but had only three seconds to choose one. She double-clicked the fountain in the atrium, and it turned into a gleaming crystal pendant, promising special powers for interacting at this level. Double-clicking again, the pendant now adorned her avatar's neck.

Forced by time limits to exit the Temple, she found herself out on the cobblestone street again. Another figure approached, this one with sneakers but cowled in white, vaguely resembling a nun from a humble order. Another avatar! An encounter with a real person!

Greetings, Lori Croft. Type scrolled across the bottom of the screen.

Persi deduced that the on-screen avatar she'd borrowed was the cyber-stand-in for someone whose actual name was Lori. Likewise, the avatar's name, Lori Croft, was probably chosen to conjure up another adventurer of fictional dimensions: Lara Croft of *Tomb Raider*. As to the sex of the virtual nun Persi just encountered, there was no way of telling for sure—not with a nun in sneakers, not with any nun this close to San Francisco. After all, the nearby city was home to the Sisters of Perpetual Indulgence—the few, the proud, the brave—*men* who every year, clad in decidedly irreverent habits, lead the parade in San Francisco's Lesbian, Gay, Bisexual and Transgender Pride Celebration.

What are you doing here? the nun asked.

Where was *here*? Did someone want to know what Lori was doing at work on Saturday, or what Lori Croft was doing in this medieval village? Persi needed to make this quick. Best to play along like she's Lori Croft. "Exploring this village, digging for clues," she typed.

Different word architecture! the nun shot back, having processed six words of diction and syntax in a nanosecond. Scary! *You're not Lori Croft! Who are you?*

There was nothing whimsical about the strange-looking nun. She— no, Persi divined, *he*—was gravely serious. Just then she heard someone approaching the cubicle area. Her heart pounded. No time to cover her tracks.

"*¿Qué pasa, María?*"

Adrenaline whipped her blood into a turbid roar, but she was able to let out one short breath of relief.

"*Cálmate, mi hija.* It's only me." It was her co-worker and friend, Imelda.

Still frantic, Persi clicked SAVE and exited the game, rudely deserting the nun in the middle of a medieval village. She could only hope someone would not come looking for Lori.

Imelda smiled, implicitly approving whatever mischief Persi had found. The two of them had arrived on the sixth floor together half an hour ago; Imelda started cleaning at one end and Persi on the other. She was about twice Persi's age, the same height but sturdier in frame. When she smiled, her high angular cheeks softened, and her dark-brown eyes radiated an infectious joy—a love of life that was strongest when she talked about her five children or her seven grandchildren.

Having seniority, Imelda carried the radio keeping them in touch with operations. She had received a call from their boss, Phil Torres— *el Jefe,* the Chief.

"He wants you to meet him up in RD Two right away. He has an emergency cleanup for you."

"Why does he want me? Since when am I an emergency cleaning specialist?" Persi asked, speaking Spanish.

"Maybe because you are *muy bonita,*" Imelda answered, smiling.

"Oh, please," Persi protested. "He's married . . . and twice my age!"

Imelda was a big tease but in a good-natured way. The line about the Chief managed to get a rise out of Persi because there was a grain of truth in it. He probably had asked for her because she was *bonita,* but that was as far as it went. He was a well-behaved married man.

Moments earlier, at 7:30 A.M., the Chief had received a computer-generated report that it was a sweltering 104 degrees inside RD 2. The sole occupants this morning consisted of four programmers on the fifth floor—with ThinkSoft's QE Deluxe legal reasonware division— who had been holed up there cranking code for seven days straight. When their microwave oven gave out and it was too early to order takeout, they solved the problem by hacking into and reprogramming the building's heating system from a PC.

Persi stepped out of the elevator on the third floor, at the same time as the Chief, to a scene that might have been a twisted remake of *Beach Party.* The wiped-out coders—all in their twenties—were wearing nothing but their colorful Jockey shorts, with the exception of the one female sporting black underwear and matching bra. A languorous slow motion seemed to govern their every gesture. Sweat streamed from their skinny borderline-undernourished bodies. One young man lay on his stomach next to a convection oven fashioned from hardware casings taken from cubicles and arranged over the floor heating vent. Dreamily he watched over a configuration of slices of Wonder Bread topped with Kraft singles ripening into glistening golden cheese-melts. Hula music swayed gently from computer speakers, courtesy of a site they found that was Webcasting from a native Hawaiian village located in the middle of a rain forest—or so Persi overheard the programmers say. While two swivel-chaired young men played imaginary slack-key guitars, the woman performed a delirious hula dance.

After Persi and the Chief arrived, the programmers decided to pack it in, go home, and get some sleep. They would neither be reported nor reprimanded; the policy at ThinkSoft was to overlook minor facility abuses *as long as they appeared to be developing code*. The Chief radioed someone to reprogram the heating system while Persi cleaned up crumbs, cheese dribblings, and such.

She returned to the cubicle area on the sixth floor of Admin 1 to finish up. She emptied the trash and began vacuuming. She noticed a memo—not there before she left—conspicuously placed in the middle of an otherwise neat cubicle she had already cleaned. More strangely, the memo—stamped CONFIDENTIAL—was written in both English and Spanish. She read it but did not dare lay hands on it as she had done with the file in RD 807 a week earlier. The memo described how to get free food in the employee cafeteria by keying into the cafeteria with a password given only to guests of the company who were "comped" during their stay at ThinkSoft. Although the easy-to-remember password was printed at the bottom, she had no intention of trying it out. Stealing food from the cafeteria was outside her investigation.

Suddenly the weekend quiet in the office hallways was broken by a frantic disturbance at the other end of the floor. It was Imelda. Persi hurried halfway down the hall and stopped where she could observe without being seen.

Imelda was being detained by a security agent with a German shepherd. The agent squinted at her; from head to toe, and then back up again, he looked her over methodically as if going through a mental checklist of symptoms. From Persi's vantage point she could see her friend was wild-eyed, behaving as though possessed. She was loudly blabbering in Spanish: "I took it . . . It belongs to ThinkSoft! . . . My young one really wants one. I didn't want you to know! . . . It's in my left pocket . . . You can arrest me!"

Persi recognized the careening speech pattern caused by the Electronic Truth Serum, but there was nothing she could do for her friend. Out in the middle of the hall someone had left a large open box with hundreds of so-called 'SOFTbabies, tiny plush toy figures ThinkSoft marketeers had dreamed up to get children to demand the ThinkSoft brand. The company had produced millions of them as premium giveaways so that kids would become lifetime habitual purchasers of ThinkSoft reasonware. 'SOFTbabies had become so popular that an entire secondary market had developed around them.

The dog barked and pointed. The security agent, dressed in a quasi-military uniform, reached into her left pocket and pulled out a single crumpled 'SOFTbaby. He then examined it, perhaps checking the product series number. The dog barked some kind of verification when the item was passed in front of its nose.

In an instant Persi knew that the box of 'SOFTbabies had been planted out in the hall. Her mind reeled when she considered the implications: Was the memo she had seen also left out as bait . . . or only the information in it? Was possession of information enough to trigger Electronic Truth Serum in her again—wherever and whatever it was?

"Your employment with ThinkSoft is terminated," the security agent told Imelda bluntly. "I could turn you over to the police, but if you agree to keep everything about your experience at ThinkSoft quiet we can avoid that. Please follow me." Hands cuffed behind her back, Imelda was led away.

‹ 9 ›

"Of course I care if they're stealing *things* from ThinkSoft! But that's not why we spent ninety-eight million in R and D on it!"

Art Newman was furious, shouting into his cell phone as he rode alone in a golf cart between the last hole and the next tee at the Burlingame Country Club. He was the guest today of his longtime attorney, Thurston Crushjoy.

"Listen! We're not developing E-Serum to guard ourselves against pilfering of plush toys—or paper clips, for that matter!" he yelled. "I want to know if employees are taking *information*, for God's sake!"

The technology was, needless to say, complicated. For E-Serum to be activated, some kind of tangible property of ThinkSoft had to be physically in the possession of the employee. To initialize self-disclosure of *intangible* property—that is, trade secrets—would require a complex set of calculations and calibrations on one of ThinkSoft's powerful mainframe computers. Art listened patiently to the explanation for a full five seconds before slamming the brakes on the golf cart.

"Just figure it out! Fast!" he bellowed. "This firewall should've been in place a month ago. Do you understand what's at stake? The Wholly Grill must be secured at all costs! Amp it up! Get it done!" He threw the phone on the floor and lurched the cart forward again.

When Art pulled up to the fifth tee, his attorney was already there. Thurston Crushjoy was a tall man, powerfully built for his sixty years, power most embodied not merely by musculature but by his legendary jaw, large enough to be seen from a distance, substantial enough for oceangoing ships to use as a landmark for navigation.

Thurston Crushjoy had missed a twenty-two-foot eagle putt on the last hole by a half inch. While Art finished putting, Crushjoy had walked ahead to the next hole with his long quick stride, a habit of his when he wanted to carefully review the "game tapes" in his head, to make sure coming up short of perfection did not recur. Meticulous analysis, preparation, and execution were the hallmarks of Thurston Crushjoy, whether on the golf course or in the courtroom.

Crushjoy asked after the condition of the offices back at Thinksoft. "The usual aches and pains," Art responded. Art teed up his ball but was troubled by a tree that posed a problem for the slice nagging his driver today. He picked up his ball and tee and moved it outside the box for regulation play to a location more his liking. "Incidentally, I was also just told that the first lawsuit has been filed against the new Wholly Grill division. We picked up on the Web a press release issued by the suing law firm. Some idiot tried to cook the free sirloin tip on his Weber. Ha! Imagine thinking his old Weber would support *our* information-laden sauce!" He took two practice swings. "Something about his little pooch catching on fire and going blind. Talk about a dog of a case! Muni Court in San Jose. Our insurance company will defend it for us."

He teed off. The ball skidded haplessly and then rolled for about seventy-five yards, landing in front of the pesky tree that now stood between him and the hole. Art recalled he hadn't taken a mulligan when he played last week with his tax lawyer. He decided to go ahead and take last week's mulligan by kicking the ball out away from the tree.

Crushjoy advanced to the center of the box and gazed out at the distant hole. "Your shrink-wrap should knock that claim out." He planted his tee in the center. "But are you sure you want to take your chances with an insurance company defending your license the first time out? All it takes is one judge to say it's invalid, and the dam bursts. As if you don't remember what happened to MicroGiant."

Crushjoy was referring to the company that had dominated the software market before ThinkSoft. MicroGiant had held a contest to see who could come up with an operating system for a new artificial intelligence software, what later became reasonware. The winner would receive the glory and a $50,000 prize. Art's son, Joon Newman, had entered the contest seven years ago at his father's direction. Unknown to Art, Joon had submitted his completed "developer's kit'" but imposed a major condition on its use: "If you employ this operating system, you agree that it belongs to no one. It shall become open source, for anyone to use, modify, and share alike with others." When Art found out, he was furious.

Meanwhile, MicroGiant ignored the precocious fifteen-year-old's conditions and relied on the terms of its contest entry package: BY BREAKING THIS SEAL AND ENTERING YOUR SOFTWARE INTO THIS CONTEST, YOU AGREE THAT ANY SOFTWARE YOU CREATE AND SUBMIT BECOMES THE PROPERTY OF MICROGIANT.

Joon Newman's operating system didn't just win. His operating system was brilliant and revolutionary. The company sent the $50,000 check and launched its product. The check was never cashed. Art Newman immediately sought the help of Thurston Crushjoy to find a way to cancel the MicroGiant agreement and make sure that Joon's freeware offer never took hold. Thurston Crushjoy made it all happen so fast in court that MicroGiant was left standing with its legal briefs down around its ankles.

Crushjoy argued that Joon Newman, a fifteen-year-old, was a minor and by law not old enough to be bound by any contract, whether under MicroGiant's terms or his own. The judge voided all deals, and Art gained control again of the rights that launched ThinkSoft.

Whenever Thurston Crushjoy counseled a legal course of action, Art was ready to listen. "What are you suggesting?" he asked the lawyer.

"We should take the strongest measures to protect the trade secrets of Wholly Grill," Crushjoy said grimly. "Send the complaint over to the insurance company to defend, and send a copy to me. I'm thinking we might set up your shrink-wrap license in concrete early on . . . maybe with a little surprise."

Without taking a practice swing, he exploded into the ball with his driver. The sky seemed to stagger back a step, sucker-punched by an improbable shot up the middle, a powerful uppercut with relentless upward thrust. Thurston Crushjoy was back in complete control of his game.

‹ 10 ›

At eleven-forty-five Wednesday morning, Will arrived back at the office from a meeting and picked up his mail at the front desk. He was walking slowly down the hall, sorting through a stack of correspondence and junk mail, when from a close distance behind a familiar woman's voice arrested him in his tracks. The sheer sound of it pierced the part of his soul that, for a long time now, had been "getting over it."

"Will?"

He turned around to face Dagmar for the first time in four months. Seeing her so near to him instantly infused his blood with an addling mix of pain and desire. As always, she was beautiful: pale blue eyes embedded like precious stones in the ivory of her complexion, delicately framed by lustrous black hair. Statuesque and dressed *à la mode*, she looked to have sprung straight from the catalog pages of Banana Republic—where she also happened to work.

"Dagmar . . . hi. What are you doing here?" he managed. Five yards away, she took three steps closer. To his unfailing awe, she always walked like a model on a runway. Her legs moved as easily as running water while her head remained perfectly still and upright. Dagmar had actually done some runway modeling.

"I'm meeting Mother. We're having lunch with Uncle Edwin today."

Her mother, Gilda, was very different from her brother Edwin. Gilda had married Detlef Brittman, a German engineer whose financial success here in the Valley was legend. He and his socially ambitious wife had become fixtures in the Silicon Valley society scene.

"How have you been?" Dagmar asked, with only a hint of guilt in an otherwise solicitous voice. They had been dating on and off for three and a half years. When they were "off," it had always been because she had been the one to say, "This isn't working anymore." He sometimes wondered which of his weaknesses did him more harm, loyalty or lust.

"Fine, fine. Edwin's been keeping me too busy for anything else. I'm learning a lot. Really a lot," he added, in a feeble effort to suggest she was asking how work was going. "How about you?"

"Good. Edwin says you've got a lawsuit of your own. What's it about?"

With Dagmar standing right in front of him, he suddenly wished the receptionist would interrupt him, shouting down the hall at him that a big client was on the phone awaiting his considered opinion on an important matter. He couldn't resist wanting to impress her—to show her he was beyond the lowly inexperience of law school. He was a real lawyer now.

There was no such interruption. He would have to improvise.

"Pretty heady stuff, actually," he heard himself say. Now he would have to back it up. "It's a product liability case that hinges on a failure to warn and the enforceability of high-tech shrink-wrap licenses."

She stared at him blankly. The heady approach wasn't working. He needed to throw some action into the mix. "It's all because there was this terrible disfiguring accident . . . Now I'm battling a huge company to force them to pay."

"Really?" She was becoming a believer now. "What happened to your client?"

"Actually it was his dog. A Chihuahua."

She snickered, both charmed and incredulous. "I can't believe you're telling me everything." Whenever she used to laugh like that, she would take his glasses off—calling him her "very own Clark

Kent"—and run her hands through his brown hair. He never knew whether to be flattered or frustrated by such cooing. Lois Lane regarded Clark Kent, the mild-mannered reporter for *The Daily Planet*, as a bit nerdy, often bumbling, and never *there* for her like Superman always was.

Determined to make it sound impressive, he added, "It's no ordinary dog. She has a real pedigree, I'm told."

She giggled again. She had often said she loved the way he could make her laugh. Funny thing was, right now he wasn't trying to make her laugh.

"I do want to hear more about what you've been up to. Promise you'll call me."

His heart leapt, but he didn't show it. "Yeah, I'd like that."

"Then I'll see you," she said with a smile, as she turned around and headed back toward Edwin's office.

She had always been able to move him that way. That she had urged him to come to work for her Uncle Edwin only half indicated the power she held over him. If she had suggested it, he would have applied to become a judge hearing drug cases in the jungles of Colombia.

"I'll see you," he echoed her. His eyes fixed on her back as she drifted down the hall and away from him. Her right hand glided up to shoulder level and floated there for one and a half seconds. He didn't understand why he could never say no to her.

‹ 11 ›

It was five-forty-five on Saturday afternoon. Persi, as weekend janitor, had punched off the clock upstairs in Building Admin 1 and then slipped downstairs to the women's room in the basement to change her clothes. At six-fifteen she had to be in Saratoga for an exclusive interview with Donald Bigelow, founder and chairman of BigChip, a giant chipmaker in the Valley. Following the interview she was invited to a dinner party at his estate, where a number of other Silicon Valley movers and shakers would be in attendance.

She had done this twice before when she had to go out immediately after leaving work at ThinkSoft. The basement women's room was a good choice because it was virtually private. (She knew nobody used it because she cleaned it from week to week, and the toilet paper was untouched from the week before.) There also was a basement exit near the lot where her car was parked, and she did not have to pass through security again.

Tonight was an occasion to trot out the one killer outfit to her name, specially chosen for evening dress-up events she attended from time to time. It definitely made it easier for these executives to talk, sometimes more than they had planned. She jumped out of her janitor grays and into a short but elegant black skirt and blood-red charmeuse blouse, which she had carefully folded into an old gym bag and carried in this morning when she was still "Maria."

She saw three glossy edges sticking out of one side of her folded wallet. They were sample photographs she had taken of the high-security lab. She decided to look at them again. It occurred to her that in each of the glass cases the lab technicians had created a 3-D version of the popular computer game *SimCity*. In fact, they had gone to some trouble to liven up what was otherwise tedious lab work, displaying the kind of unfettered whimsy only lab technicians can hatch.

The Sims depicted in the first simulated city were greeted by an overhead sign that read WELCOME TO GREEN BAY, HOME OF THE RAT PACKERS. Beneath the sign hung a collection of emblems re-creating the experience of entering an all-American city: Jaycees, Kiwanis, Lion's Club, even the "Ratary." The most popular gathering spot in town was not Lambeau Field, where the real Packers played, but "Lambone Field," a separately enclosed "indoor stadium" for the Rat Packers. Except no sports were played here. This was where the rats were exposed to thick clouds of smoke, blown in and then sucked out through a mesh of clear plastic tubes.

She flipped to the photo of the next case. Greeting "simulated citizens" in this rural community, and promising more suffering for rodent kind, was the sign WELCOME TO FREEZER FARMS, HOME OF THE COLD TURKEYS. A miniature farm was laid out. Fake snow blanketed the barn roofs and grounds. In this module the little critters were shaking, in obvious distress. Either the temperature was a bone-rattling cold or they were suffering from a terrible nervous disorder. Just looking at them again caused Persi to feel a quiver in her stomach.

She looked at the pictures of the last case. A large sign made alluring promises: WELCOME TO RATOPIA, HOME OF THE ALL-YOU-CAN-EAT BBQ. These obese rats were dining, all right, devouring splattered gobs of sauce on lettuce, insects, and pellets.

Despite the utopian theme, it was plain to see that Ratopia was a joyless environment. The inordinately fat rats appeared to be eating nonstop, as if their appetites were permanently switched on. Persi recalled a phrase from Shelley—"sick with delight"—that seemed to describe the vapid pleasures these rats drew from their licentious eating. But she still could not draw any conclusions about these experiments other than what was self-evident: This was a barbecue sauce the rats couldn't resist.

She looked at her watch and threw the photos into the bag. She applied makeup hurriedly, including the right lipstick to accentuate her favorite blouse. She then tossed her compact and janitor clothes into the bag, pulled out her black stiletto heels, and stepped into them. One last look in the mirror—she looked great—and, grabbing the bag without zipping it up, she charged out of the women's room.

Once out the door and while attempting to plant her left heel to negotiate a quick right turn out toward the main basement hall, her ankle gave way, causing her to collapse like a folding table whose leg has been kicked out. Sprawled on the floor with her ankle pulsating in pain, she spontaneously spewed out a few colorful phrases—an earthy poetry—the kind that causes biker chicks to blush.

Just then she heard footsteps behind her. "Are you OK?" the male voice asked.

"Yeah, I'm fine," she said, consciously steadying her voice to avoid a fuss.

Sitting up, she turned and saw none other than Joon Newman standing over her. He was wearing jeans and a pullover and his trademark thick glasses. Persi was horrified. The plan was for a seamless exit but, of all people, she had run into the co-founder, co-owner, and chief technical officer of the entire company. He seemed to have come out of nowhere. The reclusive inventor of reasonware must have been in the boiler room, the only room close to her.

"Can I help you up?" he asked, extending a hand. Her ankle smarted but she had collapsed too quickly to damage it with her full weight.

"Thank you," she said, as he lifted her up. The bag was wide open; in plain view was the photo of the simulated citizens of Ratopia. She gave the bag a quick nudge with her foot, and the photo fell from its perch on her clothes. Had he seen it? Unfortunately, with the photo removed, in its place appeared her ThinkSoft employee badge, still attached to the janitor top. Another kick wouldn't do it. The ID picture showed her from the shoulders up wearing her gray top with the name underneath, MARIA VALENTINO. It was a little late to start speaking with a thick Spanish accent, especially after the brief exchange with Joon, not to mention the robust expletives she had broadcast. Even if she did, how was he supposed to reconcile her humble job with the outfit she was wearing—designed for hobnobbing with executives?

She glanced up at his face for only a second, averting her eyes before his caught hers. No doubt he had seen the employee badge. Underneath his expressionless face either there were more calculations and connections being made per nanosecond than within any other person she had ever met; or maybe nobody was really home. Joon Newman had one of the most brilliant engineering minds in the world; it was safe to assume somebody must be home. The question was who.

"Word architecture familiar," he muttered, while gazing distantly, as if trying to recall something. "Not supposed to be here," he finally added, in a cool voice weighted with judgment. "There are rules."

He stared at her as coldly as a row of code in small print. She couldn't be sure if he was referring to the company rules she was breaking or something else.

"Do you know something?" he asked her. His voice was earnest but vaguely preoccupied, almost talking to himself. His hands twitched at his sides, as if manipulating phantom controls. "On this level you must reveal to me what you know."

"Excuse me?" Persi couldn't think of anything else to say. She knew he was eccentric—that is, a little off center—but she was in no position at this moment to dismiss his cryptic remarks as benign. He was referring to a *level* again, as he had done at the Wholly Grill product launch. He was either referring to the basement of the building, where this well-dressed nonjanitor had no business, or the level after level through which any fantasy role-playing gamer must thrash his way in order to reach the object of the game.

"These are clues," he said, pointing to the various items on the floor: her makeup bag, which had opened and spilled all its contents, a hairbrush, her wallet, an apple, and a plastic pint of spring water. "They are information packets," he said, classifying the items, sounding like the engineer again.

She bent over to pick up the items. He knelt down and did the same. He held the apple and spring water in his hands for a moment and examined them. "These tokens speak of harmony with nature. The apple is knowledge. The color is beautiful," he said, handing the apple to her. Suddenly she had a feeling that she was being shyly complimented, that he was referring to her blouse of the same color. She rose impulsively and smoothed her skirt with her free hand. It was all too strange.

Then he handed the pint bottle up to her, as she stood above where he was kneeling. "And the water is sublimely clear . . . crystalline," he said gently, just as his eyes met hers. "They have special powers."

She did not miss that the spring water had become "they." She knew she had done a commendable job on her eye makeup in a pinch, but she didn't expect this. The eyes she saw this time revealed another facet of this strange young man. There was something lit up, even warm inside, something she just *knew* was there in the way he regarded her—an immediate respect, enraptured from a distance—Joon Newman, the dreamer.

"There's danger here!" he spoke curtly, suddenly narrowing his eyes again at her. His tone was urgent and dispassionate. The dreamer was gone. "What information do you have? Tell me what you know!"

She was startled by the abrupt turn. "I don't know about any danger," she said, trying to smile politely. "Thank you for helping me."

She put the last item in the bag she was holding, turned, and quickly walked away from where he stood. He said nothing more. Once out of the building and walking toward her car, she took a deep breath, her mind still racing from the encounter.

She couldn't help but play over and over again the two faces she had seen. The engineer Art Newman Jr. would thoroughly investigate the employee name he had seen and find out who she was—a bug in the system—information "packets" transmitted but overlooked when she had applied for the job. Art Newman Jr. would follow procedure and report the irregularity. The dreamer, on the other hand, would not disturb the dream. Who knew? Maybe she represented a character in his fantasy computer game that brought new powers—like knowledge or crystals—to fight the forces of evil and advance to a new level. Then there was the feeling she had when he regarded her. Perhaps for that serendipitous moment he imagined himself Dante emerging from the Great Boiler Room at last to meet Beatrice for the first time. Of course, unlike the precise world of the engineer, there was no bright line defining where his dreaming left off and hers began. Besides, all that mattered now was what happened next, something entirely in the restive hands of this strange young man. Whether the engineer, trained to reduce the world around him, would take action against her, or the dreamer would let her be, she could not predict; the power was his and his alone.

Before turning the key to the ignition, she leaned on her steering wheel for half a minute to consider how far she had pressed her luck while working inside ThinkSoft. Her reasons for staying on were complicated. She could have played it safe and quit after the terrifying experience she had had in the lab, with what must have been the E-Serum, and certainly after the incident she witnessed with her friend Imelda. Since then she had carefully avoided touching anything she wasn't supposed to while on the job. But knowing, as only she did, that

E-Serum and Wholly Grill were part of the same beta testing coming out of the Neuro Group, made her all the more determined to find out the true nature of Wholly Grill. One was being tested on a handful of company employees, but the other had already been foisted on millions of unsuspecting consumers. Even if ThinkSoft caught up with her dual career—perhaps a fait accompli after today—she hoped she could use what she knew about E-Serum against the company before they used it against her. It was obviously illegal, however it worked, and they had to know it. Of course, they would deny everything, including the memo about E-Serum she had seen.

Backing out of her parking space, she glanced into her rearview mirror and saw Joon Newman standing outside the door she had just exited. The hood of his pullover was now covering his head, and he was looking out toward her car. He was close enough to know what kind of car she was driving, but he probably couldn't make out her plates from where he was. She gunned the accelerator and flew out of the parking lot.

‹ 12 ›

It was 7:50 A.M. Friday morning, and Will Swanson was pulling his car into one of the parking lots adjoining the Silicon Valley Logic and Convention Center. The lots were already filling up. From his parking spot he could see the center's electronic marquee flashing:

DISCOUNTED REASONWARE—ALL THINKSOFT OS—TODAY ONLY

Will got out of his car, locked it, and started making his way toward the convention center, joining throngs of other people headed in the same direction. As planned, he was meeting Edwin to help him do some shopping.

The new artificial intelligence was originally supposed to be purely an analytical tool for a handful of professionals—in law, accounting, medicine, and such—its uses limited and specialized. A doctor could load the digitized symptoms and test results into a computer, and the program would go to work analyzing the data and printing out the reasons for the illness, along with a treatment recommendation. Or a tax lawyer could load a client's financial and other data into the computer, and the program would come up with a tax-saving strategy or find reasons for characterizing personal expenses as business. Or a criminal defense lawyer could select a defense, and the program would spell out, step by step, under the pre-loaded facts, how to successfully implement the defense.

Most lawyers bought information products from catalogs or from traditional legal publishers, but not Edwin. "The best chefs in town go to the market themselves to select the finest produce and fish they're going to prepare, don't they?" he had said.

Will had no illusions about how different Edwin was. That his boss did not live by the conventions of mainstream—and boring—lawyers didn't trouble Will. What was beginning to bother him was that Edwin was *so* different—*so* much the loose cannon other lawyers saw him to be—that he, Will, might have to make his next career move sooner than he had ever imagined.

He was also keenly aware that it looked bad on a young lawyer's résumé to have worked somewhere for only a few months. Three to six months at one job stood out more than two full years at San Quentin. Without exception, hiring partners at law firms looked for the same thing: commitment and a willingness to do the time. He needed to spend at least a year with Edwin before putting feelers out to another firm. Accepting a new job after a full year, on the other hand, was commonplace among young lawyers.

A premature move was particularly perilous for Will. Even if he found a new job with a first-rate group of trial lawyers (estate planning and probate was now out of the question), he would still carry the stigma of "I made a mistake." That only mattered because of his father, who no doubt was eager to step up and say "I told you so." After that anguished Sunday night dinner—mother and son eating in near silence followed by his early departure—she had left a message the next day on his recorder: "Maybe it would be best for you not to come home for a while, at least until you're ready to talk to your father about what you *really* want to do with your life."

Arriving at the front entrance to the center, Will checked his watch again: 8:02. The outer parking lots were continuing to fill up fast, and people were streaming in from all sides. He unfolded the copy of the ad from the *Mercury News*:

GIANT SALE!
REASONWARE EXTRAVAGANZA
HUGE INVENTORY OF REASONS
ALL MAJOR BRANDS
ON THINKSOFT OPERATING PLATFORM
TODAY ONLY!
SILICON VALLEY LOGIC AND CONVENTION CENTER
DOORS OPEN 8:00 A.M.
DEALERS AND LAWYERS WELCOME!
ADMISSION: $20
OR FREE WITH THIS AD

With the name ThinkSoft everywhere he looked, Will briefly considered what it would be like if Lenny Milton's legal problem were a lot bigger. What if he, all alone, had to challenge the giant ThinkSoft and its legal machine head on? He shuddered to think of it. Edwin, on the other hand, with his experience and his yen for a worthy match, would delight in taking on a company like ThinkSoft. As it was, Lenny Milton's case would be referred to an insurance company, fluffed up a little by its attorneys, and, he hoped, settled. Art Newman and his lawyers would probably never even know his insect-sized claim existed.

He recognized Edwin's gargantuan German car with the vanity plates—EGO ESQ—making its way through the crowd of people streaming through the aisles of cars toward the front doors. Edwin honked, and people looked back in surprise to see a car coming through. Edwin pulled up to the side of the convention center in a NO PARKING AREA; he was absorbed in a lively conversation on his cell phone, his free hand gesticulating wildly. A security officer began to walk over to tell Edwin he could not park there. When the officer got close enough to recognize Edwin—"the doughnut maniac on Channel 58"—he must have decided it wasn't worth spending the next two years in court over it. He turned and walked back to the front entrance.

Edwin stepped out of the car, still immersed in his conversation. "That's your best offer? Life without parole?" he chortled. "Be assured, my client will be found innocent. You'll see!"

There was no mistaking what case he was talking about. It was the notorious Johnson murder case, number one on Edwin's shopping list today. Edwin had no qualms about standing in front of a bank of microphones and proclaiming his client's innocence, despite considerable evidence to the contrary.

A. J. "Big Apple" Johnson, recently retired all-star center fielder for the New York Yankees, had been stewing for some time over his failed marriage. While in the Bay Area for an autograph appearance with other former players at the Logic and Convention Center, Big Apple had stalked his estranged wife, Mary Jo Johnson, into a bank in Palo Alto and gunned her down along with three bystanders. The crime was captured on the bank monitors. Until that fateful moment, Big Apple had been a beloved television pitchman for the Washington State Apple Growers Cooperative, urging America to eat more apples. In some of the better-known ads, his wife Mary had even appeared with him as a co-pitcher.

Until the infamous crime, sportswriters and commentators had affectionately and variously referred to Johnson as Big Apple and Apple, with and without *the* preceding it. Sometimes he was revered as His Ripeness. During his peak playing days when Big Apple crushed a dinger deep into the left-field seats, driving the Yankee Stadium crowd into a frenzy, doting TV commentators couldn't restrain themselves from blurting out even more endearing monikers, like "Apple of My Eye," "Apple Dumpling," or "Yum! You Big Sweet Juicy One!"

But the homicides changed all that. To make matters worse, despite the video camera and twenty witnesses in the bank, Apple Johnson denied he had done it. Needless, to say, Big Apple was no longer a spokesperson for the apple growers. But that wasn't enough. The growers were so devastated by the ensuing negative and unwholesome images being conjured up when its namesake product was mentioned, not to mention all the Apple jokes, the growers' board conceived an emergency plan for damage control: they offered to pay its former spokesperson two million dollars if in return he, Apple Johnson, would change his legal name to Snapple. Johnson needed the money badly in order to mount a legal defense and readily agreed.

The growers insisted that the new moniker was inspired by the fact that his name was Apple and he had "snapped." The makers of Snapple drinks were furious, especially since the growers were competitors in the beverage business, with apple juice and other apple-based fruit juices. Snapple Beverages sued the growers for one hundred million dollars and tried to get an injunction to stop the Growers Cooperative from paying a criminal defendant, who had committed "a heinous crime of moral turpitude," to change his name to that of a competitor's for the purpose of "wrongfully and intentionally tarnishing its all-American image as a wholesome and beloved source of fruit beverages, including tea with plain apple juice (hereinafter 'Plains'), apple fruits, and fruited Plains." The suit alleged that "Defendant Johnson's adoption and use of the 'Snapple' name creates an unsavory association in the minds of the public between Plaintiff's refreshing and healthful beverages and Defendant's bloodthirsty murders." That's when Edwin was retained to defend both the criminal case and the case of *Snapple Beverages, Inc. vs. Snapple Johnson aka A. J. "Apple" Johnson and the Washington State Apple Growers Cooperative.*

Will was now walking beside Edwin to the front door of the convention center, practically trotting to keep up with him. Edwin continued his phone conversation, snapping his fingers at the ad Will was holding. Will handed it to him. When they reached the front door, Edwin handed the security officer the ad he had torn out while brusquely waving his finger at Will and himself to indicate both were entitled to free admission. The security officer started to open his mouth to explain that two people needed two admissions, but there was no point. Edwin would not have heard a word; he was already inside, still barking into the phone: "Last chance to make a reasonable offer! We're pulling out all the stops from this point forward!"

Edwin concluded the conversation by clapping the hinged phone shut and dropping it into his pocket. The two lawyers stopped for a moment to get their bearings. The enormous interior was like the inside of a 3-D video game—shiny machines beeping, chirping, whirring, and emitting an array of unworldly sounds. Brand names of reasonware developers and manufacturers were emblazoned in bright lights, each in its own stylized letters designed to suggest cutting-edge technology: Airtight, WhyTech, ReasEnable, 2XPlane, and hundreds more. The ThinkSoft logo was everywhere; in order to create the applications using the standard operating system, each and every one of them had been required to obtain a developer's license from ThinkSoft.

"I heard a new one on the radio this morning," Will ventured. "Why didn't Apple Johnson change his name to Vodka?"

Edwin grimaced slightly but didn't say a word.

"People might think he wanted a Bloody Mary . . . and he denies it." All the Apple jokes ended with a tagline about Johnson denying something, anything, or everything.

Edwin didn't even crack a smile. Will filled in the silence with his own halfhearted laugh, then moved quickly on to business. He had to give Edwin the bad news about what he'd found.

"I've exhausted all the research I can. The only defense is insanity, but there are obvious risks."

Edwin shook his head. "It'll never fly. I know that. Not with that book out there." Edwin was referring to the book written by his client currently in every bookstore window: *I Just Want to Tell You I Deny I'm Insane,* by Snapple Johnson.

"But that's the whole point," Will said, having earnestly tried to follow the client's convoluted decision arrows to their end. "Don't you think he must've been insane to write a book with a title like that?"

"My reputation rides on this case," Edwin pronounced, casting his eyes upward toward the flashing lights overhead. "A successful defense will require the most meticulous analysis and applied logic. No doubt the DA will argue that everything about the book was thought out and premeditated, especially when the sales figures are trotted out. No, we need something that reaches deeper. Let's take a look around and see what we can find."

Will had already devised a plan for keeping his distance from Edwin's case—a case which, by any logic, was indefensible. "I'll catch up to you. I thought I'd do some looking around on the Milton case," he told Edwin.

"Ah, yes! The blinded dog." Edwin recalled. "What's going on with that?"

"I filed and served the complaint," Will told him. "Incidentally, since the night it happened, Lenny has been able to get through on his barbecue modem. Now he doesn't want to get rid of it. He told me he actually likes the barbecue it makes."

"They'll want to settle with you," Edwin boasted. "Mark my words." And he took off toward a row of vendors.

Reaching an early settlement was fine with Will. He wasn't sure what the case was worth, but he would research that when the time came. He had heard about rules of thumb in automobile injury cases where plaintiffs—humans, not Chihuahuas—received settlements of three to five times their medical bills, plus lost wages. He wasn't sure if the same figures applied for vet bills.

In the middle of the center, Will came upon a cluster of interactive kiosks, courtesy of ThinkSoft. MEET AND TALK TO VIRTUAL ART! ASK ART YOUR REASONWARE QUESTIONS! an overhead electronic banner invited in streaming text.

Curious, Will approached the nearest one. Onscreen a half real, half cartoonlike "Virtual Art" Newman was giving his default sales spiel: "With the newest release of our reasonware operating platform, ThinkSoft-based applications offer information-rich solutions, twenty-four/seven tech support, and greater compatibility and consistency with your entire reasoning portfolio. Whether for commercial or personal applications, let us help you manage your business. ThinkSoft. What do *you* want to get out of today?"

Although it was only a digital replica hawking the company's wares, the dazzling lights, the frenzied buying, the array of slick and colorful signs and packages everywhere crying out to be noticed—all of it bespoke Art Newman's omnipresence. His son had invented reasonware, but it was Art Newman who had seen to it that everyone had to have it.

But Art Newman burst open the market to every business and household, releasing a flood of consumer applications. First, he shrewdly changed the words to help people change the way they thought about it. "Artificial intelligence" sounded so . . . artificial and user *unfriendly*, whereas "reasonware" sounded so . . . reasonable and friendly.

That's not all Art Newman had done. Since the founding of ThinkSoft, he had changed the rigorous logic in the source code of the original operating system by tweaking, reprogramming, rewriting, rearranging, overwriting, and not only skewing its weightings but perhaps abandoning altogether the core values of the software.

Now, reasonware was used wherever any kind of deductive reasoning, analysis, or explication was needed, from strategizing nuclear deployment at the Pentagon, to a lawyer defending a client, to a teenager deciding on a guest list for a party: Each step was laid out with logical precision. But by allowing ThinkSoft's operating system to cast a wider net, critics claimed it merely lowered the bar to the already-low lowest common denominator; the logic was compromised, making it nothing more than "excuseware." More often than not, these same critics were the most avid buyers, who perpetuated ThinkSoft's stranglehold on the market. Art Newman was canny. He knew what people wanted.

Will regarded the empty text box at the bottom of the kiosk screen inviting him to ask Virtual Art "anything about ThinkSoft reasonware." Maybe he would ask Virtual Art a question or two. Better yet, he would ask him about Wholly Grill, maybe even trip Virtual Art into an admission, arming Will with shortcuts to the proof he needed for Lenny's case. Best of all, he'd test his cross-examination skills on the virtual chairman of a major company. This could be good.

Looking around to see if anyone was watching, he stepped up to one of the screens. "Mr. Newman, you are the founder and chairman of ThinkSoft, are you not?" He spoke into a mike the size of a pencil eraser; his words were processed by ThinkSoft voice-recognition software, which displayed the text of his question in real time on screen under the image of Virtual Art.

Yes, Virtual Art answered, and returned text at the speed of electricity. *I'm the chairman of ThinkSoft, and it's my privilege to talk to you today about your reasonware needs—*

"But Mr. Newman," he interrupted.

Starting a new question had the effect of shutting up Virtual Motor Mouth. That was a small thrill: a sense of control of the witness, essential to any master of trial forensics.

"Does ThinkSoft use its reasonware operating system in developing all its products?"

Yes—

"Does that include Wholly Grill?"

Yes—

"Then if ThinkSoft reasonware was used"—Will was laying a foundation just like a real lawyer; he snorted a breath before continuing—"shouldn't there have been a warning about any dangers to users that were known to ThinkSoft?"

Yes. The Wholly Grill End User License Agreement, prepared by our customer satisfaction department with the aid of our newest release reasonware operating system—

"So," Will plunged on, "shouldn't there have been a specific warning about the dangers of using the Wholly Grill sauce on anything other than the Information System?" Instinctively, Will put his hands on his hips and narrowed his eyes on the witness, assuming the swagger of a Big Kahuna trial lawyer. The truth *would* be told, damn it.

Yes, as you will see. Please take a minute to read the terms. In paragraph three the end user agrees that "use of the Information Sauce on any system other than the Information System could result in injury or death for which the Company cannot be held responsible." You see? Clarity and logic from the maker of Wholly Grill that could only be achieved by using the newest version of the reasonware operating platform—

"But that doesn't warn about anything specific! Nobody's going to think they could die using a barbecue sauce on another ordinary grill! It tells you nothing!" Will railed, forgetting for the moment that he was talking to a machine.

I'm sorry. I don't recognize a question. Virtual Art paused. *I'm sorry again. I don't recognize a logical statement either. But we're here to help with all your internal logic. With the new operating system and a custom-selected set of ThinkSoft reasonware applications to suit your needs, we can help.*

Will clenched his fists tightly. The nerve of the thing! But he resisted the urge to shatter Virtual Art's pixellated jaw. Instead, he took a deep breath and composed himself, along with a question he was sure would spell checkmate for the now unruly witness: "If the maker of Wholly Grill is reasonable, as you suggest, shouldn't it have included a clear warning about dangers that are unknown to users?" Now he had him boxed in. He couldn't deny that ThinkSoft was reasonable, and, if so, he would have to admit it should have included a clear warning.

I'm sorry. You have mistaken ThinkSoft for ReasEnable, Virtual Art explained with complete certainty, referring to a relatively small rival maker of reasonware applications. *ThinkSoft is the exclusive source of the Wholly Grill Outdoor Cooking Information System, and ReasEnable has nothing to do with it.*

To be certain, Will repeated his question, taking great pains to enunciate "reasonable." To no avail. The same answer. It was possible some poor engineer who headed ThinkSoft's development team might even lose his job when it was discovered that Virtual Art had been programmed to recognize all but one among tens of thousands of everyday English words. True to the real chairman's reputation, Virtual Art had also been programmed to detect the enemy on his radar screen all too quickly when, in actuality, the threat of competition was no more than a figment of his imagination.

For now, Will had had enough. So much for his trial run at herding Virtual Art into Lenny's evidence corral, he thought. And so much for this first step into what would have to be a long haul in gaining even a journeyman's proficiency in cross-examination—what lawyers called "competence." In hindsight he realized that his last question was full of flaws; it would have invoked a flurry of objections in a real court of law. Feeling at this moment particularly devoid of competence—and in need of self-flagellation—he concluded that he should perhaps try his skill on something less challenging than a semiliterate cartoon figure; maybe next time he should cut his teeth on one of those new sock puppets McDonald's was giving away with Happy Meals. This was going to take him years, he thought ruefully.

Flustered, Will gave the marble floor of the Logic and Convention Center a sharp, jabbing scuff with his left shoe, more than was needed to make his point with himself. Maintaining his game face, he nevertheless moved away from the cluster of kiosks, limping a little and shaking his sore left foot every couple of steps.

Having lost interest in shopping, Will caught up with Edwin at the far end of the center at the QE Deluxe counter. QE Deluxe was one of ThinkSoft's own brand names for its huge catalog of information products—premium legal reasonware designed exclusively for the well-funded client. Even with deep discounts, these items were dearly priced.

Near the checkout counter Will noticed a colorful point-of-purchase display for one of the most popular titles from QE Deluxe, "I Don't Recall" 6.0. The product name, like all those in the legal market, was originally meant to be nothing more than a tongue-in-cheek nick-name—supplanting a dry and wordy identification for an irremedi-ably dense legal doctrine that poked fun at anyone who would flagrantly misuse the product. But the playful meaning was lost, or at least rarely considered, after years of habitual use in the pragmatic world of daily commerce. As with its earlier versions, the QE Deluxe "I Don't Recall" 6.0 was a known memory hog, loaded with program-ming that justified forgetfulness.

Behind the counter the portly sales clerk was bursting out of an old English barrister's outfit supplied to him by ThinkSoft, complete with a white powdered wig he wore over thick, incongruously black eye-brows. Edwin had already briefly explained the "hypothetical" fact sit-uation he was dealing with—a perfectly sane man walking into a bank and killing his estranged wife and three bystanders, all recorded on bank cameras.

"Is it safe to assume, Mr. Ostermyer, that you have an adequate budget for the hypothetical case profile you have just described?" the sales clerk asked with a bad British accent. The clerk was playing out the charade that he did not know what case Edwin could be talking about, and that he was unaware of the widely publicized report that two million dollars had been paid into the defense coffers already.

"That is fair to assume," Edwin replied, obviously pleased at being recognized.

"I think I have just what you are looking for." He reached under the counter and pulled out a box. "This is still in beta testing, but I think your situation seems ideally suited for it. The QE Deluxe 'I Didn't Do It,' Version Seven-oh. Of course, this is not for your average street hooligan."

Edwin was skeptical. "I've tried previous versions of 'I Didn't Do It' with unsatisfactory results. Why should I expect something different from this one?"

"This one was developed for QE Deluxe by a team of lawyers, former Supreme Court justices, biologists, statisticians, and logicians," the clerk said, thrusting his chin out in the manner of an upper-crust Brit as he pronounced the "ish" in *statisticians* and *logicians* with a thin, sibilant *s*.

"Come on, those are just the advisers!" Edwin retorted. "Everybody knows the engineers are the real brains behind these things."

"Granted, the guts of this thing came from a bunch of loopy engineers holed up inside one of ThinkSoft's R and D buildings, where they had to survive for six months on nothing but coffee, pizza, and take-out sushi." Serious lapses started to dissolve his accent, but he managed to end with a flourish. "But, by Jove, they succeeded!"

"Perhaps." Edwin appreciated the concession. "But did you say *biologists*?"

"Ah! That's the backbone of this new product." The sales clerk removed his powdered wig, revealing his dome-shaped head, to mop his shiny brow. "The premise of the reasoning is this: It is a biological fact that every cell in the human body is replaced every seven years. Based on this logical foundation, the team came up with the proposition that if a trial could be delayed until at least seven years after the alleged crime, the defendant could rightfully assert, 'I didn't do it; not a single cell in my body lifted a finger to hurt anybody.' Unless and

until elected officials recognize reincarnation, the courts cannot possibly find a defendant guilty of a crime under those circumstances."

Edwin contemplated this for a moment and gave a glance to Will as
though to say, I think we're making progress now.

Will bit his lip.

"But there seems to be one serious flaw," Edwin pondered. "How do
you expect to get a trial delayed for seven years? A year or two, sure.
But seven years?"

The sales clerk smiled. "Trust me. We've thought of every possible
detail. Version Seven-oh comes bundled with everything you need. Yes,
the object is to get the trial delayed for seven years. The reasonware
comes with all the ready-made motions and court pleadings you will
need. There is a motion to continue, a motion to delay, a motion to
enlarge the time in which to prosecute the action, a motion to enjoin
the use of time as a measure for calendaring the trial, and a motion to
suspend time altogether. Before you know it, you and your client are
home free . . . as in QED—*quod erat demonstrandum*, what was to be
proven: namely, your client didn't do it."

Edwin smiled broadly, obviously impressed, and turned to Will.
"What do you think? Isn't this exactly what we've been looking for?"

Will didn't want to be the one to burst Edwin's bubble, but he had
to make clear what he thought, particularly since it was likely that he
would have to take the laboring oar and set the improbable defense in
motion. "This thing is still in beta," he said, in a skeptical tone. "Don't
you think it's probably still full of bugs? Besides, it raises more questions than it answers. To me it doesn't make a lot of sense."

"Nonsense!" Edwin trumpeted. "It's just what the doctor ordered.
We'll take it. How much?"

The clerk revealed a price tag of $14,995. "That's less than you
might pay a single expert to work on the case for a week's time. A
bargain."

Edwin rubbed his hands in agreement.

"And may I offer you, sir, the QED Extended Warranty Plan? For but a pittance, the product is guaranteed to conform to specifications for the duration of any appeals, retrials, petitions for habeas corpus, and—surely an improbability in your case—last-minute appeals made to the governor for clemency."

"We'll take it," Edwin said. "We must be prepared for all eventualities." He put down his credit card on the counter, proffering it with a decisive snap of the plastic. The clerk processed the sale and dropped the "I Didn't Do It" 7.0 into a fancy chrome-colored paper bag with twine handles. The sides were emblazoned with QE DELUXE, and THINKSOFT REASONWARE, followed by the *carpe diem* tagline seen everywhere: **WHAT DO YOU WANT TO GET OUT OF TODAY?** ®

Will resolved to do some hard thinking about where he was headed with his career.

‹ 13 ›

When Edwin burst through the front door of his office, the first thing he saw was the New Receptionist holding the backs of her hands in front of an electric fan and staring at her palms. She looked like she was either reading a book or warming her hands in front of a roaring fire. The toll-free lines, unattended, were lighting up her phone console like a Christmas tree.

"What in God's name are you doing? The phones are ringing!" he bellowed.

The New Receptionist—this one had succeeded the computer solitaire player two weeks ago—was oblivious to Edwin's concerns. She had short bleached white hair with black roots pushing defiantly out of her skull. Her cold silver lipstick matched her wan complexion, and from her pierced left nostril a row of rings were arranged that had been fashioned from a recycled can of Diet Coke. But the pièce de résistance of her appearance was her curated exhibition of tattoos—on the backs of both hands, on her exposed upper arms, her ankles, and surely on other unspeakable places.

Edwin's first impulse was to march over and turn off the fan, but he reconsidered; if he were accidentally to hit the HIGH instead of the OFF button, her ghostly thin body, draped entirely in loose black clothing, might become wind-borne, catapulting her against the nearest wall.

"I just applied a tattoo gloss that's supposed to be fantastic. This is

the fastest way to dry it. Trust me. If I sit at my desk and let it dry—
wow!—it could take a half an hour, and I wouldn't be able to answer
the phone anyway. You have to keep the skin very still for it to dry
right."

She seemed genuinely convinced that tattoo glossing was right at
the core of the firm's business. Edwin tried to stay calm while setting
her straight. "It is entirely unsatisfactory that those calls are now going
through to voice mail. New clients are calling from hospitals and
county jails. Time is of the essence! They can't wait for a lawyer to call
them back. They'll call the next lawyer in the yellow pages. Do you
understand how important that is?"

"Wow, when I took this job, I was told I was the first line of public
relations, because I'm the first person they see. How I look *is* my job.
I've got to look my best. Wow! Check out these tattoos now. They
shine. Look how rich the colors are." She thrust the backs of her hands
into Edwin's face for him to see. "Wow! This is what it's all about."

Edwin reeled back a step, as if she had waved a rattlesnake in his
face. He opened his mouth again, intending to inculcate proper procedures for firm receptionists or, failing that, to fire her, but she spoke
first.

"Hey! Wow! They're dry already!" she exclaimed, sharing her scientific breakthrough. The toll-free lines began ringing again. She rushed
over, picked up the receiver, and announced to a series of callers: "Law
Offices of Edwin G. Ostermyer! Please hold!"

Edwin exhaled wordlessly, turned, and made his way down the hall,
momentarily thrown off his stride.

Will stepped out of the library to go over the calendar. He would
be appearing at an early status conference in the Lenny Milton case
next week. As to be expected, the insurance company lawyers
defending ThinkSoft had filed a motion to dismiss the complaint,
arguing that the plaintiff had not made out a legal claim. Edwin asked
Will what insurance company law firm was defending ThinkSoft.

"No stranger to this office," Will said. "Barr, Bloch, Milkitt and Cave."

Edwin was amused to hear that one of his regular rivals was defending the case. "You won't have any problem with them. After the Barr firm gets finished blowing hard with the usual posturing, needless motions, and fee-generating make-work, the insurance company will instruct them to settle. I predict they will want to settle with you shortly after the judge denies their motion."

"I've got Dr. Stone on line one!" the New Receptionist yelled down the hall. She was standing at her chair, barely covering the receiver with a finger.

"In my office!" Edwin bellowed back at her, more loudly than she had yelled at him.

Dr. Elizabeth Stone was the most sought-after psychiatric expert witness in the country. Edwin had spoken briefly with her to see if she could deliver some psychiatric defenses in the Snapple Johnson murder case. She had recently enjoyed a string of successes in some high-profile criminal cases. Of course, it did not hurt her standing with the jury that she was a popular nationally syndicated columnist and frequent guest on radio talk shows. Her daily column "What's Their Problem Anyway?" was read by millions in newspapers throughout the country. People would write in and describe the strange behavior of an acquaintance or friend, or more typically of a spouse or child, and ask Dr. Stone to render a diagnosis, preferably that identified a pathology of some kind. Dr. Stone would then respond by naming a specific clinical disorder, neurosis, addiction, or maladjustment, along with possible treatments or remedies. Sometimes she would turn the tables and respond by concluding that the writer/complainer was the one manifesting some form of obsessive behavior or suffering from one or more psychiatric problems. Her comments were always well-balanced, never overstated; she often brilliantly reinforced her own professional credibility—the voice of reason—by making no diagnosis of clinical dementia but, instead, giving some homespun commonsense advice. Her readers and listeners gobbled it up.

Edwin stood in front of the mirror behind his desk, straightened his tie, and stabbed the speakerphone button with the middle finger of his right hand. "This is Edwin G. Ostermyer."

"Yes. Mr. Ostermyer, this is Elizabeth Stone, following up with you after our last conversation. How are you today?" Her deep, almost sultry, voice seemed to resonate with authority.

"I am well, thank you. And I am sure I will be even better when you tell me you will join the Snapple Johnson defense team," Edwin added, cutting to the chase.

"I am sorry to disappoint you, but I don't think I will be able to be of service to you," she said.

"Really?" Edwin said, surprised. "Now, if you are concerned about fees, I assure you we have a budget that can pay you whatever you require—"

"No, that is not the problem here. I have given the matter some thought. I've even run the case information through PsychoLogic, the standard relational database reasonware used in our profession."

"I am familiar with PsychoLogic, Doctor," Edwin said. "But did you specifically screen for 'I was temporarily insane,' 'I was just plain insane,' 'I couldn't cope with the unmanageable amount of post-traumatic stress I was under,' and related disorders?"

"Yes, and none of them are a match. Unfortunately, there is nothing I have to say that you want to hear or that you want a jury to hear. In my opinion, Mr. Johnson knew what he was doing when he did what he did."

"But even assuming, for the purposes of this discussion, hypothetically and for argument's sake, Johnson *did* do it"—Edwin was careful to qualify—"and even if he knew what he was doing, that does not take into account the reasons he did it, profoundly deep-seated reasons resulting in otherwise inexplicably aberrant behavior, acts that find their origin deep in the psyche of an incalculably complex individual, in an *origo profundus*, a profound origin—"

"As a matter of fact"—she cut him off—"based upon my review of all of the relevant data, as well as my twenty years as a practicing psychotherapist, I have concluded that the actual reason your client killed his wife was because he wanted her dead."

Edwin was silent for a brief moment. Then, undeterred, he pressed on. "What if I asked you to assume certain facts and, for the purposes of your testimony, to ignore other facts? Assume he loved her deeply. Ignore the sensational videotape. Let me establish that foundation with evidence. The question for you is: Can you work up a psychological profile of the killer that would be a complete mismatch with my client?"

Dr. Stone laughed. "You're not going to give up, are you? Not to stray from our subject, Mr. Ostermyer, but I must say your unwavering persistence is classic behavior of a type of person I am currently studying, some of whom, you will be interested to know, are quite well-adjusted, many of whom have gone on to become quite famous. Others never make the transition to a reciprocal universe. You persist in your quest, perhaps seeking to talk your way through anything, unintimidated by some rather formidable realities. You have to overlook or filter out a lot of harsh information, either stoically or without any cognitive effort. Here, for example, your client's misdeed is coldly recorded on a bank video monitor. Don't get me wrong. You are in some good company. In some cases it can definitely be the mark of a highly successful person."

"That gives me another idea," Edwin said. "How about I get a background check on the employee who installed the bank camera? Maybe we learn the guy's a little off center. That's where you come in. You could work up a profile of someone who would install the kind of camera like we have here that should be taken about as seriously as a fun-house mirror—"

"Have you given any thought to psychotherapy?" Dr. Stone asked.

"With all due respect, Doctor," Edwin protested, "I don't think you're hearing me. I need a legal defense. I need reasonable doubt. And, by the way, I already have a veritable panoply of compelling defenses, supported by some of the top scientists in the country, including biologists—that's right, biologists!—statisticians, and very high . . . highly esteemed computer programmers. Now, I think it is all fine and well that you would suggest therapy for my client, but I seriously doubt he's much interested in facing his inner child at a point in time when, as a matter of fact, he's facing the gas chamber!"

"Actually, I was inquiring as to whether you had given any thought to psychotherapy for yourself."

"Me?" Edwin replied incredulously. "How is psychotherapy going to make me a better attorney? How is it going to help Snapple Johnson in his time of need? Wait." Edwin, who had been standing in front of his desk talking down to the speakerphone, suddenly dropped into his chair as if someone had popped the hinges behind his knees. He picked up the receiver and spoke in a slower, more subdued tone. "You're not suggesting that I actually *need* psychotherapy, are you? You would not be implying that I might be delusional because I think the Snapple Johnson case is defensible, because if you *are*—!"

"Oh, no, no, no. Not in the least." She laughed again. "But you *are* a piece of . . . well, the more I think of it, I realize you could be a valuable piece of my study. I was only asking if you had considered psychotherapy as a means of enhanced self-knowledge. But now I am thinking you could be an intriguing case study for my new book, *People Who Are All the Talk: What Makes Them Tick*. We don't have to call it psychotherapy if you don't want. We'll call it an interview for this important book. More than a hundred people are going to be part of it. Not that you would be impressed, but in addition to typical case studies some of the subjects are quite famous. Believe me, I would not be including you unless I felt you had something very important to contribute." Dr. Stone started to rattle off some of the people she planned to interview for the book. It was indeed a list of glitterati, literati, and luminati lifted right out of the pages of *People* magazine.

Just then Will ducked his head into Edwin's office. Seeing that he was still on the phone, Will held up his right palm as though to say, You're busy. I'll come back later. But Edwin waved him in and pointed to one of the chairs in front of his desk. "Excuse me, Dr. Stone," Edwin said. "You asked if I would agree to be interviewed for your book about some of the biggest movers and shakers in the world and what makes them so damn successful. I think you were telling me who else you are interviewing. You had mentioned some senators, captains of industry, and literary giants. You were about to mention a few Hollywood celebrities when I interrupted."

Edwin put the phone down again on its hook and reactivated the speakerphone. He leaned back in his chair, cradled the back of his head with his hands, and winked at Will, who was now seated; this moment was like a fine bottle of wine, not fully enjoyed unless shared.

"Please, Doctor. I won't interrupt again. Tell me more."

‹ 14 ›

From a distance, Persi was tailing an unmarked black Ford Explorer around Santa Tostada. She had not been able to resist following one of the license enforcement fleet vehicles after her janitor shift to see for herself what they actually did. Because this latest research was being performed on public roads—something any reporter could legitimately do—she figured she was safe. She also thought it might make for a good piece for the paper—working title: "Proprietary Fever Run Rampant"—especially if she wove into it the story of Santa Tostada. The heroic nineteenth-century nun had liberated a wrongfully withheld formula for eradicating a pestilence, saving the people of the valley. Persi also saw her as the unofficial patron saint of the public domain. The saint might have been the last person to walk this valley and preach that ideas were gifts from God, belonging to and enriching all.

Since her unexpected encounter with Joon Newman, Persi was more eager than ever to dig up the truth about Wholly Grill and the secrets of ThinkSoft's highly covert Neuro Group. She had decided the more information she could gather, the better armed she would be to defend herself if the ax fell—something that could happen at any time.

The German shepherd stuck his nose out the back window of the Explorer, vigilantly continuing his lookout—or "smell-out"—for unlicensed, unauthorized, and otherwise illicit barbecuing. The dog's highly trained sensors drank in the air rushing by. Whenever it detected any use of a Wholly Grill Outdoor Cooking Information System he would bark, and his handler would stop to investigate a possible violation. The dog handler she was following today happened to be the same humorless robo-agent who had appeared on the scene the day her friend Imelda had been detained and summarily fired for "stealing" a 'SOFTbaby plush toy while cleaning in Admin 2.

Based on the last stop the agent had made, Persi was beginning to think she had seen enough for one afternoon. A mom-and-pop deli had been struck. Predictably the deli owners were shocked that the "illegal" barbecuing of a few chicken breasts—the agent called it "unlicensed commercial use"—would result in repossession. The dog handler had radioed for backup, and a van arrived within minutes to load up the grill. The van, large enough to carry several grills, was boldly marked SMEL on both side doors with the full name in smaller letters beneath: *Society of Manufacturers for the Enforcement of Licenses.*

She was now following the black Explorer to an open space on the outskirts of Santa Tostada, the site of a community farmers' market. The agent pulled quickly into a parking spot that offered a strategic view of the goings-on. Shoppers who had come to buy fruits and vegetables were lined up to order burgers and Cajun dogs from a young couple who had set up the Wholly Grill via a wireless phone from the back end of their pickup. Persi wondered if the demand was due to a genuinely popular taste or curiosity stemming from ThinkSoft's media blitz, and the fact that every mailbox in America—even those of both religious and lifestyle vegetarians—had now received at least one freezer-wrapped package of Wholly Grill marinated sirloin tips.

The young couple even appeared to be savvy about what to look out for, or perhaps their little trade had been SMEL'd out before. When the dog in the Ford Explorer began barking, the young woman said something to her partner. Customers were politely shooed away as they quickly rolled the barbecue up the ramp into the pickup. The young woman had hurried to the driver's side and opened the door when the German shepherd lunged out of nowhere and, to Persi's horror, sank its teeth into her ankle. The young woman fell to the ground with a cry of pain. Her jeans torn, she lay there, bleeding and trying to shake free of the dog.

The agent hurried up, taking his time to secure the area before calling the dog off. The young man jumped out of the pickup and screamed at the dog handler. "You can't do this! Are you freakin' nuts? We'll sue! I swear to God we'll sue the shit out of you!"

"I suggest you review your Wholly Grill End User License Agreement carefully," the agent said calmly. "You agreed to K-Nine enforcement under paragraph seven, and you assumed the risk of all injuries arising from misuse of the system under paragraph eight. You're the one with the legal problems. This is a serious violation of paragraph four, which prohibits any commercial use of the Wholly Grill. By law *you* will be required to turn over your illegal profits to SMEL or be sued. The sooner you cooperate in allowing me to shut down this unlawful enterprise, the better off you'll be!" As with the previous repossession, the backup van soon arrived.

The repo van took off in one direction, and the Ford Explorer headed into Santa Tostada on its way back to ThinkSoft. Persi was sickened by what she had observed—convinced as she was that ThinkSoft's obsession with controlling and owning everything it touched or imagined bespoke the singular megalomania of Art Newman. She was about to peel off the Explorer's trail when it suddenly turned into the parking area next to the Mission Santa Tostada. The German shepherd was barking again.

On a large grassy area adjacent to the mission, a barbecue and bazaar was in progress. She decided to get out of the car and check it out herself. However, she was still wearing her janitor grays with her employee badge. The pants could pass as generic but not so the top, with its ThinkSoft patch on the left shoulder and her employee badge attached to the front pocket. She covered the evidence by throwing on a windbreaker from the backseat of her car.

The SMEL agent in the Explorer was filling out a report on a clipboard as Persi made her way toward the festivities. She paid an entry fee to a group of friendly volunteers at a long folding table. The entrance sign and pamphlets on the table announced that all proceeds benefitted homeless causes in the Valley.

She smelled barbecue but couldn't see where it was coming from. Arriving atop a gentle slope, she saw a row of grills set up against the back wall of the mission. Trays of barbecued meats were laid out on a table for people with tickets to help themselves, along with other foods brought by the volunteers. Smoke wafted from all the grills except the one at the far end. Drawing closer, Persi observed that it was a Wholly Grill—the only one there—operated by a rotund man with a Chihuahua at his heels. He wore a volunteer name tag identifying him as a MISSIONARY HELPER printed across the top; underneath, handwritten, it said *Lenny*. A modem wire extended from the grill into a basement window of the mission.

At that moment Persi reflected on the fact that this kind-looking man named Lenny had volunteered his grill in the name of homeless suffering, something the namesake of the mission would have approved. She also liked to think that Santa Tostada would have given her blessing to Persi's own vocation—gaining information in the hands of a greedy few and spreading it around for all to share. Persi shuddered, thinking that: if the saint could see what was happening here, she would be turning in her grave. Just then Persi saw the SMEL agent at the top of the slope, fifty yards away, beelining toward the fat man with the dog.

From *The Life and History of Santa Tostada*, a pamphlet freely distrib-uted by the mission:

Santa Tostada was declared a saint for her selfless work on behalf of the poor and hungry natives of the lower Santa Clara Valley and her crusade against the shameless mercenaries who took advantage of them. Born in 1787 as Evangelina Morales to a prominent family in Mexico City, she founded an order of nuns and later began her mis-sionary work in the valley before the mission was built.

When the mission was founded in 1834—originally named San Felipe—she and her order joined the padres in the missionary work. At the time there was a famine and a terrible blight on the farmlands of the valley. Not even the fathers, with their superior knowledge of agricultural matters, could figure out how to rid the fields of a pest that was destroying their corn and other crops.

Against the odds, Evangelina found a way to feed the hungry with the scarce food they had. Using extra corn she was able to harvest from the mission land, she ground it into meal and made tortillas, even finding ways to stretch the meal to make twice as many. In order to preserve them for as long as possible so that they could be delivered to hungry natives in far-reaching areas, she oven-toasted the tortillas. Evangelina's bounty saved lives. Her tostadas were legendary among the natives, who believed they had healing powers.

At this time, before the Gold Rush of 1849, there were only a few fair-skinned people living in California, most of whom quietly assimilated into the life of the frontier land. But there were a few men living in the lower valley who had come from the East; they saw the natives' plight as a chance for financial advantage. One such mercenary corre-sponded with a professor at a university in the East, who gave him a

formula for ridding the cornfields of the dreaded bug. The same formula was widely and freely used by farmers on the eastern seaboard.

The mercenary approached the padres and told them that he had a
secret formula that would kill the bug. The price he quoted was
extortionary. The padres pleaded with him to show compassion, but
the mercenary would have none of it.

One day word was sent to the mercenary's ranch that the padres had
agreed to the payment terms. The message said that the padres
would be sending Sister Evangelina with the money, since she was
making her rounds out that way.

Evangelina arrived at the ranch, wearing her ragged habit and carrying in her hands a basketful of tostadas for the daily feeding of the
hungry. The money was in the basket too. It was all the money the
padres had for a year's worth of needed farm supplies and books for
the schoolchildren.

Once inside the parlor in the ranch house, the mercenary asked to
see the money. She pulled the towels back covering the money, carefully letting the scent of the still-warm tostadas waft up to his nostrils. He could see the wads of money were there, and Evangelina
could sense he was hungry for the tostadas.

"May I offer you some, señor?" she asked. "I have plenty today."
He nodded his head.

She put the basket on the table and began breaking the tostadas up
into chips, using both hands. She was concerned that he might start
grabbing them. "It would be even more pleasing if we had something
to dip them in," she told him.

She could read his mind like a book. The kitchen and pantry were on the other side of a screen. He knew he would not be able to see her while he stepped into the other room, but he would be able to hear her as long as she was sitting and breaking the chips. His hesitation assured her that the formula was there in the parlor somewhere.

"By the way, señor, when you give me a copy of the formula, I will need you to read it to me," she told him. "Since I do not read, that is the only way I know that you have given the padres the formula and not something else with writing on it."

This seemed to assure him of her illiteracy. He nodded his OK to her request and slipped into the other room. She could hear him walking gently and opening cabinets quietly so as to be able to hear the loud crackling sound she was making in the parlor.

As soon as he stepped out of the room, Evangelina pulled the basket handle up high, having cleverly invented this concealed feature herself. Placing the lengthened handle over her shoulder, with one hand in the basket she continued breaking up the chips as loudly as she could. With the other hand she quickly and quietly moved about the parlor, opening drawers until she found what she wanted. She memorized the formula after reading it three times, closed the drawer, and returned to the table. She lowered the basket handle and resumed her two-handed labor just as the mercenary returned with a jar of stewed tomatoes and some dried chile peppers he had found.

She looked up at the mercenary as though absorbed in her simple labor. "Señor, I am thinking the padres made a mistake in sending me. Perhaps they forgot I can't read. I am going to tell them to send someone over who can read and make this trade properly. But help yourself to these chips I have broken for you."

She was showing herself to the door. Suspicious, the mercenary went over to the drawer, but nothing was missing. She was gone before he looked back. The padres never returned in her place. The bug was soon eradicated; she saved the natives from famine.
The natives knew her as Evangelina con las Tostadas *and, after her death,* Santa Evangelina Con las Tostadas. *Because Evangelina was difficult to pronounce in their tongue, she came to be known as Santa Tostada. The mission has been known by this unofficial name for over a hundred years.*

The mission was built on ground below which the ancestors of the natives had built miles of catacombs, a rarity on the American continent. Santa Tostada was buried in the chambers set aside by the missionary padres for Christians back in the mid-nineteenth century when the catacombs were still used. Out of respect for the dead buried there—not only Santa Tostada but also the early mission Christians and the natives—the padres did not allow tours of the catacombs or any other commercial exploitation of the rich history of the mission.

When she was alive, Santa Tostada taught the children of the mission that what she did was not stealing. Bread may be stolen, she said, but God gave knowledge to humankind. Knowledge is as free as the air we breathe. By her faith she saved a native people and their culture—a culture that had survived for more than a thousand years.

Suddenly the SMEL unit had overtaken the grounds. The German shepherd was barking. Picnickers in the crowd gasped at the advancing dog and the SMEL agent charging in behind. Adults and children alike tripped over themselves to make way. They stopped at the table of foods, where the agent had the dog do a sniff test of the meat to detect the presence of Wholly Grill. Then, together, they advanced toward the volunteer named Lenny.

"Is this your Outdoor Cooking Information System?" the agent asked. Bewildered, Lenny nodded that it was.

"Let me call to mind for you paragraph four of the Wholly Grill End User License Agreement." The agent was reciting from memory. "'You agree that your operation of the Wholly Grill will only be for your personal and private use and enjoyment, such as food preparation in your home. Without limiting the generality of the foregoing, you agree not to make any commercial or for-profit use of the Wholly Grill, such rights being expressly reserved to the Company.' That would be ThinkSoft. Now, under paragraph seven, I am going to proceed with repossession of the property."

The agent called the van on a phone he wore on his belt. Lenny, about to lose his grill, stepped defiantly in front and held on to it. One of the priests appeared suddenly and urged him to avoid a confrontation. "Don't worry, Lenny. We'll buy you a new one if we have to." At $1299 per grill, there wasn't going to be much in the way of proceeds to homeless causes today. Lenny backed away.

Persi couldn't stand the role of invisible observer any longer. "Look, Mr. SMEL, this is a nonprofit function. A church, for God's sake! Nobody's violated your stinking license agreement!" she yelled at him, stepping forward. The German shepherd tensed.

"It's commercial, all right," the agent said matter-of-factly, holding his ground. "Tickets are sold up front, and people help themselves to Wholly Grill meat on the trays over there. Money changes hands." He turned around and spoke to the priest. "If the mission buys its own grill, you can inquire about purchasing a nonprofit-enterprise license. There's a forty percent discount for nonprofits. But this grill doesn't qualify. It belongs to the company that licensed it. Stand back!"

As he began to roll the grill away, Persi lunged at him and wrested it away. She started rolling it back in the direction of the volunteer when suddenly a frighteningly familiar sensation took hold of her and electrified her from the neck up. She began spouting at the mouth: "The Wholly Grill belongs to ThinkSoft! I am taking it! I am stealing from the Company! And there's more I know! I looked at E-Serum files in RD One! I have Company secrets in my head—"

Only when the mission priest managed to disengage Persi from the grill did her blathering stop. He tried to calm her, putting his arms gently around her shoulders. She staggered away a few steps, painfully aware of what had just happened but not why. People stared at her as if she were a madwoman. The SMEL agent stood stiffly in the breeze and appraised her. He squinted at her face, panning down to her feet and then back up again—the same creepy once-over she had seen Imelda undergo before she was led away. Suddenly self-conscious, she looked down at what he saw. Sure enough, the telltale outline of an oversized ThinkSoft badge showed through the thin fabric of her windbreaker.

She turned and ran toward the parking lot. When she reached the slope, she glanced back over her shoulder. Everyone was watching—especially the SMEL agent, speaking into his phone, his eyes fixed on her.

‹ 15 ›

On Friday, the day of Lenny's hearing, Will was at the San Jose Municipal Courthouse when the doors opened at eight, although the case wasn't set to be heard until nine. The status conference and ThinkSoft's motion to dismiss the complaint were scheduled in Department 10 before the Honorable Robert J. Lifo, a fifteen-year veteran of the Municipal Court bench.

Having practiced law for less than four months, Will had only attended two hearings for Edwin, and neither were seriously contested—"warm body" hearings where no advocacy skills were called for. He had never appeared before Judge Lifo, but he had heard from other lawyers that he was painfully indecisive. Most judges would read the papers submitted on a motion in advance and decide how they were going to rule before the matter was called, often posting their "tentative decisions" on-line and in front of the courtroom before the hearing. The oral argument was typically nothing more than a formality, an opportunity for the attorneys to feel they had been heard and, at best, an opportunity for the judge to clarify a fine point. But, unlike other judges, Judge Lifo could not produce even a tentative decision.

Will had heard this criticism of Judge Lifo from many lawyers who'd argued in his courtroom. They griped among themselves about how he never gave them a clue as to how he might rule until his moment of decision, and even then they were left feeling that, justice having been derailed, the so-called *final* decision was really the tentative one, at least until the court of appeals set it back on track and made it final. More bluntly, his critics characterized his rulings, and the logic behind them, as "back-asswards."

At some point early in the tenure of Judge Lifo, an unidentified critic of his, while bored and sitting through an interminable morning calendar, had fixed his eyes on the brass nameplate set in front of the judge: THE HONORABLE ROBERT J. LIFO. As his mind wandered, he discovered that BOB LIFO, if read ass-backwards, was *O-f-i-l B-o-b* and could only be pronounced *Awful Bob.* After word spread, lawyers were fond of saying things like "I've got a date with Awful Bob in the morning, but I'll meet you for lunch." Or they used code to commiserate when they were within earshot of the court clerk: "*Awful* nice to see you here today" or "Your client must've done something *awful!*"

Will checked the docket sheet outside Department 10: He was number three out of nineteen items on the calendar. He would not have a long wait, but if it did not go well an entire courtroom full of lawyers would witness the humiliating dismissal of the only case that was his sole responsibility. "What are the chances of that?" he reassured himself. After all, this was a straightforward negligence and product-defect claim—failure to warn. This judge had seen thousands of negligence claims—car accidents, slip-and-falls—and it would be unheard of to dismiss. Will recalled Edwin's comments that the Barr firm was just running up some fees to bill the insurance company, huffing and puffing and acting like it could blow the case down. After that tactic failed, the insurance lawyers would be ready to deal. That was fine with Will. He wanted to put some money in Lenny's hands as soon as possible.

The attorneys were all filing into the courtroom as the calendar was about to begin. Will looked at his notes one more time. He wanted to convince the judge right away that the motion to dismiss was empty and nothing more than tough talk from the defendant. Until now, Will had not decided between the words *obligatory* and *perfunctory* in describing what was really nothing more than a knee-jerk motion directed by the insurance company—*knee-jerk,* of course, being a little too strong. He crossed out one of the words on his notes, settling on *perfunctory* as conveying the right attitude toward the defendant's legal maneuverings.

"All rise! The Honorable Robert J. Lifo presiding!" the bailiff announced. As all the attorneys stood up, Will noticed that Fred Guernsey from the Barr firm was in court to appear for ThinkSoft. Fred looked a little bit like Detective Columbo, except that he had a well-developed paunch and, even more than Columbo, he invariably looked disheveled. Fred could be wearing a new suit, and it would look as if he had slept in it.

Judge Lifo swept into the courtroom and took the bench. With most judges the robe served its purpose well of conferring an air of solemnity and authority, a redundancy in the austerity of a courtroom. But with Judge Lifo somehow the standard-issue judicial garb looked different. Will could not help but think that on this judge the robe, which hung down to his feet, looked more like a black pleated muumuu than anything else.

"Good morning, everyone!" he announced amiably. With big ears but a small head and mouth, Judge Lifo seemed prepared to listen, unlike many judges Will had heard about. "We have a long calendar again today, and I ask for your cooperation in getting through it as quickly as possible. Better yet, if the attorneys for both sides would like to go out in the hall and talk settlement, that would be just fine with me. Those of you who have appeared in my court before know my policy. If you settle your case and pass a note so advising my clerk, your case will be taken off the calendar. You are then free to go next door to the jury assembly room and help yourself to freshly brewed coffee and sweet rolls. For those of you who are morning indulgers, there's candy, although more popular with the afternoon calendar: Oh No bars, Butterfingers, Snickers, and Milk Duds, my favorite—all this at no expense to the taxpayers, I might mention. But let me issue a stern warning! If you don't settle your case, no candy for you!" The judge smiled in appreciation of his own good humor. "Now, with that offer made, do I have any takers?"

No one moved. All the attorneys stared straight ahead, some squinting at the judge as though trying to make out a railroad timetable in a developing nation.

"All right, then," the judge continued. "But if you change your mind—and that's quite all right in this courtroom—just let my clerk know and excuse yourselves."

Judge Lifo struggled through the first two cases on the calendar. Each time, rather than come to a decision, he took the matter under submission; that is to say, he decided that he had come to the decision that he would decide the matter later and let the parties know of his decision in the mail.

"Line item three: *Lenny Milton versus ThinkSoft Corporation*," the clerk announced, and handed the file to the judge.

"Ah, yes," the judge said, opening the file. "This is a negligence case brought by one Lenny Milton against ThinkSoft. Plaintiff's dog was rendered blind by Defendant's barbecue sauce, which caught on fire. Plaintiff alleges that Defendant failed to adequately warn of the dangers of using defendant's barbecue sauce with anything other than Defendant's laser barbecue grill. Now, counsel, is that an accurate summary of Plaintiff's claim?"

Both Will and Fred Guernsey had arrived at counsel tables with their briefcases and nodded affirmatively. The judge seemed pleased to get some agreement. On a roll, he continued to set the stage. "I have read the motion brought by ThinkSoft, who argues that Plaintiff cannot make a claim recognized by law and that said complaint should be dismissed."

The judge paused, as if realizing he had stated the conflict and, unless he was going to hear argument, he would have to decide the matter. He dropped his shoulders, along with the file in his hands. "Can't you fellas work it out? Why don't you just settle this thing? I'll let you go out in the hall, and if you can't work it out, I'll call your case at the end of the calendar."

Both Will and his adversary stood in front of the judge, stiff as statues.

"Let's see then," the judge said, casting about for an alternative. "I suggest we proceed with a hearing on this. That's what we'll do. Counsel, state your appearances for the record."

"Good morning, Your Honor. Will Swanson, Law Offices of Edwin G. Ostermyer, appearing for the Plaintiff, Lenny Milton."

"Fred Guernsey, Barr, Bloch, Milkitt and Cave, appearing for defendant, ThinkSoft Corporation. Your Honor, our firm is now substituting out of this case on behalf of Defendant and will henceforth be represented by new counsel, whom I expect to arrive shortly."

That struck Will as odd. Why would an insurance company change lawyers at this point? It would only result in more expense, since another law firm would have to get up to speed.

"And who would that be?" the judge asked.

"ThinkSoft's chief outside counsel, Thurston Crushjoy."

Will had a distinctly sinking feeling. Something was up. What would the great Thurston Crushjoy be doing here? This was a garden variety injury case in Municipal Court. The attorneys in Crushjoy's international megafirm would have reason not to know Municipal Court existed, since only cases with amounts up to $25,000 could be heard here. Crushjoy's firm often handled cases in the hundreds of millions, never smaller than a few million. Not to mention, at the hourly fees they charged, who could afford to have them handle a case worth less than $25,000?

Just then the door into the courtroom opened. A few small waves of pin-striped associates rippled into the courtroom and fanned out. Will felt himself widen his stance slightly and curl his toes, instinctively trying to grab sand under his feet before the looming tsunami hit.

Thurston Crushjoy towered at the door, paused, and then strode down the center aisle. His long powerful gait was familiar from television, where reporters were often seen trotting beside him with a microphone to get a comment on one of his high-profile cases. Fearing for his fragile career, Will suddenly wanted the same protection that a few scattered briefcases were receiving. Sloppily dropped in the aisle and in jeopardy of a terrible kicking, they were being plucked to safety by their owners. He wished Edwin would appear in the courtroom and do the same for him.

"If it please the court," the newcomer boomed, "allow me to introduce myself. Thurston Crushjoy and the firm of Kilgore, Crushjoy, Clubman and Howell for the defense."

"Hardly necessary, Mr. Crushjoy," said the judge, who seemed impressed—even a little humbled—by the presence of the great defense attorney in his courtroom.

"Your Honor." Will launched into his prepared argument. To his chagrin, his voice sounded weak and fraught with uncertainty. "This is a perfunctory motion brought by the defendant, an attempt to dismiss what is a straightforward negligence and product liability claim. It—"

"I have read the papers," the judge interrupted. "And I have decided that the complaint is indeed entitled 'Complaint for Negligence and Product Liability.' I am firm on that."

Will was not sure if the judge was agreeing or making fun of him, or whether anything had been decided.

"But as Your Honor intimates"—Crushjoy seized the opening and took over—"the complaint is a mere exercise in form over substance. And precisely because the complaint masquerades as a negligence claim, when it is not, Your Honor is invited to examine the merits. Upon closer scrutiny, you will see that dismissal—clearing this groundless claim from the court's overburdened calendar—is the ineluctable course that sound jurisprudence demands."

Crushjoy measured each word as if, knowing of an imminent milestone wedding anniversary, he was laying out exquisite necklaces on black velvet for the judge and his wife to consider. Even the other attorneys in the courtroom, who had been creating a low murmur of chatter, were silent and raptly attentive.

"Let's take a look at what this is really about," Crushjoy continued. "As you will see, this is about Mr. Milton's rights under a contract. In essence, he is suing for breach of contract when he, the plaintiff, is the one in breach. He agreed when he opened the free sirloin tip that he would only cook it on the Wholly Grill Outdoor Cooking Information System. Then he entered into another agreement when he purchased the Information System itself." Crushjoy read from the shrink-wrap license: "'THE COMPANY WARRANTS THAT THE INFORMATION SYSTEM AND THE INFORMATION SAUCE WILL OPERATE IN CONFORMITY WITH THE USER MANUAL AND DOCUMENTATION SOLD HEREWITH. OTHER THAN SUCH WARRANTED USE, YOU'—that would be Mr. Milton here—'AGREE THAT THE COMPANY SHALL NOT BE RESPONSIBLE FOR ANY MISUSE OF THE INFORMATION SYSTEM OR THE INFORMATION SAUCE OR ANY DAMAGES OF ANY KIND OR NATURE'" . . . Crushjoy paused to heighten the impact of the self-serving terms—"'AND YOU ASSUME THE RISK OF ANY INJURY OR DEATH WHATSOEVER ARISING FROM ANY SUCH NONCONFORMING USES.'

"Quite recklessly, it was plaintiff who used his nonconforming Weber grill with the Information Sauce, contrary to these explicit terms. I would offer this license agreement between Mr. Milton and my client into evidence as Exhibit A and supplemental to our motion to dismiss. I am sure that there is no dispute by plaintiff that this agreement was part of the sales transaction," Crushjoy said, turning to Will to cue his compliance.

"It's true, with a mountain of manuals and such, it was there," Will started, "but—"

"There was a license agreement to buy a barbecue grill?" asked the judge, in a voice of bewilderment.

"I am sure Your Honor is familiar with shrink-wrap licenses," Crushjoy continued.

"Judging by the sound of it, I would imagine they are airtight agreements," the jurist observed.

"Indeed they are. And I am sure Your Honor is familiar with the purpose and effect of shrink-wrap licenses," Crushjoy continued, engaging the judge at every turn.

The judge paused for a moment to think, then held his hands out in front of his chest as if he were holding an invisible beach ball. "To lock in the freshness, no doubt," he said.

"That's exactly right," said Crushjoy. "And to preserve the agreement of the parties. When the plaintiff purchased the Wholly Grill system and opened up the free sirloin tip, he elected to enter into the license agreement by breaking the seal on the shrink-wrap."

"Well, Mr. Swanson, it sounds as if this particular kitchen wrap will stick to most anything you try to dish up in your complaint. Doesn't seem fair that your client should try to shrink away from his promises now." The judge smiled, pleased that his wit matched his command of the facts and legal principles. "After all, a deal's a deal, wouldn't you agree?"

"But Your Honor . . . "

Will was shaken, yet he was determined somehow to gain control of this hearing. He instinctively thought of Edwin, who would never let Crushjoy just take over like this. What would Edwin say?

"This case is *not* about some agreement foisted upon the plaintiff," Will began. "And Lady J—the pedigreed Chihuahua who is the subject of this lawsuit, and has been cast into a realm of eternal darkness—did not agree to any terms and conditions of a so-called license. She is just a victim of Defendant's failure to warn about a barbecue sauce that would blind a dog when used with the wrong barbecue grill. Mr. Milton assumed no such risk. Our laws cannot be so perverted." Will heard the words coming out of his mouth and saw the court reporter taking them down, but he didn't know where they were coming from.

Judge Lifo nodded his head at Will but didn't seem to understand his argument. At best, he still seemed anxious to avoid making a decision for as long as possible. "Why should assumption of the risk apply to the injuries of the dog, who didn't agree to anything?" he asked, turning to the defense.

"As Your Honor indeed knows," Crushjoy said, "under the law, a dog is merely an item of property. A dog is not a person. Only a person—here, Mr. Milton—can agree, and did agree, to the terms."

The judge pulled his chin as though contemplating a vexing legal issue. "Can you cite me any legal authority I should follow on this case, Mr. Crushjoy?"

"Indeed I can, Your Honor. On the assumption-of-risk issue, I refer you to volume three, section one-seventeen, of *Claims Refusal . . .* which is directly on point."

When Will saw the starstruck look of the judge, he knew it was over. The judge had just been referred to the definitive treatise for defense lawyers in civil cases, *Crushjoy on Claims Refusal.* The venerable defense lawyer had just pronounced it "*ref*usal," as he always did, intimating that plaintiff's claim, or any claim for that matter, was so much toxic waste in need of swift disposal, without which a plague would ensue, followed by the upheaval of institutions and the collapse of society as we know it.

Before Will could open his mouth to suggest contrary authority, Crushjoy pressed forward. "The treatise cites the case of *Splatford versus Experimental Parachute Club of Greater Idaho Falls, Inc.* The plaintiff in *Splatford* signed an agreement upon joining the club. He then, by and through his bereaved, made the same argument that Mr. Milton makes—that is, he was not bound by his agreement to assume all risk. I have taken the liberty of photocopying and high-lighting the precise ruling in that case. If I may, I would like to share that with the court."

Crushjoy handed the clerk the photocopy. Pliantly the judge took the piece of paper and read aloud: "'Plaintiff here is grasping at air in his efforts to convince this court that his claim should not be barred under the doctrine of assumption of risk. Make no mistake, this court is sensitive to the terrible tragedy which has befallen Plaintiff, but his argument—that he should not be bound by the agreement he entered into—falls flat on its face. Accordingly, Plaintiff's complaint is hereby dismissed.'"

As the judge spoke, Crushjoy watched the court reporter taking the words down. Will was paralyzed with horror at what—unquoted, unqualified—had just gone into the record.

"Thank you, Your Honor," Crushjoy said, in a deep tone of grati-tude, when the judge was finished, "and let me say that my client—like you, a champion of disciplined reasoning in its field—thanks you for the courage of your convictions." Thurston Crushjoy turned and walked confidently out of the courtroom, his retinue of associates falling in behind him.

The judge looked up, evidently not sure what he had done. Then a faintly smug expression crept over his face, eventually ripening into a stoic squint. "What's next? More tough calls to make, no doubt. Clerk, call my next case!"

As humiliated as he was, Will kept his head up as he walked out of the courtroom. He mistakenly made eye contact with a few lawyers still waiting for their cases to be called. The looks were sympathetic but in a strangely ambivalent way, as if Will were being wheeled out of an operating room following elective brain reduction surgery.

Out in the hallway he collapsed onto a bench in shock. His first case—the first court hearing that was all his—and he had failed igno-miniously. He had really wanted to do the right thing for his first client. He couldn't stand to think how disappointed Lenny would be. And what would he tell Edwin? Edwin would want to read the tran-script from the hearing, and he would see that Will had lost control from the get-go. It might be months before he got another chance to prove himself in court.

Will heard a gavel sound across the hall from Judge Lifo's depart-ment. He stood and glimpsed through the portal window into the courtroom; for an instant this judge bore a striking resemblance to his own father. Unable to hear through the door what the "Honorable Roderick Swanson" was saying, Will's imagination filled in: *At sen-tencing you were remanded into the custody of the Tax and Probate Penal Colony. You failed to surrender yourself as ordered. I find you in contempt*!

Will slouched back down on the bench. Although today he had been prepared to argue—and had foolishly thought he knew everything about—"failure to warn," he was ill-prepared for the ambush visited upon him by Thurston Crushjoy. As for the motion sickness churning in his stomach, he had only himself—with help from Judge Lifo's topsy-turvy seat-backwards carnival ride—to blame for that. He felt just *awful*.

‹ 16 ›

Persi walked out of the elevator and into the offices of the *Golden West Business Journal*, located in a downtown Los Angeles high-rise. The routine was that she visited the offices of the paper every other week from her new home in Silicon Valley. There were no more weekend shifts as a ThinkSoft custodian. She had called in her resignation the day after the episode at the mission barbecue, when she had inexplicably succumbed to the mysterious E-Serum.

Before she arrived at the front desk, she ran into Karen Branson, the weekly paper's associate editor. In her late thirties, Karen had been a rising star right out of college, just like Persi. She had proven to be both friend and mentor for the young reporter. It was Karen who had lobbied to hire Persi and was responsible for her early promotion to resident correspondent in Silicon Valley.

"Persi! We need to talk."

"What is it?" Persi said.

Karen stepped into an alcove where they could speak privately. Tall and willowy, she leaned against the wall from nearly two feet away, but at such an angle that she could speak more intimately with the petite reporter. "A guy was here not ten minutes ago, looking for you and asking questions. Said he was a private investigator, and if you were the Persi Valentino he was looking for, you stood to inherit some money. He was a lousy liar."

Persi had an uneasy feeling. "What did you tell him?"

"Nothing," Karen said. "But hold on. I haven't told you the creepy part. He brought a dog in here with him!"

Persi's mind began to race. ThinkSoft was hunting her down with a bloodhound! "What was he doing with the dog?" she asked.

"He had something in his hand, something for the dog to smell. He said that the dog could verify whether you were the same Persi Valentino he was looking for by having the dog crosscheck the smell around your old desk. Can you believe that? He wanted to sniff around your chair! Creepy!"

Persi didn't show her alarm as the danger signals shot through her head.

"He's a creep, all right," Persi said. "I have to go."

"Persi, are you in some kind of trouble?" Karen asked. "Talk to me."

"No," Persi said, as she did an about face. "We'll talk later. Gotta run."

Instinctively, she knew she had to get back on a plane. The heat was on here in LA, and she needed to clear out fast. Out on the street, as she was opening the door to her rented Mustang convertible, she noticed a man, across the street and thirty yards away, in a black Ford Explorer, the same kind of car from the SMEL fleet she had tailed a few weeks earlier. The crew-cut driver had turned around and was staring intently at Persi through military-style dark glasses.

Suddenly the Explorer roared and squealed out of its parking space. The driver started to negotiate a U-turn but quickly braked to avoid a collision with a car coming in the opposite direction. She knew he intended to pin her into her parking space. She jumped into the car, fired the engine, and screeched out just in time. She looked in her mirror; he was right behind her. The German shepherd craned his neck out the window of the backseat with his nose leveled at her car.

She knew she wasn't going to lose him with speed or head fakes alone. She headed across town, weaving in and out of traffic, doing fifty-five in a twenty-five zone. While driving she put the Mustang's top down and, reaching into her purse, put on the impenetrably cool LA shades she only wore in southern California.

She rounded the corner onto Hill Street and saw the studio trailers. Having lived and worked in LA for two years, she knew a car chase or some other scene was being shot at this location for one television show or another at least three out of five days a week. Several of the trucks today were marked in giant letters SPELLING PRODUCTIONS.

The street was barricaded, and she expected she would be asked to turn around by the security people. If she had to turn around, he would have no trouble cutting her off. He hovered about twenty yards behind from where she stopped.

Two security men held their hands up for her to stay put in front of the barricades. One was signaling for her to turn around; the other walked up to the driver side of the car. She had the music turned way up, and her hair was recklessly askew . . . just so. Her image could have been the lead in a fashion magazine pictorial entitled "Ten Secrets to Windswept Insouciance."

She turned the radio down. "Hi, it's me," she said to the security guy, lowering the shades on her nose a smidgen to let him take in a pair of languorous eyes that spoke of untouchable status. "Dionna," she said, in a hushed voice, as if it were their little secret—and surely the thrill of a lifetime for him. "I'm doing a cameo in this scene, but you know that. Where's makeup?"

He wasn't convinced, but she could tell she was getting close. She glanced over her shoulder and looked annoyed. "Say, that guy behind me . . . he's been following me. I think he's a celebrity stalker. He gives me the creeps. Would you be a doll and get him off my back? I don't even want him near the set." The security guy took one look at the creep in the Explorer who was staring at Persi while hovering from a distance of twenty yards with a German shepherd in his backseat. That did it. He signaled for the barricades to be drawn back.

As she drove through, she saw a flock of security guys descend on the Ford Explorer. They opened the door, pulled him out of the car, and slammed the door. He was yelling, and the dog—all fangs and claws against the glass—was staging a fierce protest.

Persi breathed a sigh of relief and turned down the radio. She drove half a block and made a right into a side street to head straight for the airport. Why had they tracked her down in Los Angeles and not Silicon Valley where she lived? It was true that the address in her ThinkSoft employment records was not accurate, whereas finding the offices of the paper was easy enough. But it didn't make sense that one of the biggest infotech companies in the world couldn't have found her current address.

As she rolled up to another stop sign, two new black Explorers roared out left and right, cutting her off fore and aft. The agent in front jumped out with a dog. The dog was straining at the leash to get a whiff of Persi. With the convertible top down, he had no problem. He barked and pointed.

"Affirmative that you are both Maria Valentino and Persi Valentino," the agent announced, in the same dry tenor as the man who had hauled away her friend Imelda and had witnessed her bizarre behavior at the mission barbecue. "As an employee of ThinkSoft, your license to be on the premises was only to perform your assigned duties. You gained your license under false pretenses and then exceeded its strict limitations. Be advised of your status as a trespasser, both on land and in the realm of the mind."

He thrust a dreadful-looking document in her face. Shocked, she took it and glanced at its title: NOTICE OF BREACH OF LICENSE AGREEMENT. It contained pages of legal mumbo jumbo. She had certainly never considered her employment was governed by some kind of license agreement while on company grounds.

"You also terminated your employment with ThinkSoft without following proper procedures," the agent droned on. "You failed to turn in your company security badge. Turn it over now."

"I don't have it. I don't know where it is."

Just then a low-flying black helicopter roared over a nearby stand of eucalyptus trees. An agent in dark glasses leaned out and trained what looked like a giant zoom camera on her.

"The papers you are holding are also company property, and you have no right to them."

Persi nearly gasped, realizing she had been set up. That wasn't a zoom camera. Whatever it was, she had a hunch that the aim was to activate the E-Serum and make her blather. They wanted to empty the contents of her mind one more time. She had been tricked into holding an item of company property. But the awful wave that had overtaken her twice before never came. A few seconds passed; she was still clear-headed.

"Then take them back," she said. "What makes you think I'm going to read this dreck anyway?" He didn't take them back. Within seconds the chopper and the two Explorers vanished.

She was no longer in a rush to get to the airport. She had to return to the office and talk to Karen. She found the associate editor in her office.

"Can we talk now?" Persi asked at the door.

Karen looked up. It was apparent from her face, as pale as Persi's must have been, that she had already been contacted.

"I wish you had talked to me before," she said. Her voice was pained.

Persi nodded slowly, advancing a few steps into the office. "I wanted to tell you, but knowledge is . . . dangerous. You can't be on the spot. Especially now, you have to be able to say you don't know anything I know."

"They haven't wasted any time on that," Karen said. She waved a fax letter she held in her hand. "We just got this. It's from the legal department at ThinkSoft. First they threaten us with a lawsuit if we ever publish anything you learned while employed there. Then they say that if all we do is continue to employ you after receiving this letter, they will assume that we approved the *subterfuge,* and will hold the paper legally liable."

Persi felt a chill.

"It gets worse. They say, 'We have reliable information that Ms. Valentino accessed confidential trade secrets with the intent of exploiting the proprietary information in news stories for commercial gain. In fact, we have located unauthorized fingerprints on trade secret files in a Level One Security lab. We are in the process of electronically transmitting those fingerprints to an FBI lab for identification. The full force of criminal prosecution can be diminished if Ms. Valentino comes to ThinkSoft, gives a complete statement, and signs a nondisclosure agreement on our terms and conditions. Absent such cooperation, once we have fingerprint verification, we will proceed with the filing of criminal charges against Ms. Valentino for theft of trade secrets and violations of the federal Economic Espionage Act.'"

Persi shook her head in defiance. "No way! Believe me, bad things are going on. The truth about Wholly Grill has to come out."

"I believe you," Karen said. "I don't have to read between the lines. Listen to this: 'Notwithstanding the above, we deny in advance anything Ms. Valentino claims to have seen.'"

Karen put the letter down, stood up, and walked around the desk. Without a word she put her arms around Persi and gave her a hug. "You know I have no choice? I have to let you go."

"Of course," Persi said. "You have to. The paper can't afford to get into a legal war with ThinkSoft."

As they made their way out to the bank of elevators, Karen offered to help Persi if she could in finding a new job.

"Do me a favor," Karen added. "Before you do anything, promise me you'll get yourself a good lawyer."

"I promise."

"You'll be OK?"

The elevator doors opened. Persi stepped in, turned around, and faced her former boss with a confident smile. "I'll be fine. Don't worry. Hey, I'll bounce right back. You've been great, Karen. I've loved it. Thanks for all you've done for me."

Karen raised her right hand softly, a quiet salute to her young protégée. When the doors closed, Persi's smile wilted as quickly as cling wrap in flame and melted into tears. She had really loved that job.

‹ 17 ›

To: wswanson@ego-law.com
From: persivalentino@earthlink.net
Re: Your long-lost client
Hey Will Swanson!
Hope you haven't forgotten your first client. I've
just moved here to Silicon Valley. I'm between jobs
right now. In fact, there's a bit of a legal problem
I'd like to talk to you about. But I've got something much bigger that I want to steer your way—
maybe big bucks! (You sure didn't make any money
getting your editor/friend out of trouble in college!) I'm going to be downtown Monday morning. Any
chance you can meet me for coffee around 11? How
about the Amalgamated Mocha on the 400 block of
First?
You're still my lawyer, right?
Persi

Will hadn't seen his college friend Persi Valentino since he graduated over three years ago. It had been a breath of fresh air hearing from her Friday afternoon after his disastrous experience in court that morning.

He also liked that he had an excuse to get out of the office: a potential new client. Since arriving at the office this Monday morning, he had wanted to escape. A fax greeted him from one of Thurston Crushjoy's minion associates. Although presented as a settlement offer, it was what lawyers referred to as a *dog bone*—a token thrown at the plaintiff to reward a final surrender where, due to a court ruling or the development of fatal evidence, the plaintiff found himself bereft of any leverage. In exchange for Lenny's consent to a judgment declaring the shrink-wrap agreement valid and binding, along with his waiver of any appeal, ThinkSoft would pay him $750. It was a Chihuahua-sized bone at that.

After Will had reported what happened in court on Friday, he was not anxious to show Edwin the dog bone slipped under the firm's front door . . . with strings attached. Edwin was already furious: at Will for letting it happen, at Crushjoy for doing what he did to Edwin's young associate, at ThinkSoft for getting away with it, and at the New Receptionist for reasons not entirely clear. Edwin seemed reluctant to express any anger toward the Honorable Robert J. Lifo, possibly because he wanted to maintain faith in the judge. After all, his motions to delay the Snapple Johnson case were going to be heard by Judge Lifo.

Edwin gave the settlement offer a dismissive wave of the hand, not to bother him further. Will would just have to handle it as he saw fit after talking to his client. Edwin was busy preparing for the first motion in the Johnson case. It was obvious, however, that Edwin hated the fact that Crushjoy had prevailed, even if it was a small matter.

Will had been unable to reach Lenny all afternoon following the hearing to let him know what happened. Lenny's Mattress Mutual line had been busy every time he dialed it.

After mulling over the settlement offer, he decided to pay his client a personal visit. Lenny was only ten minutes from downtown. Mercifully, that would remove him from the office tension even sooner. Every time he saw Edwin in the halls, Edwin averted his eyes as if politely concealing his disgust. By leaving a little after nine-thirty, Will wouldn't have to resume his skulking until after lunch.

Lenny lived by himself in a small one-level house he rented. A postage-stamp lawn was bisected by a walkway to the front door with box hedges on either side.

Lenny's front door was slightly ajar when Will arrived. He knocked three times, but there was no answer. He decided Lenny must have left the door open to allow business visitors to walk right in, like a "real" office. Will stepped into the house announcing himself with a "Lenny?"

A television, out of view, was chattering away in the living room. As he took another step into the house, Will could see a computer monitor was on in the home office to the left, displaying Lenny's calendar for the day. In addition to updating insurance quotes for mattress brokers on his Web site, Lenny had a long list of telephone calls to make but no appointments.

The kitchen, to the right of the home office, appeared eligible for federal disaster relief. The sink was loaded up with kabob skewers, tongs, barbecue forks, and more grill paraphernalia than Will had ever seen. There were dirty meat platters in the sink but no plates. A hip-high kitchen garbage can was loaded to the top with bottles of Wholly Grill sauce. An old box for a desktop computer had also been pressed into service. It was loaded with the bones of birds and beasts: flanks, legs, chops, ribs, and racks.

On the kitchen table were a dozen computer magazines, including the most recent copy of *PC Computing* opened up to a full-page ad—the same one seen in magazines everywhere and plastered on billboards throughout America. It showed a bottle of Wholly Grill Barbecue Sauce, its front label depicting an ironclad horseman—part medieval knight, part cyborg—with his laser-tipped lance extended and taking aim at a smoking lamb chop. Underneath the picture of the bottle was the familiar copy:

Wholly Grill ®
Wholly Smoke!
Wholly Delicious!

Now with Smoke Crystals ⁽ᴿ⁾
For a Burst of Hickory Flavor!

Will came around the corner from the kitchen and saw Lenny behind a sliding glass door hovering over his barbecue. This was his second grill, replaced as promised by the mission priests after the first one was repossessed. A telephone line ran from the office across the living room, out the door, and into the modem of the high-tech grill.

Lenny was working on a drumstick fresh off the grill. After devouring it in two bites, he rubbed the bone on some sauce spilled on the grill surface. Then, to Will's quiet astonishment, he massaged his gums with the end of the sauce-dipped bone.

When Lenny finally looked up and noticed someone standing in the living room, he seemed taken by surprise, but he slid the door open a foot.

"Lenny, I didn't mean to startle you," Will said. "The front door was open."

"Oh," Lenny said uneasily, "I was just coming into my office." A platter of uncooked wings remained on the outside table. From behind Lenny a Chihuahua appeared—Lady J—and walked straight into the partly open glass door. Lenny slid the door all the way open and stepped in with his dog.

"Smells good. Early lunch today?" Will said, in an effort to defuse the awkwardness. It wasn't even ten in the morning.

"Yeah, I've got two long back-to-back meetings to go to in a little while, and I won't have time for lunch." He glanced at his watch as if to confirm his schedule. "Yeah, these grills are just great. You just baste some sauce on your meat once and hit the START button. Dial up. That's it. Perfect every time. When you're busy and in a hurry, like I am, it's faster than making a sandwich. They're great. Really."

"So long as you use their grill, I guess," Will said.

"Well, I'm not saying they shouldn't have warned me better about the dangers. But it's true. If you use the sauce on their grill, there's no flame-up at all. It doesn't even make any smoke. Amazing." Lenny wasn't looking at Will as he spoke. He was facing the grill outside.

"Listen, Lenny, I need to talk to you about your case," he said, in a tone lacking any verve. He told Lenny what happened in court Friday and about the meager settlement offer. "All things considered, I have to recommend that you accept. If it's any help, I want you to have the whole thing. Remember, at first I was going to help you on a pro bono basis anyway. Maybe that will help pay the vet bills." Will looked down at Lady J, who was now lying on the floor under a table.

"So the judge says Lady J gets nothing. That doesn't seem fair." Lenny seemed disappointed, but he didn't express the great upset Will had anticipated. He'd expected that Lenny would ask endless questions in an effort to fathom the bewildering legal process. Instead, Lenny seemed more preoccupied than anything else.

"Go ahead and settle the case then," Lenny told Will. "And thanks for giving me a break on your fee. That means a lot to us." He bent over and scratched under Lady J's ears. Then he looked at his watch again. "I better start getting ready for my meetings. You're welcome to stay while I go put a tie on. You can use my personal phone over there if you want to call your office. No smoking, though. It gives Lady J a terrible cough." Will said he had covered everything necessary, and he would show himself out.

On the way to his car, Will remembered that he had brought a copy of the settlement offer for Lenny to see for himself. He walked back through the front door, into the kitchen and was about to announce he was leaving it on the front table when he saw Lenny standing in front of the television laughing. He was laughing so hard at a television comedian that he was breathless and gasping for air. Will blinked in disbelief at what he saw next. From Lenny's nostrils a strange milky-white fluid began to flow, covering his upper lip and streaming down the sides of his mouth. The remote control still in one hand, Lenny used the other forearm's shirt sleeve to mop his face.

Will didn't say anything. Sidetracked by repulsion at what he just saw, he turned and automatically walked back out of the house. Realizing when he was outside again that the papers were still in his hands, he decided to leave them on the table without any announcement.

Back inside, he saw Lenny was now standing in front of the open cabinet at the far end of the kitchen with his back to Will. On the upper shelf there were a few dusty wine bottles and six-packs of soda. On the lower shelf, to Will's amazement, were bottles of Wholly Grill, at least eight across and four deep.

Lenny suddenly closed the doors to the upper shelves and saw Will through one of the mirrors adorning the outside of the cabinet. When Lenny turned around, Will could see that he was embarrassed.

"I'm just making a quick list of things to pick up after my meetings," he said. He closed the lower cabinet doors and put his hands behind his back.

"Thought you'd want a copy of the letter I told you about. I'll leave it here," Will said, leaving it on the front table. "See you around, Lenny. Take care of yourself." Will hurried out the front door as fast as he could.

‹ 18 ›

Inside the Amalgamated Mocha on First Street in downtown San Jose, Will found Persi had arrived before him. Her coffee drink was half empty, and she was absorbed in her notebook computer.

It occurred to him that they could have been meeting after class three years ago when they were both at UC Santa Barbara. The only difference was her hair was a little shorter and she had upgraded the low-end notebook she had in college. Her dress was no-nonsense as always: sweater, leggings, and flat shoes, together with no makeup, something her olive complexion, bright hazel eyes, and pristine facial features made redundant anyway. He had forgotten what a stand-out beauty she was. Or maybe he hadn't paid attention before; at the time he was friends with Persi, he had just begun dating Dagmar.

They had met Will's senior year—Persi's junior year—while taking an English lit class together. He was majoring in business with the goal of law school and a downtown San Francisco firm. Persi had always had her sights set on a career in journalism. That year she was editor of *The Daily Nexus*, the UCSB student paper.

She introduced herself to him after he was pointed out to her as someone "pre-law." That was close enough for her. She could have used a full-time lawyer on staff at the paper if its budget permitted. As an editor prone to taking risks, Persi had a knack for getting her hands on confidential memos from faculty committees and the administration—even highly sensitive and politically charged material concerning the Board of Regents of the University of California—and she would publish them, highlighting their impact on student well-being. When trouble escalated, she would call upon her newfound friend—the would-be, will-be, wanna-be lawyer—to help her find some way to inoculate her reporting against a lawsuit.

On one occasion the university regents announced they were cutting off funding of an internationally acclaimed research project using computer models that examined the root causes of human rights violations. When Persi reported that the claimed lack of funds was a fraud and that millions of dollars in revenue was available, a powerful group of regents and like-minded politicians decried her "journalistic irresponsibility."

She again called on her friend Will. Not yet a lawyer having the power of subpoena, he learned how to use Freedom of Information laws to get his hands on university financial records and uncovered millions of dollars of unaccounted-for revenue. When he reviewed the books from the university's enormous patent portfolio, he turned up millions in patent royalties that were "off the books"—the university received little more than some worthless trade, in exchange for which private companies were licensed to use university patents on a royalty-free basis. Persi turned the editorial heat way up in the paper when Will discovered that one of the regents—an outspoken critic of the human rights project—owned a large block of one of the companies with the sweetheart royalty deal.

Will had found it exhilarating doing whatever it took to take the heat off Persi and keep it on the bigwigs: rudimentary legal research, reviewing mountains of financial records, and getting free legal advice from alumni attorneys in the community sympathetic to their cause. Armed with Will's findings, Persi didn't take long to get the regents to back off completely and commit to renewed funding. She'd playfully nicknamed Will "Super Chill," her one-man force blown in from San

Francisco who, with the same ability as the famous fog of shrouding its power, could make the hot and bothered headed her way *chill out fast*.

After college Will had gone north to the University of San Francisco for law school. Following a short exchange of letters, they lost touch. He was the one who dropped the ball, due to absorption in his studies or, more accurately, the kind of *self*-absorption endemic to places of postgraduate learning where a lot of law books are found. Graduating a year after Will, Persi had gone south to Los Angeles to work for the *Golden West Business Journal*.

"So you didn't answer the question in my e-mail. You still my lawyer or not?" she asked with a mischievous smile, after he sat down. She ordered another Hot Molten Java, a Vesuvius-sized triple, under whose frothy white peak stirred a thermal reaction. Thinking a Hot Molten Java might melt his own pancreas, Will ordered regular coffee.

"What kind of trouble are you in *now?*" he asked jokingly.

The levity of old friends catching up vanished when she launched into a whirlwind account of her custodial job at ThinkSoft. She described her clandestine discovery of the highly secret Neuro Group, which developed both the popular Wholly Grill and the E-Serum, the latter technology still unavowed by ThinkSoft. She told him she had gathered information about Wholly Grill: some through public sources, some through her employment at ThinkSoft which she could only share with an attorney. She described how she had been hunted down and ended up losing her job at the paper.

"It was a risk I took," she said, "although going into it I hadn't figured on being attacked with E-Serum." It was obvious that Persi was being stoic about the loss of her job with the *Business Journal*, a position she had dreamed of in college.

At the first mention of ThinkSoft—as shocking as her account was—Will managed to maintain his composure, but he knew immediately that this conversation was on a collision course with his own entanglements with ThinkSoft and, more chilling, what he had just seen at Lenny's house. He was in no hurry whatsoever to share his knowledge, especially the fact that he had lost miserably in court and was about to settle for a dog bone, unless she pried it out of him.

"You need to talk to an experienced criminal lawyer right away," Will advised. "I'll set up a meeting with Edwin."

"That's not the reason I contacted you. I don't want to just defend myself. I want you to help me expose the truth about Wholly Grill."

"What's to expose about a barbecue sauce?"

As if mentally backing up, Persi waited a second before answering. "The first thing you need to understand is who the mastermind behind the Wholly Grill is."

"That would have to be Art Newman."

"Please. Mention his name and I want to bathe again." She shuddered. "And that insipid techno-veneer! He's so unctuous he makes Exxon look like the Audubon Society. Yes, that's exactly who I'm talking about!" She was erupting; Hot Molten Java was roaring through her veins. She jumped up—a habit familiar to Will—paced around her chair, and leaned on it; he knew she would even stand on it if necessary to make her point. "Art Newman would sell his own mother down the river. No, he'd do better. He'd figure out how he could make more money by shrink-wrapping his mother and *licensing* her down the river! Just look how he treated his own son."

"I've heard some rumors that Joon was not happy growing up," Will said. "Any truth to that?"

"Trust me, Joon had to do more than finish his vegetables to get his dessert," she said. "He'd have to sing in code for his supper. Art used to make Joon sit in front of his computer screen for twelve hours at a time without food until he solved problems Art had invented. He would out-and-out starve him! Turns out, that was the kind of inspiration that drove Joon to invent reasonware."

"Where'd you learn all this?"

"Speaking Spanish with my co-workers had its advantages. They knew women who worked as maids for Art Newman. And get a load of this." She leaned over, pulled a microcassette out of her purse, and put it on the table. "I got a copy of a training cassette for Grace Telemarketing, Art's company before ThinkSoft. It's a demo of how to sell by calling right at the moment people sit down for dinner. Classic Art Newman." She flipped the switch on and sat down, leaned back, and crossed her legs, her free foot fluttering wildly while the tape hissed a brief prelude.

"Hello, is this Mr. Smith?"

"Yes, it is."

"Mr. Smith, I am calling you on behalf of Global Telecom Long Distance Services. Is this a bad time for you to talk?"

"As a matter of fact, yes. My family and I just sat down to dinner."

"I am so sorry, Mr. Smith. Of course, I should have paid attention to the fact that you and I are in different time zones, and it's the dinner hour where you are. I tell you what. I'll switch your long-distance service for free. But that's not all. I'd like to buy dessert for you and your family tonight as a way to make it up to you for my thoughtless mistake. How do four pints of gourmet ice cream sound?"

"God, it sounds really good right now. I'm starving. But—"

"You bet it sounds good. And I owe it to you. What are you supposed to have for dessert tonight?"

"I think I saw Jell-O pudding with sliced bananas."

"It just so happens, Mr. Smith, that a representative of Global Telecom is prepared to swing by in a refrigerated truck in the next hour to let you select your four pints of delicious gourmet ice cream. All you will need to do is sign an authorization to switch your long distance carrier, and you and your family can have an ice cream feast tonight. Can I do that for you?"

(Sound of licking lips) "Can he make it in twenty?"

"Thirty max. It's the least I can do for my clumsy error, Mr. Smith. I know you will be happy with Global Telecom."

Persi turned the recorder off. A nosy woman in a business suit who had been packing a briefcase at a table nearby descended on them.

"Hi. I'm Abby Willis. I'm regional director of marketing for Amalgamated Mocha. I couldn't help but overhear your training tape. I assume you are with Global Telecom. I think the telemarketing with the ice cream is just the best! If you ever want to start calling at six in the morning, I would love to do business with you. Here's my card. Don't you think your long-distance service and our espresso drinks make for a marketing marriage made in heaven?"

"No question about it. And I'm sorry we didn't talk to you sooner" —Persi looked up at her, wearing an expression of feigned disappointment—"but we already signed an exclusive deal for the early morning slot with a company that manufactures a highly caffeinated granola and yogurt blend."

"Of course! But promise you'll keep me in mind if that doesn't work out," she said, before she disappeared into the back of the store.

"So you get the—shall we say—historical perspective of how Art Newman has learned to manipulate people with food," Persi said. "It's a life obsession."

Still chuckling over her charade with the interloper, Will resolved again she was going to have to come up with more than innuendo before he showed any of his cards. "Art Newman is shrewd, all right, probably the envy of every would-be entrepreneur in America. Now he's marketing the hell out of Wholly Grill. Is there some crime in that?"

"Let me ask you something, counselor," she said. "Don't you think that if the Wholly Grill does a fraction of what Art Newman says it does, he could have gotten a patent on it?"

"Sure. So what?"

"Then why didn't he? Why is he trying to hold on to his property rights under trade secret law rather than applying for a patent? Rather tenuous, isn't it?"

"A trade secret is good for as long as you can keep it a secret: a week, a year, or a hundred years," Will recited, as if the bar exam were yesterday. "A patent you own for twenty years. But in order to get that kind of lock on it, you have to disclose everything about it to the Patent Office. Are you suggesting——?"

"Art doesn't want anyone to learn the secrets of the Wholly Grill."

"Why do you say that?"

Persi took a deep breath—the first since the coffee, or the mention of Art Newman, had jump-started her nerves—and leveled with him. "Wholly Grill is addictive. Really physically addictive. Users get hooked like on heroin, cocaine, or any other drugs. I am convinced it was designed to work on people that way."

At first he felt a deep chill, his legal mind-set giving way to an experience of evil he could only imagine up until now. What he had seen at Lenny's house was disturbing. But was it merely aberrant behavior or something frighteningly intended, as Persi insisted? If he accepted what she was saying, everything would change. What was supposed to be a simple case in small claims court would invite bewildering, untested legal issues, and the scope of his undertaking on Lenny's behalf might take on staggering dimensions. The lawyer in him, trained to reject the unproven, rose again and presided over his thoughts. She would have to come up with more than mere hunches.

He leaned back in his chair, shook his head, and laughed. "Come on, Persi. What kind of evidence do you have? People who eat a lot of barbecue and aren't in control? We could go after all purveyors of snack foods." Will waved his hand at the inside of the store. "Why not Amalgamated Mocha? This place is crawling with junkies."

Persi was unfazed. "So far the evidence is mostly circumstantial . . .

anecdotal, I admit. Too soon for any hard medical evidence. But it's just a matter of time. Where there's smoke, there's fire, so to speak. It's out there. That's where you come in."

"How's that?" Will lifted his eyebrows.

"Your firm would be perfect at the forefront of this. Edwin G. Ostermyer—I know because I've checked—belongs to those trial lawyer organizations that share information. You can see what information may already be in on this. Somebody may have already filed a suit on behalf of one person, and there are other ways your legal ticket can get information that I can't. When you find it—and I know you will—you'll be sitting pretty to file a monster class action against Art Newman's company. All you need is one class member to file it, and the rest will follow."

"And what exactly do you picture this class-action lawsuit will claim?" asked Will, maintaining his tone of skepticism, while pangs of realization were gnawing away inside.

"First of all, only a fraction of Wholly Grill users are addicts. It's unknown at this point why they alone are affected. What the legal theories are I leave to you, but these people are indeed heavy consumers; they eat barbecue almost to the exclusion of everything else. They lie about their use, hoard the stuff, and have uncontrollable cravings that run their lives. Family relations suffer, careers are put on the back burner—that kind of thing. Symptoms sound familiar?"

She had no idea *how* familiar they were. Will was all but hallucinating: sitting here with Persi, whom he had not seen in three years, yet it seemed like yesterday; having just seen it all played out at Lenny's. He even thought he felt a Chihuahua banging into his ankles and the chair legs . . . .

"All right. Just suppose we got our hands on medical and scientific proof of this *and* premier expert witnesses to deliver it. Do you have some people in mind who might volunteer to be the lead plaintiffs in such a class action?"

"Don't worry about that right now." She waved a dismissive hand. "By the time the proof is there, we'll find the right person. Right now it's not easy. The ones who have a problem, like other addicts, are in complete denial that anything is wrong."

"Oh, this is good!" Will scoffed. "Not only is there no scientific evidence, the entire class I'd be representing would be denying that the defendant did anything wrong. I'd say that's a problem, all right."

After his sarcasm gushed out, he knew it had come on too strong. She'd just lost her job and come asking for his help. He didn't want to sound cold.

"Look, Persi, I don't know if I can help you. First of all, you should know I'm just now getting my first courtroom training as a litigator. Even if there is a case, I don't know if I'll be around to see it through. By the time it gets to trial, I'll probably be at a new firm doing estate planning and probate work. That's what I studied in law school." He had no such intention, but he wanted to convince her.

Persi looked at him incredulously. "Are you kidding? Death and taxes? What a waste."

"It's an interesting realm of the law. And you can jump into it right out of school without years of training. I happen to be good at gathering information, research, and applying schedules." As he spoke, he became conscious of how insincere if not preposterous he sounded. "All right, maybe I won't be doing probate work, but I'm not sure I'm cut out to be a trial lawyer. It takes years and years and, even then, a knack for turning a mountain of diverse information into a something a jury can get instantly."

Persi nodded her head in an expression of confidence. "Seems to me that's exactly what you can do. Graphically, even! Just ask Ward Braxton." She laughed; she was referring to a few political cartoons Will had concocted for *The Daily Nexus* mocking Ward Braxton, the regent who benefited from the royalty-free patents at the expense of the human rights project. In one, a line of starving and beaten people were queued up for HUMAN RIGHTS as the clerk—Ward Braxton—was shutting the counter with a sign: CLOSED INDEFINITELY WHILE STAFF ATTENDS FREE LUNCH.

Persi grew earnest again. She reached across the table and squeezed his fingers gently. They were very warm, more so from the passion of her convictions than the hot coffee, Will thought. "They've said they're going to file criminal charges against me," she said. "Listen. It's as simple as this. I need to get as much on them as I can through legal channels. And you need to be at the forefront of what may be one of the biggest manufacturer liability cases of all time. Will, just agree to the next step. Let's take it to Edwin."

Will felt himself nodding his head involuntarily.

"Yes! Super Chill strikes again!" She jumped up again, saluting him in a tongue-in-cheek demonstration. "Oh," she added, dropping back down in her chair. "There's one other symptom I didn't mention. Something Art Newman, despite the best-laid plans, couldn't have foreseen. Very curious. When addicts laugh really hard, a milky fluid comes out of their noses. I mean, even when they haven't had any milk to drink. Tell me *that* isn't weird!"

Will leaned way back in his chair, balancing on two legs almost to the point of no return, as the vivid image of Lenny came to mind. He rocked forward, bringing the front legs of the chair down with a thud, and began rubbing his brow with both hands. The moment had arrived. He would have to tell her now about his big client Lenny Milton, the blind Chihuahua named Lady J, and all he had learned while forced to grovel at the feet of Thurston Crushjoy about the legal niceties, or not-so-niceties, of shrink-wrap licenses on free packages of sirloin tip, on bottles of barbecue sauce, and on outdoor cooking information systems.

Why hadn't he followed that dream of a wonderfully dull practice in probate court? he thought to himself.

‹ 19 ›

Dr. Elizabeth Stone had decided after her third telephone interview with Edwin G. Ostermyer that she had to stop. It wasn't that he had nothing to add to her work in progress, *People Who Are All the Talk: What Makes Them Tick*. Quite to the contrary, he was definitely the most humility-challenged individual she had ever met and a perfect case study for her book.

But another interview? She was simply unable to resist calling him, now for an entirely superfluous *sixth* time. With each succeeding interview, and with increasing intensity, she had experienced a strange feeling—a feeling of letting go, of relinquishing the kind of control to which she was accustomed—that he managed to stir up in her. After first ducking the truth—something she sternly discouraged in her own patients—she had plumbed her own psyche to discover the cause of a compulsive behavior she was famous for revealing in others.

When she was six years old, she had played doctor with the neighbor boy, Theo—a year older than she—a beautiful child with an angelic face and an almost grim obsession. She often played with Theo, though curiously she never got to be doctor. Theo was the doctor. She was always the patient. She recalled how he would subject her to imaginary procedures that were so complicated, so dangerous, so intricately delicate that she, too, was swept up and carried away into his make-believe world.

The boy's highly acquisitive mind had managed to pick up a small library of medical terms that he would intone in a low sweet voice while performing an "operation" on her. She had no idea what he was talking about but had found his medical babble—and the things he did to her—to be comforting, nurturing, even thrilling. Theo was blessed with hands that, at the slightest touch, could lift up and transport her. He didn't know it, but he took her to a place within, a private place full of secret pleasures, one she might have told him about if he had ever really noticed her. But he didn't, self-enamored as he was, like the mythical boy (from whom the eponymous Narcissus complex that now so keenly interested her), absorbed by his own reflection in the river, unaware of the wood nymph nearby who pined away for him.

Abruptly, Theo and his family moved away. She never saw him again. The loss left her empty inside. It occurred to her during her own psychoanalysis that she might have compensated for the loss by becoming a doctor herself.

She decided to try something different in her interview today. For her own sense of identity, she had to reestablish the professional upper hand. Rather than have Ostermyer talk about himself—a subject that for him was the verbal equivalent of a perpetual motion machine—she decided to try a new tactic: to ask him to talk about others, or at least how he saw himself *in relation* to the rest of the world. She was an expert on relationships, she reminded herself; she would stay in control.

Determined, she picked up the phone and dialed his office. "This is Dr. Elizabeth Stone. I would like to speak to Mr. Ostermyer, please."

"Are you sure?" asked the bland-voiced receptionist, a different one from last week.

She experienced a mild shock, unsure if it was the raw impertinence of the questioner or the chilling thought that she might have misdialed and reached her own conscience. She reminded herself that she could handle it.

"Greetings, Elizabeth."

"Mr. Ostermyer, let's explore today, if we might, how you respond to other people when *they* talk. I'd like—"

"That's the key to my success," he said. "I really *listen*. Then, after they hear what I have to say—that they have rights beyond their dreams—they know they have come to the right lawyer. But you have to listen. Sometimes, for example, it is not the right move just to file a lawsuit for a client, particularly those clients who are squeamish about confrontation. Those clients are best served by a well-orchestrated series of threatening demand letters graphically depicting the severities of litigation. You see, that's when I can thrash out an amicable settlement, thus avoiding the needless escalation and ill will often born of a lawsuit."

Despite the best of intentions, she felt herself giving over to that feeling again. She was losing control. It was irrational, forbidden, yet darkly delicious. Nevertheless, the doctor in her pressed on. "You say you listen, but do you really think you are an effective listener? And when I say *effective listener*, I mean—"

"Exactly—listening to what I'm saying."

He interrupted again. He was incorrigible, hopelessly unreachable. She was letting go, slipping away to that private place . . . .

"My law practice is all about possibilities and making them realities. I tell that to my clients. And I have to practice what I preach. To be an effective listener, it is not enough to listen to my clients. I have to listen to what *I* am saying. Like right now." He paused as if to let the full meaning of his words sink into his ears. "I am saying that anything is possible—even something as seemingly unachievable as my becoming a more effective listener—but if I am saying that, and if I am listening to what I am saying, I have to put it into practice. That's the art of being a dynamic listener. I'm sure you know exactly what I am talking about."

"No, but I'm listening." She had no idea what he was talking about. It didn't matter. She took a deep breath and let it slowly pass through her lips. If she closed her eyes and yielded to the reverie, she could hear the plainsong of the boy and feel his hands upon her.

"I knew you would," he went on. "The possibilities are always there. To be a truly great lawyer—a real professional in the communications business as we both are—it is not enough to give lip service to yourself. You have to be focused on what you are really saying. You have to be disciplined and block everything else out."

"Yes, I think I am following you." She got more comfortable in her home office swivel chair. Its leather was smooth and pliant. He was going to take her there.

"Which invokes my overriding philosophy—"

"Oh, yes, I've been meaning to ask you. I want your philosophy *inside* . . . between the covers of my book. But you must explain it to me in all its rich, manifold texture . . . " Her voice was near breathless.

"To understand my philosophy, you have to understand my worldview, my Weltanschauung." He began to thrum.

Dr. Stone turned the phone volume up, depressed the MUTE button, rendering her breathing inaudible to him, and leaned back in her chair. The hot air palpated her ears and fanned gently over her skin like a tropical breeze.

She had asked him to expound on his philosophy. For the next hour and twenty minutes, with scarcely an interruption, he gave it to her.

‹ 20 › .

Will should have known that Edwin would practically be tripping over himself to get into a class action—with a shot at a big payoff in what would be named the Barbecue Addiction Litigation—as soon as he and Persi had briefed him on it. When they suggested to Edwin that he contact his trial lawyer associations to see if any similar claims had already been made, he vowed the last thing he would do would be to notify his competitors about this lead. "And tip them off so they can beat me to court? Not on your life!"

With class actions it was often a matter of who was first to file on behalf of the class. When a class action was filed against a company in New York, for example, followed the next week by the same suit in Florida, and then California, the trophy litigation more often than not was awarded to the lawyers in New York who were first to file.

Although Edwin had been at the forefront of more than his share of ground-breaking liability cases, he regretted he had been a latecomer on some choice opportunities. He had missed out recently on the class action filed on behalf of bad back sufferers who bought the popular "mini-hammock," which was supposed to attach to the railing on a studio apartment balcony; if it didn't break off the railing, it permanently contorted postures with a V-shaped resting surface. If Edwin had filed earlier in the class-action securities litigation involving inflated stock of Gloria Rothschild Liposuction Surgery Centers—the action that the press jokingly referred to as having been filed on behalf and for the sake of the "class ass"—he would have been living off the fat of the land with the other plaintiffs' lawyers.

Edwin solemnly swore never to miss out on the big ones again. "I have said that. I must hear what I am saying," Edwin said.

Will had no idea what he was talking about.

The idea presented to Edwin was that the firm should research, investigate, and build a case with experts through available legal channels and then, *and only then,* file suit if it all came together. But Edwin flatly refused to risk tipping his hand or losing out to rival lawyers. On top of that, the prospect of going after ThinkSoft seemed to cast an intoxicating spell on him, not to mention the media coverage that would accompany it. Some quick research conducted through on-line databases revealed a Wall Street forecast that ThinkSoft would gross over a billion dollars this year on its Wholly Grill business alone. Edwin ruminated that, if this was found to be unlawful, perhaps the entire amount would be a suitable monetary judgment under the legal remedy of "unjust enrichment."

When Will described Lenny's behavior at home, Edwin had heard enough. "Lenny's an addict. He needs help. We need to do whatever we can for him."

Again, Will suggested research and investigation that, if productive, could be presented to Lenny.

"No," Edwin snapped. "This can't wait. His condition cries out for a lawsuit, a class action, nationwide in scope. Will, get Lenny on board right away."

Will called Lenny and told him to meet him at the office. Rather than tell him what it was he needed to talk to him about, Will merely said he wanted "to go over some new evidence" before signing the settlement. Since that new evidence concerned Lenny's diet, Will purposely suggested, as a means of observing Lenny's eating habits in action, that they meet for a brown bag lunch in the office conference room.

For all intents and purposes, Edwin had cast Will in the role of an addict interventionist, something that took years of training to be successful; even then, it required joining forces with the user's friends, family, and even co-workers. It was reduced to this: He and Lenny needed to talk and have what Will code-named to himself the Big Discussion.

He offered to order a bag lunch for Lenny, but Lenny declined, saying he would bring his own lunch. Will was not surprised, expecting he would show up with a bag full of barbecue from home. At least that would make it easier to demonstrate to Lenny that he was out of control.

To Will's surprise, Lenny arrived in the office conference room dressed in a business suit and carrying a briefcase. Will was impressed with how professional he looked and what a favorable witness he would make on his own behalf should the matter ever go to trial, something that seemed rather remote.

"I've got another meeting downtown I need to go to," Lenny said, glancing at his watch. Will remembered that Lenny had claimed to have pressing engagements last time when he did not, but he really looked convincing in his suit.

"Well, put your briefcase down and have a seat. Where's your bag lunch?"

"It's in my briefcase." Lenny put the briefcase on the conference table, opened it up, and pulled out an appliance that looked like a smaller hi-tech version of a hibachi. "It's the laptop Wholly Grill, the Wholly Grill Junior. I just got it a week ago." Judging by its wear and tear, it looked like the mini-grill had logged—or logged on—a lot of time in just one week. Will pictured Lenny at home running both the big grill and the junior at the same time, with both the home and business lines tied up, doubling the credit card charges. "I swear it's easier than making a sandwich and perfect for eating on the run." It was hard to imagine Lenny—all 370 pounds of him—making *a* sandwich for lunch. It was even harder to picture him running.

He opened up the top of the jet black appliance, exposing a grill large enough for two or three fast-food burgers. The unit was hot-stamped with WHOLLY GRILL, JR., underneath which appeared the words OUTDOOR COOKING INFORMATION SYSTEM: INSIDE EDITION.

"Do you need to plug that in?" Will asked. "What about a modem connection?"

"No. It's wireless. But only four hours of battery life," Lenny boasted modestly.

"Say, Lenny, that's not going to smoke in here, is it?" Will asked, nervously smoothing his favorite silk tie while cycing the building's sprinkler system overhead.

"Not a chance," Lenny said confidently. "That's one of the beauties of the Wholly Grill system. The sauce has Smoke Crystals." Lenny uttered the words *Smoke Crystals* slowly and expressionlessly while fixing his eyes on the grill. As soon as Lenny had begun setting up, he became absorbed with the details of preparing the altar for whatever sacrifice he had brought along. "I think the way it works is, the laser flame hits the Smoke Crystals and absorbs the smoke. There is absolutely no smoke," he said, pausing to give Will the chance to consider how perfectly sublime this feature of the product was. "But I'm telling you it makes the smoke flavor even stronger. God, it tastes good!" Lenny seemed calmer now than when he first arrived, perhaps comforted by the imminence of gratification.

Lenny next produced a box from his briefcase. The front panel depicted a bunch of regular guys sitting around a living room having an inordinate amount of fun watching a football game and eating sausages. Large stylized letters identified the product as WHOLLY GRILL®LINKIN' BUDDIES® with "six all-beef sausages pre-basted with

Wholly Grill® barbecue sauce with Smoke Crystals®." Lenny tore off the shrink-wrap, opened the box, and pulled out the inside plastic tray of six ready-made sausages.

Will picked up the box to look at it in disbelief. "This box of sausages has a warning that says it's sold under a shrink-wrap license."

"All Wholly Grill stuff is sold with those licenses," Lenny said, removing one of the sausages from the tray. The meat was so thickly encrusted with sauce the actual sausage could have been as thin as a pencil and the end user wouldn't know until he'd bitten into it. The sauce was blood red with hundreds of charcoal-colored specks the size of peppercorns. These must be the celebrated Smoke Crystals. Lenny placed three sausages snugly on the grill, closed it, pushed a number of buttons on a small computer screen, and hit START." Will heard the modem dialing up the Wholly WORD at ThinkSoft and then a whirring sound, which must have been the scanning and digitizing of the sausages for transmission to ThinkSoft so the laser flame would be correctly modulated.

Lenny opened the grill, turned the sausages over, and closed it again. Amazingly, no smoke was coming from the meat, although the sizzling sound and bubbling sauce revealed it was at least as hot as any conventional grill. The Smoke Crystals on the cooked side were now twice the size as on the uncooked side.

A beep sounded and Lenny opened the grill again, removing the sausages to the wax paper in which they came packed in the box. He attacked one of them with the "traveler" Wholly Grill barbecue fork in his briefcase. He took a bite of the sausage and chewed, ravenously at first, then slower and slower, extracting greater and greater gratification, perhaps as the effect kicked in, with each moment.

"Think about how far we've come," Will said. "I guess it was the caveman who discovered fire that invented the first wireless grill." He was trying to warm up a tough audience before launching into the Big Discussion, but Lenny was too preoccupied to respond. Will's own thoughts were free to drift off and consider the evolution of mankind, the discovery of fire, as well as cave paintings of primitive outdoor cooking information systems.

Will realized that he was in as deep a trance as Lenny seemed to be and that his musings were only causing delay. He had let tens of thousands of years elapse without getting down to business. That was a lot of time. Worse, he could only bill a few minutes of it to Lenny's case. Edwin had admonished Will about uncaptured time. He simply couldn't put off the Big Discussion another minute.

Lenny moaned faintly as he engulfed the remainder of his second Linkin' Buddies sausage. "Lenny, we need to talk about your case," Will started.

"Did you want to have me sign some papers to finish the settlement you told me about?" he said, obliviously talking with his mouth full.

"Actually, we have another approach on your case we want to discuss with you. It seems there are some other aspects of Wholly Grill that may be the basis of a class-action lawsuit against ThinkSoft." Will proceeded to tell Lenny about his friend Persi and what she had learned thus far. When he told him there were Wholly Grill addicts out there, Lenny didn't even flinch. Instead he scraped sauce off the fork, rubbed it into his gums with his index finger, and smacked his lips.

Finally Will took a deep breath. "Lenny, I think you are one of those afflicted . . . addicted, that is," he stammered. "You're an addict. Nothing to be ashamed of. But in terms of your lawsuit, we need to rethink the settlement on the table. There's another legal course I think you should consider."

Lenny, who was absorbed in his work on the third sausage, suddenly stopped. His eyes grew big and his face red. "That's ridiculous!" he said, raising his voice. "The whole thing is ridiculous. I don't know about these other people who have a problem. I don't have a problem. I just like the taste of it and I like to cook with it. I like the taste of a lot of things." Lenny was angry and his feelings were hurt. The anger Will felt directed at him spoke of an insensitivity Lenny had endured for many years before Wholly Grill came along. Will felt awful.

"I meant no disrespect, Lenny. I'm sorry. I just want you to give it some thought before you sign a release for ThinkSoft. Maybe you are being used in a way you hadn't considered."

Just then Edwin walked into the conference room and greeted Lenny. It was obvious that Lenny admired Edwin. The redness drained from his face, and he smiled when Edwin spoke to him. Will got a quick glance from Edwin telegraphing that Edwin could see the Big Discussion was not going over well with Lenny.

"Sorry I couldn't join you for your meeting," Edwin said to Lenny. "I am preparing for another hearing in the Snapple Johnson case. As you probably read in the paper, my motion to continue the trial was successful. Now I am moving to suspend the entire action indefinitely. Things are going quite well, if I do say so." Lenny asked some questions about the Johnson case, clearly pleased to be talking to the great trial lawyer handling a high-profile murder trial.

"I'm a little more familiar with the Wholly Grill since our last visit," Edwin told Lenny. "In fact, Snapple Johnson has one in his backyard and loves to cook with it."

While Edwin was there, Lenny loaded two more Linkin' Buddies into the grill, demonstrating to Edwin that there was no smoke. After expressing how impressed he was with the gadget, Edwin excused himself and went back to his office. Lenny was in a calmer mood when the conversation continued.

"Lenny, how can you dismiss this out of hand?" Will persisted, but he was not enjoying his task. He genuinely liked Lenny, but he was telling Lenny everything he didn't want to hear. "You are an exact match of the profile addict. Whether you decide to sue or not is up to you. But you need to take a hard look at this. This is your life."

"You bet it is. I like my life, and I *am* in control of it." He opened the grill and turned the two sausages. His face was puffy and his eyes were a rounder shape than when he had come in. He looked strangely different, like someone who wears glasses looks when seen for the first time without glasses.

"Forget about control," Will said. "What about that milk coming out of your nose when you laugh? I saw you when I was over at your house. We believe that's a symptom. How can you deny it?"

"It's no big deal when that happens," Lenny said, dismissing Will's point with halfhearted conviction. "My doctor *has* told me I have a problem with cholesterol. In particular, I need to cut back on dairy products—especially pizzas . . . too much cheese . . . ." Will was left on his own to reach the improbable conclusion that the etiology of the milky effluent was a lifetime overindulgence in pizzas.

The electronic beep sounded again; Lenny opened the grill. As he speared the first of the two perfectly cooked sausages, the fire alarm blared with a deafening ring. The overhead sprinklers exploded, spouting water all over the table, the chairs, the carpet, and the two of them.

"Let's get out of here!" Will yelled. Lenny was trying to cover the open grill with his hands, apparently more concerned with saving the sausages than himself.

By the time they had scrambled out of the room, Lenny looked like a walrus in a business suit. Will felt like a dog just come in from the pouring rain; he wished he could shake it all off. Office workers came running to the area. Seeing there was no fire, they pointed at the two of them, some smirking. Edwin arrived at the same time as the building engineer, Tom Peterson, who immediately looked around with a radio in his hand.

"No fire suppression! Repeat! No fire suppression required on eight," he barked into the radio. "Notify tenants on all levels via emergency PA that we will not be evacuating the building." He started to put the radio down, then brought it back up. "Deactivate sprinklers in conference room on level eight. Dispatch a crew here with mops and carpet dryers." Peterson put the radio in its holster and walked over to the Wholly Grill, Jr., still on the table, opened up with two soaking wet sausages. The Linkin' Buddies box was open and full of water, a lone Buddy floating face down. Steam was rising in the conference room from where the water met the hot grill.

Lenny, who was still stunned, blurted out, "It wasn't the grill! No smoke comes out of that thing. I swear! Right?" He looked at Will to back him up.

"It's true. I didn't see any smoke," Will said.

"We didn't see any smoke," Edwin observed.

"You have to understand that the deadliest smokes are the ones you don't see at all," Peterson concurred gravely. "The detectors in these offices are state-of-the-art. They pick up not only fire smoke but emissions other systems would miss. If there is Legionnaires' disease or some other unknown or undocumented toxic intruder, our system will send an alarm pronto, activate the sprinkler to suppress whatever it is, and ask questions later. I don't know what tripped the system today, but I assure you it is nothing to fool around with. I am going to keep this room sealed and have my crew wear gas masks until it is cleaned up. Stand back, everyone!" Peterson closed the conference-room door, radioed some further instructions, and departed.

Edwin turned to Will. "This barbecue is deadlier than we ever imagined," he said grimly. "We need to document this at once! Call Stanley on his cell phone. Tell him to get up here right away and take pictures, draw diagrams, and interview witnesses."

Stanley Harper was the firm's private investigator. Whether it was an intersection accident or a class-action securities fraud case, Stanley Harper—ever vigilant—was there to take pictures, draw diagrams, and interview witnesses.

"Lenny, I know you need to get home as soon as possible," Edwin continued. "But I know you are equally anxious to see that the wheels of justice are set in motion. These merchants of misery—these syco-phants of human suffering—must be brought to justice. Come with me to my office. The papers have been prepared. You only need to sign them and you are on your way."

Lenny was not only soaking from the impromptu shower, his eyes were swimming in his head from the events. "If I agree—if I sign on saying I am addicted to whatever this stuff is—do I have to quit or can I think about that?" His voice quivered slightly. It was apparent that he was more frightened of quitting than continuing to load his body with unknown toxins.

Will was about to tell Lenny that Persi had found a few twelve-step programs already or he might want to talk to a psychologist, but Edwin preempted him. "No. You can do whatever you want. All you have to do is say you are addicted."

Lenny thought for another moment. "Could I get more money to take care of Lady J?"

Edwin smiled reassuringly. "Just follow me."

Will called Stanley while Edwin had Lenny sign the new paper-work. Still soaking wet, Will dropped by Edwin's office to let him know he was heading home to change into some dry clothes. While waiting for the elevator, Will decided to go back to pick up the draft complaint so he could work on it at home and get it filed the next day.

The original negligence lawsuit in Municipal Court would be vol-untarily dismissed, making way for a new lawsuit filed in the federal courthouse in San Jose only a few blocks away. The old complaint would be recycled into the new complaint, along with a fresh array of untested and highly charged claims, all of which hinged entirely on proof of an undisclosed and insidious addiction. The new legal theories would include false advertising, false labeling, unfair and deceptive business practices, constructive battery, and intentional infliction of emotional distress.

While doubling back through the office corridors, Will halted his steps when he overheard Edwin having an uncharacteristically jovial telephone conversation in his office. "You were brilliant! I owe you for this, Tom Peterson. 'Unknown or undocumented toxic intruders'? A superb performance! You get an Oscar for acting, an Oscar for original screenplay, and, of course, one for special effects—a sprinkler system screaming *Danger!* just like a real emergency!"

Will couldn't believe what he was hearing. He decided to reach his office by another hallway, retrieve the papers, and get home. As he began to retrace his steps, he could still hear Edwin crowing on the phone. "You were a hit. An unwilling client, who dearly needed a reason to believe, was inspired by your performance!"

< 21 >

The giant solid-mahogany doors to the firm of Kilgore, Crushjoy, Clubman & Howell opened like floodgates, allowing Thurston Crushjoy and an entourage of six associate lawyers to pour into the office. The attending lawyers scurried around Crushjoy as he strode across the expansive marble floor to the client waiting area. There were four more lawyers-in-waiting in the reception area, hoping to get a few seconds of his time, a few golden drops of advice he might dispense on the way to his first meeting of the day.

When the lawyers-in-waiting started to advance toward him, Crushjoy lifted his hand to ward them off for a moment. He picked up a copy of *The Legal Institution*, the daily trade paper, to see how it was dealing with the case of *Milton vs. ThinkSoft*, newly filed in federal court. The general press had sensationalized the story and actually given the ridiculous addiction claims just enough credence to tease the population into imagining there could be some merit to the lawsuit.

Before being purchased by a media and entertainment conglomerate a few years back, *The Legal Institution* had been considered a respected and intelligent daily publication. But that reputation had gone downhill since the entertainment peddlers had purchased it. Crushjoy noted that the lead article on the new ThinkSoft lawsuit had been written by Alfred Woolsey, a fine young contributing writer for *The New Republic* before moving west to join *The Legal Institution*.

Crushjoy hoped that would bring some journalistic integrity back and paint the lawsuit for what it was: a frivolous, unprecedented, and groundless claim.

He lowered his glasses on his nose to read the headline story, tilting his head back slightly to read through the bifocals, causing him to thrust out his jawbone.

WHOLLY GRILL IS JUNKIE FOOD, SUIT CLAIMS

CLASS OF ADDICTS SUES THINKSOFT FOR DAMAGES

BY ALFRED WOOLSEY

A CLASS ACTION WAS FILED YESTERDAY AGAINST SANTA TOSTADA–BASED THINKSOFT CORPORATION, WHICH RECENTLY FORAYED INTO MANUFACTURING OUT-DOOR COOKING INFORMATION SYSTEMS, FORMERLY KNOWN AS BARBECUE GRILLS. THE SUIT WAS BROUGHT ON BEHALF OF AN UNSPECIFIED NUMBER OF INDIVIDUALS WHO CLAIM THEY HAVE BECOME ADDICTED TO THE POPULAR WHOLLY GRILL SYSTEM AND WHOSE SYMPTOMS INCLUDE UNCONTROLLED CRAVING, OVEREATING, OVERSPENDING, ANXIETY DISORDER, AND "MILK" FLOWING FROM THEIR NOSES WHEN INDUCED TO LAUGH IN AN EXCESS OF MIRTH.

COUNSEL FOR THE CLASS EDWIN G. OSTERMYER STATED THAT THERE WERE AN ESTIMATED TWENTY MILLION USERS OF WHOLLY GRILL IN THE UNITED STATES ALONE AND THAT THE CLASS WAS ESTIMATED TO BE AT LEAST 10 PERCENT OF USERS. WHEN ASKED HOW MUCH MONEY WAS SOUGHT, OSTERMYER SAID, "AT LEAST THREE BILLION DOLLARS IN COMPENSATION. BUT THAT'S JUST FOR WHAT THEY OWE ANYWAY. WE WANT TO DELIVER A MIGHTY STING TO THINKSOFT TO MAKE SURE THEY NEVER DO ANYTHING LIKE THIS AGAIN. WE WANT A SHOCKING AMOUNT OF PUNITIVE DAMAGES—AN AMOUNT SO EXCESSIVE, SO FINANCIALLY CRIPPLING, AND SO HIGHLY OFFENSIVE TO THEIR OUTMODED NOTIONS OF COMMON SENSE THAT ALL THE FINANCIAL OFFICERS OF THINKSOFT, AND COMPANIES LIKE THEM, WILL SUDDENLY BECOME DREADFULLY ILL AND BEG TO GO ON SICK LEAVE. THAT WOULD BE A FAIR AMOUNT."

AMANDA JAMES, ASSOCIATE GENERAL COUNSEL FOR THINKSOFT OVERSEEING LEGAL AFFAIRS OF THE WHOLLY GRILL DIVISION, SAID SHE HAD NOT SEEN THE COMPLAINT. AFTER PORTIONS OF THE COMPLAINT WERE READ TO HER, SHE SAID, "IT'S MIND-NUMBING." SHE WENT ON TO STATE THAT THE ALLEGATIONS OF THE COMPLAINT WERE "THE STUFF THAT DREAMS ARE MADE OF." SHE SAID THE COMPLAINT HAD BEEN REFERRED TO THURSTON CRUSHJOY, CHIEF OUTSIDE COUNSEL FOR THINKSOFT.

T. OSWALD BARTHOLMEOW, A LAW PROFESSOR AT THE SANTA TOSTADA SCHOOL OF LAW AND AN EXPERT ON CLASS ACTIONS, SAID HE HAD NEVER HEARD OF A LAWSUIT LIKE THIS. WHEN TOLD OF AMANDA JAMES'S COMMENTS HE SAID, "'MIND-NUMBING'? 'WHAT DREAMS ARE MADE OF'? SHE APPEARS TO BE DESCRIBING AN OPIATELIKE SUBSTANCE. WITH CONCESSIONS LIKE THAT, PERHAPS ALL THAT IS LEFT IS A TRIAL ON DAMAGES. I'VE NEVER HEARD OF THAT." BARTHOLMEOW SAID HE HAD NO IDEA—

Thurston Crushjoy dropped the paper to the table; he had read enough. Another promising young writer had become *institution*-alized, as he and others in his firm referred to it. As for Professor Bartholmeow, there was much he didn't know. He lived in an ivory tower, far removed from the courtroom battlefield so familiar to the veteran trial attorney.

"Good morning, Mr. Crushjoy," the firm's concierge greeted him. The concierge had her own office but was out in the reception area to oversee details of a number of meetings in progress. "Mr. Newman and Ms. Amanda James are here, with others from ThinkSoft. They have been set up in the East Conference Room."

The East Conference Room was the premier meeting facility at the firm, offering, with its floor-to-ceiling windows, a steep and stark view of San Francisco Bay as seen from the forty-seventh floor of Edgewater Towers. A visiting client could not help but morosely fantasize a misstep and a death plunge into the cold waters below. As far as Thurston Crushjoy was concerned, an inspired and healthy fear was a good reference point for any discussion with clients on how they should deal with their predators.

Inside the conference room, Art Newman was going over a copy of the complaint with Amanda James. Amanda had worked at Kilgore Crushjoy for five years right out of law school before going in-house with ThinkSoft. There were six other Kilgore Crushjoy attorneys gathered around the long teakwood table. Crushjoy sat down at the far end, picked up the complaint in front of Art Newman, and leafed through it.

"There's nothing here, no evidence—just claims that the product is the subject of some vague druglike addiction and fanciful symptomatology. We can knock out one or two claims in a quick motion to dismiss that can be heard in the next month or so, but eliminating the rest of it—and I am confident we will do just that—will have to wait for a motion for summary judgment. Realistically, that's another six to eight months down the line. There's no way, as I see it, that this case will make it all the way to trial."

"The lawsuit is absurd!" Art Newman fulminated. "Meanwhile, the public sees this and believes that because someone has filed a piece of paper with the federal court—someone they have seen eat doughnuts on television and who represents a notorious killer—they think this might possibly be real. Let me tell you something. You understand the legal system and how such things could happen. I understand technology. But I see this gnat-sized nuisance of a lawsuit to be like a computer virus if not dealt with swiftly and decisively. If allowed to persist, a seemingly innocuous but virulent pest can trigger a system-wide catastrophe."

"A virus. A systemic catastrophe," Crushjoy repeated, turning to his attentive associates. "We might describe it to the judge that way." He had started to take some notes himself on a yellow pad. Not satisfied with the ballpoint pen at the table, he put it down and raised his right hand with his palm open at shoulder level. An attendant rushed over and placed a MontBlanc in it.

Amanda James looked at Crushjoy and continued where Art Newman left off. "Given the nature of the claims, we assume the plaintiffs' lawyers are going to ask the judge to make us turn over all of our recipes, formulas, and the highly secret operating system of the Wholly Grill. As you know, we have millions in research and development invested in the Wholly Grill intellectual property. These trade secrets are vital to our future."

"This technology has moved us beyond hardware and software," Art gushed. "It's even beyond reasonware. I like to call it . . . *cookware* . . ." Art drifted into his thoughts, then quickly added, "*Reinvented and reengineered* cookware, that is."

"An outdoor cooking information system, to be exact," Amanda pointed out.

"It's pure information," Art added. "Wholly Grill is the medium of the Information Age more so than any other ThinkSoft product. The grill and the sauce are licensed—not owned—because it's nothing but information. The result: pure information embodied in a side of ribs, much like a computer program, another form of pure information, is embodied in a software diskette. We all know that information is perceived through the senses. With Wholly Grill, you smell and taste it, and you never forget the touch—the Wholly Grill–ripened Smoke Crystals, exploding on the roof of your mouth." He paused, spellbound by his own rhapsody. "Once beyond the mouth, it continues to inform the senses and the total system, nutritionally and in every way. That's what we mean by information."

"And there is nothing addictive about it as far as you know, right?" Crushjoy posed the question bluntly, looking straight into Art's eyes.

"Absolutely not!" Art turned to Amanda, as if continuing an earlier conversation between the two of them. "What do they mean by addiction anyway? From what I know, addiction isn't a stand-alone accessory. It comes bundled with the rest of the addict's makeup. There's nothing inherently wrong with the act of eating, but with certain personalities overeating becomes a problem." He turned back to Crushjoy. "Even if they drag a few of those types into court who have that kind of problem, that doesn't mean Wholly Grill is responsible."

"I would not count on keeping their hands off the trade secrets," Crushjoy observed grimly. "But if the judge lets them have access to the trade secrets, he has to give us a protective order making them keep the information secure and confidential. Anything hypersensitive should be limited to attorneys' eyes only."

"That's completely unacceptable!" Art fumed. "Why should I have to reveal my trade secrets to the maniacs who filed this lawsuit? What about our shrink-wrap license? It specifically says users will never have any right to see our trade secrets, even if they sue us."

"I know. It depends on the judge," Crushjoy said. "I think a judge would typically let the attorneys see the trade secrets and take all the information into consideration before deciding whether the shrink-wrap license is enforceable. If he enforces the license, he will exclude the trade secrets from evidence and order that the material never be referred to again. If he doesn't enforce the shrink-wrap license, there is a real danger your secrets will no longer be secret."

"Who *is* the judge in our case?" Art asked anxiously.

"Judge Ignatius P. Wetherborne," Crushjoy said. "A thirty-year veteran of the bench. An independent thinker. Can be a little rough around the edges. Sees himself as a no-nonsense type. That's good for us."

"Clerks who have worked for him," Amanda chimed in, "have said, for example, that he has a standing instruction to them that they black out about a hundred recurring words from lawyer's briefs before he will read them—words like *clearly*, *egregious, moreover,* and *accordingly.* Some briefs are cut in half. Some prove to have nothing to say."

Crushjoy added a more sober observation. "He also has an unpredictable, ill-tempered side. We know something about his trigger points. His courtroom do's and taboos, otherwise inscrutable, can mean the difference between winning or losing."

"How do you know this stuff?" Art asked, pleased. He loved unshared inside information.

"I have appeared before him many times. There's also this strange coincidence," Crushjoy added, smiling confidently. "Six of the fourteen lawyers so far assigned to the Wholly Grill defense team clerked for Judge Wetherborne." On cue, six figures across the table, taking notes, began preening.

Art Newman tilted back in his leather swivel chair and smiled as if finally seeing, to his satisfaction, how the playing field was likewise tilted in his favor. "Let's not just win. Let's win big. Let's send a message to all the would-be bloodsuckers out there about who delivers a mighty sting." He turned to Crushjoy and nodded. "Whatever it takes."

‹ 22 ›

"Hi. I'm Frank," said the lanky man in his late fifties awkwardly planted on a small plastic chair behind the makeshift card-table reception desk. He took a long drag of his cigarette and blew half of it out before saying, "Is this your first time at Wholly Grillers Anonymous?"

"My second. His first," Persi said, nodding to Will. Indeed, Persi had quietly dropped into a meeting a few weeks ago.

"Names?" His Magic Marker was poised over a stack of blank stick-on tags.

"I'm Persi."

"I'm Will."

Frank wrote down the names and handed them their tags. "Welcome to WGA. We just have a few rules. You guys clean?" Will looked down at his spotless shirt and then at his pressed pants, not sure what to say.

"We're clean," Persi said.

Frank took another deep drag of his cigarette. "Good. Just so we're clear, the grill drill is the same as kickin' the swill. No Junior out in the car. No Linkin' Buddies stashed in your coat pocket. The rules are for your recovery and to protect the others here who are tryin' to clean themselves up. And, of course, everything here is confidential; nothing leaves the meeting. Got it? Good. Go help yourself to some coffee."

Will and Persi stepped into the adjoining room in the basement of

St. Paul's Presbyterian Church. There were twenty more plastic chairs set up; more than half had been staked with sweaters or other personal belongings. Most people seemed to know one another, judging by the lively exchange coming from a large cluster in one corner. Will wasn't sure if he was going to make it through the meeting with all the cigarette smoke in the room, though Persi didn't seem to mind.

When Frank walked in and sat in the secretary's chair, everyone took a seat. "Welcome to the Tuesday-night seven-thirty-every-evening-except-Saturday meeting of Wholly Grillers Anonymous. My name is Frank, and I'm a Wholly Grill addict."

"Hi, Frank!" they chorused.

"In case somebody has to leave early, don't forget we have a picnic on Saturday at the beach in Aptos. There will be beverages, but bring picnic food to share."

"Can we bring a barbecue grill and cook?" asked a short pudgy man in a sweatshirt. "I mean old style, with briquettes and everything."

"No, no, no, Devlin!" Frank shook his head. "That'd be a bad idea—like AA members getting together and throwing down nonalcoholic tequila shooters. That's a slippery slope. Come on, guys!"

Devlin dropped his head, suitably chastised.

"Where was I?" continued Frank. "Oh, yeah! Let me begin by thanking Ellen for doing such a great job chairing the meetings on Sunday and Monday." Ellen stood up, received a rousing ovation, and sat down as Frank continued. "I couldn't be here last night"—he paused for an aside—"I was able to catch a downtown meeting." He rolled his eyes. "Imagine an army of tongheads in blue suits!"

A spontaneous round of laughter ensued from everyone except Will and Persi. Will just shuffled his feet and grinned foolishly. Just as quickly the laughter stopped, except for one young man in the back who continued to laugh riotously. Everyone turned around to look. He was now holding his breath, trying desperately to suppress tickles of delight, his fleshy cheeks swelling to the size of Alaskan tomatoes.

Finally he gasped for air, lost it altogether, and, burying his face in a handkerchief, burst into convulsions of laughter.

"Come on, Billy, for God's sake, it's not *that* funny!" Frank coaxed. When, his excess of jollies having subsided, Billy still would not look up from his handkerchief, knowing glances were exchanged.

"Billy, do you want to come clean with us about something?" Frank asked sternly. Billy separated himself from his handkerchief and looked up. His expression was sheepish but his nose, which had taken on a life of its own, was lactating like a prize Holstein. The way the spilled milk was spread all over his otherwise cherubic face could have earned him the modeling job as the "Got cookies?" poster child.

"Billy, we all know what it means when one of us does an Elsie the Cow. You've been using in the last few hours."

Billy stared down at the ground in shame.

"Who is Billy's sponsor?" Frank asked the group.

"Tom," someone said. "But Tom's not here."

Frank looked at Ellen. "Ellen, would you be good enough to take Billy into the other room? Work with him. See if he's holding. If it'll do any good, have him chew on some smoked salmon. You know what to do." Ellen jumped up and escorted Billy out.

The room was somber following Billy's departure. Then a brown-skinned man with a mustache in the front row asked, "Why is it we laugh hardest sometimes when we don't want to laugh?"

Frank thought about it a moment and then waxed philosophical. "Good question, Carlos. I suppose it's because it's not supposed to be funny. There's a thin line between laughing and crying. In Billy's case his laughing was a cry for help. It's the third time he's fallen off the unmarinated-meat wagon. He was too embarrassed to call his sponsor, so, whether he intended it or not, the only way he could tell us was the way he did. We're all struggling to deal with something that's more powerful than we are. We can't explain it to our families, our co-workers, anyone. We can't explain why a barbecue grill took control of our lives but not theirs."

"I sometimes wish I were an alcoholic, or even a dope fiend. At least people would understand," a woman volunteered. The others muttered and nodded, confirming the shared experience.

There was a momentary lull. Persi seized the opportunity and stood up. "Good evening, folks, my name is Persi, and I want to talk to you about something very important——"

Frank interrupted her. "Persi, you are welcome to be here, but if you want to share your story, you begin by saying, 'My name is Persi, and I am powerless over Wholly Grill.' Now—from the top, friend."

"Well, actually, I am not powerless." A small shock wave rippled through the meeting room. "I began looking into this as a reporter." A larger shock wave rolled through the room. "I lost my job over it. Let me assure you of complete confidentiality. Nobody is going to be mentioned in a paper or anywhere else unless they OK it. I'm here with Will Swanson, an attorney in town, who has filed a class action against the makers of Wholly Grill claiming it's addictive, that there's no warning, and they should pay for what they've done. Will?"

"Thanks, Persi." Will stood up and looked at the group. Inside a second or two the room before him seemed to quiver along a narrow spectrum of facial expressions: surprise, distrust, antagonism, and curiosity.

"Listen, we know you didn't choose to become addicted to Wholly Grill and have your lives, careers, and relationships put in jeopardy. We invite you to join in our class action to do something for yourself, but, more importantly, we need you as witnesses, who can explain to a jury what it means—like what your friend Billy is going through—so we can prove our case, help others avoid it altogether, and create a fund to pay for education and treatment programs. What I would like to do——"

"Wait a minute!" a woman shouted out. "You promise us complete confidentiality, but you want us to join a lawsuit or testify in court in front of cameras and media. What are you talking about?"

"Yeah, why do you think we have the word *anonymous* in our name?"

someone else chimed in. "We don't even list our meetings in the local papers. It's strictly word of mouth."

"We wouldn't have meetings anymore," said a grandmotherly voice filled with sadness. "I would miss you all."

"You make the personal decision to go public or not," Will said. "We don't want to interfere with your meetings. We're just offering you the opportunity to say something to those responsible and do something about it."

Frank weighed in. "We *are* doing something about it. We are taking responsibility for our lives, not blaming others. A lawsuit is the *last* thing we're interested in."

There was a chorus of "yeah!" and "that's right!" Spurred on, Frank pressed his point.

"Let's give them a taste of the kind of confidentiality they're offering us. Why don't we take one of our 'secret ballots' on whether to join the suit. Shall we?" he said, prompting the others with a wink.

In unison the entire room gave them the big thumbs down except that, in what appeared to be a well-rehearsed sight gag, they each covered their southbound thumbs with the grips of their other hands. Will and Persi, technically at least, were spared the sight of overwhelming rejection.

Lest there be any doubt, Frank announced the results of the secret ballot: "The votes are in, and you guys are out!" A chorus of anonymous grillers continued to cheer the vote as the two visitors quickly and ignominiously made their way out the door.

Back on the street Will shook his head in frustration. "The ones in denial think the suit is about the ones in recovery, and the ones in recovery want no part of it. I see what you mean. It may be awhile before we find any witnesses besides Lenny to come forward."

"I guess this is one of those rare moments when you're grateful that the wheels of justice grind so slowly," Persi said, in search of a silver lining.

‹ 23 ›

"Quiet, or Judge Wetherborne will hear you!" the courtroom clerk, Mr. Danning, shouted above the noise. "The judge is reviewing papers—and he needs to think!" Mr. Danning held his glare for a moment to remind the attorneys, spectators, and reporters gathered in the cavernous room that the full force of federal law was behind him. One bat of his eye, and a federal marshal would materialize. A disquieting calm settled on the court.

Mr. Danning was not just any courtroom clerk, he was the surrogate of the Honorable Ignatius P. Wetherborne. In no other courtroom was it necessary to maintain a hush *before* the judge entered because he *might* hear a noise from his chambers where he was busy thinking.

Will, who was now seated at counsel table with Edwin, ready for the first hearing, knew that Judge Wetherborne was both feared and respected by attorneys and that he was notoriously inscrutable. Although Will had never appeared in Judge Wetherborne's courtroom until this day, he had consulted with an old family friend, a grizzled veteran of the federal court with a wry sense of humor. The lawyer had raised his eyebrows and shaken his head slowly to express his bewilderment. He then had taken out a piece of paper and drawn a nearly perfectly round circle that did, in fact, closely approximate the shape of the judge's completely bald head.

"It's like this," the lawyer had explained, while drawing two smaller circles for eyes within the larger circle. "This is Judge Wetherborne. His eyes are in a constant state of vibration. Beware the right one taking a bead on you. That means he is after you. The left eye, however," he said, drawing an arrow to it, "is a wandering eye. It gets up out of the socket and moves around. It is not just after you. It's agitated and not to be reasoned with. The key is to weave your way in and out of the judge's line of vision, like an open-field runner, in a way that causes the judge's eyes to focus on the other guy—the left eye, if possible."

An old salt, the lawyer had then written at the top of the paper: *Orientation to Courtroom J, United States District Court for the Northern District of California.* He rolled the paper up as if it were a nautical chart and handed it to Will. "Take this to court with you. It will help you to keep your bearings."

It was 9:25 on Monday morning and the judge had not yet appeared for the 9 A.M. status and scheduling conference. The judge was *thinking.* Even the members of the press, ordinarily a boisterous group, kept their voices to a whisper. Edwin, who was not one to sit for long, paced back and forth behind the counsel table for the plaintiff, reviewing his mental notes. A phalanx of attorneys clustered around the counsel table for the defense. Thurston Crushjoy was calmly seated there, issuing instructions and commentary to his minions.

Will did not recall so many associates coming into the courtroom with Crushjoy. It was as though Thurston Crushjoy had arrived in the courtroom with six or seven lawyers in attendance, placed his smooth Italian leather briefcase on the table, released the polished brass latches—*thwack! thwack!*—and out popped seven more freshly scrubbed young associates who had somehow been spring-loaded into its interior.

"All rise! The Honorable Ignatius P. Wetherborne presiding!" Mr. Danning announced. In walked the judge, followed by six law clerks who took seats in the jury box. To Will's surprise, Wetherborne was probably no more than an inch over five feet, his robe dragging on the floor. However, although he was in his mid-seventies, he sprang onto his seat like an old cowhand to his steed. Rather than immediately start the calendar, there was another moment of awkward stillness as his large and imperious head surveyed its domain.

"Good morning, Your Honor. Edwin——"

"I know who you are, Mr. Ostermyer." The judge spoke slowly and methodically to interrupt Edwin while continuing to take in the room before him. "And I know Mr. Crushjoy here for the defense." The judge smiled distantly; he must still be thinking because his eyes were not directed toward anyone in particular. He then nodded toward a group of associates from Kilgore Crushjoy in a way that suggested he knew them too.

"Yes, I believe I recognize everyone here. Except"—and he turned his attention back to the counsel table for the plaintiffs, his right eye suddenly taking a bead on Will—"I don't believe I have had the pleasure of making your acquaintance, sir."

Will looked up, stunned that somehow he was in a class by himself. "Uh, Will Swanson, Your Honor. This is my first time in your—" He stopped; everybody already knew that. "I'm appearing for the plaintiff too . . . with Mr. Ostermyer."

"Is that a yellow tie, Mr. Swanson?" the judge asked.

Will looked at his tie, completely at a loss as to what this was about. "Yes, Your Honor," he replied, in a tone that was half answer, half question. "Mustard, actually. Not to quibble."

"I see. What is the pattern on it? I can't make it out from here."

Will looked down at his tie again. "They are . . . uh . . . bunnies." He heard a scattering of snickers. Floundering for a means to kick the judge's attention in another direction, Will added, "For what it's worth, Your Honor, you should know they are rather *abstract* bunnies."

He looked to Edwin for help, but Edwin had his eyes fixed on the judge in search of clues.

"*Abstract* bunnies." The judge ruminated. "You know, Mr. Swanson, while I was reviewing the papers on this case, I was caused to do some thinking on the subject of what is *abstract* . . . in the sense of *difficult to understand,* or *theoretical* as opposed to *real.*" Will glanced over and saw smiles of derision at the Crushjoy table. He was mortified.

The judge's eyes suddenly changed focus, as though the yellow tie colloquy had never occurred. Solemnly he turned to his clerk. "Mr. Danning, let us proceed. Announce the matter on calendar."

Mr. Danning stood and, holding the docket sheet before him, enunciated, "*Milton versus ThinkSoft Corporation*, Civil Action Number 348789 IPW."

"All right, this is the first Status and Scheduling Conference in this case. Plaintiffs have asked that I certify this as a class action on behalf of all persons who have become addicted to defendant's Wholly Grill outdoor cooking information system." The judge leaned forward and looked at Edwin, only vaguely intimating the skepticism of a moment ago. "What kind of scheduling and time line did you have in mind, Mr. Ostermyer?"

Edwin stood and addressed the judge, occasionally turning to make sure the press seated behind him could hear and take down what he had to say. "Your Honor, regardless of any delays that may be urged by the defendant, we don't see any reason why the class cannot be certified within the next six months. We recognize that, due to backlog, civil cases in this district are not scheduled for trial in less than one year, and class actions are typically twice as long. However, we believe we can certify the class and complete all necessary discovery in an expeditious manner such that this can be set for trial within eighteen months."

"Really," Judge Wetherborne mused, his mind apparently taking off in another direction. "Setting aside, for the moment, how or when I might certify such a class, what kind of discovery do you feel is necessary?"

Edwin clearly relished the opportunity to convey to the court, to ThinkSoft, and most of all to the press the kind of resources he was prepared to commit to this case and that he was ready, willing, and eager to go toe-to-toe with giants like ThinkSoft and powerhouses like Kilgore Crushjoy. "Depending on initial documents and responses we get from the defendant, we expect that there will be fifty to one hundred depositions, not including expert witnesses. But the first order of business will be to require that ThinkSoft turn over all of its testing, formulations, and recipes as well as its animal and human studies and experiments relating to Wholly Grill. We submit," Edwin said, raising his voice and turning slightly to put that extra garnish on the delicious sound bite he had cooked up for news reports on the Barbecue Addiction Litigation, "that the evidence will show that ThinkSoft knew what it was doing and that it knowingly, methodically, and in conscious disregard of the health and safety of trusting consumers proceeded with a perilous course of action, foisting a new and heinous addiction upon the unwary public." And Edwin pointed a bony finger at the ThinkSoft table.

Thurston Crushjoy, brought to center stage by Edwin's gesturing, did not miss the opportunity. "Your Honor, the bedrock of my client's business is reason, which, in turn, depends for its foundation on the facts." His deep voice boomed throughout the courtroom. "What we have here is nothing more than paranoid conjecture. And it is not just unreasonable, it is sheer lunacy! That's why we've asked for sanctions. To think that anyone can have access to the trade secrets of my client—an innovating technology company that has invested millions and millions of dollars in research and development—by waltzing into the federal courthouse with a piece of paper that contains entirely unsubstantiated claims—"

"But we don't have to prove our entire case in order to get the evidence to which we are entitled," Edwin countered. "That's the point of discovery. They can't hide the truth from us!"

Crushjoy shook his head. "The logical extension of plaintiff's misreading of the law is that they could have filed the same lawsuit against Coca-Cola, claiming its popular beverage was dangerously addictive and Coca-Cola should turn over a formula whose value cannot be estimated—a formula that has been a jealously guarded trade secret for well over one hundred years."

"That's right," the judge concurred. "I'm going to have to be convinced of some compelling need for that information before I order the defendant to turn it over. Why should I treat intellectual property differently from any other property? Should I turn over the defendant's factories to the plaintiffs just because they say it would help them to prove their case? I daresay not." The judge was speaking directly to his clerks, who all nodded back at him as if this was something they had heard the judge say in chambers moments ago when he was *thinking* out loud.

Seizing the moment, Thurston Crushjoy nodded to two associates in the back of the courtroom standing guard next to a large visual display leaning against the wall. As Crushjoy spoke, the display was moved to the front for the judge to see. "Your Honor, there is a more fundamental problem with the plaintiff's asking for these materials. Lenny Milton agreed to the terms of the shrink-wrap license that came with the system." The associates tore away the paper covering the display as though they had been given the go-ahead to unveil the latest-model Chrysler. "I present to you Exhibit A." Crushjoy read aloud the giant print: "YOU AGREE THAT ALL FORMULATIONS, RECIPES, TESTING, STUDIES, MANUFACTURING DATA AND SPECIFICATIONS AND OTHER KNOW-HOW RELATING TO THE INFORMATION SYSTEM, THE INFORMATION SAUCE, AND THE WHOLLY WORD ARE THE INTELLECTUAL PROPERTY AND TRADE SECRETS OF THE COMPANY"—Crushjoy went into high gear with his ballgame-is-over voice—"'AND UNDER NO CIRCUMSTANCES SHALL YOU

HAVE THE RIGHT TO INSPECT OR HAVE ACCESS TO SUCH TRADE SECRETS, EVEN IF YOU BRING LEGAL ACTION AGAINST THE COMPANY."

Edwin snorted. "Your Honor, this self-serving cake-and-eat-it-too so-called shrink-wrap license cannot be enforced under the facts of this case."

"And that's because you say you need the documents and records to support your case? Am I right, counsel?" the judge asked, evidently off on his own set of conclusions.

"That is correct," Edwin responded.

"But you only need those records to prove your claim that ThinkSoft acted knowingly and willfully. We can decide that later. You claim your client is addicted. He either is or is not. No records anywhere will change that. And I cannot decide whether to enforce the shrink-wrap license until I have heard more of the facts. Mr. Ostermyer, you say that you would be prepared for trial sooner than is customary?"

"Yes, Your Honor, we feel our time line is quite feasible, provided we get the records we are asking for in a timely fashion and—"

"I'm not going to give you those records!" Judge Wetherborne bellowed. "Not until you show me your client has been injured in some discernible way as a result of wrongdoing by the defendant. You're not going to get them if I decide the shrink-wrap license is enforceable!" The judge's eyes were moving around in his head again. It was as though he began hearing music, his eyes pulsating to a strange rhythm. "You want those documents? You want them sooner, not later? Fine. We will go to trial a great deal sooner, which I am sure will be to your liking. A trial on just the pivotal issues of whether the plaintiff Lenny Milton is an addict and whether I should enforce the shrink-wrap license." The judge paused and smiled solicitously. "Fortunately, we have an opening in my calendar. Mr. Danning, did we receive confirmation that our criminal trial scheduled for next week has been resolved?" the judge asked his clerk. Mr. Danning said it was confirmed. "How about you, Mr. Crushjoy? Are you available next week?"

Thurston Crushjoy turned to look at Art Newman, who was seated behind him. Newman smiled, apparently pleased, and made a short-hand affirmative gesture; Crushjoy addressed the judge. "That is agreeable to the defense, Your Honor."

"Excellent. Then we will begin a jury trial on Monday at eight-thirty A.M. Unless there is anything else . . . ?"

Edwin was on his tiptoes with his arms held stiffly to his sides; he was leaning forward like a world-class Norwegian ski jumper, defying gravity in his efforts to get in the judge's face. "Your Honor! You can't do this! We have to be given a chance to gather evidence from the defendant and from others who may have it. This isn't fair!" Several members of the press were already racing out of the courtroom, dialing their cell phones to report the sudden trial date.

Judge Wetherborne looked down unfazed from his throne. "Of course it's fair, Mr. Ostermyer. It's not only fair, it is a golden oppor-tunity for you. If you win—if your client has become as perniciously addicted as you've alleged in your complaint—I will certify your class sooner than even you wanted. But you have to show me you've got the goods. You have to convince this court that your claims are bona fide before Mr. Milton is going to be named the lead plaintiff"—the judge scoffed—"for millions of other allegedly destitute addicts in a suit seeking billions of dollars. Of course, if you don't prove your case, and I determine that your complaint was filed without sufficient factual basis, I will grant the defendant's motion for sanctions and make you and your colleague there, with the abstract theoretical bun-nies, pay all of ThinkSoft's attorneys' fees."

Judge Wetherborne was notorious for liberally granting motions for sanctions—legal fees incurred by the party adjudged innocent to be paid by attorneys who bring unwarranted claims. Will glanced over at the swarm of smiling young lawyers at the ThinkSoft table in expensively tailored suits and shuddered. They hadn't even started trial prep, and they were well into six figures.

"But Your Honor——" Edwin persisted.

The judge's hand shot out in a rigid gesture demanding silence. "Let me put it to you this way, Mr. Ostermyer. This is what I'll do." His demeanor softened but offered no comfort. "Today is Monday. If you dismiss your complaint by Wednesday at five, I will deny the defendant's request for sanctions. My calendar will be clear, and neither you nor Mr. Crushjoy and your clients will have to be here next Monday. Seems to me everybody will be happy."

He smiled enigmatically for a moment at no one in particular. Then, as he narrowed his gaze on Edwin, his eyes and lips began to quiver, his face oscillating with light and shadow cast upon him by a force unknown.

"But if you decide to go forward next Monday and you don't deliver"—The left eye was pounding in its socket—"be prepared to face the consequences!"

The judge grabbed the gavel with both hands. For a split second it seemed like a tug of war was under way before the left hand won out. He banged the gavel loudly. "This court is . . . adjourned!" he shouted, his voice rising as if competing against a din of unearthly music.

‹ 24 ›

Persi's knees were locked together and her back was perfectly straight. Looking across the desk at the gray-haired editor of *Tech Weekly*, she sat in his visitor chair, not too far forward, not too far back. She had made a convincing presentation of what she had to offer the paper. Now she was listening to the editor speak. He had agreed to meet with Persi as a favor to a friend of a friend. He acted as though he was genuinely concerned, not just for the paper but for Persi and for the greater good, including "the technology community at large."

"You have all the skills we want at *Tech Weekly*. However."

She knew exactly what was coming next. It was the same thing she had heard from all the others. Even though she had disclosed her predicament with ThinkSoft without going into confidential details, her gut told her it was unnecessary. He'd already been spooked, and she had a hunch it was through nefarious ThinkSoft channels. The reach of Art Newman's company angered and frustrated her.

"I'm a little concerned that your legal difficulties with ThinkSoft may have an adverse impact on perceptions of this paper's ability to be objective. As you know, we write about ThinkSoft on a continuing basis. We have to be fair. . . ."

The message never ceased to be chilling. She had no difficulty reading between the lines. She'd heard it before:

No technology paper will hire you. We'd be sued for reporting something you said, even if we had no way of knowing it was confidential. Or ThinkSoft could damage us by using its direct access to our readership to call our objectivity into question. Besides, we need their advertising dollars.

He leaned over his desk to underscore that he was speaking to her colleague to colleague. "It's a changing industry. You know that. We have to be careful. Sometimes it's not just about getting the stories. These days we have to be thinking more about our shareholders."

It was as though his words were being fed into a translation program on the editor's desktop PC and projected onto the blank wall behind him:

ThinkSoft is one of the largest information technology companies in the world. Reasonware controls how information is gathered, distributed, and interpreted. They could cut us off and destroy us. An information conglomerate like ThinkSoft might be interested in buying out our parent company in the future at an inflated price. We need to be on their good side.

Persi managed not to lose her professional demeanor, not to wince from the unseen welts beneath her skin's surface. What was happening was as protracted and tortuous as a death sentence before a long-winded judge. From interview to interview it was being revealed to her that she was unemployable—effectively blackballed from the career of her dreams by ThinkSoft's malevolence.

"Incidentally, your writing is exemplary," the editor complimented her. "You could do a great service to journalism. Have you thought about going into teaching?"

"Mr. Ostermyer, this is Dr. Stone. So sorry to call you outside of our regularly scheduled interviews."

"Now, please, no need to apologize, Elizabeth. I so enjoy our little phone talks—little 'tele-têtes,' if you will. You see, it's not just you who's benefited from them. I can tell you quite honestly that I too—"

"Mr. Ostermyer, that's not the reason for my call today. It's about my book. For some reason, I have been so distracted that I neglected to obtain a privacy release from you when we started the interviews. Now the publisher cannot distribute the book until I secure that release from you promptly. As a lawyer, undoubtedly you're aware that this is standard procedure for books of this nature."

"Of course, and I'm glad to hear from you. The timing of your call is excellent. As I'm sure you've read, I just filed the complaint in what the media has dubbed the Barbecue Addiction Litigation. At my urging, and given the exigencies created by ThinkSoft, the case is headed for trial next week. Here's where you come in. I'm going to need a world-class expert to render an addiction diagnosis, together with an exposition of symptomatology."

"I hope, Mr. Ostermyer, that you are not trying to take advantage of a situation. If so, I must express my dismay. In any event, the answer is no. And this time I have to be even firmer than when I said no in the Snapple Johnson murder case. I uniformly decline getting involved in forensics based on medical or psychological theories that are highly speculative."

"I knew you'd see your way clear to help out—"

"Actually, I said no, didn't I? If I can just fax this release to your office—"

"Splendid. I'll state the case in legal terms. Then you'll say the same thing, but in psychological terms."

"Mr. Ostermyer, please, when you ignore my words, it's hard—"

"In a moment I will share with you my opening statement, powerful yet sublime in its poignancy. Yes, my opening statement, more than anything else, carries the full gravamen of what I'm saying. Now I don't expect for you simply to testify at length with a lot of psycho-legal mumbo jumbo about the etiology of Mr. Milton's predicament. Naturally, you must actually agree with everything I'm saying. You, in the position of expert, must be as comfortable with the strong legal position I've taken as I am with my own so that you can lay down the undergirding for its considerable heft. Stated in plain terms, my potent argument is in need of some nice buttressing that only you can provide—a need that will only be satisfied by means of learned expert opinions, puissant as yours will seem."

"Mmm . . . yes. I need . . . my release—"

"As you request, I will release you of any and all liabilities, causes of action, and claims whatsoever, whether now known or hereafter arising in the future, including, but not limited to, invasion of one's privacy—"

"Yes. You're releasing me—"

"And, in the matter of my upcoming trial, you will give me oral testimony about what triggers certain eccentric cravings people suffer."

"Yes."

"Splendid. Now, as promised, let me deliver my statement:

"Ladies and gentlemen of the jury, this is a case of naked, manipulative power systematically exerted over people who are weak or trusting or easily swayed, ordinary people who've been tricked into giving up not just their hard-earned money but their ability to freely choose. Today I'm going to tell you about one of those sorry people. Used and abused to a degree that will make you shudder, this exploited individual is the one who—more so than any sizzling hot sirloin tip you may hear about—was treated like some cheap piece of meat—"

"Oh, yes! That's . . . it's . . . so exquisite. Don't stop!"

Will had, for lack of a better description, napped between 2:30 and 5:30 A.M. a few hours earlier, with papers scattered everywhere in his apartment. Even that sleep was fitful. He'd then arrived at the office at 6:45. He was a wreck.

He was trying to research and put together a trial brief, jury

instructions, motions to be heard before jury selection, witness pro-
files, exhibit books, and a host of other materials in a few short days.
What he had to do alone he knew that the Kilgore Crushjoy firm had
an infantry squad of young lawyers to do.

After the stunning initial-status-turned-final-pretrial conference
yesterday with Judge Wetherborne, Edwin had sent him back to the
office with a long list of trial readiness tasks. Will was past anxious—
closer to delirious—to know what the strategy was going to be, what
legal theories would be advanced, what evidence would be presented,
and who all the witnesses were going to be—in short, whether they
even did have a case. Edwin had said he couldn't think about those
things right now; he needed to prepare his opening statement first and
only then give some thought to those matters. Edwin often preached
that, barring a major blunder late in the game, cases were won or lost
with the opening statement.

While brewing a pot of office coffee, Will heard the fax machine
ring. It was from Persi. It had upset him to learn she couldn't get
another reporting job. It troubled him that someone with her talent
could be prevented from finding new work. Nothing she had ever
gotten him mixed up in before compared to this. He had always managed to extricate themselves from whatever trouble she found . . .
until this case, a case that was feeling less like Lenny Milton's and
more like *Will Swanson versus The Known Universe*.

The fax was coming from Persi's home with a cover sheet on which
she had written:

> *Hi Will!*
> *No one wants to touch me with my ThinkSoft problems, but that*
> *won't stop me from reporting. Here's an article I freelanced for a*
> *Web-based publisher on the speedy trial date. I'm as frustrated as*
> *you that the judge won't let us have their lab tests. We've got to do*
> *something about that. I've got some ideas. Meanwhile, I can't wait to*

see my lawyer have his way at trial with ThinkSoft and that paper
tiger by the name of Kilgore Crushjoy! I'm counting on you. Persi.

He understood the way the legal system worked in ways that Persi didn't. With only five days until trial, there wasn't enough time to do anything. He scanned over her article:

In a dramatic development in the Barbecue Addiction Litigation, U.S.
District Judge Ignatius P. Wetherborne ordered the case to an imme-
diate trial beginning Monday in federal court in San Jose. In the class
action filed by Lenny Milton it is claimed that users of ThinkSoft's
Wholly Grill Outdoor Cooking Information System develop uncontrol-
lable cravings and that it is ThinkSoft's intention to addict Wholly
Grill users.

The judge ordered that a jury will decide whether the lead plaintiff
Lenny Milton is in fact addicted. The judge also said he would decide
whether to enforce the terms of the license agreement—the so-called
"shrink-wrap license"—sold with the cooking unit. ThinkSoft main-
tains that there is no such addiction, and in any case the license
terms absolve ThinkSoft from any responsibility.

"We are confident that we will prove our case to the satisfaction of a
jury," Will Swanson, attorney for plaintiff Lenny Milton, told a reporter.

He did not remember giving that quote when he called Persi right after the hearing yesterday to describe what had happened. In fact, he recalled nothing in the few hours following the hearing except that he was catatonic and, owing to a general default in his cerebral cortex, unable to group even monosyllabic words together into coherent sentences. Nevertheless, he really liked the no-nonsense self-assurance of the Will Swanson he was reading about, and he only wished the Will

Swanson in the article did not seem so purely fictional. The real Will Swanson felt like he was furiously pedaling his Pee-Wee Herman bicycle down a railroad track on a collision course with a freight train by the name of Kilgore, Crushjoy, Clubman & Howell.

It was Tuesday morning; he and Edwin had until tomorrow night at five to complete the reality check on this case and decide whether to make the white-flag call to Thurston Crushjoy. Federal court rules made plain that the lawyer who signed the complaint—in this case, Will—certified that the complaint had merit. If found sufficiently lacking, the judge could order Will alone to pay hundreds of thousands of dollars in sanctions. Should the judge decide the lawsuit was unfounded and hold the plaintiff's lawyers responsible, Will imagined he would become indentured to ThinkSoft for the remainder of his so-called career.

Alternating from free-floating anxiety to a session of corrosive self-punishment, he made himself imagine what it would be like trying to borrow the money by calling his father:

> Hi, Dad. It's your son, Will. Say, listen, you may have heard I'm getting off to a slower than expected start in my career as a trial lawyer. I know you told me to take the estate planning job at McKenna Covington, and you aren't talking to me because I went to work for a maniac, but here's the reason for my call. I need to borrow a couple hundred thousand dollars real fast to pay off a fine for what the judge called a run of inexcusably stupid lawyering. Maybe you'd like to take it out of the house or put off your retirement for a while. And since I'm now unemployable as a lawyer, I could wait tables and pay you back over, say, seventy-five years.

He was on his own and way over his head. It was also clear that Edwin was not going to broach the subject of the judge's ultimatum. Will would have to do it.

Edwin arrived at the office lobby and walked briskly past the week-old New Receptionist. She was reading a statement prepared by Edwin and his publicist in the event the press called the office directly. Holding a typed double-spaced piece of paper, she was reciting its final lines into her console headset with a halting voice: "As always, I will not rest my case until I can look myself in the mirror and say, '*Well done.*' More than any other case in my fulfilling legal career, with the Barbecue Addiction Litigation . . . I find myself on the cutting edge of the law . . . a risk I dutifully accept. Once again, I can truly say my reputation is . . . a steak."

Edwin was about ten feet beyond the New Receptionist's desk when the words *my reputation is a steak* burned his ears and brought him to a painful halt, as though someone had stuck a giant fork in his back. He turned around and glared at her.

"To whom were you just reading the prepared statement?" he demanded.

"That was Associated Press," she announced proudly. "And I have read the statement this morning to UPI, Reuters, CNN, and a bunch of other really cool ones. Actually, that was the second time Associated Press called. The first time there was only one person. He called back with a bunch of his friends on the line just now. They laughed out loud, especially at the end. Were you trying to be funny?"

Edwin grabbed the press release from her hands. His temples were throbbing. "It says *stake*—S-T-A-K-E!" he yelled, hoping all those news services would hear it as well.

"That's what I said," she replied calmly.

"But it's supposed to say *at stake, not a steak*! The *t* was obviously omitted, a simple typographical error. What were you thinking?" he continued to fume.

"I was just asked to read it," she said matter-of-factly. "I'm not paid to be your publicist, spin doctor, or editor. I'm supposed to answer the phone and greet people. Why don't you tape it yourself and I'll just play the tape for them. That way you can tell them yourself exactly how you want your steak, or whatever it is you're trying to say!" She thrust the prepared statement at him. The phone rang and she answered it before Edwin, who had opened his mouth, could issue his indictment.

"My opening statement is a masterpiece," Edwin boasted to Will, buried in books in the library. Indeed, Edwin was so enthralled with his overture that he had already recovered from the debacle with the New Receptionist. "The rest will fall into place. The key is Lenny's testimony and a world-class expert to back us up. Other witnesses are window dressing. But the right expert is going to make or break this case."

"What expert, much less *world-class* expert, is going to testify for us on such short notice?" the young lawyer asked dubiously.

"It just so happens," Edwin said, bird in mouth, "that Dr. Elizabeth Stone owes me. As you know, she requested that I be a case study for her new book. She has even told me that her coverage of me is pivotal to the book, which is at distribution centers as we speak. But as fate would have it"—Edwin paused to savor the circumstances—"she has been so caught up in my robust philosophy that she has only now asked me for the release she needs to include me in the work." Edwin picked up the release on his desk and waved it around. "No signed release, no legal distribution of the book. Happily, she has agreed to testify about the clinical addiction suffered by one Lenny Milton."

It was obvious from Will's expression that he wasn't worked up to a froth in the same way Edwin was. "We need to talk about the judge's deadline for . . . disposing of this case," the young lawyer began.

"I have given it all careful thought," Edwin said. "I will not let that deadline come and go if I determine a call is warranted."

‹ 25 ›

The Kilgore Crushjoy legal machine was in full production, two dozen lawyers working tirelessly along with countless clerks, paralegals, secretaries, text processors, investigators, information management personnel, process servers, and gofers. At 4:15 P.M. on Wednesday, the team of lawyers received an e-mail from Thurston Crushjoy:

```
I just received a voice message from Mr. Ostermyer
asking me to call him back before 5. If you can
promise to keep your mouths buttoned, I'll share the
call with you on speakerphone in the East Conference
Room at 4:45.
```

"Now if this call is what I think it is," Crushjoy announced to the lawyers assembled in the conference room, "I don't want you to stop working—and billing—this case until we have it all in writing, which should be by no later than tomorrow morning." He smiled, in full control of his dominion.

Crushjoy's secretary dialed the number on the speakerphone.

"Hello?" a confused female voice answered.

"Is this the Ostermyer law office?" Crushjoy's secretary asked.

"Yes, but I'm busy right now." *Oprah* could be heard in the background. "Can you call back later?"

"Mr. Thurston Crushjoy is holding for Mr. Ostermyer. He is returning Mr. Ostermyer's call, and it is extremely urgent," Crushjoy's secretary persisted.

"Oh, are you the hair plug company?" the voice asked.

"No. It's not about that," the secretary said. Snorts of laughter were barely repressed. "It's about a case, and it's very important that Mr. Crushjoy speak to him at once."

"OK. Sorry. I'm new here and . . . oh, I just lost another call. Please hold. . . . "

Two minutes later a familiar male voice announced, "This is Edwin G. Ostermyer."

"Yes, Mr. Ostermyer. Thurston Crushjoy returning your call," he said, looking up at the grinning faces surrounding him.

"Thank you for getting back to me," Ostermyer began. "I assume you are still interested in disposing of this case?"

"Of course," Crushjoy replied politely, as all the gathered faces beamed.

"I am pleased to hear that," the plaintiff's lawyer continued. "I have given a lot of thought to this case over the last day and a half. We are also prepared to dispose of this case. But there are a few things we will need to do. Naturally I'd like to do something for my client."

Crushjoy was amused but maintained his polite demeanor. "Lenny Milton, of course. Something for his poor little pooch—what's her name? Lady J. Blinded I know, but no doing of ours. Unfortunately, the offer made when this case was in Muni Court is no longer available. But maybe something can be done—what with the vet bills and such—provided there is confidentiality about everything. What did you have in mind?" Crushjoy glanced around the room. The previous offer was $750. Legal fees were accruing in the vicinity of five thousand dollars an hour just to listen to the phone call.

"Actually, I was talking about the class and not just Mr. Milton,"

Ostermyer replied. "Here is what we want, in exchange for which you will receive a release and dismissal. First, the cash. We think that when all is said and done the full class will be awarded around four and a half billion dollars, including punitive damages. We are prepared right now to settle for nine hundred seventy-five million dollars. Second, and over and above the cash, we want you to open and fund one hundred addiction treatment facilities throughout the country, and of course you will immediately discontinue the entire Wholly Grill line. Third, and last, we want an admission of wrongdoing and an apology suitable for dissemination to the media. Now, I understand you'll want to talk this over with your client. But, bear in mind, this settlement demand is good until Friday at noon, after which it is withdrawn and future demands will be dramatically higher."

The gasps could not be suppressed. Thurston Crushjoy's massive jaw seemed to be disembarking from his stoic face, a nuclear warship being deployed on a grim mission.

"I'll see you in court Monday," Crushjoy said, fuming. "And don't forget to bring your checkbook."

<　26　>

STUDIO ANCHOR: *Welcome back, everyone. I'm Janet Jones in New York, and this is the Lawsuit Network bringing you live coverage of the Barbecue Addiction Litigation. Let's go back to our reporter and commentator at the San Jose Federal Courthouse, trial attorney Ben Griswold. Ben, you've given us the lineup and the questions to be decided by the jury. We're about to hear Mr. Ostermyer give his opening statement. What does he need to do to be successful?*

TRIAL COMMENTATOR: *As I have said, Janet, these are novel claims, and they will be difficult to prove. As lawyer for the plaintiff, Mr. Ostermyer needs to take advantage of going first. He needs to cement an emotional connection with the jury right away—make them believe he understands ordinary people, what it means to be a little vulnerable—and give to his story a real human perspective, so that perhaps the jurors will be sympathetic, rather than doubtful, about these scientifically unproven claims he is making on behalf of his client, Lenny Milton.*

" . . . And when all the evidence is in, I am confident you will agree that I am right and what I have told you is right," Edwin pronounced, in concluding his opening statement.

So as not to attract the attention of the jury, Will was fluttering both index fingers under the table at Edwin's peripheral vision, trying to get him to turn around. Edwin had turned his back 90 degrees from the jury and was taking his case right to the LNTV camera. Edwin pressed on.

"So, is it right to conclude from that evidence that my client has been rendered a helpless addict at the hands of Defendant? There is no other conclusion. I am right in saying that Lenny Milton is a victim and that he has been used, abused, and made a guinea pig in Defendant's cruel and sadistic 'science project.'"

Edwin cast a glance over at Lenny, who was seated next to Will at counsel table. Lenny, sitting up stiffly in his business suit, seemed frozen with fear at what was taking place.

"From the beginning Lenny Milton only wanted to enjoy a little bit of backyard barbecue, a small slice of a great American tradition. Instead, he was swallowed up in the maws of the ravenous predator that is ThinkSoft"—he paused for effect—"a predator that does not see Lenny Milton as a person but rather as an object of its own insatiable appetite for money! You will see evidence that, in order to satisfy its own unquenchable thirst—billions of dollars already received with billions more to come—ThinkSoft set about to enslave and did enslave Lenny Milton to an addiction which you will see and come to recognize for yourself. You will see and conclude what I already know. I am right. You will return a verdict for the Plaintiff."

As Edwin returned to his seat next to Will, there was a hum of animated voices in the packed courtroom. During the course of Edwin's opening, Will was frantically thumbing through the pages of the trial notebook trying to find some support for some of the assertions Edwin made. He finally gave up—exhausted from lack of sleep—and turned to Edwin, now seated, to offer him a stroke of encouragement. "Great opening." Edwin was still smiling at his fingernails.

Judge Wetherborne then invited the opening statement for the defense. Will had found Crushjoy's calm, both before and during Edwin's opening statement, to be unnerving. During jury selection the day before it was even more unsettling; in questioning potential jurors the legendary defense lawyer had engaged with each of them in a way that made them feel as though they were honored guests in his own living room.

Instead of beginning his opening statement, Crushjoy stood up and announced, with a voice that thundered throughout the courtroom, "Your Honor, Defendant moves at this time for a nonsuit." He stretched out the pronunciation of the word *nonsuit* for maximum effect.

An associate in a corner of the courtroom with one of the dozen brand-new laptop computers brought by ThinkSoft had finished summarizing Edwin's opening statement and was waiting for the full text of the motion to be noiselessly generated from a laser printer. Will and Edwin had a single notebook computer—state-of-the-art a year ago, now badly outmoded. When the associate was finished printing, she stapled it together and passed it to a junior associate, who handed it to a senior associate, who delivered it to Crushjoy. Mr. Danning, the judge's clerk, handed the papers to the judge.

Rather than dismiss the jury, the judge read the papers quietly to himself, giving the jury ample time to ponder the word *nonsuit*. Will could feel their eyes burning into him and Edwin, but he did not look up. Did *nonsuit* mean that the two plaintiff's lawyers were not dressed in regulation federal courtroom attire, or did it mean the dramatic opening statement they had just heard was much sound and fury, signifying nothing?

Edwin rose to argue against the motion. The judge told him to sit down. "The plaintiff in his opening statement must refer to evidence he has, which, if established, would be sufficient to support a judgment in his favor. If the opening statement comes up short on evidence and long on wind—and I am not ruling on that yet"—the judge carefully avoided looking at Edwin—"I can end the case here or I can allow the plaintiff to supplement his opening statement with additional references to evidence, if any he has." The judge then gave Edwin a stern glance. "I am taking this motion under advisement. I shall rule on it at a later time. At this time I would like to complete the opening statements, should the defendant care to give one. Mr. Crushjoy?"

Crushjoy, taking his cue from the judge, announced, "In light of our pending motion for nonsuit, and in view of the fact that the burden of proof in this matter rests entirely on the shoulders of plaintiff, the defendant reserves the right to make an opening statement at the commencement of its case, should this trial survive to that stage."

"As you wish," Judge Wetherborne said. "We will hear the evidence now. All right, Mr. Ostermyer, call your first witness."

Edwin stood. "I call the plaintiff, Lenny Milton."

Lenny, who was stuffed into his best suit, lumbered sheepishly up to the witness stand. Will thought Lenny must have been gaining ten pounds a week since he first came into the office five weeks ago. During the week before trial, the stress must have had Lenny grilling round-the-clock.

Edwin took him through his testimony methodically, starting with the free sirloin tip and the frustration of trying to connect to the Wholly WORD that fateful first night.

"I tried everything to make it work. Couldn't get through. I called tech support. I couldn't get through there either. I had to eat."

Lenny described how in desperation he fired up his Weber and put the pre-marinated meat on to cook. When Lenny described the explosion and searing injury that blinded Lady J, he wept. Will noticed several jurors became teary-eyed witnessing Lenny's pain.

"I felt I should try to get it to work one more time before taking it back," Lenny said. "Then, sure enough, I got through. The lasers came on. I sauced up some meat and put it on. When I opened it up, the

Smoke Crystals were swollen. I . . . can't describe it. It was just too delicious."

Lenny recounted how his cravings quickly took control of his life. He would make up excuses to tune out business or social engagements so he could turn on the grill all day. Edwin walked him through his credit card bills; at $3.95 an hour to be connected to the Wholly WORD, it would have been less expensive to eat out at a pricy restaurant every night. He was going bust, but OmniCredit kept sending him new credit cards anyway.

Throughout Lenny's testimony, Edwin deftly played his own client as the reluctant witness, encouraging Lenny to act ashamed, speaking publicly of this aberrant behavior for the first time: "I know this is embarrassing for you, but please tell the jury. . . . " Lenny, for his part, was indeed embarrassed, hesitated to answer, and at times waited for prodding from Edwin.

Some eyes on the jury grew wide when Lenny described how he would scrape a little sauce off from each meal and put it in a vial he carried around with him. To satisfy his cravings between meals he would dip his finger in the vial and rub the sauce around his gums. "The Smoke Crystals burst around the gum line and under the tongue, and it gives me a quick feeling of calm and well-being. It only lasts for a few seconds but—well, it keeps me going."

Edwin then moved in for the dramatic finish. "Are there any other symptoms of your chronic use of Wholly Grill that you have not told us about?"

"Yes."

"And what is that?"

"When I laugh too hard, milk comes out of my nose," Lenny said, staring down at the floor.

Crushjoy bolted up. "I move to strike," he said, causing Lenny to cower in nameless dread. "There most certainly isn't any evidence of a connection between or among the sauce, the grill, the laughing, the milk—if indeed it is—or that any of this has anything to do with addiction. These are fanciful musings, not science."

"Denied," the judge said. "You can cross-examine on that."

Edwin turned back to Lenny. "Even when you have not had any milk to drink?"

Lenny nodded his head. Edwin pointed a finger at the court reporter, prompting Lenny to muster up a meek "Yes."

"Have you had any Wholly Grill today?"

"Yes."

"What precisely did you have?"

"I had a breakfast goose stuffed with half croutons, half barbecue sauce."

"Have you had any milk today?" Edwin wisely did not pause to explore the difference between a breakfast goose and, say, a snack goose.

"No."

"I know you would prefer not to, but would you please now demonstrate to the jury the phenomenon you have described: namely, milk issuing from your nasal passage?" Edwin asked Lenny from the attorney lectern.

Will was leafing through his copy of the trial notebook. He and Edwin had never discussed a demonstration or gone over it with Lenny. Persi had a lead on a videotape someone had which they hoped to use later in the trial depicting the phenomenon. However, Edwin was undoubtedly so pleased with the way Lenny's testimony had gone in, he must have been sure there would be a payoff for going for the dramatic demonstration right now.

Lenny stared dumbly at Edwin, then looked at the jury peering at him strangely. He looked back at Edwin. "Something would have to make me laugh," he finally said, trying to be helpful.

"Then go ahead. Think of something funny," Edwin said, smiling at Lenny, appearing confident that a little encouragement was all that was needed.

It did not look like Lenny was going to think of something funny on his own. As if to reinforce himself on that, he looked meekly up at Judge Wetherborne. The dour judge, seated on high in the solemn federal courtroom in a black robe with a wooden sledgehammer in easy reach, had to be the personification of Not Funny.

"I can't think of anything funny right now," Lenny said, "but maybe you can make me laugh."

The eyes of the jury were now entirely on Edwin. Edwin paused for a moment, then pressed ahead. "All right, so an itinerant sales representative walks into a tavern subject to the jurisdiction of Alcoholic Beverage Control, and the proprietor therein asks him—"

"Objection!" Crushjoy stood up. "He is telling jokes. The procedure in this court is question and answer."

"Sustained!" the judge ruled. "Mr. Ostermyer, you will confine yourself to a question-and-answer format. Proceed."

"But Your Honor," Edwin implored, "I am merely trying to provide demonstrative evidence of a phenomenon that is pivotal to the plaintiff's case—"

"Enough!" the judge sounded the gavel. "I have ruled. You can introduce evidence through traditional channels, but you are not going to turn this courtroom into a lowbrow comedy club. Do you have any other questions of this witness?"

As bad as it was, Will was grateful Crushjoy had objected when he did. Edwin's wretched delivery of a punch line would have prompted Lenny unconsciously to do an impression of Mount Rushmore. The defense lawyer, for his part, was playing it safe and smart, making sure there would be no evidence introduced of any side effects.

As the momentum deflated, Edwin rallied with a few more questions about whether any of the effects he had described were listed on the license or the packaging to Wholly Grill as a warning. Receiving the orchestrated "no" to each of the questions, Edwin announced he had "no further questions at this time."

Lenny failed to conceal his terror when Crushjoy rose up and filled the entire courtroom with his presence. But, to Lenny's obvious relief, Crushjoy began his cross-examination with a few softball questions; in fact, you would think he just wanted to be friends with Lenny and forget about all this nasty trial stuff.

"So you really do like that Wholly Grill, don't you?" he asked, as if he were acknowledging how irresistible it was. Responding to the friendly giant, Lenny gave a nervous laugh and said he did.

"Does it make you hungry for some right now, just thinking about it?"

"Yeah, sure does."

"I see it's almost noon. You're always hungry about this time, aren't you?" Crushjoy asked, continuing to verbally sidle up to Lenny.

"Sure. Who doesn't get hungry for lunch?" Lenny agreed, directing a nervous smile at the members of the jury, whom he must have expected to agree with him.

"But you just really like the taste of Wholly Grill. Isn't that it?" Crushjoy asked suggestively.

Lenny, apparently uncertain as to whether this was another purely friendly question, paused to think about it. After first looking to Edwin, he answered in a mechanical voice as though by rote. "At first it was about the joy I got from the taste. Now my compulsive . . . ingestion of Wholly Grill is only about . . . blunting the pervasive craving I must now live with." The jury looked curiously at Lenny and then over to Edwin. Edwin, as if sitting in the director's chair, appeared pleased with Lenny's performance.

"But you're saying there's something about Wholly Grill, something strangely irresistible about it, that makes you incapable of controlling your appetite for it. Right?"

"That's right."

"And now I've made you hungry and you just have to have Wholly Grill right now. Is that right?"

"I can hardly wait for lunch. I brought my Wholly Grill, Junior," Lenny said. After a glance at Edwin, he added, "I'm dyin' for some Linkin' Buddies."

"I see. Well, I don't have any Wholly Grill barbecue, but—" Crushjoy wheeled around. Miraculously, a large platter of wedge-shaped finger sandwiches appeared on his counsel table—roast beef, turkey, tuna, and chicken salad. Inside the same second he had picked it up and was offering it to Lenny. "Would you care for some?"

"Objection!" Edwin sprang from his chair; Crushjoy had wandered too far from Edwin's script. The judge ordered the attorneys to come forward for a sidebar. Will followed Edwin to the side of the bench away from and barely audible to the jury. Crushjoy was calmly explaining why it was perfectly relevant, and the judge was nodding his head in agreement.

"They can't do this! This is a mockery of rules of evidence . . . and courtroom procedure!" Edwin kept interjecting.

"Enough!" The judge cut Edwin off. "You claim this case is about some kind of addiction. Well, they have a right to explore whether it's really about that or something else, like a personal eating disorder, or maybe even something perfectly benign like *it just tastes good*. The question is relevant. Unless you can cite some law to the contrary, Mr. Ostermeyer, the defendant has a right to ask on cross-examination if Mr. Milton cares for or, for that matter has a craving for, a medley of tea sandwiches."

"Indeed, I *can* cite legal authority forbidding this," Edwin proclaimed. He pointed a long finger at a metal sign on the side wall of the courtroom. "Your own laws, Your Honor! And I quote: *During session no talking or noise from electronic devices, including pagers and cellular phones. At no time is any food or eating permitted in the courtroom.* Defendant's flagrant violation of the law should be met with the strongest possible sanctions!"

The judge smiled distantly—perhaps pleased, perhaps amused—not looking directly at Edwin. "You are a real scholar of the law, Mr. Ostermyer." A cloud darkened his brow. He leveled his eyes on Edwin. "Your objection is overruled!" he snapped. "Now back to work! Let's keep this trial moving!"

During the sidebar exchange, Will had barely noticed a subdued ripple of laughter making its way around the courtroom. He had been too focused on the argument to pay any attention to it. Now, walking back to their table, Will and Edwin looked over and saw Lenny deftly inserting the last two finger sandwiches into either side of his mouth. Neither Will nor Edwin had noticed that Crushjoy, before approaching the bench, had left the platter at the witness stand in the custody of Lenny.

"I withdraw my last question to the witness: namely, 'Would you care for some?'" Crushjoy beamed, evidently pleased with Lenny's nonverbal response. He also had to be pleased with his caterer's handiwork and the timing of the senior associate in the firm's Sandwich Practice Group. "The question is now moot. Let the record reflect that the platter of non–Wholly Grill food items I offered has been vacated, being entirely consumed by the witness." Full-bodied laughter erupted freely from the packed courtroom. Even members of the jury snickered among themselves.

"The record will so note," confirmed the judge, making no effort to conceal his satisfaction.

Edwin glowered at Lenny. Lenny, finally suspecting he had been set up, stopped chewing, his cheeks the size of tabletop pumpkins.

Crushjoy encouraged Lenny to take his time swallowing and then continued with his questions. He spent the next several hours, before and after the lunch break, methodically and painstakingly walking Lenny through his own medical records, which ThinkSoft had subpoenaed—a sorry history of compulsive destructive oral gratification since childhood with unheeded warnings from countless doctors. The only medical advice he had ever followed was to quit smoking, which he had accomplished just in the last six months. His doctor had told him he would have a coronary if he didn't stop. Unfortunately for the plaintiff's case, an entry in his medical chart just before his purchase of the Wholly Grill showed he had already started gaining weight precipitously, which the doctor had noted was common for ex-smokers.

"Mr. Milton, you purchase your groceries at Food Farm supermarkets, correct?" Thurston Crushjoy was holding up and examining a thick printout that he had not identified.

Lenny nodded. "Yes."

"And you have a Food Farm Frequent Buyers' Club card, don't you?"

"Uh-huh," Lenny uttered, then remembered he needed to use words. "Yes."

"Whenever you insert your card, the clerks always tell you about a favorite food that's on sale, isn't that right?" Crushjoy continued to examine the printout, not looking up at Lenny.

"Come to think of it, they do," Lenny said.

Crushjoy leafed through the printout slowly. The courtroom remained hushed. "You joined the club a year ago. Now, you wouldn't quarrel with me, Mr. Milton, if I told you that, between a year ago when you joined the club and when Wholly Grill was introduced just recently, your monthly grocery bill increased—let's see—by more than sixty-two percent?"

"I guess not." Lenny gulped nervously.

"Including a dramatic increase, for example, in your purchases of Ben and Jerry's ice cream. Right?" Crushjoy did not look up.

"That's probably true." Lenny shifted uncomfortably in his seat.

"But you're not suing Ben and Jerry's for any addiction, are you?"

"Uh-uh." Lenny said, as if in full agreement, then added, "No."

Crushjoy lowered the printout for the first time and fixed his eyes on Lenny in the witness box. "You're aware, aren't you, that whenever you insert your card, the words 'I'm a food addict' appear on the checker's screen along with your . . . singular preferences?"

"Objection!" Edwin shot up from his chair. "Hearsay! And it's the opinion of—a cash register!"

At the sidebar Crushjoy explained that the Frequent Buyers' Club software and reasonware were developed, installed, and maintained by ThinkSoft and that he would be introducing into evidence the printout of Lenny's consumer profile designating him a food addict.

"But it's sheer hearsay!" Edwin protested. "Who or what am I to cross-examine?"

"Nonsense!" the judge rebuked Edwin, his left eye pulsating. "Mr. Crushjoy has represented to us that it is conventional reasonware. Really, Mr. Ostermyer, what next? If defendant were to cite the law from a bound volume of the official reports, are you going to insist on cross-examining the printer? The paper supplier? Enough! Let's move on!"

Over Edwin's objection, Crushjoy entered into evidence the consumer profile of Lenny. Shame-faced, Lenny admitted he did not know that the checker terminal, or the ThinkSoft reasonware that tracked his every dietary whim over the course of a year, thought he was a food addict. The profile showed that Lenny was incapable of saying no to any offer of his favorite snack foods: ice cream, frozen pizza, potato chips, cookies, sweet rolls, tamales, and burritos. Automatically, using the data-driven marketing solutions generated by the ThinkSoft reasonware, the checker offered Lenny a couple of his favorites that happened to be bundled together at a special price right at the cash register. Lenny would tell the checker to toss them into his cart and ring him up.

Commandant Crushjoy moved to his last line of questioning.

"It is true, isn't it, Mr. Milton, that no medical doctor, other than perhaps some expert witness paid for by your attorneys, has told you that you have some kind of addiction to Wholly Grill?"

"Yeah. I guess it's true."

"In fact, it wasn't until someone told you you were addicted, just before your filing this lawsuit, that you began believing it?"

Will turned and whispered furiously into Edwin's ear. Unless this line of questioning was averted, Crushjoy was about to elicit that Will was the one who first confronted Lenny about his problem. Except the jury would not see Will as any angel of mercy. Crushjoy was going to make it sound like Lenny was convinced by a bunch of conniving lawyers that he had an addiction problem, and the greedy lawyers had convinced him to file suit so they all could get rich siphoning money from an innovative, respectable, tax-paying American icon among revered corporate citizens. Under his skillful cross-examination—the suggestive language, the selection of questions, the sequence and pacing, the tone of voice—how could the jury not see it that way? Crushjoy was a masterful craftsman with courtroom evidence; as such, relativity was not just a theory, it was a power tool. The jury would surely adopt his point of view, resulting in Lenny's case being ground up and left as so much sawdust on the courtroom floor.

Lenny hesitated to answer and then said, "I was told I was addicted because I really do have a problem." He glanced at Edwin as if looking for further inspiration for the right words. "I was in . . . denial."

"By the way, who *did* tell you that you had this problem?" Crushjoy must have smelled blood but he carefully soft-pedaled the question, always keeping his options open, always in control.

"Your Honor, we object to any questions to the extent they may call for attorney-client communications," Edwin asserted, without revealing in his bearing whether Crushjoy was close to causing melt-down of his case.

"I will then remind the witness that any communications he may have had with his attorneys should not be disclosed pursuant to the attorney-client privilege." The judge's expression revealed that he already tracked and subscribed to Crushjoy's point of view. "Bearing that in mind, let's have the question again."

"Mr. Milton, I don't want to know about any secret or embarrassing discussions you may have had with your lawyers. Can you promise me that you won't reveal any of those discussions?" Crushjoy asked with feigned solicitousness.

"I promise."

"Thank you, Mr. Milton. That's excellent," he said. Will knew in an instant that the sequel to this touching scene—the friendly giant extending the helping hand to the cowering man—was *The Hammer of Doom*, starring Thurston Crushjoy. Will put on his best "everything-is-fine" demeanor for the jury and held his breath.

"Now, Mr. Milton, you have already testified that you started to believe you had an addiction problem just before filing this lawsuit. And that was because someone said you had this problem. Now here is my question: Did anyone *other* than your own lawyers tell you that you were an addict prior to filing this lawsuit?"

Lenny looked to his lawyers to throw him a gargantuan life vest. The jury also looked at the lawyers, both of whom continued to display no signs of ruffled feathers, especially when the jury was scrutinizing them. Edwin seemed to do it effortlessly. In spite of his external composure, Will's internal organs screamed for triage.

"Not that I recall," Lenny finally admitted.

"Thank you," Crushjoy said, in a tone that bespoke the confirmation of his suspicions. "No further questions." Crushjoy returned to his seat and to the gleaming faces of adulation on his troops. Will started to do another head count of the troops to roughly calculate the hourly fees he was going to be asked to pay; then he stopped, realizing he was torturing himself senselessly.

Edwin did a commendable job of trying to rehabilitate Lenny on redirect examination. His questions focused on the symptoms of Lenny's addiction, again bringing them out in high relief, suggesting it did not matter who may have told Lenny he was addicted; he either was or he wasn't.

Upon completion of Lenny's testimony, the judge adjourned the trial for the day. Edwin seemed to see Crushjoy's cross-examination of Lenny as just a few unavoidable hits, all in a day's work. Edwin would soon enough have the chance to cross-examine ThinkSoft's witnesses and return the favor. He was looking forward to the next day and the chance to call his ace-in-the-hole witness, Dr. Elizabeth Stone. She would mesmerize the starstruck jury, spell it out for them, and make their fact-finding charge an exercise in coloring by numbers.

Will did not feel the same way at the end of the day. Once again he could not help but lament his passing up a career where he could have been dispensing tax advice from quietly sequestered offices or administering an estate in probate court. That sounded especially good right now: clients who were totally predictable and always under control—in short, clients who were dead. They would never in a million years, if not minded for the blink of an eye, create catastrophes like spontaneously gorging themselves with an entire platter of finger sandwiches while court was in session, reducing to crumbs what little evidence had been built up in their favor.

Probate lawyers didn't know how good they had it.

‹ 27 ›

After court adjourned for the day, Will waited for Persi to pick him up two blocks from the federal building. The two of them had decided it would not be prudent to have her come into the courtroom or be seen with him, not when ThinkSoft was threatening both civil and criminal prosecution against her. ThinkSoft's people would assume that she was feeding unauthorized information to the plaintiff's lawyers, which would only trigger more legal action. Will, likewise, had to be careful; if seen with Persi, the Kilgore Crushjoy lawyers would no doubt accuse him—no matter how unfairly—of unethically and illegally gaining information the judge had ruled off limits.

When Persi's silver Honda Accord pulled up to the curb, he tossed his briefcase in the backseat and hopped in. To brief her on his day, the first thing he did was let out a long melodramatic groan.

"I thought so," Persi said. Persi had watched the proceedings all day on LNTV. "That definitely counts as one rough day. Thought you could use a smoothie." She smiled and handed him an ice-cold strawberry banana smoothie in a large, brightly colored cup.

Will laughed in appreciation. "Oh, yeah. Just what the doctor ordered. You knew."

What started out as a joke had, over time, become a tradition between them. If Will emerged from a killer exam, or if Persi had pulled an all-nighter to get out an issue of *The Daily Nexus*, the one surviving the ordeal was treated to a smoothie by the other. A blend of fresh fruits, ice cream, and other cheerful ingredients, there was something irresistibly pure about a smoothie that made it the perfect midday relief, at least whenever the two of them met up. They professed their belief that a smoothie possessed mood-altering benefits undocumented by science. Even if nothing more than an act of kindness, the offering never failed to smooth out the rough spots in ways only friendship can.

Will took a big gulp and emitted an exaggerated "ahh!" as if he'd thrown down a shot of whiskey. The smoothie tasted a world better than the pencil he'd been gnawing on for the last two hours in court. He felt even better when he realized she had known what it would mean to him. After three and a half years apart, she, like him, still had faith in what the two of them had discovered in the time they were together.

Just the sight of Persi lifted his spirits. In contrast with the dark courtroom suit and tie in which he was still bound, he could not help but admire her: hair held back with a purple elastic scrunchy, wearing a comfortable orange cashmere sweater and blue jeans that covered her noticeably attractive, slender legs. While nursing the smoothie with a straw, he continued to drink in her profile—welcome relief after watching Edwin and the scowling judge for two full days—while she focused on the road.

She drove them out of San Jose and across the Bay by way of the Dumbarton Bridge. Touching down in the East Bay, Persi headed north on their way to a chemical lab near the UC Berkeley campus. She checked her rearview mirror again, a habit she had developed since being hunted down in LA by a gaggle of Explorers, dogs, and helicopters.

"Hey Will, you gotta get into the action. Edwin needs your help. He just doesn't realize it yet."

"Right," he said, stretching the word out with a satirical tone. "I'll just tell Edwin I'm taking over the billion-dollar class action. After all,

I've been practicing for nearly four months now." Changing to sound level-headed, he added, "Look, you have to understand that a trial is scripted like a play. There's room for improvisation, but just because I'm cast in the role of second chair doesn't make me Edwin's understudy. For me to jump into the fray right now is more like someone in the chorus stepping into the lead on a few hours' notice."

"Whatever. You know what I'm saying. Crushjoy needs to be double-teamed. You've got to somehow escalate." As if stomping her foot to make her point, she hit the accelerator and shot up to 85. "As it is, Crushjoy and his army are having their way with you and Edwin."

"No wonder it hurts to sit down," Will joked. The last thing he wanted was a serious discussion with Persi after eight lugubrious hours in court.

"Very funny," she said.

"Look, I *am* helping. I'm doing my job," he said. "I'm the Young Associate. My job is to handle the paper and research. That's what the second chair is supposed to do. That's what I'm paid to do . . . Do you have directions to the lab?" he asked, before she could continue the discussion.

"I need to call him," she said. "I just remember he's on Telegraph Avenue. Hand me the piece of paper in the console with his number on it."

Will didn't want to talk about his role in the trial. It made him crazy to think about the case. Everything was so far beyond his control. Nothing was going as planned. He had pictured this case going forward like the lawsuit by Health's Fury when he was in law school— the case brought by a health advocacy organization against an oil refinery for groundwater contamination. As a legal intern in that case he'd seen that time was allowed in a lawsuit for depositions to flush out what the other side was claiming, time for research and analysis, and, all importantly, time for interviewing and hiring premier academic experts to offer scientific proof.

When the judge announced the "rocket docket" trial a week ago, while at the same time denying the plaintiff access to ThinkSoft's lab tests and formulas, Edwin and Will conceded it was too late for any meaningful chemical lab work. Ordinarily, that would have been completed before suit was filed, but in no event less than four months before the trial. But Persi insisted it was still not too late, at least for some preliminary results. All she had told Will was the name of the chemist she found: Frederick P. King.

He located the number and handed it to her. "And by the way," he said, continuing to veer away from his role in the trial, "I couldn't find that name listed in any of our expert witness databases. Who is this guy?"

"He's not into that academic stuff." Persi waved her hand at him as if it wasn't important. "He runs his own chemical lab. He's just known as Sky."

Red flags went up and fluttered wildly in Will's brain. He rubbed his forehead in dread of what was to follow. This guy was neither a doctor nor a professor, nor was he a professional expert. He didn't even use his real name!

Persi dialed the lab, using the car speakerphone, and spoke to Sky. "I have your address. How far out on Telegraph are you?"

"Far out!"

"OK." She didn't flinch. "How late will you be open?"

"The door is always open to the people. Just come in and make yourself at home," he offered, in a kind voice.

"Thank you. And how long will you actually be there?" she asked.

Sky said he would be there another half hour before he had to go out to pick up a new meth-laced batch of ecstasy for testing. He described it as some particularly "bad shit" that had just hit the streets. Persi said they would be there in less than twenty minutes.

The name of Sky's establishment was the People's Open Door Chemical Lab. When they arrived, Sky was labeling vials and putting them into racks. He wore a faded white lab coat with a Grateful Dead skull-and-roses sew-on patch on one shoulder, an old pair of khakis, and wire rim glasses. His blue eyes were in a constant state of wide-eyed wonder. When he spoke, somehow he stretched them wider yet. He was balding but still managed to maintain a long pepper-and-salt ponytail. Led Zeppelin was blaring from a cassette player. The lab was cluttered and dirty, a far cry from the "clean room" labs so familiar in Silicon Valley.

Sky's diplomas and licenses hung off to the side, taking a position of less prominence than a framed Jimi Hendrix poster. As a graduate of the University of California system himself, Will tried to imagine what it would have been like to be in college when Sky was. He was indeed a homegrown phenomenon, with an undergraduate degree at Stanford and a doctorate in chemistry from Berkeley.

"We need you to do a chemical analysis," Persi said.

Sky turned the music down. "Fer sure I can do it. But if you folks have some kind of illegal shit you want me to look at, I need to get clearance. The authorities," he said, emphasizing the word *uh-thor-ities* while widening his eyes in disbelief, "have been hassling me."

"No, these are not illegal drugs. This is barbecue sauce, but we think there is something chemically addictive in it," Persi said, pulling the bottle out of a bag she was carrying and placing it on the counter.

"*Whoa!* I've never tested barbecue sauce before. But I've done some of that stuff myself. It's good shit. My friend Jimbo has one of those grills with the sauce. He cooked up some Garden Burgers once when we had the munchies *real* bad. It was outrageous. Since then those billboards always make me hungry." He lifted his head up toward some imaginary stage lights in the ceiling as though about to recite his favorite passage from Shakespeare: "'Wholly Grill. Wholly Smoke. Wholly Shit!'"

"It's Wholly— never mind." Will abandoned the idea of setting him straight. He was 180 degrees off. The word was *Delicious.*

"We'll need this right away," Persi said.

"Wait!" Will interjected. He needed to say something. This guy was going to do tests and no doubt come up with something ridiculous. Maybe he could get Sky to decline the work after all.

"Before we ask you to do this," Will continued, "I want to be perfectly candid with you about what we are asking you to do."

"What is it, man?" Sky asked.

"Even though it's not an illegal drug, you may be in legal trouble just by performing a chemical analysis of it."

"Huh?"

Persi let out a breath, suggesting he was wasting time, but he pressed on.

"You see, I represent someone who may have agreed to use this bottle of barbecue sauce under the terms of a license agreement. The license says the sauce is a trade secret and my client, or anyone acting with him—that's us—agrees not to have it reverse engineered. That would include a chemical analysis."

"Yeah, well, true, but you should also know the company is run by a megalomaniac who's convinced he owns your thoughts," Persi added.

Will maintained his unamused lawyer demeanor. "If we do this and make your findings public but the license holds up in court, do you understand that we all could be sued by one of the largest and most powerful companies in the world for millions of dollars on charges like *conspiracy to misappropriate trade secrets?*"

Sky scratched his head and smiled curiously. "Come on, man. Why would anybody sign such a tripped-out thing?"

"He didn't sign anything," Will confided, leaning forward and closing in on the most far-reaching but real risk of all. "They say he agreed to all that just by breaking the seal on the product shrink-wrap. And so did your friend Jimbo and millions of other buyers of Wholly Grill. And because of what they agreed to, you and I are about to become outlaws if you do this." With a matter-of-fact expression, he looked squarely into Sky's wide blue eyes.

Sky rocked on his heels, taking in all that he heard, and then burst into laughter. "You are too much, man! You head-tripped me good! Merry Pranksters got nothin' on you. That whole trip is . . . unreal, man!"

"Are you sure?" Will maintained. He flashed a look at Persi of *Don't tell me I didn't try to tell him*. Sky was holding his head with both hands and rocking with laughter.

Persi produced a Tupperware tray, explaining to Sky what was in the series of containers. As Sky emptied the smaller containers into vials and labeled them, he then made sure to distinguish between containers of Linkin' Buddies that were uncooked and laser-cooked. Will pointed out to him that the cooked Smoke Crystals adhering to the meat were twice as large as the uncooked ones.

Sky said he would have some results to report by the next day. "I don't know what they put in this barbecue sauce, but if it turns trippers into freaks like you . . . *whoa*, man! I can't wait to try this stuff with my old lady this weekend!"

Outside, as the two of them walked down the sidewalk, Persi poked Will in the ribs with her index finger. "Nice work in there, Mr. Hotshot Lawyer. If you were just trying to show off what command you have of the material, you did a nice job. All the more reason that when Sky demonstrates he has something to testify about, you're going to handle it. Right?"

They were heading toward the car parked on a side street to Telegraph. "You're still pushing that, aren't you?" Will said, walking close to the edge of the sidewalk.

"Yeah, you better believe I'm *pushing* it," she said, giving him a frolicsome shove off the curb, sending him a step down onto the street.

"Oh, so that's what you mean by *escalate!*" he said, bouncing back onto the sidewalk, grabbing her with both arms, and pulling her toward the curb as if the thrill of a swimming pool awaited. She resisted fiercely but playfully, doubling over, clawing, and squeezing his hands around her waist. Finally, the two fell off the curb. Both landed on their feet, but Will lost his balance slightly, letting go of her and stumbling farther into the street just as a dark SUV roared by within two feet of him.

"Look out!" Persi yelled.

Instantly sobered, Will made light of it nonetheless. "Whoops! Almost ambushed again by *Crushjoy*."

It was obvious from Persi's expression that she thought he'd almost been killed—nothing funny about it. "Be careful," she said. Then she narrowed her eyes, abandoning the levity of the moment before, staring off at the disappearing vehicle as if it were one of the SMEL vehicles. "With ThinkSoft it's always about ambush, surprise, the strongarm. Sky, Lenny—anyone, everyone—*should* ignore that thing."

"Thing? You mean the Wholly Grill End User License Agreement?" he said.

"Yeah, that thing. That's some arm's-length agreement," she said. "At ThinkSoft, be aware, *end users* is not merely what they call their licensees. It's a standing order—not to be carried out, of course, until said users are at the end of their money."

Will laughed at the cutting hyperbole.

"I mean it, Will, we gotta get you into this." She started in again. "I understand you've got to do your job and Edwin has prepared all the other witnesses. But he hasn't even met Sky. He's *your* witness. The jury would eat up whatever Sky says if *you* were questioning him." She paused. "Look, all I'm asking now is this: If—make that *when*—Sky has testimony that will help us, promise me you'll handle his questioning and evidence, not Edwin."

Will didn't want to say no, but he didn't want to argue with her either. His few hours' off would soon be over. He wanted to keep things light and easy. Now was not the time to tell her about his conversation with Edwin shortly before he left court. Edwin had approved of his meeting and interviewing this unknown expert witness proposed by Persi, and Will had actually suggested it might be appropriate for him to conduct the direct examination of the witness should evidence come of it. Edwin had bluntly dismissed the idea but, in what probably was intended as a compliment, he told Will that he would be ready to assume such active courtroom roles in big cases within the next twelve to eighteen months. In any event, the chances of Sky coming up with anything usable were close to zero; he would never be a suitable expert witness in federal court.

They had arrived at the car, Will stood outside the passenger door, Persi on the other side.

"That's not a problem," he said. "I'll do it. That is, *if* he comes up with something, and I hope he does. In fact," he added, not being able to resist a little white lie, "I've already spoken to Edwin about handling this expert if he comes through."

"I knew you'd do it!" she said, jubilantly banging the top of her car with an open hand. "Now just you wait. I bet Sky gets us the goods on Wholly Grill."

They drove across the Bay Bridge, planning to stop for dinner in San Francisco before heading back down the peninsula to San Jose. She was going to drop him off at his office, where once again he would research and prepare papers for the following day. She had selected a South of Market restaurant—a hot spot in the city's trendiest district—that specialized in a hybrid California-Asian cuisine. The restaurant, Asia SF, described its servers as "trans-gender illusionists." Sure enough, after they sat down, they were approached by someone in a short glitter cocktail dress. "Good evening. I'm Maya, and I will be serving you tonight." She—or he—was an Asian beauty who could have been a flight attendant for Singapore Airlines.

After taking the drink orders, Maya described the evening's specials with a flourish in savory open verse that stirred Will's appetite. He hadn't eaten anything but food in cartons and plastic containers for a week.

Persi seemed more at ease and happy than ever. She was particularly proud of having located Sky when no other labs would go near the case. Her hands were flat on the middle of the table, palms down. Instinctively, Will placed his hands on hers and rubbed them lightly.

"Your help's been great," he said. "Thanks."

Persi smiled and turned her hands over, holding his fingers delicately. "I have a stake in this too, don't forget. And hey, we're working together again for the first time since college. Just like old times, right?" She added, "Although it's *different* now, isn't it?"

He couldn't be sure if by *different* she meant the working world or what until now had been a simple uncomplicated friendship. He had a strong hunch that he'd want to conduct some R&D, to explore his feelings for her and any she had for him, but right now, in the middle of the trial, there was no time for that. The demands of the courtroom would take every measure of his energy, time, and focus to save, if possible, Lenny's case, Persi's reputation, and his own fledgling career from going up in flames.

Maya returned and placed their drinks on the table. Will was warmed by the fact that Persi did not quickly let go to take a sip. When Maya stepped away, a woman suddenly appeared in the vacated spot. It was his old girlfriend, Dagmar.

"Hi, Will!"

Abruptly, Will withdrew his hands. Persi was discernibly discomfited. This clearly registered on Dagmar's face.

"Dagmar," he said. He felt Persi's eyes on him, but he didn't look back at her. He noticed—in the nanosecond it took—that the two women discreetly scanned each other head to toe. They both looked back at Will. Glancing at their eyes, he could see they had each taken on at least another 100,000 megabytes of information, apparently an inconsequential load on their systems.

"I'm Dagmar Brittman," Dagmar said to Persi, grinning and extending a stiff right hand that resembled a four-barrel shotgun.

"This is Persi Valentino," Will said.

Persi shook her hand. "Hello."

"Persi is working with me on our case," Will explained.

"Oh, are you a lawyer?" Dagmar asked, with a slight hint of jealousy. Persi shook her head slowly, eyes fixed on Dagmar.

"Persi's a reporter," Will said. Realizing the next question would be where, he added, "She's between jobs right now."

"Sorry to hear that." Dagmar looked down at Persi consolingly but evidently couldn't think of anything else to say. She turned back to Will with a smile. "I'm here with my gang from Banana Republic. We just had to get away from work. This place is so . . . *on!* You know what I mean? Don't you just love it?"

"It's quite a scene," he agreed. An elevated strip of floor in the center of the restaurant served as both the bar and a model runway for performers. Maya was on right now, lip-synching to Diana Ross, hips undulating to the rhythm, singing sweetly about the joy and anguish of love.

"Will, I thought I was going to hear from you. What happened?" Dagmar said coyly.

"I meant to," he was quick to offer. "But this case. I haven't had time for anything—"

"Well, promise me you'll call," she said.

"Promise," he heard himself say. The word leapt out of his open mouth with the ease of a trained dog jumping through a hoop. Without looking over at Persi, he could feel her stare searching through his wreckage for signs of taste, common sense, a brain, or a spine, all unaccounted for. He couldn't bear to look back at her.

"Hey, I saw you on LNTV highlights last night. You were sitting at the lawyer's table when Uncle Edwin gave his opening statement." Dagmar glanced over at Persi, as if to make sure the latter got the blood connection. "Wasn't that an incredible opening statement he gave?"

"Yeah. Not to be believed." Will nodded. "I'm sure he'd love to hear that from you. You should tell him yourself."

"I did," she said. "I called him on his cell just before coming over here. He said you'd left an hour before to go meet an expert who might testify. By the way, you must be doing great over there in his office, Will. I asked him how the new trial lawyer is coming along. You know what he said?"

Will went blank, momentarily struck dumb. He couldn't believe where this conversation had veered.

"I want to know," Persi asked with a polite smile, her reporter's nose no doubt smelling blood. "What else did Edwin say?"

"He said that Will here and he just talked about that, and they agreed that Will would probably be ready to handle his first witness in court, all by himself, in about a year and a half. Isn't that something?"

"Oh, yeah, that's really something, all right," Persi said.

"Gotta run," Dagmar said. "Call me, Will."

As soon as she was gone, Will attempted damage control. "Persi, I can explain."

There was a moment of weighted silence, its cause unspoken. He could see where she found herself: an unscheduled stop at an awkward, vulnerable place. He should have met her there; he'd wanted to, but he'd been completely thrown when, out of nowhere, Dagmar had horned in.

"You know what?" she finally said. "We probably should go. You need to get back to the office. You have papers to shuffle around and hundred-year-old-cases to catch up on. You seem terribly distracted, and we're not accomplishing anything here." She got up and reached in her bag.

"I've got this," he said, producing his wallet.

She stared in a direction away from him. He dropped a bill on the table.

"Persi, I tried. I really did."

"I know. You have to play the role of second stool, right?" she said. "And you're perfect. That's why they call it typecasting."

She took off toward the front door.

‹ 28 ›

"Plaintiff calls . . . Dr. Elizabeth Stone!" Edwin announced the next day, sweeping his hand toward the courtroom doors like a late-night TV host welcoming his featured guest.

Dr. Stone entered wearing a double-breasted gray Armani pantsuit and a set of Tiffany's pearl earrings and necklace, so simple and understated it cried out she was on top of her universe. About five-foot-eight, she was thinner than the television cameras made her out to be. Her brunette hair, with only a hint of gray, was pulled back into a perfectly coiffed ponytail. Fashionable eyewear framed, but did not hide, brilliant emerald eyes that shone like high-voltage grow lights, their intensity increasing when she spoke with passion and certainty.

After being sworn in, and with a measure of comfort unlike Lenny's the day before, she settled into the witness chair. Edwin was so intoxicated by his star witness that he scarcely seemed to notice that at first she was asking and he was answering all the questions.

"Now, Dr. Stone, tell the jury about your educational background in the field of psychology," Edwin began.

"Academic training, or courses I've taught at universities throughout the world?" As soon as she spoke in her assured and familiar voice, the jury regarded her as though the female personification of Walter Cronkite had taken the stand to tell them "the way it is."

"Let's start with academic training," Edwin replied, delighted.

"In the interests of time, can I limit the answer to *advanced* degrees?"

"Yes."

"And I'm sorry, but do you want me also to include *honorary* advanced degrees?" she asked, glancing at the judge, as though apologizing for the sheer unwieldiness of her curriculum vitae.

"By all means," Edwin coaxed her. Dr. Stone clearly enjoyed being center stage and spreading around her erudition. Will looked for any sign that she resented having to testify at the trial because of the release she needed from Edwin.

By the time the members of the jury had heard a detailed review of her résumé, including a heavy list of scholarly publications, they were hungry for a spoon-feeding on the diagnosis and treatment of clinical addiction. Will was beginning to appreciate what Edwin had said—that trials, by their nature, had their up days and down days. Things today were looking up.

"Did you have occasion to observe and evaluate the plaintiff in this case, Lenny Milton?" Edwin asked.

"Yes. I spent about four and a half hours with Mr. Milton, which I divided evenly between Sunday afternoon and Monday night. I interviewed him, observed him, and evaluated him in his home—in his natural habitat—where I felt I could gather the most data."

"Let's pause here, Dr. Stone, before you tell us about the data you gathered *in the field*—right in the midst of Mr. Milton's habitat," Edwin emphasized, perhaps hinting that Dr. Stone could be likened to Jane Goodall, bravely going it alone to Lenny's cavelike bungalow out in the middle of the suburbs. "Instead, please tell us what, in your estimation as a world-renowned expert, defines a chemically dependent addict."

"Such an addict can be defined as one who engages in habitual—*in extremis*—consumption of a substance, over and over, in spite of the plain evidence that there are self-destructive consequences. Three big signposts help us recognize the addict." Will jumped up to unfold in front of the jury an oversized chart with three words in large print: TOLERANCE, WITHDRAWAL, and CRAVING. Under each word appeared bullet points describing the characteristics. The jury leaned forward to take this all in.

"Continue, Dr. Stone," Edwin said.

"Tolerance is shorthand for the phenomenon common to all addicts—when the addict needs an ever-increasing amount of the controlling substance to get the desired effect. Alcohol, heroin, and cocaine are examples of such notorious substances." She was using a laser pointer from the witness stand to walk the jurors through her chart. "Withdrawal for the addict is the painful cessation of the addictive substance. The higher the tolerance, the more painful—physically, psychologically, and emotionally—can be the withdrawal." She circled the last word with the laser for a few seconds for dramatic punctuation. "And craving is the habitual, compulsive need for the substance in order to re-create the desired experience. Craving is the engine that drives the addict's behavior."

"Now, based on these definitions and these scientific indicators, what did you observe of Mr. Milton that, in your opinion, would tell us whether or not he was engaged in addictive behavior?" Edwin asked. "Let's begin our inquiry with any evidence you found of tolerance as you have described it."

Will was in charge of operating the video projector directed toward a large screen. In her two interviews, Dr. Stone had taken along a videographer and prepared a professionally edited video recording of Lenny's activities. There was Lenny marinating the meats and laying them out on the grill. Absorbed with and in control of the details, he was captain of his ship. There he was dialing up ThinkSoft with the grill's modem and connecting to the Wholly WORD. Even though it wasn't necessary to "check the meat"—it was the subject of continuous onscreen digital readouts culminating in a *beep* when it was done—there was Lenny hovering around the grill. Although he looked like he would never abandon his watch, it struck Will as strangely tragic that all the instruments in the Wholly Grill had made Captain Lenny obsolete.

"In my interview with Mr. Milton I learned that he had started out cooking the equivalent of two pork chops or two hamburgers at a time to achieve the desired effect that the barbecue seems to produce for him. Some stimulants, like nicotine in cigarettes or caffeine in coffee—both of which can be addictive substances—act as *reinforcers* that chemically trigger brain reward mechanisms such as increased alertness, improved mood, and reduced anxiety. Mr. Milton, by radically multiplying his intake of the substance many times over, seemed to be motivated in activating such reinforcers." The video provided just enough candid shots of Lenny gorging himself with large trays of barbecue so the jury could perceive his behavior as indeed markedly abnormal, but there were not so many shots that the jury would be repulsed. They saw the bottles of Wholly Grill sauce squirreled away, and they caught a few equally unstaged glimpses of Lenny rubbing his gums with the cooked sauce. The jury regarded this with both amazement and shock.

"Did you have any occasion to determine whether Mr. Milton was subject to chemical withdrawal as you described that hazard of addiction moments ago?" Edwin posed, rolling his shoulders back in a way that lifted and dropped his suit jacket back where it started.

"Yes," she responded, on cue. "After our visit on Sunday, I asked him to abstain until my return approximately twenty-four hours later."

"What did you find upon your return the next day?"

"First of all, it appeared accurate that he had abstained for the duration of my absence. He related to me he had. And I put my hand on the grill, and it was cool to the touch."

"How did he appear?"

"Mr. Milton's eyes were apprehensively wide, and his pupils were sharply dilated. He was showing signs of severe anxiety. He complained of a sensation of unrequited hunger."

"Had he eaten anything that day?"

"He'd eaten a large quantity of food, none of which was the barbecue he continued to crave. For example, I think he had eaten a number of sandwiches." she said, glancing over at Crushjoy in a thinly disguised effort to undo some of the damage done by Crushjoy's demonstrative evidence that ensnared Lenny the day before.

"What else did you observe?" Edwin continued.

"He seemed deeply distracted and incapable of focusing on anything besides his barbecue. I asked him to wait at least another hour before becoming a user again so that I could observe him. Since he could not barbecue, he exhibited further and related signs of an obsessive disorder. He washed the housing of the grill and towel-dried it. Then he hoisted it up and performed some meaningless work underneath it. His pathological obsession with the machine itself corroborated my findings," she pronounced. The female members of the jury were bobbing their heads affirmatively as if they were in a coffee klatch with Dr. Stone—waiting for their turn to share anecdotal evidence. Dr. Stone then described how in her opinion Lenny's behavior had resulted in his sacrificing his work and a normal social life in favor of the Wholly Grill.

"Have you formed an opinion, Dr. Stone, as to whether or not Lenny Milton is a chemically dependent addict to Wholly Grill?" Edwin asked.

"Yes, I have."

"And what is that?" Edwin asked, as if he did not know the answer.

"Objection, Your Honor." Crushjoy finally spoke. He had been sitting there acting like he was patiently listening to nonsense. The truth was, and he knew it, the jury was now completely under the sway of Dr. Elizabeth Stone. "The question lacks foundation. There has been no evidence of any chemical, much less *addictive* chemical, in Wholly Grill barbecue sauce."

"But Your Honor, the testimony has elicited *circumstantial* evidence of such a chemical," Edwin countered.

Even Judge Wetherborne appeared to have been favorably impressed with Dr. Stone; his eyes were becalmed, not focused on any one thing. The judge rubbed his chin for a moment and then ruled. "I will allow the question, making reference to a *substance addict* and not a *chemically dependent addict*. As so rephrased, the objection having been sustained in part and overruled in part, the witness may answer the question."

Dr. Stone cleared her throat and turned to deliver the gospel directly to the jury. "In my professional opinion, Lenny Milton has become not just a substance abuser but a substance *addict*. That substance is Wholly Grill. He has achieved a markedly high degree of tolerance, one that is a serious threat to his physical and mental well-being. And he exhibits a traumatic withdrawal reaction that is clinically significant—commensurate with the high level of tolerance. The craving he suffers is constant and in my view is physiologically based." Dr. Stone had a wonderful way of using big words that was not pretentious; her words just rang true and clear. "More specifically, although the causes of substance addiction are typically multifactorial, it is my firm opinion that the overriding and source cause of Lenny Milton's addiction is not any behavioral or even biological predispositions unique to Mr. Milton but rather the substance itself." She gave the jury a grave expression before delivering her final blow. "Wholly Grill is a dangerously addictive substance."

"Thank you, Dr. Stone. No further questions." Edwin sat down, but he seemed to be hovering above his seat, so pleased was he with Dr. Stone's performance. Will passed him a note: *Bravo! Crushjoy's got his hands full now.*

"You may proceed with your cross-examination, Mr. Crushjoy," the judge said, nodding to the defense table.

Unlike Lenny, Dr. Stone was sphinxlike in her calm while awaiting—perhaps eagerly awaiting—any attempts by Crushjoy to challenge her authority. The veteran defense lawyer leafed through his yellow pad of notes of her testimony, giving the impression to the jury he was looking for a hole he could not find. He then stood up.

"Now, Dr. Stone, you have stated your opinion that Wholly Grill is a dangerously addictive substance. Let's take a look at the label of the bottle so that I can understand what you are saying."

A slick 3-D image of the Wholly Grill barbecue sauce was flashed onto the screen; the gleaming bottle rotated on its base so the entire label could be observed by all. The graphics on the front depicted the horseman with laser lance aimed at the smoking lamb chop. The bottle rotated to the back where the ingredients could be read.

"Looking at the ingredients, Dr. Stone, I want you to tell the jury exactly what ingredient is addictive. Is it the water?"

"No, I seriously doubt it." She smiled and shrugged dismissively.

"Do you think it's the tomato sauce? Or perhaps the fructose sweetener?" Crushjoy pressed his point, the list of ingredients plain as day on the screen.

"I know the sauce in toto is an addictive substance," she said. "I do not know the precise particulars of the biochemical sequelae. It could be the combinations of ingredients; it could be the so-called other spices and seasonings, or it could be something in the Smoke Crystals."

"Oh, you think maybe it's the hickory smoke flavoring listed here?"

"I told you I don't know. What I do know is that your client was asked to turn over that kind of pertinent information and refused to do so," she added.

"Move to strike the last remark!" Crushjoy barked, turning to the judge.

"Motion granted," the judge ruled. "The jury will disregard Dr. Stone's last statement." But the jury had heard it. Dr. Stone had shrewdly strengthened her position while casting aspersions on ThinkSoft.

Crushjoy signaled an associate and the screen was turned off. He moved on. "The bottom line is that you can't tell us what component of Wholly Grill is addictive?"

"No."

"Now Dr. Stone, it's true, isn't it, that the field of psychology recognizes a variety of addictions?"

"Yes."

"For example, psychology recognizes gambling addiction and shopping addiction. True?"

"Yes."

"And there are addictions to everything from computers to relationships to the need for power?"

"Yes. There are all varieties of nonsubstance addictions."

Pausing, perhaps to challenge her qualifying remark, the defense lawyer forged ahead instead. "And, of course, psychology recognizes sex addiction. Right?"

Without losing her composure, she darted a furtive glance at Edwin, who missed it. Will had no idea what was going on between Edwin and the witness. "Yes. That is a recognized addiction."

"But you are not of the opinion that God should be sued for a product defect because He installed *those* components in the manufacturing of human beings?"

"Objection! Argumentative!" Edwin shrilled.

"I'll withdraw the question," Crushjoy politely offered. The jury giggled in appreciation of his sarcastic humor.

"Psychology also recognizes what it refers to as food addicts. True or false, Dr. Stone."

"True. There are food addicts."

"Wouldn't you agree that, even under the principles of psychology to which you subscribe, worst-case scenario, Lenny Milton is nothing more than a food addict?"

"No. I disagree," she said, with great certainty. "The symptomologies are so pronounced in this case with and without Wholly Grill that it is clearly specific to the substance. The reaction is so substance-specific that, as I alluded earlier, it appears to involve a brain-reward mechanism, where neurotransmitters in the brain are triggered to stimulate the desired experience—"

"Move to strike," Crushjoy interrupted her. "There is no foundation for those remarks. The witness is an expert in psychology and psychiatry, but is not qualified to speak on the subject of neuroscience or brain chemistry."

The judge hadn't yet ruled when Dr. Stone continued. "I'm sorry, did I forget to mention that I also have a PhD in neuroscience from the University of Ottawa School of Medicine? I was the Cornelius Rumford Lecturer on *Neurochemical Self-Encryption in the Chronically Forgetful,* which was published—"

"Thank you, Dr. Stone," the judge interrupted. "I am going to ask that you wait for an inquiry about that. Motion granted. Next question."

Having posed the last series of questions from the well—the space between the jury and the witness—Crushjoy returned to the defense table, where an associate handed him a large tabbed three-ring binder.

"Bottom line, Dr. Stone, if you were not hired to act as an expert witness here by the plaintiff's attorneys, these would not be your opinions. Isn't that true?"

She scoffed. "No. That's *not* true."

"More to the point, if Lenny Milton were *your patient*, and not the plaintiff whose attorneys hired you, you would not blame Wholly Grill; you would tell Lenny Milton he is entirely responsible for his actions. Right?"

Dr. Stone, evidently accustomed to this kind of suggestion of bias, remained unruffled. "No. I stand firmly by my statements."

"Well, while we are on the subject of where you stand, Doctor, let me refresh your memory." He opened the three-ring binder and began an exhaustive review of statements made by Dr. Stone from her daily newspaper column, radio call-in programs, and guest television appearances. Not letting Dr. Stone explain the context of any of her statements, Crushjoy presented the doctor with a long series of apparently inconsistent statements made to interviewers or call-in participants. She referred to various addictions as "ultimately lifestyle choices"; one call-in self-proclaimed addict was told by her to "get a life"; a number of others were told to take responsibility for their lives.

With Crushjoy's carefully orchestrated questions and the playing on cue by his associates of radio and television clips on the big screen (displaying the text of the radio remarks in large print when the audio clips were played), the defense team effectively portrayed Dr. Stone as being more in the entertainment business than in the practice of serious medicine. In one dramatic video clip, a close-up of Dr. Stone showed her rolling her eyes in disbelief bordering on derision, when a woman in the television audience described her uncontrollable addiction to a certain brand of "ranch seasoning" potato chips. Crushjoy managed to milk a number of rhetorical questions out of the scene while running the video on continuous loop.

Will swallowed hard during this line of questioning. Although her testimony was being systematically chipped away, Dr. Stone held on to the core with her strong bearing. Will was stunned by the amount of work that went into this sequence. Under the court's order, each side was required to give the names of their expert witnesses three days after the trial was set. The Kilgore Crushjoy team had managed, in half a week, to subpoena and actually listen to hundreds of hours of tapes. Not just listen—a dozen associates, under the guidance of more senior lawyers, had gone over to all of this material with one mind, interpreting, sorting, and compiling the segments under the brilliant direction of Thurston Crushjoy, the single purpose being to discredit the preeminent Dr. Elizabeth Stone. Just when Will thought he had understood the staggering scope of the legal fees for which ThinkSoft sought to hold him responsible, the possibilities were still as dizzying and nerve-wracking as a broken slot machine spinning, spinning, ever spinning . . . .

A brief lull followed, intimating that Thurston Crushjoy was about to mount his finish. He was now wearing an expression that bespoke disbelief, amused bewilderment, and disappointment in the well-known doctor. He was handed a printout from an associate working on one of the computers.

"Dr. Stone, let me represent to you, and at the same time make an offer of proof to the court," he said turning to the judge, "that we have fed your testimony on direct examination into state-of-the-art analytical software from ThinkSoft. This software is capable of digitizing your testimony into logic strands, decompiling it, and tracing the precise source, if other than your own. Specifically, it can trace any use you may have made of proprietary reasonware. Let me show you the exact reason it identified that you made." The screen was filled with the following words: I'M NOT RESPONSIBLE. THE [fill in the blank, e.g., psychoactive drugs, Twinkies, etc.] ARE ADDICTIVE. IT'S THEIR FAULT.

"Do you agree, in essence, that this is an accurate shorthand summary of your testimony today, having filled in the blank with *Wholly Grill?*"

Dr. Stone shifted her posture, appearing a little uncomfortable for the first time. "Shorthand, I suppose, without the scientific support I gave; otherwise, I would say it is accurate."

"And it's true, isn't it, Doctor, that the words you see on the screen—and the reasonware you used—are from a program called *Psycho*Logic?" He stressed *psycho* as though she got her opinions from the crazed killer in the movie of the same name. Nor did he deign to look at her; Crushjoy looked directly to the jury, as if to convey his aversion to this type of pandering testimony.

"I did use PsychoLogic in preparing my testimony; it is a standard source material in the profession," she said. "In this case it merely verified my opinions."

"PyschoLogic is made by a company called *Creative* Psychology *Unlimited?*" Again, Crushjoy stretched the pronunciation of the company name to make it sound as long as Self-Serving and Entirely Made Up out of Whole Cloth, Incorporated.

"Yes. That's the company's name," Dr. Stone answered tersely. She had moved beyond uncomfortable and was now angry. Crushjoy was twisting everything around. The jury would have no way of knowing that Creative Psychology, maker of reasonware for use in legal proceedings, was a reputable company whose engineers were the creative ones, not its mainstream professional advisory staff.

"One more thing, Dr. Stone," Crushjoy began, as if as an afterthought. "You have just completed a new book, haven't you?"

Dr. Stone flinched for the first time. The jury leaned forward to hear what that could be about. "Yes," she answered, endeavoring to maintain her composure, again darting a glance at Edwin.

"And the title of that new book is *People Who Are All the Talk: What Makes Them Tick*. Am I correct?"

"That is correct."

"Now, your new book interviews and discusses at length the plaintiff's lawyer, Mr. Ostermyer. True?"

"Yes. That is correct." Dr. Stone did more than glance at Edwin this time. She glowered at him briefly. Edwin didn't notice. He was beaming proudly at the jury with a look that said, Pretty impressive, huh? Will had that sinking feeling again. There was nothing the ThinkSoft network did not know.

"Tell me, Doctor, isn't it true that your book is printed and sitting in a warehouse right now?"

"Yes."

"And the reason it has not been shipped to bookstores yet is that you need to get a privacy release from Mr. Ostermyer before it can be distributed. Right?"

"Objection!" Edwin finally snapped out of his reverie. "This has no relevance to the expert opinions this witness has expressed."

"Indeed it does," Crushjoy nodded to the judge. "Goes to the bias of this witness."

"Overruled!" the judge decided. "You may answer the question."

It was apparent that, for a brief moment, Dr. Stone had hoped that the judge would cut these questions to the quick. Not to be.

"Yes," she responded, a discernible hiss in her voice; her anger was now overt—both at Crushjoy for his questions and at Edwin for putting her in this position.

Crushjoy turned the heat up. "The deal was this: Once you do Mr. Ostermyer's bidding and testify for the plaintiff in this case, he will give you the release you need. Isn't that true?" He was now filling the courtroom and the outer hallway with his booming voice.

"Yes. That's our arrangement." Dr. Stone crossed and recrossed her legs. She looked at Edwin for help, to no avail. The judge dropped a pen he was using and rocked back in his chair, dramatizing for the jury his own disgust.

"Previously, you had turned down Mr. Ostermyer when he asked you to help him in the Snapple Johnson murder case, hadn't you?"

"I declined to get involved in that case. Yes." She had taken her glasses off now and was rubbing her eyes.

Crushjoy let the jury take in the sight before his final question. He tilted his head back so as to take aim at her with his massive jaw, creating the illusion that he was looking down at her from where he stood in front of the jury. "Admit it, Dr. Stone. You would not even have considered—not for a moment—testifying in this case but for the fact that your book was being held hostage?"

Fortunately Edwin did not object to the question. It would have only drawn more negative attention to him. There was total silence in the court. Dr. Stone looked up with her glasses still off, her eyes fatigued and watery. Her emerald-green eyes were soft and vulnerable. She seemed burdened by an inexpressible shame. "Under the circumstances . . . " She paused, then conceded, "It was a mistake, a lapse in judgment. I . . . can't explain it."

"That's all, Dr. Stone. No further questions," Crushjoy announced, returning to his seat, his hardened face revealing no sign of self-congratulation. Instead, his icy blue eyes serenely reassured the jury: This was just another day at the office for Thurston Crushjoy. Not so his client in the front row. Art Newman made no effort to conceal his exultation at Crushjoy's performance.

‹ 29 ›

After Dr. Stone's testimony, Edwin called several secondary witnesses who were supposed to support the testimony of Lenny Milton and Dr. Stone. The witnesses were clerks or owners of liquor and convenience stores. They testified about customers they had observed who made unusually large and frequent purchases of Wholly Grill barbecue sauce or Linkin' Buddies. One clerk was prepared to testify that one such purchaser laughed at a joke at the cashier stand, then started spouting milk through his nostrils. Crushjoy objected that there was no way of knowing if the purchaser had not swigged a quart of milk out in the car before coming into the store. The judge agreed and refused to allow the testimony. Without any of the milk getting into evidence, the afternoon testimony was bone dry. Some jurors could barely keep their heads up.

After the day's court session, Judge Wetherborne called the attorneys into his chambers. He was not happy, and it obviously had not escaped his attention that if there were bookmakers for jury verdicts, they were not betting on the plaintiff in this case by any spread.

"Mr. Ostermyer, although I have none for you, I do have some pity for your sadly misled client. Based upon what I have heard, I have strong reason to believe that you, or Mr. Swanson"—he frowned at Will—"convinced Mr. Milton he was an addict who should file a lawsuit without any scientific proof. You then filed a lawsuit on behalf of not one but *millions* of addicts. I have yet to see one! You put your client on the stand, and we see quite plainly that he has a garden-variety eating disorder. But that doesn't stop you! You then use strong-arm tactics—threats of economic ruination—to get an expert witness to sing whatever tune you call." The judge maintained a calm voice but leveled his throbbing glare at Edwin. "For that stunt I am reporting the matter to the State Bar. I am also asking the U.S. Attorney's office here to see if a federal crime has been committed—using litigation as a racketeering enterprise or something of that nature." Crushjoy nodded his head in agreement.

Will began feeling nauseated again, but Edwin remained entirely unflummoxed. "But Your Honor, those *were* her opinions. In fact, after she'd agreed to testify, I asked her if it was OK to explain the issues at length and she said to me, 'It would be my extreme pleasure.'"

"I am not finished!" The judge cut Edwin off, raising his voice. There seemed to be some correlation between the decibel of his voice and eye movement; the left one was pumping scorn at Edwin. "The only reason I have not granted the defendant's motions and concluded this case once and for all is that this case is on LNTV. That's right, *because* of the television coverage! I want everyone—every hare-brained would-be plaintiff out there, every hare-brained would-be plaintiff's *lawyer*, every child thinking of going to law school—to see all the ways the court system should not be used! To see what happens in the end to those who think that they can use the court system like a lottery ticket every time they think they might get lucky because maybe the judicial system is insane enough." He reached a pitch, then lowered his voice. "When they find out what happened to the lawyers who brought this case—what it cost them in money and professional standing—they will know exactly what they should *not* do."

"With all due respect, Your Honor," Edwin began, as if he had barely heard a word the judge said. "Save for a few hiccups, to be expected in a jury trial, our case is proceeding quite smoothly. Let me share with you what I saw before coming into chambers." Edwin downshifted into an even lower gear of imperviousness. He smiled and leaned forward as though he and the judge were having a drink after work, trading stories. "I caught a glimpse of juror number two, who, by the way, is my bet to be foreman. I saw him stand up and move his elbow in a way that you could not help but read as a thumbs-up sign for the plaintiff, which I am sure he was directing at me. If we are connecting with the jury like this already, this bodes well for the next phase of this suit, the full class action—"

"Mr. Ostermyer, you and I are different species. We do not speak the same language. I am going to try and have a rational discussion with your associate. You are excused from my chambers!"

After Edwin left, the judge looked sternly at Will. "Mr. Swanson, I have many grounds in this case to grant the nonsuit and award sanctions. Let me address with you one or two that particularly trouble me." His left eye widened to three times the size of the right and beaded on Will. "The forum jockeying! You should have filed in small claims court, but you chose Municipal Court. I have read the transcript of the hearing."

Will felt the humiliation all over again but endeavored not to show it.

The judge continued. "The case was thrown out on grounds I am being asked to decide again. You lost. I am not your court of appeals!"

Will could see out of the corner of his eye that Crushjoy was shaking his head in disgust. "But this is a class—" Will started to explain.

"It will *never* be a class action unless I say so!"

Will remained silent. It would be foolish to argue with the judge about what powers he had.

"And since you signed the complaint, Mr. Swanson, you know the rules allow me to hold you fully responsible for the defendant's fees. You, who filed and argued the Muni complaint, should know best how ill-advised the new complaint is." The judge reflected a moment. "I strongly suggest that you have a talk with your client about dismissing this lawsuit tomorrow morning. That will go a long way toward minimizing sanctions and saving your own career. Do *you* understand me?"

"Yes, Your Honor," Will replied humbly.

‹ 30 ›

Outside the judge's chambers in the courtroom hallway, Edwin expressed resolve to get even with Crushjoy for the insinuations about PsychoLogic reasonware. "Go see what ThinkSoft's QE Deluxe line of reasonware has that we can use," he said to Will. "Let's turn their own weapons against them."

Ever since Edwin had been introduced to QE Deluxe reasonware at the Silicon Valley Logic and Convention Center, he had been hooked. His use of the "I Didn't Do It" 7.0 on behalf of Snapple Johnson had been hugely successful. Judge Lifo had just announced that he had granted all motions to delay *nunc pro tunc*—literally "now for then"—bypassing time altogether and deciding the case as if it were already seven years later. Accepting the premise that if every cell in Snapple Johnson's body would be replaced by then, the judge agreed with Edwin that Johnson was innocent under the law because foresight revealed that not a cell in his body could be held accountable for the heinous crime committed more than seven years earlier. Johnson was set free, and a public uproar ensued. Edwin was receiving more new client calls than ever on his toll-free lines.

"You won't have time to shop while we're in court," Edwin said. "You'll need to download it off the QE Deluxe Web site after hours."

"I haven't been able to visit any Web sites," Will told Edwin. "Our Internet access has not been working."

"That's outrageous!" Edwin fumed. "Who's our provider now? Do they know who they're dealing with?"

"We're on the ThinkSoft Network," Will said. "I've reported it several times. They keep promising to get us back on-line, but nothing has happened." Edwin didn't speak a word, evidently gathering the dark implications. He just shook his head in anger and stalked away.

Because Lenny had already left the courtroom to go home, Will called to let him know he was coming. He told Lenny they needed to talk. Will then left a voice message with Persi to let her know where he would be. Persi called back and said that Sky had to come over from Berkeley to San Francisco for a meeting at the Haight Ashbury Free Medical Clinic. He had told her it would be no "hassle" to swing by Lenny's—some forty miles out of his way—on his way to the Haight.

After Will had found out Edwin had staged the sprinklers going off in the conference room, he'd felt duty bound to tell Lenny about it the next day, regardless of what Edwin might think. Lenny's attitude about Edwin then was not much different than the first day he came into the office. "Did Mr. Ostermyer do that? He's a genius, a one-of-a-kind lawyer. I knew it when I first saw him on TV. Let's face it, I never would've moved off my butt to do something about Wholly Grill if he hadn't shaken me up the way he did. He's the best."

When Will arrived at Lenny's house it was plain that Lenny anticipated a serious discussion. Discreetly abstaining from Wholly Grill, Lenny had laid out on the table a few different kinds of "regular" sausages with crackers and cheese for his guests. The sausages seemed to be of keen interest to Lady J, who, according to Lenny, would not touch scraps from the grill that had blinded her. She sat up next to Lenny and trained her nose on the movements of the sliced sausage from the plate to Lenny's mouth.

Will repeated the judge's harsh remarks and asked Lenny what he wanted to do. "I am more convinced than ever we are right. The judge is wrong. You have been great, Will, but I know I can't lose with Mr. Ostermyer on my side. Wait until he starts cross-examining *their* witnesses. He'll eat them up!" Lenny said, conjuring up the image of Edwin devouring doughnuts on TV.

"It's your call, Lenny," Will said, not sure whether to be relieved at Lenny's decision or filled with dread that he wanted the trial to continue.

When Persi arrived, she said she had just come from trying to recruit witnesses at other meetings of Wholly Grillers Anonymous and Grillanon, the latter a support group for codependents of Wholly Grill addicts. She'd still had no luck.

Persi looked angry and frustrated, for good reason. Now not even her freelance articles were being picked up. Because she faced massive legal problems with ThinkSoft, no one would touch her *or* her work. Every publisher saw her as a liability, a time bomb waiting to explode.

She also remained cool to Will following last night's fiasco. That didn't mean she was about to abandon Lenny—or her own interests, for that matter—just because she was unhappy with Will. So she'd come to a diplomatic peace with him, if nothing else. The terms of the accord: Will said Sky would testify *if* he delivered any valuable new evidence, but she had to accept that Edwin would be the one to examine Sky.

When Lenny got up to answer a call in the other room, Persi announced defiantly, "I've got it. *I* will testify. What do I have to lose? I'll tell the jury about the shivering rats at the Home of the Cold Turkeys and the behavior I saw. Don't tell me something addictive isn't involved up there in that lab. Let ThinkSoft try and give some innocent explanation. I'll bring in the pictures I took, too."

"No way." Will was firm. "Even though it was in plain view for any janitor to see, ThinkSoft is claiming, and the court order says, anything you saw—anything having to do with animal or human experiments—is a trade secret. And the photographs are completely off limits. ThinkSoft will multiply your problems if they find out you took pictures."

"I don't care! I want to help Lenny. I want to help the others too. What do I have to lose? They've destroyed my dream of being a journalist."

She was no doubt going to vent more of her anger when they heard a thunderous drumbeat coming from the front of the house. Someone was flailing away on the front door, incorporating the knocker in rhythmic time. Will recognized the improvisation as a segment of the drum solo from the acid rock paean "In a Gadda Da Vida."

Lenny opened the front door to a man's voice. "*Whoa*! Sky out here. You must be Milton in there. I've got a chemical cornucopia fresh from the Sky Lab. What, you ask, can you do in the name of science?" His voice was inside the door now. "Why, yes, you can bring me a beer. You're a cool dude, Milton. You and I are going to be beautiful together." It was obvious from the silence that Lenny had just stood there dumbstruck.

Sky waltzed into the living room with his satchel, greeted Persi and Will, and sat in a chair across from them on the other side of the coffee table. Another chill shivered through Will's body. The charade of consulting Sky, a human chemistry experiment gone awry, as a possible expert witness continued. At some point if he actually had something substantive to say, Will would have to say no to Persi. That wouldn't be easy.

Lenny brought Sky's beer and resumed his seat next to Lady J. Sky opened his satchel and put two labeled jars on the coffee table. "OK. Here's what we've got so far. Jar number one here is the uncooked shit. It's light gray but a little more heavy-duty than the other. Jar number two is the cooked shit. The cooked Smoke Crystals are black as night, but super fine—light, almost like dust. If Iron Butterfly were a chemical . . . " He held the black jar up for contemplation.

"So, what can you conclude at this point?" Persi asked anxiously.

"It is my informed opinion," Sky began in mock self-importance, raising a pedantic index finger and pointing it up, as if he were going to speak from a pretension he had rejected ages ago. "Nay, it is my *carefully considered* opinion, that indeed . . . they must have done some kind of *trip* on it." He nodded his head and pulled his chin, inviting the others to share in the broader philosophical implications of his conclusion.

No one said a word.

"Exactly what kind of trip do you think they did on it?" Will finally asked.

"Lasers, man. Did you know the word LASER comes from 'Light Amplification by Stimulated Emission of Radiation?' Way tripped out! Lasers have radical power. They can change the chemistry big time. The ingredients on the back of the bottle could definitely be different after being zapped with a laser. Like I told you, the full chemical analysis is going to take a lot longer to complete."

"We know," Persi said. Her legs were crossed, and her raised foot was fidgeting wildly. "But is there any other test you can do short of the full chemical analysis that might tell us something more about the sauce and what's in it?"

"Thought you'd never ask!" Sky lit up. "There's one test I've been dying to try, but I didn't have time back at the lab." He jumped up, pulled a mirror off the wall, and laid it out on the coffee table. Will and Persi both were momentarily stunned into speechlessness at what they were seeing. Poor Lenny had not regained the power of speech since the people's chemist arrived in his home.

Sky carefully poured out a portion from the black jar, then parceled it out into two long lines with the edge of a credit card. The jar was left open and on the mirror, which suggested, to Will's horror, that Sky might already be thinking of going in for seconds.

Finally Will blurted out, "Stop! What are you doing? You're not going to snort that, are you?"

"Fer sure! Best way to find out exactly how trippy this stuff is!"

"You could get sick! How do you know you won't die?" Persi pleaded.

"Trust me," Sky assured. "If there were anything lethal in here, Milton here would've OD'd a long time ago. It's not that kind of toxic."

Before any further protest, Sky swooped down on the mirror with a rolled-up dollar bill, snorting up a long line like a human Dirt Devil. He lifted his head up and, for one second, looked like the wind had been knocked out of him. Then he sneezed violently, kicking the table and knocking the open jar over. Before anyone could catch it, the jar rolled to the end of the table and fell right in front of Lady J's nose, raising a small cloud of black dust. Suddenly Lady J started gagging and wheezing spasmodically, at first haphazardly, then continuing until settling into a strange but predictable rhythm of wheezes every two seconds.

"Oh, shit! Sorry, man!" Sky apologized. He was down on his knees with Will and Persi trying to deal with the mess on Lenny's carpet.

"Poor Lady J!" Lenny was petting Lady J in an effort to subdue her wheezing but had not moved from his chair. "You're coughing just like my smoking used to make you. Calm down, girl."

"What?" Will asked.

"It's the same cough she had that got me to stop smoking. The vet told me she was terribly allergic to the smoke. That's what finally got me to quit." Lady J's wheezes were starting to die down.

"Is it only cigarette smoke that makes her cough that way?" Will asked Lenny.

"Oh, yeah," Lenny answered. "She's been around campfires and all kinds of smoke. It was only cigarette smoke that made her wheeze."

A string of lights switched on in Will's head. "Lenny, you're a heavy ex-smoker. If there were nicotine in the cooked sauce, you would be predisposed—"

"*Whoa!* You're talkin' chemistry," Sky said.

"Yeah! That would explain it!" Lenny said, his head vibrating in agreement. "That's it!" He begin petting the dog furiously. "Good girl, Lady J!"

"It fits," Persi chimed in. "If it's nicotine, or nicotinelike, it's addictive all right! And you wouldn't believe how many people I've seen stand up at these WGA meetings and say they had taken up smoking again, never thinking there might be a direct connection between one craving and another. And the lab experiments in Building RD—"

"'Welcome to Green Bay, Home of the Rat Packers.'" Will recalled the first control group in the lab where the rats were exposed to smoke under glass that Persi had been unable to smell. "It was cigarette smoke. Packers: like in one, two, and three packs a day."

"And the Cold Turkeys," Persi added. "Those rats were going cold turkey on nicotine until they arrived at Ratopia Restaurant, where they got hooked on Wholly Grill. All very cute, Art Newman, you sicko!"

Will nodded in agreement. "ThinkSoft makes other illegal competitors look like choirboys. Using technology to prey on people's brains . . . to increase market share! Sick, all right."

He pondered for a moment, then took a mental step back. "Wait! Time out. Are we deluding ourselves? What kind of trade-secret witches' brew are we now accusing Art Newman of cooking up? I mean, is it even possible that there could be a strong nicotine reaction without having to smoke it?"

Sky leaned forward and looked at Will. "You dig what computers can do? They're nothing like the real thing. This thing, man"—pointing to his temples with both of his index fingers—"is the ultimate virtual-reality head trip. Who needs head*sets* when you've got a head and a universe of chemicals both inside and outside ready to combine and switch you on? Listen up! I know my chemistry, and the most incredible chemistry in the universe is going on right here. You've got three pounds crammed right between your ears that's nothing but—I shit you not—electrochemically bonded Jell-O."

"Jell-O?" Lenny perked up, always ready for dessert.

"Yeah, can you dig that? I say Jell-O, not *gel-like mass*," he said, with imaginary quotes, not hiding his contempt for the way his colleagues would so aridly describe it. "Jell-O. Hey, it's *fun*—dig it—and it's full of *colors*, man. Did you know that they are wrong when they call it 'gray matter'? It's only gray in a dead man's head—that's right—when all the blood is drained out. When it's alive, man, it's a trippy deep reddish brown. And with a universe of chemicals to play on our mind's eye, the light show of colors is so far out, so beyond limits. . . . " He paused, looking up, absorbed by his own vision. Then he came back to Lenny's living room on earth. "So you want to know if it's possible for barbecue sauce to do a head trip? Since I've now scientifically field-tested it, I can tell you categorically the answer is yes."

"What kind of head trip?" Persi asked.

"Dopamine. A definite hit of dopamine," Sky said with authority.

"Dopamine?" Will repeated incredulously. "How could you know it's dopamine and not one of dozens of other brain chemicals? How can you be sure it's anything like that at all?"

Sky shrugged. "Don't ask me how I know. Some cats taste wine and know. I'm a connoisseur of head food, and I am telling you that was a monster hit of dopamine. In fact, you may be right about what's in this shit. Dopamine is exactly the brain chemical that nicotine trips off in a tobacco freak's head. You wanna try some?" Sky held up the black jar and nodded his head at the mirror.

"Dehydrated laser-zapped barbecue sauce inhaled through my nose?" Will verified the offer. "No, thanks. I've been trying to quit." Persi burst out laughing. Sky laughed, too.

"The point is, man, it's all totally possible. Some day they'll be able to get computers to do more than just the electro in *electrochemical*. It starts with figuring out how the head works. Whoever figures out how to get computers to reach in and flip on the pleasure switch in the head—not just for fun but for profit—is going to be one mighty fat cat!"

"Art Newman!" both Persi and Will chimed in unison.

Will wasn't sure how much Sky knew about Art Newman. "Art Newman is founder and head of ThinkSoft. He has used his monopoly of the reasonware operating system to dominate key segments of the entire software market—"

"He's a pig, man."

"Yeah, that's what I was trying to say," Will said. "For Art Newman, Wholly Grill has to be the first piece, the key that opens the door in the quest you describe—"

"Some quest!" Persi hissed. "Such a quaint and time-tested business model, based on perfidy and abuse. Same old grift." Then, as if responding to someone else who'd spoken the last words, she added, "So *that's* what Art Newman means by 'ThinkSoft innovation.' "

Sky announced he had to leave but promised on his way out that he would narrow his search, given the new information as to the possible nature of the laser-cooked Wholly Grill Smoke Crystals. However, it would still be a week or more before he had a full chemical analysis.

Standing in the walkway in front of Lenny's, Persi called out to Sky, "Hey, Will here is going to need you to testify in federal court. Can you do it?"

Will was startled by Persi's request. He had no idea what facts she expected him to establish, or how.

Sky looked over the top of his VW bug with the door open. "You people are cool, but federal court? The big stone palace? That's a c-o-old place, man! I mean, they got uh-*thor*-ities in there, don't they?"

"No getting around it, the place is crawling with them," Persi replied.

Sky hunched his shoulders. "Fer sure. If you call, the Skyman will be there," he promised, as he lowered himself into his pod, fired his engine, and launched himself down Lenny's street.

After Sky disappeared, Lenny excused himself and retreated to the back of the house. Will turned to Persi. "What do you mean, we'll be needing him as a witness? That's entirely up to Edwin. No decision has been made—"

"You can't back away from this now," she said, with a look both incredulous and wounded. "This is your only shot. You said—"

"Wait. I said *if* he came up with something we can actually use,"

Will said. "Trust me. The mirror test won't play well in Judge Wether-borne's court."

"Are you kidding? The jury will love it. They'll see the differences between the cooked and uncooked vials, hear about the experiment and what triggered a smoker's hack in Lady J. Then Sky delivers an expert opinion on what the brain target is: dopamine. And that last bit will nicely complement Dr. Stone's testimony."

"You must be insane! We'd be laughed out of court and asked to check our licenses at the door. And *complement*? What's to comple-ment? Crushjoy destroyed her." He winced at the memory.

"No," Persi corrected him, kicking some dirt loose with her shoe near the front walkway. "All Crushjoy did was impeach her credi-bility—temporarily. What she said is still in the record. He didn't dis-prove a word of it."

"Whew! Am I relieved to hear that! Dr. Stone gave us brilliant tes-timony. Just one small problem: The jury doesn't believe a word she said!" He laughed sarcastically; then he spoke in a more serious tone. "Look, I may not be that experienced, but I know how scientific evi-dence is normally presented."

Persi wasn't laughing. "What? You don't think what Sky has to say belongs in a courtroom? This is your chance to make something happen!" Her Italian blood was rising now.

Will could hear from the back of the house the telltale sound of the Wholly Grill being rolled out onto the patio tarmac for takeoff, fol-lowed by the lid flying open.

"Look, I've told you from the first day that this would be Edwin's trial, that I'd be doing the legwork, the support stuff. I like Sky, don't get me wrong, but I can't recommend him as an expert, based on what I've seen."

She stared back at him, waiting for something more. Finally, she said, "You know, maybe you should've taken that tax and probate job after all.

A legal pallbearer. How perfect. Pat little baby steps. It comforts Lenny and me to know that you'll be there to carry us out——"

"Persi!" Will snapped, his own frustration rising. "You don't understand! I'm doing my job."

"I understand," she said, play-acting empathy. "You've got to play it safe. Maybe you can afford to. I can't. I suppose you think it will help Lenny. I doubt it. As for me, I need to turn the heat up, reclaim my stolen career. However, whoever. Someone who won't flinch."

Her words pierced him. He felt like he was bleeding. There was silence.

She'd hit her target. He hadn't realized until now how important her approval was to him. That she had been pushing him to take risks—jump out of that cozy second chair, or have a crackpot "expert" testify—only complicated matters.

She stepped up to him and took both his hands. He let her because the feeling of anger was supplanted by another. For that moment he wished she were drawing him in rather than letting him go.

"Good luck, Will. I really do hope everything—in particular, the trial—ends up OK for you."

A wave of gloom swept over him, but he said nothing. Her words were sincere. He was the one losing faith. It was sinking in quickly that he was on his own now. She would press on elsewhere and without him. He was saddened and confused by where he found himself. There were forces—rules, procedures, protocols, job descriptions, and expectations—bigger than he was, tying him down with what he knew were restraints of choice, governing what he could and could not do.

Walking to her car, she turned to him one more time. "You've got to get out from under Edwin's shadow. In a word, I say GO-BOSH: *Go Big or Stay Home*. What're you waiting for?"

‹ 31 ›

Will had trouble getting out of bed and arriving at the office early to prepare for another day in court. But it wasn't from the usual nausea-producing thoughts, like when he felt the Kilgore Crushjoy legal fees rising rapidly in his stomach. Rather, he was still haunted by his parting with Persi last night.

He met Edwin out in the hallway before trial started up and told him about Lady J's reaction to Wholly Grill Smoke Crystals. Edwin expressed a keen interest in the possible involvement of nicotine or a substance like it. However, based on the description Will gave him of Sky, Edwin wasn't the least interested in calling him as an expert witness. He was not "in the same league" as Dr. Stone. "But the nicotine angle gives me some other ideas," Edwin started to say, before he was interrupted by a courtroom delivery of documents.

"Have you seen Professor Timmons?" Will asked, after Edwin signed the delivery man's receipt. Professor Timmons was a cultural anthropologist at the Berkeley campus who was scheduled to testify about the role of ritual in addictive behavior and how well-known addictive products and their paraphernalia were successfully designed to promote and engender addictive ritual. The professor had concluded that Wholly Grill had successfully cultivated such ritual through its alluring product design, user instructions, prescribed procedures, and reinforcement through product advertising.

"I have decided not to call Professor Timmons," Edwin said.

"What?" Will was shocked. They had no other witnesses who could testify on the issue of addiction. Will had spent the early morning researching the admissibility of the professor's testimony in anticipation of Crushjoy's objections. It was their last chance to save the addiction claim. Professor Timmons was leaving for Europe tomorrow. "Then who are you going to call next?"

"I'm going straight to McCloud."

"Are you kidding?" Will protested. "McCloud's a secondary witness on a secondary issue. We need to build the addiction case or we're dead."

"I need to score extra points with the jury today," Edwin insisted. Will knew that Edwin wanted to goose Crushjoy in the worst way. "Besides, this will make them more prone to believe the evidence we have put in already. They'll believe it's addictive if they hear just how nefarious ThinkSoft really is."

Edwin walked into court for the start of trial. Will followed him, but he was angry. So much was at stake: his career and his future, not to mention total financial ruin courtesy of the judge, losing face to his father, and disappointing Persi more, if that were even possible. Will had not even been consulted on this tactic, and he dreaded to think where it might lead.

STUDIO ANCHOR: *Good morning. I am Janet Jones in New York, and this is the Lawsuit Network bringing you continuing live coverage of the Barbecue Addiction trial. Welcome to day three. Let's go right to our reporter and commentator at the San Jose Federal Courthouse, trial attorney Ben Griswold. Ben, what can we expect today?*

TRIAL COMMENTATOR: *Janet, yesterday we saw Thurston Crushjoy deliver what might have been a TKO to the plaintiff's star witness, Dr. Elizabeth Stone. Today we understand the plaintiff's attorneys are changing their focus, but they surely will come back to the addiction evidence. You'll recall that the judge wants two questions decided: one, whether Lenny*

Milton is actually addicted to Wholly Grill as his lawyers have claimed, and two, whether the judge should enforce the license agreement that came with the barbecue. Today we expect to hear evidence for the plaintiff to attack the license agreement and attempt to persuade the judge that ThinkSoft should be held accountable even if the agreement clearly says the company is not responsible.

STUDIO ANCHOR: *How is Mr. Ostermyer going to do that, Ben?*

TRIAL COMMENTATOR: *He's going to try to show that the agreement is so completely one-sided and unreasonable—what the law calls "unconscionable"—that it should not be enforced. He needs to do more than show Mr. Milton ran up a lot of vet bills. To prove ThinkSoft is overreaching, we're told he is going to call one of ThinkSoft's own witnesses as a "hostile witness"—that is, a witness friendly to ThinkSoft. Ostermyer is going to call Special Agent Jim McCloud, who runs the K-Nine investigations for ThinkSoft. He is the one who apprehended Lenny Milton for violating the no-commercial-use provision of the license agreement.*

STUDIO ANCHOR: *You mean a barbecue bust, . . . in a manner of speaking? What happened?*

TRIAL COMMENTATOR: *Agent McCloud confiscated Milton's grill. The priests at Mission Santa Tostada ended up buying him a new one. ThinkSoft insists its license and enforcement tactics are reasonable. We'll see how unreasonable Mr. Ostermyer can make this out to be.*

STUDIO ANCHOR: *Thanks for the preview, Ben. I can see there is going to be more sizzling action today in that San Jose courtroom!*

Before the jury was brought in, the judge addressed Will directly. "Did you speak to your client, Mr. Swanson?"

"I assure you I did speak to him, Your Honor," he said, standing up as he spoke.

"And does the plaintiff have anything to announce this morning?" the judge asked in a not-so-subtle hint at what he wanted to hear.

"Yes, Your Honor." Edwin stood up to intervene. "Plaintiff is pleased to announce that his next witness is Special Agent Jim McCloud, who is being called as a hostile witness."

"Fine. Just fine." The judge smoldered. "You've called the tune, Mr. Ostermyer; I hope you and your associate are prepared to pay the piper. Summon the jury."

Calling Field Agent McCloud presented no surprise for Crushjoy. Edwin had given written notification of his intention to call McCloud and formally requested that the witness appear at trial this morning. Crushjoy no doubt had prepared his witness for the questions he might be asked.

"Do you agree that Mr. McCloud is a hostile witness?" the judge asked Crushjoy. Appearing to be magnanimous, Crushjoy acknowledged that the Society of Manufacturers to Enforce Licenses was indeed a wholly owned subsidiary of ThinkSoft, and therefore Agent McCloud of SMEL was acting on behalf of ThinkSoft at the time of the incident.

McCloud, an ex-marine in his mid-thirties, strutted in as if he were still in uniform. He was wearing a no-nonsense cheap dark suit, white shirt, and dark tie. If the Drug Enforcement Agency had a DEA Retail Catalog, that's where McCloud could have bought his suit. When he stated his name and was sworn in by the clerk, he stood stiffly at attention with his hand up as though taking the oath to become a Green Beret. His impassive eyes were set deeply in his head and were almost as difficult to see as the blond hair on his all-but-shaven head.

Edwin was looking at a résumé of the witness. "So, Agent McCloud, I see that you were in the Marine Corps."

"Yes, sir." Although his demeanor suggested he hated his interrogator, it was instantly clear that his military training would make him a well-behaved witness.

"And in the Marine Corps you learned the importance of following proper procedure, didn't you?"

"Yes, sir."

"By the way, Agent McCloud, your résumé, which I show you and which has been marked into evidence, says *decorated Marine* on it. Let me represent to you that I have here a printout of your service record"—Edwin was waving around a report, documents delivered to him moments ago in the hallway, to demonstrate to the jury that ThinkSoft's attorneys were not the only ones doing in-depth background checks—"and it's true, isn't it, that the reference to *decorated Marine* is a false statement?"

"No, sir," McCloud responded, explaining in flat affect, "it's just incomplete. Somehow you must have gotten the first draft of my résumé. It should say *decorated Marine facilities.* My detail was to decide where the metal desks went, straight-back chairs, regulation file cabinets, flag with stand . . . depending on where the door was . . . for Quonset huts and portable field offices. It should also say that I received commendations for my decorating work."

"I see," said Edwin, eager to move on. "And you worked as an investigator for ASCAP, the American Society of Composers, Artists and Performers. Right?"

"Yes, sir. That's where I first began working to enforce intellectual property rights. I worked mostly in the food and beverage industry. I looked for bars and restaurants that had not secured necessary licenses from ASCAP to play members' music protected by copyright. I was later assigned to retail stores and shopping malls."

"And in working for ASCAP you again learned the importance of following proper procedure, didn't you?"

"Yes, sir."

"If you personally identified music performed in a bar that was controlled by ASCAP, you would document evidence of it before offering to let them pay for a license or filing suit against them?"

"Yes, sir. That was procedure."

"And then you went to work for SMEL, the Society of Manufacturers to Enforce Licenses, specifically the canine division thereof. Is that right?"

"Yes, sir. When Mr. Newman invited me to head up the K-Nine division of SMEL, I looked forward to the opportunity to get back into the food industry."

"Now, did you conduct an investigation as to whether license violations were occurring at the church picnic at Mission Santa Tostada?"

"Yes, sir. That is correct. I was driving back to headquarters at ThinkSoft when I became aware that there might be a Paragraph Four violation in progress at the church. I exited my field utility vehicle with my K-Nine officer to investigate. Paragraph Four forbids use of the Wholly Grill for any commercial purposes. Only ThinkSoft has the right to use it for profit."

"Even a church fund-raising barbecue where families, including the disabled and elderly, scrape together the small admission fee—maybe their last few dollars— and all the proceeds go to charitable causes designed to ensure the continuing dignity of humankind?" Edwin managed to stretch out the question in feigned disbelief.

"Yes, sir. An agreement is an agreement. The terms of the license must be strictly enforced."

Edwin breathed out a contemptuous guffaw. "The church must get permission from ThinkSoft?"

"Yes, sir. No exceptions, unless a written waiver is obtained from ThinkSoft in advance."

"So then, on the day in question, you arrived at the picnic and people were helping themselves from trays of cooked meats. Correct?"

"Yes, sir. The infringing barbecue was in plain view. Having determined that it was a violation of the license, I photographed the cooked meats with the grill unit of the Wholly Grill Outdoor Cooking Information System as a backdrop, and then I proceeded to effect repossession of Mr. Milton's system and confiscate the products of the unlawful enterprise."

"You repossessed the grill?" Edwin acted as if he hadn't read the shrink-wrap license a hundred times.

"Yes, sir. Paragraph seven says that any material violation of the license will result in repossession. That's the company's right. They own it."

Edwin shook his head to underscore the unfairness, then pressed on. "But on this occasion you didn't follow procedure. You had no way of establishing that the meats were barbecued on the Wholly Grill, did you?"

"They were laid out on trays next to the grill."

"But *you* didn't see them cooked on it, did you? You didn't witness it like the music that *you personally heard* when you worked for ASCAP. Isn't that right?"

"No, sir. That wasn't necessary. I did better. My highly trained K-Nine officer verified that the meat was Wholly Grill cooked."

"So!" Edwin was grandstanding. "Your testimony is that a dog told you it was Wholly Grill?"

"A highly trained dog. That was our top K-Nine officer on the western front, Dwight Eisenbowser."

"Your Honor, I move to strike the witness's statement. The only proof he can offer that the meat was cooked on a Wholly Grill is that he was so informed by a dog. It's classic hearsay."

Crushjoy rose and waved a dismissive hand. "Nonsense. The dog is not testifying. As the witness can further establish, the dog is essentially a highly trained precision instrument with extraordinary sensory capabilities. It is no different, but probably more accurate, than a police officer relying on a Breathalyzer for determining blood alcohol. It is perfectly legal and proper."

Judge Wetherborne had heard enough. "The motion to strike is denied."

"But Your Honor!" Edwin hesitated in the face of the judge's admonishing scowl. "Very well!" Edwin changed his tactic. "Then, if you are going to allow it, I have a right to examine the source of this information. Even if it's like a Breathalyzer, due process affords my client the right to examine the instrumentality relied upon."

A sidebar discussion ensued. Will had researched a related issue only a month before, and he was able to pull up from their trial notebook computer a string of cases irrefutably confirming Edwin's position. Reluctantly, the judge ordered that Dwight Eisenbowser be delivered to the courthouse. The dog was twenty miles away at K-9 headquarters in Saint Chip. The judge scheduled the dog to be available at 2 P.M.; there would be a short recess, followed by a few minor witnesses called by Edwin, with lunch in between.

Because Edwin immediately was on his cell phone at the break, Will did not have a chance to ask him exactly what he intended to do when the dog arrived. Dutifully he had set the stage for Edwin by coming up with the key research. But that was it. He was now determined to act on what had kept him awake all night, an idea that had ripened into a decision after the infuriating conversation with Edwin before the trial started. Things had managed to deteriorate further. Edwin was now going to cross-examine a German shepherd. Will stepped into a phone booth and called Sky.

Will left a message that he needed Sky in court the following morning and to please leave a voice mail message that he would be there. In the interim he would figure out how he would get it by Edwin. He then left a message on Persi's voice mail telling her he was bringing Sky in and imploring her to help turn the heat up on ThinkSoft, "whatever it takes."

While Edwin was still on the phone, Mr. Danning announced that the break would be extended another half hour because Judge Wetherborne had to attend to an emergency. While waiting for court to resume, an e-mail popped up on the trial notebook from Persi:

```
To: wswanson@ego-law.com
From: persivalentino@earthlink.net
Re: The Quest Continues
Great that you're calling Sky! You won't regret it.
"Whatever it takes." Yes! That's what I wanted to
```

hear. I'm exploring some uncharted directions and
invite you to join me. I've arranged to meet with
someone who doesn't know much about Wholly Grill but
I think knows a lot about the bigger picture. I
can't promise you this person has "evidence" of anything, but I'd like you to be there. Meet me at the
Marriott in Saint Chip by 5. Room is in my name.
Persi

Will welcomed the invitation. He had already decided he needed an excuse to leave the trial, even if it was to chase down a nonwitness. Anything had to be better than what Edwin had in mind.

Will spoke to Edwin outside the courtroom. "Persi wants me to meet her in Saint Chip. She's arranged a meeting with someone. I don't have any details yet, but there may be vital evidence. She needs me to be there."

"I need you here for a demonstration this afternoon I was about to discuss with you. Send Stanley down there," Edwin said, referring to the firm investigator who was trained to take statements from wit-nesses, draw diagrams, and take pictures of intersections.

"Sorry, but I have to be present. Why don't we have Stanley here for your demo?" Although he was curious as to what demonstration Edwin had in mind, Will did not ask, since that might suggest he was avail-able. Edwin called Stanley Harper about the demo, speaking to him in a hushed voice.

At 2 P.M., Dwight Eisenbowser, followed closely by Agent McCloud, barged into court on a taut leash, sniffing everything and everyone in reach. Under questioning from Edwin, McCloud explained that Officer Dwight was a five-year-old German shepherd, one of 250 dogs nationwide in the K-Nine division of SMEL and one of the first to be trained for Wholly Grill. Edwin questioned Agent McCloud about the identification procedure, and McCloud gave a demonstration of the dog correctly identifying one lamb chop cooked with Wholly Grill and one that was not.

"So let me review," Edwin summarized. "You give the dog the command HICK!—which is how you ask the dog, *yea* or nay, if it is Wholly Grill cooked meat. Is that right?"

"Yes, sir."

"And if the dog identifies it as Wholly Grill, he will bark twice and point with his right forepaw. Is that it?"

"Yes, sir. As he just demonstrated."

"And if the dog believes it is some other brand, he will sit still and do nothing?"

"Yes, sir. And that's what Officer Dwight just did with the other barbecued meat."

"Thank you, Agent McCloud. I would like to do my own verification now." Edwin turned and signaled to the back door. Into the courtroom rolled Stanley Harper with what appeared to be hotel room service. He wheeled his cart down the aisle and into the nave of the courtroom where Edwin was standing. Stanley pulled the warmers off of the two plates, revealing two grilled pork chops. A bottle of Bull's Eye barbecue sauce was displayed between the two plates.

Once again Will did not know what his boss was up to, not having been in the loop when Edwin decided on this piece of demonstrative evidence. He held his breath, hoping Edwin was not taking another ill-advised risk. Almost out of evidence and witnesses, Edwin was shooting entirely from the hip.

"I will represent to the court that this pork chop was cooked with Bull's Eye barbecue sauce on a regulation Weber grill." He sat the plate down in front of the dog, who was located on the floor in front of the witness stand between the jury and the judge; Edwin raised his right hand and commanded "Hick!" The dog made a passing sniff at the pork chop and sat on his hind legs, perfectly still.

"Thank you, Officer Dwight. I am now going to show you another pork chop, which I will represent to the court has also been cooked with Bull's Eye sauce on a regulation Weber grill but with one difference: As an experiment, the coals for this chop were sprinkled with not hickory sticks but unfiltered nicotine-laden cigarettes." Will braced for what might follow; perhaps Edwin thought he had little to lose. If Officer Dwight confirmed it was not Wholly Grill, Edwin was not really any worse off than before, given the judge's ruling. But if the dog identified it as Wholly Grill, aspersions would be cast.

Crushjoy looked up from some notes he was casually taking, but he remained inscrutable, unmoved by the demonstration. Art Newman, on the other hand, was scribbling on a pad of paper and whispering to Crushjoy at the same time.

Edwin placed the plate in front of the dog. He raised his right hand and asked, "Now isn't it true, Officer Dwight, that the pork chop you are now inspecting is Wholly Grill?"

"Objection, Your Honor!" Crushjoy was paying attention. "The question misstates plaintiff's own offer of proof; it lacks any foundation. Mr. Ostermyer just said it's *not* Wholly Grill!"

"This is cross-examination, Your Honor," Edwin countered. "I have a right to ask leading questions . . . and I haven't even finished the question yet."

The judge was not entertained by this sideshow. "Just finish the cross-examination, Mr. Ostermyer! The commands only. Be done with it!"

The jury's eyes remained fixed on the dog, the room service cart, and Edwin. The jury paid no attention to Art Newman's agitation, but Will could tell by Edwin's renewed delight that he had not missed it. Obviously pleased that he'd touched a nerve with Art Newman, Edwin raised his right hand again, this time with a dramatic gesture, and spat out the command: "Hick!"

The dog scanned the plate with his nose. He neither barked nor sat still. Instead he punctured the quiet in the courtroom with two brief but piercing whines, stepped lightly on both front feet, and looked at

McCloud as if for guidance as to what to do. He started to raise his right forepaw but, in a gesture reminiscent of Dr. Strangelove, just as quickly drew it back. He then whined again in shriller protest, his brow deeply vexed.

Edwin was exultant. "So, Officer Dwight Eisenbowser, you can't tell us one way or another whether you are beholding a Wholly Grill pork chop. Isn't that a fact?"

Officer Dwight sniffed the pork chop again, breathed out a deep groan of resignation, and rolled on his back, pawing the air, undoubtedly preferring to be scratched on his belly than badgered with perplexing questions. McCloud jumped up and came to the dog's rescue.

Edwin turned triumphantly to the court reporter. "Let the record reflect the facts as I have stated them!"

He turned next to the judge and clicked his heels. "No further questions!"

He then turned to the jury and bowed his head—once—slowly and with exaggerated self restraint, escalating the effect with each turn like a beloved stage performer taking a curtain call.

The judge bolted for his chambers after first calling a short recess—perhaps to allow time to have the plates and carts removed or perhaps he felt a sudden urge to get out of his own courtroom.

Will, who also couldn't wait to get out of the courtroom as fast as possible, packed his briefcase and told Edwin he needed to get going to meet Persi in Saint Chip if he wanted to make it through afternoon traffic. Edwin was still enjoying his afterglow and barely heard him. McCloud was leading Officer Dwight out of the courtroom on a leash; the dog paused a second to sniff, then whisked by Edwin, who was leaning back in his chair at counsel table, preening himself on his performance.

"*That's* what cross-examination is all about! Did you get a load of what I did with their star witness?" Edwin pressed, nodding toward the dog. "I ate him up!"

‹ 32 ›

Will left the courtroom a little after two-thirty although he needed less than forty-five minutes to make Saint Chip for his five o'clock meeting, so he decided to pay Lenny another visit at home.

As expected, Lenny was in the backyard when Will arrived. Lenny no longer tried to justify his excesses. He was beyond that. Nor was it like that first visit, or the visit in the office when he still seemed so thrilled by the new toy. Like the diners at Ratopia Restaurant that Persi had photographed, it was gratification without joy.

"Mr. Ostermyer said he'd call me when he wanted me back in court," Lenny said, following instructions unquestioningly.

Will didn't even know what Edwin had in mind. "Lenny," he began, "I guess you know we have . . . a lot of problems with the judge and your jury." That might have been an understatement, but he saw no point in saying it any more harshly.

"I know you're doing the best you can," Lenny said. He was a gentle soul. "But if we could just find a way to do something for Lady J. That's all I ever wanted," he added, in a voice fraught with pain and sadness.

Will nodded his head but didn't speak. What could he say? Everything had gone so far awry from that first meeting in his office.

"Make yourself at home," Lenny said. "I gotta run down to the cleaners and get another shirt if I'm going back to court today." His blue shirt was crumpled and sweaty from sitting in court and worrying. It had moons under his armpits the size of basketballs.

After Lenny left, Will gravitated to the patio's centerpiece, the Wholly Grill. Although pictures had been shown during the trial, there hadn't been any reason to roll the big black tech box into court and mark it with an exhibit tag.

Impulsively, Will reached out and pressed START, activating the dialup. When the screen asked for his password, he typed in LADYJ as Lenny had described to him. WELCOME, LENNYM27, it said, greeting him with Lenny's screen name. WHAT ARE YOU HAVING TODAY? it asked cheerfully. He couldn't resist a snide response. He typed in HUMAN SUFFERING and threw on one of Lenny's marinated sausages. He closed the lid and hit the GRILL command.

Instantly the screen responded: WE DO NOT RECOGNIZE HUMAN SUFFERING AS ONE OF YOUR REGULAR BARBECUE SELECTIONS, AND IT IS NOT WITHIN THE PURVIEW OF OUR DATABASE. PLEASE PROVIDE ADDITIONAL DATA SO THAT WE MAY USE OUR ANALOG TECHNOLOGY TO CONFORM WITH YOUR PREFERENCES. Following the ORDER and GENUS prompts, Will typed in PRIMATE and MAMMAL.

THANK YOU, LENNYM27. THE WHOLLY GRILL IS NOW DIGITIZING YOUR HUMAN SUFFERING AND TRANSMITTING IT TO THE WHOLLY WORD FOR PROCESSING. PLEASE STAND BY.

Will watched in morbid fascination as the screen displayed a constant stream of data—letters, numbers, graphs, diagrams—that meant nothing to him, along with banner ads for ThinkSoft reasonware and software products. After a few minutes a ring sounded, and the screen proudly announced: YOUR HUMAN SUFFERING HAS BEEN PREPARED TO PERFECTION! JUST THE WAY YOU, LENNYM27, WANTED IT. BON APPETIT!

Will opened the grill and stared at the bubbling meat, fried with lasers. It could have been Lenny's brains for all the computer cared.

Predictably, his caprice with the keyboard had plunged him into another bout of depression. ThinkSoft was getting away with crimes that could neither be seen nor proven. But that would have to change, and fast.

Approaching his destination, Will's eyes fixed upon a small official-looking sign he had never seen before, as many times as he'd driven these roads. It was newly attached below the larger, more familiar one:

WELCOME TO SANTA TOSTADA
"SAINT CHIP"

The words at the bottom of the welcome sign melded at the edge of his vision with a billboard right behind it hawking the latest PC, registering in a blur of geo/demographics: *pop. 12,980 alt. 1123 RAM 256MB lines of resolution 1024 x 768 battery life* . . . However, the smaller sign, the one that demanded his attention, he could not help but READ CAREFULLY:

By Entering Saint Chip and Accessing Its Publicly Financed Amenities, You Manifest Your Agreement to Abide by All Rules of the Road, Health/Safety Ordinances, and Private Property Laws, and, When Charged, You Agree to Reimburse the City Any and All Public Funds Expended in Your Successful Prosecution. Enjoy Your Visit!

Instinctively, he gunned the engine and blew on by.

The Marriott at Saint Chip was in the commercial hub on the western side of the sprawling ThinkSoft campus. On the other end of ThinkSoft, on the eastern side, was Old Santa Tostada, where the mission was located, and Old Town, the historic remnants of the original pueblo. The Marriott was located on hospitality row, comprised of four hotels, all of which faced ThinkSoft. The rest of western Saint

Chip, part of the Municipality of Santa Tostada, was covered by one-, two-, and three-story glass buildings, as well as sanitized white buildings, housing both the start-up and established high-tech businesses spawned by ThinkSoft. The fading sun, reflecting off the glass buildings, was just setting when Will pulled into the parking lot at the Marriott a few minutes after five.

Having called Persi from the lobby, Will knocked at her door. She opened it in her bare feet, wearing jeans and a casual shirt. Using both her hands to put on earrings, Persi held the door open with her foot. "I'm changing. I'm outa here in ten minutes. We've got a lot to talk about. Are you ready for this?" At the bedside table she pressed a key on her notebook that displayed an e-mail. "This is where I'm going."

He looked at a message she received a few hours ago.

```
To: persivalentino@earthlink.net
From: gamemaster@thinksoft.com
Re: Meeting
I would like to meet with you, too but you must be
alone, and it must be secret. I need to do some
reconnoitering of my own. Meet me where we met
before—in the basement of Building A at 5:30
tonight. The boiler room there is open. Go inside.
There is a small room that adjoins it from the
inside. Knock three times, then enter.
```

Will read the FROM line out loud. "Gamemaster at ThinkSoft?"

"Yeah, him!" Persi was shouting from behind the wall in the dressing area next to the bathroom.

"Who?"

"Remember I told you about the game *Secrets and Solutions* on the company network? I recalled that support questions were directed to that e-mail address. I took a flyer that it was Joon, and e-mailed him this morning."

"Joon Newman!" Will blurtcd out, stunned. "The co-founder of the company? Are you insane? You're meeting *him*?"

"That's right. That is, if he shows up."

"I don't believe it! You contacted him? What were you thinking?"

"I couldn't figure out why they chased me down in Los Angeles and not here at home. Remember the ThinkSoft lawyers said they were transmitting fingerprints electronically to an FBI lab to nail me? They wanted to file criminal charges against me immediately. My fingerprints are on those files, all right. What ever happened to that transmission? Possibly someone—with access, expertise, and a reason to do it—hacked into the ThinkSoft system and misdirected, or redirected, e-mail to and from the FBI. Who would do that? It could only be Joon Newman. Ever since that day I ran into him, I've thought he might like me, even though he knew I was a mole."

"I suppose it's possible," he said, still a little overwhelmed. "But you have no proof—"

"It's a leap of faith, I admit. But what do I have to lose? I have to do this."

"So what did you say in your e-mail?" He sat down on the bed, trying to take it all in. He was understanding for the first time that there might be more to the Persi–Joon encounter than security issues.

"First, I reminded him of how we met. By the way, he has nothing to do with Wholly Grill. That's Art Newman's baby. I'm hoping he cares, that even if he is a little emotionally . . . "—she waggled her hand—"he won't stand behind Wholly Grill if he learns the truth about it. I told him, without mentioning my connection to you or the lawsuit, about all the evidence I had that a nicotinelike substance might be involved in Wholly Grill." She emerged from the dressing area, presenting herself with a curtsy and a mischievous smile. "I just laid it all out for him."

To Will's astonishment, she was wearing a red charmeuse V-neck blouse and an elegant but tight black skirt . . . so tight, in fact, he couldn't help but notice it was slit well over half a foot up the side.

"What . . . is . . . this?" he mouthed slowly.

Persi laughed. "You like it? When I ran into him that day, this is what I was wearing."

"You never told me that."

"Since when did you take an interest in my clothes?"

"That's not the point. Why? Why this?" He was floundering.

"Look," she began, hand on hip. "I want to make sure he recognizes me, doesn't doubt I was the one he saw that day. He's a recluse, kind of skittish. I don't want him to take flight."

"*Recognizes* you?" he repeated. "Jeez, I sure hope he's able to pick you out of the crowd milling through that closet adjoining the boiler room."

"My God, Will, you're jealous, aren't you?" She was laughing a little, leaving her mouth open in exaggerated disbelief.

He suddenly realized that's exactly what he sounded like. "No, of course not." He backtracked. "It just seems so . . . unnecessary, that's all."

"Unnecessary?" She laughed. "Listen, if this will encourage him to talk to me and deal with the reality of what's going on at his company, believe me, it's necessary. Besides, with the company after me, what do I have to lose by contacting him? I'm hoping he's the eye of Hurricane ThinkSoft. If I'm wrong and he's there just to turn me in—well, at least I'm sure to be the best-dressed outlaw they've ever had."

Persi seemed fearless. What she said made sense. But the comment she challenged—that her dressing up was unnecessary—was precipitated more than anything else by a new awareness he was too embarrassed to identify. Persi mounted a pair of killer black stiletto heels and let her full weight—all 105 pounds—sink slowly into the carpet. His mixed emotions—about the case, about Persi, about her clandestine meeting with Joon Newman—were being stretched in so many unnatural directions, he nearly groaned out loud.

An unending moment of quiet followed Persi's last statement. "What's going to happen?" he finally asked.

"I don't know. I just told him I wanted to talk to him off the record. He hasn't spoken directly to the press, without his father present, since he was sixteen, and that was for *Teen* magazine. He may not show. Or it may be a two-minute meeting, and he's gone. I may be arrested, in which case I'll call you. Or maybe something will come of it. In any event I'm glad you're here. I may need you."

She was putting the finishing touches on her eye makeup and was going in for the matching red lipstick. Before today he had never noticed Persi's makeup for the simple reason it was so understated. During college it had been nonexistent. The coloring she wore tonight caused her light olive complexion to glow. He was confounded. He knew he should be thinking about evidence and the danger to which she was exposing herself; instead, he was thinking how her highlighted face reminded him of a favorite Botticelli painting.

Seated before the vanity mirror, Persi finished teasing her hair out a little, stood, and walked over to the full-length mirror. After viewing herself, she turned to him. "So how do I look?"

For a split second he vacillated between the complete truth and a serviceable half-truth—between *I've been sucker-punched by your killer beauty, leaving me breathless, sick, and begging for more* and—

"Terrific," he managed.

There was a knock at the door. Persi answered it and handed a delivery person a tip. "I assumed you would want to watch the rest of the afternoon court session. I asked the concierge to have it taped for you."

"You did? Thanks."

"Gotta go," she announced abruptly, looking at her watch. "Can you believe it? I've got a date with a twenty-two-year-old billionaire. Even if it doesn't work out, it's all about contacts here in the Valley, right? Wish me luck."

"Good luck with your . . . meeting." To his own surprise he could not bring himself to say the *d* word she'd used, even if she was being facetious. She opened the door, smiled, and waved at him on her way out. "I'll wait up for you," he added, in an effort to keep it light, but she was already gone.

He tried to focus on something else. He took off his suit jacket, turned on the television and VCR, and inserted the tape. He quickly fast-forwarded it to where he left the courtroom. Watching on television rather than from counsel table gave a very different perspective. Following a long commercial break right after Will had left and while the court was still in recess, the LNTV commentator picked up some action right outside the courtroom:

STUDIO ANCHOR: *Although the trial has not resumed, we have a report from our expert commentator, trial lawyer Ben Griswold. Over to you, Ben.*

TRIAL COMMENTATOR: *Thanks, Janet. I'm standing outside Judge Wetherborne's courtroom right now, the scene of a dramatic confrontation only moments ago. As they were leading K-Nine officer Dwight Eisenbowser out of the courtroom, another witness, plaintiff Lenny Milton, arrived with his dog—the one whose blinding injuries started this historic lawsuit—Lady J! We understand she's here to give some kind of demonstration about Wholly Grill. But when the two dogs faced off, they were straining at their leashes, having "words" with one another.*

STUDIO ANCHOR: *I'll bet that was quite a scene. What does it all mean?*

TRIAL COMMENTATOR: *Based upon my thirty-two years of experience as a trial lawyer and the fact that they were viciously growling and baring their teeth at each other, I can tell you it was something in the nature of mutual disapproval. Meanwhile, Eisenbowser has left the building while Lady J waits outside here until she's called as a witness, which we understand will be later this afternoon. Back to you, Janet.*

STUDIO ANCHOR: *My, my, do we have a dispute on our hands! Stick around, Ben, to give us more. We'd be flying blind without you to guide us through this trial.*

Uh-oh, Will thought. That's is why Edwin sent Lenny home to await

instructions. Edwin was taking more risks, hoping to cast more aspersions on ThinkSoft without offering much in the way of scientific
proof.

He fast-forwarded through the next witness—the substance of
whose testimony was not disputed by ThinkSoft—a distributor who
had sought permission from ThinkSoft to sell bottles of barbecue sauce
to retailers without the shrink-wrap license. Unlike old "economy"
stores, computer and electronics stores had become accustomed to,
and very comfortable with, selling software and electronic media with
shrink-wrap licenses. But grocery stores—which sold meats, vegetables, canned goods, and such—got nervous finding themselves to be
purveyors of vaguely defined intellectual property rights. They wanted
to sell the bottles of popular barbecue sauce, but they wanted to sell
them like Bull's Eye or Heinz. The distributor's request that the licenses
on the bottles be removed was emphatically refused by ThinkSoft.

He fast-forwarded the tape again, and the trial proceeded silently
with a real yet dreamlike quality devoid of the angst that had thus far
attached itself to his experience: extended sequences of lips moving
followed by comic herky-jerky movements around the courtroom. It
was all intimately familiar to Will, yet detached from what was now
occupying his consciousness: Persi and Joon Newman in a steamy
boiler room annex. A point of evidence must have been disputed,
because the tape ran a prolonged exchange with Edwin, Crushjoy, and
the judge outside the presence of the jury. Will did not hit the PLAY
button to find out what it was; he was more interested in playing out
the line of questions in his head.

What kind of exchange had there been between Persi and Joon
when they first met in the basement that day? Why hadn't she mentioned what she was wearing? How exactly had Joon looked at her?
Who in her position would not be interested in the prospect of a
liaison with the richest man in the world under twenty-five?

His thinking was so clouded by the strain of the trial and his newfound feelings for Persi that he only now realized he could run afoul of rules of legal ethics. Joon Newman was an officer of ThinkSoft; the rules prohibited Will from speaking to the opposing side if it was represented by counsel. If Joon showed up—a very big *if*—Will would have to excuse himself.

On the tape, Lady J was being led into the courtroom by Lenny. Will hit the PLAY button just as Edwin was addressing the court.

"We will begin this demonstration by observing the reaction of Lady J when exposed to a small amount of laser-cooked Wholly Grill Smoke Crystals reduced by one of the most prestigious chemical laboratories in the United States. To understand the scientific evidence, we reserve the right to expose her to actual nicotine-rich cigarette smoke and to have the hacking diagnosed and explained by a renowned doctor of veterinary medicine."

Stanley Harper handled the demonstration for Edwin. First he dumped the contents of Sky's vial of cooked Smoke Crystals onto a small flat tray. He then approached Lady J, who was sitting on the raised surface built into the front of the witness stand—the same surface upon which Crushjoy had left the tray of sandwiches for Lenny. A tiny amount of Smoke Crystals would have re-created the ambient cloud her sensitive nose had experienced at Lenny's the night before. Instead, Stanley aimed the tray at her nose an inch away, took a deep breath, and blew a dark cloud right at her.

Lady J gagged once. Her eyes rolled up toward the ceiling and she stiffened and then collapsed, falling from her perch to the floor. The jury gasped in horror.

Lenny jumped up and ran to the little dog, his hulking mass kneeling over her. Stanley Harper looked into the camera with a terrified expression, holding the tray gingerly balanced on the tips of his fingers as he cast about for a place to dump it. The television cameras were rolling.

A coroner appeared who'd been testifying in a murder trial down the hall. She bent over, checked for Lady J's pulse with two fingers, and then stood and solemnly announced, "She's dead."

"No!" Lenny burst out, tears flowing.

Judge Wetherborne adjourned court for the day and stalked off to his chambers, shaking his head. The jury filed out. As the day's coverage concluded, Will could see Art Newman and Thurston Crushjoy still inside, huddled together. There was an ease in their expressions—even in the way they gently shifted their weight as they spoke—that told him the progress of the trial was like a dream come true, especially with an enemy that was killing itself with friendly fire.

The LNTV studio anchor, before signing off, said that plaintiff's lawyer Edwin G. Ostermyer had reportedly run out of witnesses and would probably rest his case the following morning. Will knew it was true. In fact, if Lady J had not dropped dead, compelling the judge to adjourn immediately, Edwin would have been without any other witnesses. Without so much as a breath—much less a cough—from Lady J, there was no point in having the vet talk about her smoker's hack. The end of the case, in turn, would prompt the judge to commence with a decision on Crushjoy's motion for nonsuit, followed by more dreaded rulings.

As the credits rolled, the studio used as a backdrop an eerie freeze frame of Lady J at the moment of her demise. The expression told it all. Her blinded eyes were cast stoically upward as if, in an odd way, attempting to rise above the folly of human affairs. It broke Will's heart to see Lenny mourn the loss of his beloved friend and companion.

Will heard a rap at the door. He opened it to find Persi, still beautiful and seemingly alone. He was about to speak when a young man emerged from Persi's side. He was wearing navy blue sweat pants, a matching sweatshirt with the hood over his head, and comic-book-super-hero wraparound sunglasses. He reminded Will of the widely circulated Unabomber sketch but with updated shades. Persi and the young man hurried into the room and closed the door.

"Joon Newman?" Will asked, stunned.

There was no response. The young man walked over to the window, looked out, and then scanned the room nervously. Will could not believe he was in the presence of the inventor of Reasonware, a technology that had revolutionized the analysis of how business was transacted around the globe, how government decisions were made, how justice was administered, and how people managed their everyday lives. Although nobody would compare him to Kant, Hegel, John Stuart Mill, or the other great philosophers contributing to humanity's understanding of reason and logic, Joon Newman's engineering brilliance assured him a place of prominence in the same history books with those great masters of reason.

"Joon Newman, this is Will Swanson." Persi gestured toward Will and excused herself to use the bathroom. Will ordinarily would have walked across the room and extended a handshake, but he could see there was no point. Joon was distracted; the fingers on his hands were fidgeting as if manipulating imaginary controls. Compulsively he picked up the video remote that Will had left on the bed. He turned it on, did a lap through the channels, and turned it off.

"Who does your wardrobe?" Will asked, in an effort to break the ice.

"Did I overdo the incognito thing?" Joon grinned vaguely.

"It's OK, except bombing suspects never wear cool shades," Will replied, relieved that he could actually connect in some modest way with the famous visitor.

Joon's face took on a grave expression again. "These clothes are all you're given at this level. No weapons, no crystalizers. You're pretty much on your own," he conceded grimly. "Except for this." He lifted up his sweatshirt and showed Will a handheld computer strapped to a utility belt.

Will knew about computer games. In law school, when he needed to escape from the study grind, he had tried his hand at them. As a game contestant he too, at least for those few hours, had lived vicariously through heroic figures on the computer screen who were supplied with a finite amount of weaponry or more fantasy-driven accessories—like rings, potions, or stones with magic powers—for battling demons, solving puzzles, and dealing with a host of obstacles.

"What level are you talking about?" Will asked, unable to resist being drawn into this conversation spoken in tongues. "What game?"

"*This* one," Joon stated matter-of-factly.

Will ventured further. "What's the object?"

"To gather clues, to uncover secrets, to find answers in the adventurous quest for knowledge. To find the Holder." He opened the bedside drawer, picked up the Gideon's Bible, and, grasping it by the binding, shook it as if trying to dislodge something inside. Finding nothing, he became absorbed in a passage for a moment, then put it down. "There should have been a clue in there."

This exchange was too much for Will. He couldn't decide what he was dealing with, a paranoid schizophrenic, an idiot savant, or someone afflicted with a manageable form of autism. None of these amateur diagnoses offered an encouraging prognosis for meaningful dialogue. In this brief encounter, Joon Newman's mental clarity seemed to flicker episodically between all there, a little there, and not at all there, like an unnerving fluorescent light—the kind that, with enough tortuous waiting, will eventually either come on, burn out, or drive a person insane.

Will was reminded of a debate he had followed that raged among game developers: Could computer games ever compete for the public's favor with mainstream storytelling art forms like books or movies? They carried a plot line and brimmed with action and spectacular effects. But, according to the naysayers, there was something critically, almost painfully, missing: Computer games were devoid of emotion.

It was not for Will to ponder now. His time was up. "I hate to be the rude host, but the fact is that rules of ethics forbid me as Lenny

Milton's lawyer to speak to you, an officer of ThinkSoft, since your company is represented by attorneys. As Persi has no doubt told you, I come from the otherworld, the world of trial lawyers. But that's my problem, not yours. You're welcome, of course, to stay here with Persi." Will was aghast to hear himself invite the competition to stay the night in a hotel room with the woman he wanted. Sometimes it more than just hurt a little to do the right thing, it sucked.

"Wait!" Joon said.

He pulled back the hood of his pullover, revealing a wild tuft of strawberry-blond hair sprouting out of the top of his head. Fumbling awkwardly, he removed his dark glasses and replaced them with a pair of thick bifocals he was wearing around his neck under the pullover. Behind the boyish look, the nervous gestures, and the thick glasses, Will could see intelligent eyes, narrowly focused but far removed.

"I need your help to get through this," Joon added.

"You need *my* help?" At least for the moment, Will abandoned his attempt to distinguish whether Joon was describing his path through the levels of the imaginary game he was playing or something else.

"I know all about the rules of the game," he said, evidently referring to Will's concern for legal ethics. "The rule you refer to doesn't apply here if there's a waiver."

"That's true. So?" Will replied. Oddly, when Joon became more lucid, Will became even more confused. There were many too many games going on, all with complicated rules and level upon level of play.

"I have reason to believe that at my level—the highest level that's been achieved—you learn that the Sorcerer and the Manufacturer of the game are one and the same. There is a systemwide error, a manufacturing defect, but the game is so defective I am not getting the message from the operating system alerting me to the error. It's a monstrous bug! I am going to have to hack into the operating system of the game myself to find out if my hunch is right." He caught his own image in the full-length mirror and seemed startled. "I'm going to have to fix the defect myself. The Sorcerer is cheating, So your rule doesn't apply."

"I'm not following. Who is the Manufacturer?" Will was stubbornly behaving as though he were involved in a sensible conversation.

When Persi emerged from the bathroom, Joon, without excusing himself, drifted in and closed the door.

"So far, I figured out that his father is the Sorcerer," Persi whispered. "His father is also the Manufacturer of the game . . . and of him. You know, procreation is a form of manufacturing." She rolled her eyes, as did Will. "I know," Persi continued. "I'm not sure if anyone is home . . . or, if so, who it is. But this much I understand from him. He believes there may be some kind of crime against life going on at ThinkSoft. He seemed concerned about all the details I gave him—particularly the lab rats. I think they are the Creatures of the Realm. As far as your talking to him is concerned, he's saying he thinks there's a crime going on and he urgently needs to have us help him investigate. Because a crime might be involved, he's saying your rules don't apply."

"You've been able to figure all that out?" Will asked incredulously.

"I had a head start. By the way," she whispered, "I was right in guessing that he stymied Security's computer information about me."

If Persi was also right about Joon's remarks, Will was dumbfounded, not just because of their eccentric nature or even the reference to a crime in progress. Joon's complete comprehension of a fine point of legal ethics astonished Will. Although he spoke from a strange and distant place, it was possible Joon's spongelike mind had learned as much law in one afternoon of speed reading as Will had learned in three years of immersive study.

"What kind of help do you need from me?" Will asked, when Joon emerged from the bathroom.

Joon produced a large map from under his shirt and spread it out. On it was printed a fanciful rendition of the ThinkSoft campus, but the name ThinkSoft appeared nowhere. Instead, in medieval type, it was entitled Map of the Kingdom.

"My best strategy right now is to break into the castle. The rules say I have a right to go wherever I want in the kingdom." Joon picked up a pen and drew a line from the western edge of the campus, where they were located, to a building labeled CASTLE; he circled it. Will assumed the castle was Building RD 1 in Joon's alternate world. Unquestionably, the "rules" allowed him to go wherever he wanted at the company; he was an owner and executive officer. "But there's a deadly risk if I go into the castle through the front gate," he warned. "The Sorcerer will be alerted, and that will mean heavy losses for all of us. We need to get into the castle without the Sorcerer's being alerted. I need your help to do that."

"What's the rush?" Will sensed from Joon's fidgeting there had to be some kind of hurry.

Joon replied grimly. "Just a short while ago, I used my dwindling allotment of all-access magic to post a query on the kingdom network searching all databases for secret information. The query was FIND: WHOLLY and/or GRILL and SECRET."

Joon assumed a brave pose.

"When the Sorcerer becomes aware of what I have done, all existing secret information will be covered up, if it hasn't been hidden already." He turned to Will. "Can you help me?"

"Don't worry, he'll come with us," Persi assured Joon, without looking at Will.

"If you're telling me you need my help, let's go." Will had made up his mind before Persi's coaxing. He owed it to Lenny.

It was six-fifteen when they left the hotel, walking briskly across the ThinkSoft compound to the eastern side where Building RD 1 was located. It was getting dark, but the pathways and buildings were well lit. Joon wore the hood up on his sweatshirt. Will, still in his suit and tie, walked on one side of Joon and Persi walked on the other side. Before embarking on their mission, Persi had changed into her old janitor clothes. She hoped that if she were found somewhere off limits, she would be in a better position with an employee uniform on to lull Security into believing she had a right to be there.

In the back of Building RD 1, Joon directed them to a huge metal plate lying flat on the ground, an industrial trapdoor designed to be raised by a machine for making basement deliveries. Joon glanced around to make sure no one was watching. "We can get into the basement from here. The three of us should be able to lift the door after I disable the electromagnetic lock mechanism." It seemed the more Joon became focused on a task at hand, the more coherent his speech became.

Joon whipped out the small computer attached to his belt and began tapping away. The giant plate popped up about an inch, signifying that he had successfully hacked into the controls and released the electronic magnet that held the door shut.

"There should be a garbage can within thirty feet we can use," Joon said, staring at his screen. But Will had already seen the sturdy plastic prop and dragged it over on its side.

The three of them struggled to lift the metal plate and finally managed to raise it nearly three feet. Persi let go and, under Joon's direction, rolled the garbage can underneath; the others eased the trapdoor down. The can squished but was sturdy enough at its base to leave a gap that was just enough to crawl through.

They scrambled under the metal door one at a time on their bellies, stood up, and walked down a ramp to an unlocked door leading into a basement hallway. Joon checked for activity and signaled for them to follow him through the door and down the hall.

"There's a security guard on the top floor where both elevator and stairs enter the floor," Persi whispered to Joon. "How are we going to get by him?"

"Yes, the human moat," Joon said. His right hand formed into a fist and moved stiffly and precisely in the space in front of his chest, as if he were using an imaginary joystick to guide them away from the obstacle. "There's a way, a small utility elevator that goes all the way to the top floor into the main lab where the Wholly Grill electronic nerve center is located."

Joon was not kidding when he said small. The utility elevator was a glorified dumbwaiter—a box five feet wide, three feet deep, and three feet high, not designed for people-moving.

"I'll need to go first," Joon said. This made sense. If someone were in the lab when Joon emerged from the utility elevator, he was in a better position to justify his presence in the secret lab than an undisguised intruder or Persi, even in her uniform.

About to break into the high-security lab, Will felt surprisingly calm. He'd endured three days of Edwin, Crushjoy, and Judge Wetherborne tapping out his adrenal glands, perhaps to the point of desensitization. Joon, on the other hand, was plainly agitated, a strange circumstance for a company official who had a right to be in the building. How much of his agitation was attributable to being mentally disturbed, to justified trepidation about his father, or to his preoccupation with the imaginary game was difficult to say.

Joon climbed into the utility elevator, reached out to press the button for the eighth floor, and closed the sliding door. A minute later Will and Persi both sighed in relief to hear the elevator being returned to the basement; the coast must be clear. Persi went next, followed by Will.

The utility elevator was pitch-black inside and moved slowly, but it provided nonstop service directly into RD 807, the large lab room Persi had cleaned several weeks earlier. When Will climbed out of the elevator, he could see the three large glass cases that contained the Wholly Grill experimental rats. He could also see that Joon must have finished inspecting them. He was plainly disturbed by the animal mistreatment he had now seen for himself. "Creatures of the

Realm are being abused. We must stop it," he said, more determined than ever. "Follow me."

Joon led them into an adjoining room that was filled with computers and unfamiliar electronic devices. The first thing he did was rifle through the file cabinets. When he saw files he liked, he would copy them with a scanner built into his handheld computer and put them back. Persi snooped around the room looking at the electronics while Will stood and watched Joon.

After Joon had scanned a number of files, he walked over to a large computer and signaled for Will to join him. "This is the main server for Wholly Grill. Here I will find a complete backup to the Wholly WORD." He reached around behind the computer and pulled out a black electronic device, roughly the size and shape of a cigar tube with copper plating on one end.

"What's that?" Will asked.

"Knowledge. It's the next-generation information storage device. It's called an *information vessel* because it's hollow. Here." He handed it to Will. It had a hard plastic casing but was lightweight and hollow inside.

"This thing backs up the entire Wholly WORD database?" Will asked, amazed. Persi peered at it from the side.

"Yeah," Joon said. He did not appear to be boastful or even proud of having developed another breakthrough technology. He seemed dissociated from it. "The inside wall of an information vessel contains holograms from billions of combinations of intersecting microscopic lasers. Just one info vessel can hold a million phone books. It's pure information."

"Wow," was all Will could say. He didn't want to seem ignorant by asking Joon what he meant by *pure* information, so he said, "What does it do? What's in it?"

"That's my mission to find out," Joon said. "The Wholly WORD should be contained in that information vessel. The Wholly WORD is what drives the Wholly Grill."

Will started to hand the information vessel back to Joon but was motioned off. "You hold it," Joon said, pulling a little at the side of his sweat pants to show he did not have any pockets.

Back in the lab room, Joon climbed back into the utility elevator first, again to make sure the coast was clear in the basement. Waiting quietly with Persi in the lab room, Will heard only the receding whir of the elevator stopping eight floors below and making its return.

When the elevator returned, Persi took off her shoes and climbed in. Will put the information vessel in his pocket so he could close the sliding door and activate the elevator. He was about to hit the basement button when he heard a noise from the hallway outside. A security guard! Although the nightlights in the lab were dim, the guard had no difficulty seeing the figure of Will at the far wall.

"Hey, you!" the guard shouted, rattling the glass doors. He drew his radio and started fumbling for his keys to get into the lab.

Will thrust the elevator door open and pulled Persi out. "We've got company!" he said. "We're riding tandem."

Persi looked startled, but then she saw the security guard too. "I know that guy!" she whispered hoarsely. "Blanchard. A total jerk!"

Will sprang into the elevator, flat on his back, with his head crooked up against the wall. Persi jumped on top of him belly-side down, reached out to hit the button, and slid the door shut. Just as the lab door flew open, the elevator began to move. They held their breath in the complete darkness.

"Burglary in progress in RD Eight-oh-seven!" Blanchard shouted into his radio. "Two suspects—one possible male, one possible female—headed for basement or ground floor in utility lift."

It was quiet now, but there was no way of knowing if Blanchard had left the room or was putting his ear up to the elevator shaft to listen for clues. Will started to breathe, as did Persi, her weight settling on him. Although he could not see her face two inches from his, the smell of her perfume and her warm breath was too much to stay focused on their serious predicament.

"Damn!" They heard Blanchard's muffled cry, self-flagellating and whiny, from two floors above them. Spontaneously, Persi and Will started to giggle.

Then they were silent for a moment. Persi's voice was first to venture into the darkness. "One *possible* male?" she asked. "Is that an information vessel I feel, or are you just glad not to see me?" She was whispering and giggling at the same time.

"Which one?"

"That one"—shifting her weight just enough.

When the elevator door opened, they both climbed out, still giggling a little.

Joon stared at Persi, temporarily speechless. "Are you people crazy? I heard the human moat through the shaft that leads to the tower. Let's go!"

"How are we going to get out of here?"

"The same as any other information storage and retrieval device. Garbage in, garbage out," Joon said. Will looked to see if he was trying to be funny. He wasn't.

The three of them backtracked to the door where they had entered. It was too late. They could hear the sound of barking security dogs nearby. Joon and Will hurried to the top of the ramp and peered out the trapdoor. A dog straining at his master's leash less than thirty feet away caught their scent; he was released and charged at them, barking fiercely. He would have squirmed under the plate and sunk his teeth into one of them, but Will and Joon yanked the garbage can toward them, causing the heavy door to fall with a decisive thud.

"Now what do we do?" Will gulped, his giddiness evaporated.

Joon pulled out his computer and conducted some quick calculations. "Escape," he said. Back in the hallway he ducked into a janitor's closet. Finding a flashlight and a mop, he hurried down the hall to a boiler room with Will and Persi at his heels, past the "real" elevator, which would soon be descending from the first floor to the basement with reinforcements.

In the boiler room Joon motioned for them to follow him to the far side, where a door to an outdoor stairwell led to ground level. He began furiously rubbing his hands all over the push bar on the door. "Need to distract the dogs to give us time," he said to the other two. He turned. Will could hear him mutter to himself, "I'll outsmart the Sorcerer yet."

Joon then commandeered a four-wheel dolly near the door, and, using the mop as an oar, he knelt on it and "rowed" himself over to a remote corner of the room. Standing on a metal grate, he pushed the cart back and threw the mop at Will. With Persi in position on the dolly, Will was about to reach down for the mop. Unknown to him, the information vessel had been creeping up and out of his front pocket. When he leaned over to pick the mop up for Persi, it fell out and onto the floor. Instinctively Persi reached down and picked it up.

Barking dogs and men's voices resounded at the end of the hall.

"Careful with that!" Will said.

Just then Will saw a frightful registration in her face, the E-Serum seizure she'd described to him that would cause her to rat on herself. Persi stood up on the dolly.

"This belongs to ThinkSoft! I have no right to this! I must tell them where we are!" She stepped down off the dolly on her way to the hallway. "This is the Wholly WORD—"

Will grabbed her and wrested the vessel away from her before she could get to the hallway.

"*I'm* holding on to this!" he said. She was still stunned, but he managed to get her back to the dolly and guided the two of them across the room to the grate where Joon awaited them. With a shove of Joon's foot, the dolly with the telltale scent was rolled back in front of the door as a decoy.

With the dogs approaching the near end of the hall, Will and Joon lifted the grate up. Persi jumped first, then Will, followed by Joon, dropping about twelve feet onto some loose, forgiving soil. As each rolled away from the landing spot, they gathered together in a corner of a dark space. They could hear dogs with men burst into the boiler room. There was a pause (dogs sniffing?), then barking again (dogs at the door handle), followed by quiet, all masterfully directed by Joon. *Exeunt omnes*.

Joon turned his flashlight on and pointed it at Persi. "What force possessed you back there?"

"E-Serum. I was—am—a guinea pig."

"What kind of receiver are you wearing?" he said.

"Receiver?" she repeated.

Joon inspected her all over with the flashlight, settling on the outline of the oversized ThinkSoft employee badge she had put in her back pocket.

"Let me see that," he said. He examined it carefully with the light. "It's a receiver *and* a retransmitter, targeting neuro receivers in the brain," he announced, tracing some otherwise inexplicable raised lines on the back of the badge with a stylus from his utility belt.

"Oh, my God! So *that's* why I didn't sing for the creeps in Los Angeles when they zapped me from the helicopter. The badge wasn't on me," Persi realized.

"I did some research into electronics and neurophysiology two years ago. We were going to use the R and D for some medical applications. Then I was told the project was scrapped. Instead, they used the research for this." Joon was grim.

"How does it work?" Persi asked.

"You have to be touching or connected to the retransmitter and have a conscious thought that you are holding ThinkSoft property without authorization. With that, the effect is analogous to a truth serum. Take this," he said, handing her back the badge. "Can't leave it here. They will find it. Take it with you and then get rid of it. Be careful. The transmitter must have a reach of twenty miles, so don't touch any ThinkSoft property."

SECRETS OF THE WHOLLY GRILL

"Count on it," Persi promised.

Joon went over to another area and began poking around in the dirt with the tail end of the mop. "Here it is," he announced. "We need to scrape the dirt away from this. Gamemaster used this years ago when the Kingdom was built. Getting to another level is our only way out now."

Joon was fully adrift in his alternate world, having emerged for a few moments to examine the security badge. Once again, Will noticed that when Joon was presented with a technical question or grounded by a specific task, his freewheeling identity was at least temporarily suspended.

They removed enough dirt to uncover an old three-foot-square piece of thick plywood. When they lifted the piece of wood, the flashlight revealed another open space sloping about ten feet down. Becoming adept at interpretation, Will now understood Joon's last Gamemaster remark. It refered to himself. When ThinkSoft was built, young Joon put plywood over this hole in the ground but probably hadn't been back in years.

They each crawled through; Joon replaced the plywood overhead. At the end of the slope, and with the flashlight creating fantastic illusions around the walls, they found they had descended into what was the end of a long narrow tunnel.

"Where the hell are we?" Will asked.

"*Bienvenido a la casa de las almas eternas.*" Joon spoke slowly and with a native Spanish accent. "Welcome to the House of Eternal Souls. I am Evangelina Morales." Joon had taken his thick glasses off and pulled his hood back over his head. "I hold knowledge."

"Who are you?" Will wanted to know. He glanced at Persi: *Here we go. We're getting into this deeper and deeper.*

"That's the birth name of Santa Tostada," Persi told Will. With the glasses off and the dark hood up, Joon's boyish face did resemble a cowled nineteenth-century nun.

"I will be your guide in these parts," Joon said, in a thick Spanish accent, squinting his eyes as if in touch with deep truths. He had *become* Santa Tostada. She was his avatar. True to form, avatars are typically colorful characters, acting as cyber agents for real people—but they were supposed to be digital. Will had never seen one in the flesh.

"We are in the catacombs of Santa Tostada," Persi said. "The catacombs stretch to nearly a half mile radius around the mission. Some of it—like where we are now—reaches into the property sold to ThinkSoft. I've seen the deeds. Where there were catacombs, the priests spelled out that they were only selling the surface ground. They didn't want to sell any of it, but they needed the money for their relief work."

"This is the world I now inhabit, a mere shade," Santa Tostada announced. "I have been expecting you."

The last remark gave Will the chills. Signs of death were everywhere. Joon's game, if it was one, was turning toward the macabre. He was pointing the flashlight beyond where the three of them were standing, into spaces no more than six feet high. The long narrow passageway was punctuated with recesses carved out from the walls on either side, entire families buried together behind simple stone vaults.

"Come, let me show you," Joon's newest manifestation invited them.

Without the slightest hesitation, Will yielded to the deepened surrealism. What choice did they have? Clicking SAVE and exiting the game was not an option. Both he and Persi were entirely dependent on Joon to find their way out, by whatever means he offered.

They set out along the tunnel, "Santa Tostada" leading with the flashlight, using the mop as a walking stick. After a stretch of some fifty yards, they stopped. The saint pointed out that they were standing in the oldest portion of the catacombs, where natives of the valley were interred.

"The ones you see were buried here long before I walked this valley. They believed in two gods who controlled *la vida y la vida futura*, life and the afterlife," their guide explained. "The God of Ideas, who controlled all waking activities of human life, was both revered and feared. No human act was without an idea behind it. He could visit terrifying ideas on the lives of humankind, or he could give to the living new and useful ideas for farming, hunting, toolmaking, and building, without which the human race would not survive." The cowled nun straightened her posture momentarily in a quiet gesture of righteousness and announced, "The formula I liberated from the mercenaries, to be rid of the corn blight, was such an idea.

"But the God of Ideas was a jealous god—*muy envidioso*—who vied against another god, the God of Sleep, who reigned over both slumber and the afterlife, a merciful and kind god who gave rest to weary humans. In order to have rest, the God of Sleep only asked that humans let go of all the ideas that troubled them." In keeping with the historical figure, Joon's avatar was highly educated and spoke both English and native Spanish.

"Let me guess," Persi said with delight, apparently reveling in the notion that she was communing with the heroine she long admired. "The God of Ideas asked for something in his name? A burnt offering?"

"*Sí*." The saint nodded with lugubrious determination. "*El temor.* Fear. People's ideas that they would die, that they would fail, that they would be forgotten, to name a few. This put them in their place. This was homage to him."

"Sounds like a kind of existential slavery. How depressing." Will shook his head. Was there any escape, any room for the human spirit?

Their guide held the flashlight under her chin and pointed it up, illuminating her face beatifically against the dark walls of the catacombs. "The merciful God of Sleep was the giver of dreams. You see, since dreams are born of sleep, they were not the domain of the God of Ideas. To be sure, he both hated and coveted what was not his. The people were free to take their dreams into their daily lives and build upon them without having to cede any rights to the God of Ideas." There was a pause and a flicker of pain, perhaps a glimpse of the real person behind the avatar. "They, at least, could have their dreams, and their spirits could be lifted." The fingers twitched slightly.

Will noticed that where the tops fastened on each of the small wooden coffins and the larger more deluxe sarcophagi, they were sealed with an imprimatur of wax, below which was an identical stone-engraved inscription in the alphabet of a dead language. "Do we know what this says?" Will asked, pointing to the inscription.

"*If ye should open this and look upon the face of death, ye shall enter into a covenant of death with the God of Ideas,*" the avatar saint recited, in a tone that revealed a moral repugnance for such arrogance.

"In other words," Persi elaborated, "if you open the coffin and look upon the body inside, you will be tormented to the point of insanity or death by horrible ideas . . . like terror, visions, and hallucinations. It's a time-honored—and still exceedingly popular—convention for controlling people."

Will laughed. "Think about it! The God of Ideas was the first in Silicon Valley to ship product with shrink-wrap licenses."

"Yeah, the old coffin-wrap license." Persi laughed. "And as high-handed as ever."

Will turned to their guide. "But what did he gain? There's nothing of value inside."

"The God of Ideas watches over his province, always on watch for control, to make what belongs to no one his," the saint explained. "What he can't control, he controls the ideas about. He never sleeps."

After another thirty yards they walked through a heavy wooden door. Persi explained to Will that the old catacombs were separated from the ones used by the Christian natives of the mission buried where they were now standing. Sure enough, they started to see crosses and Christian artifacts, signaling their arrival in the new catacombs. Santa Tostada stood in front of a large sepulchre as still as a statue and stared distantly. Persi read the inscription in Spanish and translated.

"It says this is the tomb of Evangelina Morales: *Beloved among the people as Santa Tostada.* She was the last person to be buried in the catacombs. In 1849."

"My time is fading. Up those stairs to your next level," Joon's avatar announced, pointing the flashlight to a stone staircase twenty-five yards away. Then the saint looked at Will. "I hold knowledge. What is it you want to know?"

Will had become so caught up in the adventure, he'd forgotten it was only so real. He wanted to be a sport and play along. He also sensed he was being encouraged to ask questions about what he *really* wanted to know.

"What should I do?" Will asked. A single open-ended question— the kind mediums like—was what was called for. There was nothing to pin down. This was a long way from a courtroom.

Just then they heard the sound of dogs through the half-open door coming from the end of the passageway they had entered. The dogs had doubled back and picked up their scent.

"Go with what you have." Santa Tostada spoke in earnest. "Everything you need is right in front of you."

Will glanced down the passageway just as the board that covered the hole fell down to the ground. Flashlights washed the dark interior. The dogs, louder now, seemed to be screaming, *They're in there! They're in there!*

"Let's hit it," Persi declared.

Will nodded at the sound of the dogs. With the behemoth ThinkSoft breathing down their backs, he nonetheless asked another question. "How do you deal with forces more powerful than you?"

Santa Tostada slammed the large wooden door. Ever resourceful, she seized the mop, like a magic staff, and used it for a doorstop, with the head propped against the door and the handle end buried in the dirt. "The mercenary was easily fooled, thinking I was just an old woman with a basket of tortillas. He believed, to his undoing, that I was unable to read or devise. Because of that, I was able to gain the knowledge that would eradicate the blight and save the people." The humble nun stood up and brushed the dirt off of her knees. She looked directly—and with a saint's ardor—into Will's eyes. "They will under-estimate you. That is your advantage. Use it as I did."

There was a bang and rattling against the door. The dogs' piercing whines announced how close they were to the three intruders.

Joon pointed to Will's pocket. "You can't have that. Give it to me now!" The accent was gone. Santa Tostada had vanished. Will reached into his pocket and handed over the information vessel.

"You asked me—" Will started, almost apologetically.

"Out of time!" Joon shouted urgently, pushing Will and Persi toward the stairs. "To the next level! Then select EXIT! Go now!" Men were pushing against the door; the staked end of the mop was moving in the dirt, about to give way.

Joon held the flashlight in one hand, pointing toward the stairs. When Will reached the stairs, two steps behind Persi, he turned around and saw Joon begin to make his way down a dark passageway, moving away from them. Ten yards out, he took off his sweatshirt and threw it down another passageway—a red herring for the dogs—and continued until he dissolved into black.

The stairs led up to the sacristy of the mission. It was a little after seven; Will could hear the murmur of the six-thirty mass in Spanish still in progress. He and Persi emerged from behind and to the side of the altar. The priest was raising the sacramental chalice, but he didn't seem to notice them.

A small door in the front was marked with a modern electronic EXIT sign, just as Joon had promised. They ducked out of the church. A cab was pulling up with two tourists arriving to take flash pictures of Old Town—the mission surrounded by white buildings with Spanish tile roofs and flanked by palmettos. Before the tourists could close the door, Persi and Will had jumped into the backseat.

"The Marriott," Will instructed the driver.

‹ 33 ›

```
To: sky@peoples-chem.com
From: wswanson@ego-law.com
Re: Testifying As An Expert Witness
I left a recording on your answering machine, and
I'm sending you this to make sure you got my mes-
sage. I urgently want to take you up on your offer
to testify. Would you meet me in court tomorrow
before 9? Please e-mail me or leave a message on my
office voice mail to let me know you can make it.
Thanks, Sky. I really need your help.
```

Will sat on the edge of the bed in the hotel, read the e-mail he had composed on Persi's notebook, and then pressed SEND. When he heard a knock, he got up to answer the door. It was Persi; she had gone straight to her car to retrieve a bag when they arrived back at the Marriott. She had decided to stay there overnight rather than drive north. Will was going back to the office to work up a direct examination of Sky.

"Did you get hold of Sky?" she asked.

"I left another phone message, and I e-mailed him."

"So will you be able to get him on the stand when he appears?"

"I can force Edwin's hand only if Lenny backs me up. And Lenny was pretty excited the other night about what we discovered. He's the client. It should be his call."

"What changed your mind?" she asked.

"I did a lot of thinking today. Edwin's out of control, a case of crash 'n' burn just like you called it. I have to step in and do whatever I can for Lenny. I owe it to him. That means I gotta go with what I have. Sky is what I have."

"Sky will be terrific!" she effused, obviously pleased that Will had come around. "And I'm glad you're heeding the advice of your elders: *Go with what you have.* That's what I heard you being told by—"

"Joon. Or was it really Santa Tostada?" he filled in. "Or did I imagine the whole thing?" He shook his head in disbelief.

Persi laughed as she slipped off her shoes. "Was that unreal or what?"

"Unreal," he agreed. "You were right in not promising me any evidence would come of this. But it was worth it. I'm not sure what I can tell Edwin I did after I skipped out on him. I'm not sure, even if I could tell anyone about it, I'd be able to explain it." He took another deep breath to underscore his wonder. "An unforgettable few hours. The most brilliant multifaceted character I've ever . . . interacted with."

"Interacting? You sound like you didn't actually exit play-mode back at the mission after all," she kidded him. "What kind of real-life computer game was that anyway?"

He pondered a moment. "Adventure and virtual reality. But if you're looking for it in the store, you'll find it in the edutainment section."

"*Edutainment?*" she echoed, amused. "And why is that?"

"It was much more than entertainment."

The truth was that the Joon experience was rapidly dissolving into the back of his mind. Persi was standing in front of Will right now. Before embarking on their adventure, she'd hastily changed out of her elegant skirt and into the baggy pair of janitor pants; underneath, her bare feet were still tightly wrapped in nude-colored hose. He desperately hoped she was interested in the same kind of information he was. He looked into her face for a sign.

"It was highly educational. That is to say, its content was loaded with *information*," he embellished, tongue firmly in cheek.

"What kind of *information*?" she asked, catching on and playing along.

"*Pure* information," he said, in a mock-serious tone, drawing a smile of mischievous delight from her.

Then their eyes connected. At a million bits per second. The advice to go with what he had now carried only one all-consuming meaning: THE GREEN LIGHT. Inside that moment those bright hazel eyes owned him completely. Instinctively, he moved toward her and put his arms around her. She reached a hand out behind his head, and they pulled each other in.

They held a long drenching kiss . . . contact between two live wires standing in a pool of warm water. For Will it was shock treatment, welcomed with open arms, numbing his overtaxed brain. He felt one thousand volts of hot-swappable charge from his head down through the lower extremities, electrifying every piece of conductive metal in the room. Embracing, they fell back on the bed, spontaneously peeling like a couple of overripe oranges.

At that moment the screen saver on Persi's nearby laptop computer activated on its own, revealing a pageant of flying toasters and household appliances with wings drifting through cyberspace and off the edges of the display terminal. At the same dream-begotten moment, and borne by natural electricity, the computer screen morphed into a much larger 3-D multi-streaming media sequence of flying shirts, pantyhose, and underwear sailing in slow motion to the corners of the room. Will reached up to squeeze the brightness control on the bedside lamp—dimming it, then dimmer still—until all that remained were two glowing icons, now merged together, brightly embedded against a field of darkness . . . .

‹ 34 ›

A phone rang. Will opened his eyes, startled. Wherever he was, whatever was going on existed in the uncharted world, between sleep and . . . .

"Hullo?"

He heard Persi's groggy voice and instantly remembered just enough of where he was and what he was doing to be comforted.

"It's for you."

"Huh? Who is it?"

"A woman. Don't know," Persi muttered, handing him the phone and collapsing back into a pillow.

"Hello?" Will mustered. The bedside clock said 4:30. He and Persi had finally succumbed to sleep about four hours ago.

"Will Swanson, this is Angela De Nuevo—De Nuevo and Cooper. I'm calling because. . . . I'm sorry, can you please hold for one second?" Muffled voices could be heard.

Will knew the name well. Angela De Nuevo was one of the most respected lawyers in Silicon Valley. One of Silicon Valley's very few Hispanic lawyers—and a woman—who was a player in the high-tech industry, she had advised the Justice Department in Washington on antitrust matters before moving back to Silicon Valley, where she had built a successful corporate law practice. But that's as much sense as Will's brain would deliver. Sleep-starved, he began conjuring up what he hadn't been told yet: that there was a hearing going on right now for a case he didn't know about involving Angela De Nuevo, and the judge was angry that Will was not present. Based on a recurring but vivid dream, Will was asleep enough to think he was at risk of showing up at the hearing in his underwear.

"Sorry to wake you like this, Will, but this is urgent," the caller continued. "I am Joon Newman's personal lawyer. That's hush-hush, of course."

His mind was starting to waken and focus. It was known that ThinkSoft engaged in the practice of "conflicting out" the major legal talent in markets around the country. Just in the Bay Area, although its mainstay firm was Kilgore Crushjoy, ThinkSoft had passed around small pieces of work to almost all the major law firms in San Francisco and Silicon Valley; when ThinkSoft sued a company in the area, all those law firms would have to decline to represent the defendant because of conflict of interest. As a result, ThinkSoft monopolized all the big talent. For some reason, De Nuevo & Cooper had never picked up any work from ThinkSoft. Now Will knew why. It had been declined without explanation because the firm already represented the highly secretive client; because of Joon's disagreements with his father, a conflict of interest would arise in representing the company as well.

"I guess you know I went on a little escapade with Joon last night," Will said. "I told him, before—" That caught Persi's attention. She rolled over and propped herself on one elbow to listen.

"Don't worry," Joon's attorney said. "This is not about you doing something wrong. I'm calling you at this hour because Joon wants to testify. He just left my house. With the trial going on, and given his own plans to investigate, I'd told him to call me at any hour. He sure took me up on that." She chuckled. "Now he's gone to his place to examine the information vessel on a special computer. Regardless of what Joon might actually want to say, I don't need to tell you there is a raft of risks and complications. Legally, there's his responsibility to the company and whether he can disclose anything. I can comment as a corporate lawyer as to what he might be able to say, but ultimately it's up to you, a skilled trial lawyer I'm sure, to get any of this into evidence."

Will was about to protest the generous description but skillfully bit his lip instead.

"And on the personal front," she continued, "there's his relationship with his father. He needs to take a stand in the company he co-founded and co-owns. That's been my opinion all along. Whether he ever will or can act on that . . . ?"

The voice on the phone was silent for a moment.

"I guess the biggest wild card is what he is going to say and how he is going to say it. I'm sure you know what I mean. He's deeply plugged into alternate reality. People have no idea what he's talking about. There's no telling how that might play out in a federal courtroom. That's a risk you'll have to decide to take or not. It could backfire. . . ." She paused. "With all that in mind, would you be interested in meeting to talk this over?"

Will didn't hesitate. "I'll be at your office in an hour."

When Will arrived at the federal court building at 8:40 A.M., members of the media were already arriving in greater numbers than the day before. Many of the papers had carried either the photograph of Lady J's moment of apoplectic epiphany on the witness stand or the photograph of her being unceremoniously removed from the building in a body bag by federal marshals. Public interest was heightened by speculation as to whether the Wholly Grill laser-cooked Smoke Crystals—albeit in concentrated powdered form—had actually caused her death.

Coming out of the elevator, Will could see on his right the throng of people gathering in front of Judge Wetherborne's courtroom. Edwin was holding forth before a number of media interviewers. Will took a left turn and sat down on a bench near the elevators, away from the crowds. He opened his briefcase to review his notes one more time.

Following an hour-long meeting with Joon and his attorney, Will had used the library at De Nuevo & Cooper to outline his strategy and conduct some research. He hoped the jury didn't mind that he was wearing the same clothes as the day before. Given his low profile so far in the trial, it was unlikely anyone would notice. Luckily, although his pale blue shirt had seen crammed utility elevators, flights through catacombs, and crash landings on hotel floors, it remained serviceably unwrinkled.

He looked up to see Persi stepping out of an elevator. She was beaming. Before she could reach him, twenty feet away, Art Newman emerged from the elevator opposite hers. The two came face-to-face.

"Well, if it isn't Persi Valentino of the *Golden West Business Journal* . . . or formerly employed there." Art Newman was not performing for a TV camera or a product launch, so his smile matched the maliciousness of his comment. "Covering the trial for the want ads?" He chuckled as if she were fair game and he had said something truly funny. "We've missed you at press events, but your being here today couldn't have been timed better."

He turned and walked over to the crowd of Kilgore Crushjoy attorneys, spoke to Thurston Crushjoy, and pointed at her. Crushjoy, in turn, spoke briefly to a young associate who opened up his briefcase, pulled out a stack of papers, and approached Persi. She had stood her ground but not said a word.

"I understand you are Persistenza Maria Valentino. Is that right?" he asked, awkwardly and stiffly mispronouncing her name.

There was no secret about what was coming. "Close enough for someone who's only fluent in dweebese," she said, lifting her head proudly. "But the name is—*Persistenza Maria Valentino*." When she spoke her name, she took it up a chord and in perfect pitch, a lilting musical phrase with an accent so delicately beautiful it seemed impossible to believe someone would want to bring harm to her.

"You are hereby served with this summons and complaint in the case of *ThinkSoft versus Valentino*." He handed the papers to her and walked back to his crowd.

Will was stung by the scene.

Persi walked over to where he sat. Holding the complaint, she was bravely trying not to show the hurt she felt, but Will could see it beneath the surface. He recognized the anger and fear any mortal feels when a giant insensate corporation delivers a high-voltage shock that says, *We are going to take away your property and your rights. We will use our might to cost you a lot of money and tie you up in court for a long time. We mean to cause you endless heartache.*

"Looks like I'll need a legal defense after all," she said stoically. She dropped the complaint on the bench next to him and wiped her hands around the waist of her pantsuit while pursing her lips in exaggerated disgust. "Yuck! This has Art Newman's slime all over it! I need to go wash my hands. Then I'm going to see if our witness is here."

Before she turned around to leave, she stared at Will and then spoke in a deadly serious tone. "Will." She waited until their eyes met and locked fully. "Stop them."

He nodded slowly and gravely. She turned and left. The pain emanating from Persi compounded his own. He'd been humiliated in Municipal Court by Crushjoy. ThinkSoft had abused Lenny and denied it. And now Will bore witness to how they purposely hurt the person he cared about most.

He picked up the complaint—date-stamped that morning—and thumbed through it. ThinkSoft claimed misappropriation of trade secrets, trespass, fraud, and concealment. It sought millions and an injunction preventing her from ever writing about ThinkSoft again, relying on the seldom-used Doctrine of Inevitable Disclosure, a theory used in rare and aggressive cases where employers sought to prevent former employees from working in the same field if shown that their new employment duties would "inevitably" result in disclosure of their former employers' trade secrets.

"Will?" It was Lenny. His eyes were puffy and red.

"Lenny, I am *so* sorry about Lady J. Something has come up. I need to fill you in quickly before we start today."

"I miss her around the house," Lenny said, almost starting to cry. "Whatever you say. Just do something for her, OK?"

"OK."

"Thanks, Will." Lenny turned and walked slowly back down the hall, hanging his head. Will closed his briefcase, stood, and moved down the hall into the crowd gathered around Edwin in front of Judge Wetherborne's courtroom.

"Excuse me, Edwin. This is important."

Will pulled him aside from the media circle he was hosting. His boss was wearing a small earphone plugged in on one side with a cordless mike—the size of a timed-release capsule—attached to his tie.

"I met Joon Newman last night. He has agreed to testify in our case." Will briefly described his contact with Joon Newman.

"You should have told me right away," Edwin scolded.

"There wasn't time," Will said with a dismissive hand. "I barely had time to get my arms around this. And I've spoken to Lenny. He's OK with it."

"I was going to rest our case this morning, but this could be good. I better handle it, though. Give me your notes."

Although expecting this reaction from Edwin, Will was in no position to tell him what to do. He could only try to convince him. Just then Mr. Danning opened the doors to let the crowd into the courtroom. Edwin, followed by Will, moved toward the doors.

"It's important that I handle this," Will said. "Believe me, if you don't know Joon Newman as I do, you'll be at a loss—"

"Mr. Ostermyer, what's that you're wearing?" Mr. Danning asked, when they reached the door to the courtroom.

"This?" Edwin asked, as if genuinely unsure whether the courtroom clerk was referring to the cordless mike or the silk tie. "I'm outfitted with a live remote to bring my perspective closer to my audience."

"It is absolutely forbidden!" the clerk said sternly, reminding Edwin that he was indeed the alter ego of Judge Wetherborne.

"But I remind you, sir, this is a public court!" Edwin insisted.

"And no place to be courting publicity!" Mr. Danning countered, with obvious contempt. "Once you step across that threshold, you can't be a lawyer *and* a talk-show host at the same time. Which, sir, do you choose?"

Edwin, frustrated and conflicted, turned his attention back to Will.

"Trust me. I've got this under control," Will reassured him, maintaining his resolve.

"I think I'll go down to the media assembly room to finish up a piece of business," Edwin said.

Watching the experienced attorney on Lenny's team turn and walk away suddenly brought home the reality to Will of what he had done. He was on his own now. He didn't have Edwin nearby to pick him up if—or when—Crushjoy knocked him down.

Before Edwin could change his mind, Will made his way into the courtroom with the others. It was 8:55 A.M. He set up his papers on the table, receiving a curious look from Thurston Crushjoy, who was watching the young lawyer at the lead counsel chair. It may have been the first time Crushjoy had realized that Will was actually an attorney, not a legal bellhop.

"All rise. The Honorable Ignatius P. Wetherborne presiding," Mr. Danning announced. The judge had not ordered the jury to be brought in yet.

"Good morning, counsel." The judge did a double take when he saw that the plaintiff's table was being soloed by the young associate. "Are we waiting for Mr. Ostermyer?" he asked impatiently.

"No, Your Honor," Will responded. "We can proceed."

"Once plaintiff rests, I will excuse the jury so I can rule on various motions that may prove terminal to these proceedings." The judge looked sternly in the direction of plaintiff's table and then at Will. "Perhaps we can start that process now without bringing the jury in. Since you are ready to proceed, I assume, Mr. Swanson, you are standing in for the formality. Is that right?" The judge had the same bias that Crushjoy no doubt had; it could not be that Will was positioned at the lead counsel chair to do anything more than parrot the words "plaintiff rests" on cue.

Will recalled the words that Santa Tostada had spoken to him when he visited her level: *They will underestimate you. That is your advantage. Use it.* He took a deep breath, stood erect, and addressed the court.

"Your Honor, the plaintiff has subpoenaed and now calls Arthur Newman Junior—Joon Newman—as his next witness."

Pandemonium broke out at the mention of the name. People jumped up and shouted at one another. At the same moment Joon Newman walked into the courtroom and stood in the back, surveying the scene. When Art Newman saw his son, the color drained from his face top to bottom like a high-speed electronic hourglass.

"Order!" the judge boomed, pounding the gavel. Automatically, Judge Wetherborne was looking to the defense for a handle on what to make of this.

Crushjoy was on his feet, towering above Will, his legendary jawbone thrust ahead— massive, hardened, and steely as the hood of a 1972 Cutlass Supreme. "Your Honor, to say we merely object to this unprecedented blindsiding would be a gross understatement," Crushjoy thundered. "This is the first we have learned that this witness was subpoenaed. Joon Newman is under a strict employment agreement with the company; that contract contains pages of confidentiality provisions. There is very little, besides his name, that is not protected by confidentiality or trade secrets."

Will spoke when the judge turned to him. "Your Honor, I certainly don't want to get into a row with Mr. Crushjoy over this. Let me discuss this with him off the record for a moment and see if we can't work it out."

The judge surveyed the scene impatiently, suspiciously. "Then talk.

But let's move this along!" Momentarily off the record, the judge turned and spoke to his clerk.

Before Will could turn to speak to Crushjoy, Joon drifted from the back of the courtroom up to Will, looking like a lost tourist. He was snappily dressed in a blazer and turtleneck. "Excuse me," the young man said to Will within earshot of the defense table. "I was tagged with this a few hours ago." He waved the subpoena in his hand. "What am I supposed to do?"

As usual, Joon was inscrutable. After meeting with him and his lawyer that morning, Will had announced he wanted to serve a subpoena on the witness. It would look better to have the witness testify that he was "forced" to appear in court. But was Joon hamming it up with his question or was he somewhere else? "Thank you for appearing, Mr. Newman," Will replied. "Wait here a moment. We'll let you know."

Crushjoy spoke to Will loudly enough for Art Newman, standing nearby, to hear the discussion. "So, you have subpoenaed Joon Newman. Congratulations on being able to find him. But we are not going to let you ask him anything confidential. Period. End of discussion. And frankly, even if you can find a question that doesn't call for trade-secret disclosure, good luck on getting a straight answer. You're wasting your time."

"I see what your concern is," Will said, as if he had not given much thought to these matters. "Are you suggesting I stipulate that I won't ask anything that calls for legally protected confidential information?"

"That's correct." Even Crushjoy, the grizzled defense attorney, seemed a little surprised to have encountered such smooth sailing, compared to the constant storm he experienced with Edwin. Crushjoy looked over at Art Newman, who hunched his shoulders.

"That's fine with me," the father said. "Not that he knows anything about Wholly Grill."

"Then no need to waste time. That's what we'll tell the judge," Will said.

Before they could get Judge Wetherborne's attention, Art Newman muttered scoldingly to his son, loud enough for Will to hear, "You were served with a subpoena this morning and you didn't tell Legal? Just like your mother. Some things are serious, young man. Don't give me that distant smirk, like you're going to try and pull some dirty linen out of one of my clean rooms! This isn't some game! You know nothing about Wholly Grill. You just better tell the truth about that!"

Joon did not look at his father or respond to him. Instead, he picked up Will's softcover copy of the California Civil Code at the end of the table. Will had Post-Its marking the section with the rules on contract interpretation. Joon flipped to another section, picked up a pen, and circled something in the book. Art Newman paid no attention to the open book on the table. Instead, he glared at his son, now walking to the back of the courtroom.

Will leaned over and saw that Joon had circled Section 3510, one of the Maxims of Jurisprudence:

When the reason for a rule ceases, so should the rule itself.

When the judge finished speaking to the clerk and saw that the attorneys were waiting, he told the court reporter to go back on the record. "Your Honor," Will said. "Mr. Crushjoy has explained to me the limits of what this witness may say. Therefore, I have stipulated that no questions will be asked of Mr. Newman that call for legally protected confidential information."

"Very well," Judge Wetherborne said. "That stipulation will become an order of the court. Bring the jury in; let's proceed with the witness."

Joon Newman was sworn in. Surprised by the appearance of the reclusive witness, the crowd tittered and traded gossipy glances.

"What do you do for ThinkSoft?" Will asked.

"I am Merlin in the Kingdom," Joon began.

Obviously, Will was going to have to be the magician to reel Joon into the real world. The jury stared blankly at the witness. The judge dropped his pen and rubbed his brow.

"As such, my mission is to create new technology. I am Chief Technical

Officer. Today, at this level," Joon said, looking around the courtroom, "my mission is to battle the Dark Sorcerer. Here I am armed with an unlimited amount of the Forces of Truth and Reason." He looked up at the judge. "Right? Truth and Reason have special powers here?"

The judge, who was speechless—he appeared to be on the verge of a stroke—could only nod his head affirmatively. It was obvious from Crushjoy's grimace that he was dying to make some objection but did not want to suggest to the jury he was opposed to Truth and Reason.

"I take it you are familiar with the Wholly Grill technology?" Will asked, jumping right in, hoping to catch Crushjoy off guard and, more critically, to get Joon to move away from pure gamespeak and into the realm of admissible evidence.

"Objection. The question lacks foundation," Crushjoy was on his feet.

"Approach the bench," the judge directed the attorneys, requesting a discussion outside the ears of the jury. Will gulped. It was going to be a long morning trying to move testimony under Crushjoy's watch. Or was it all going to be quickly cut short by the judge?

"Didn't we just agree that you were not going to ask confidential information?" The judge scowled. "It seems to me that this line of questioning is going exactly contrary to that order. I am not going to sustain the objection, only to have you persist by asking another question calling for the forbidden subject."

"I am not going to ask him anything covered by the court order, Your Honor. This is my first . . . courtroom examination," Will confided, a little sheepishly.

Crushjoy did not hide his condescension toward Will. "Mr. Swanson may be innocently unfamiliar with rules of evidence—perhaps having missed that episode of *Sesame Street*. But if the proper threshold questions were asked, he would find out that this witness has no more knowledge about this technology than the average citizen. I request that the objection be sustained. Let him ask the foundational question and find out that this witness knows nothing. We'll be done sooner."

"The objection is sustained," the judge ruled.

As the attorneys returned to their tables, Will was handed a note by a messenger from Edwin:

I am in the LNTV trailer across the street from the federal building. I am watching the trial and commentating on national television. If you need help, just call for a recess or use the phrase "Isn't it a fact?" twice in one question, and I'll hurry back.

Will relaunched his examination of Joon, opting for a simple yes-or-no question. "Mr. Newman, do you have any knowledge of the Wholly Grill technology that you have acquired at ThinkSoft?"

"Yes."

"And how did you acquire that knowledge?"

"There is knowledge media located in the Tower of the Castle."

"Would that be the top floor of Building RD One, the electronic nerve center for Wholly Grill?"

"Yes. At the eastern edge of the Kingdom. Last night there was a mission. As a result of that mission, I now have knowledge."

Art Newman's eyes bulged, ready to explode. He punched Crushjoy in the side in a not-so-subtle effort to prompt action. A man smaller than Crushjoy would have been felled.

"Your Honor, this line of questioning should be terminated now!" Crushjoy bellowed. "As shocking as it is to report, there was a break-in last night to the ultraconfidential Wholly Grill lab, Room Eight-oh-seven. The would-be spies got away. But now we are told that information was taken—"

The jury was spellbound by these developments. Things had steadily improved for them in this trial's sheer entertainment value, at least since the veterinary bills were itemized one by one and read into the record.

Crushjoy continued. "That's a theft of trade secrets, a felony under the Economic Espionage Act of 1996! To allow counsel to ask further questions would sanction 'harvesting the fruit of the poisonous tree,' which rules of evidence forbid!"

"Allow me to ask the witness whether he knows anything about that before you rule, Your Honor," Will suggested to the judge.

"Ask him," the judge said.

"Were you in that lab last night, and did you take those files?"

"Yes. I conducted that mission last night." He turned to Crushjoy. "I *harvested* the knowledge myself."

"That's it!" Crushjoy exclaimed. "The witness either stole those files or is in possession of stolen property—that which is the rightful property of ThinkSoft only. There should be no further questions until a criminal investigation has been completed!"

Will looked at Crushjoy and shook his head calmly. "But the witness is defendant's chief technical officer. He has a right to be in that lab and to look at those files."

The judge nodded in agreement. "As a principal of ThinkSoft, indeed he has a right to look at it. But that's not the same thing as the right to *reveal* what's in those files. The court order still stands."

"Did you bring anything with you today?" Will pressed on.

"The forces of Truth and Reason," Joon replied matter-of-factly. "And the knowledge I acquired while up in the Tower." He reached under his shirt and produced a standard file containing printouts of documents he had scanned in the lab.

Crushjoy looked at Will, and then Joon, and then back to Will. "Your Honor, I request a recess. I think a perfidious collusion is at play. I smell a rat!"

The word *rat,* although without mention of mistreatment, seemed to energize Joon; he leaned forward in the witness chair with determination.

"There will be no recess now," the judge said. "We will address this examination one question at a time. Mr. Swanson, if you are involved in any collusion with this witness—if you know something that you are not supposed to know—I assume you are prepared to meet the consequences from ThinkSoft. But let's get on with this testimony. If you have something you can ask this witness without running afoul of the court order, do it. Otherwise, conclude your examination or I will do it for you."

Will knew the next question was make-or-break. If the judge decided the next question called for off-limits confidential information, he was finished. The judge had complete power to decide at what point he was asking company trade secrets. Will had read a famous trial lawyer's book on winning strategies for getting evidence in—not unlike the hundreds of strategy books on how to succeed in computer games. The trial lawyer called it the *drip method*: If you can just get a drop or two in, the rest will follow; try to pour too much in and you'll be shut off for good.

"Mr. Newman, without saying how Wholly Grill is manufactured or how it works, what was the general nature and product type ThinkSoft intended to create with it?"

"Objection, Your Honor!" Crushjoy bellowed. "This is a Trojan Horse to get through the gate. I assure you my client's plans and intentions are jealously guarded trade secrets."

Will acted surprised by the objection. "I'm just asking what they intended to create, not how they did it. The example of the Coca-Cola trade-secret formula was cited at an earlier hearing. It's no secret, and never has been since Coca-Cola hit the market, that they intended to create a refreshing and sweet carbonated beverage, which at the time they could promote as having medicinal benefits. The recipe is still a secret. Now that Wholly Grill has hit the market, I am simply asking a company officer for the same kind of product profile."

Judge Wetherborne's eyes rolled around. Will hoped the half-crazy eye would settle on him.

"Overruled! You may answer the question, Mr. Newman."

"This is the black magic revealed in their own words," Joon answered, in his otherworldly way. Without opening his knowledge file, he handed Will a page of printout that had been clipped to the front jacket. Will sensed that Joon wanted to help but just couldn't bring himself to exit the game.

Will took the page, his heart pushing up against the back of his throat. He adjusted his glasses and read it to himself first. It contained a smoking-gun admission about the company's intentions that would break the case wide open. "Let the record reflect that the witness has handed me a page from files he obtained from inside Building RD One at ThinkSoft." Will began to read out loud: " 'The Neuro Group will launch a new line of consumer food products—' "

"Move to strike!" Crushjoy interrupted. "This testimony lacks foundation! This witness—company officer or not—has not shown us any personal knowledge of a so-named Neuro Group we're hearing about for the first time."

"Is that true, Mr. Newman?" the judge leaned over and asked him directly.

"I only know what was revealed to me in the knowledge file," Joon answered the judge in earnest.

A sidebar ensued with a relentless Crushjoy. "The court has not and should not change its confidentiality order. This witness has no personal knowledge. In the eyes of the law, he is incompetent!" Crushjoy seemed to take special relish in describing Will's evidence, and no doubt Joon personally, as "incompetent."

The judge waved Will off before he could argue. "He's right, Mr. Swanson!" His left eye was fluttering rapidly. "It is not competent evidence."

"Thank you, Your Honor," Crushjoy continued, taking control. "Given that ruling, this witness should be forthwith excused."

The judge pondered. "The motion to strike is granted. This witness has admitted he has no personal knowledge of the files he brought. Furthermore, the files no doubt contain off-limits trade secrets. I will advise the jury that there will be no further questions of this witness."

"Before you do that, Your Honor," Will began, trying to suppress in his voice the desperation he felt. "I should have a right to verify what Mr. Crushjoy has claimed as fact. If these are trade secrets, then fine, it's off limits. But I would ask that the court not rule until we hear it directly from a company witness—not its lawyer—who can verify the trade-secret status of Wholly Grill."

Crushjoy started to protest, but the judge stopped him. "I think, Mr. Crushjoy, the plaintiff has a right of simple verification." The judge turned to Will. "But I won't allow you to ask it of this witness. He is plainly a disturbed young man and seems to have some inexplicable bias against his own company. What reliable representative of ThinkSoft will it be to tell you what you've already been told? I won't tolerate further delays!"

Will cast about the courtroom. "How about Art Newman Senior? He is present."

Crushjoy scoffed. "Go ahead! He'll tell you it's secret, but that's all he knows and all you can ask him!" The judge nodded in agreement.

Joon stepped down from the witness stand.

Back at the defense counsel table, Crushjoy explained quietly to Art Newman why he was being called as a witness. The chairman of ThinkSoft shook his head, wearing a faintly smug expression. He was no doubt pleased to see not only that his son had been excused but that his testimony would be stricken. After being sworn in, he settled comfortably into the witness chair.

"Now, Mr. Newman, are you familiar with something at ThinkSoft called the 'Neuro Group'?"

"Oh, yes," he said gravely, as if regretting to see that particular cat out of the bag. "Extremely hush-hush. I can't tell you *anything* about that. As much as I'd love to tout life-saving miracle medical cures—"

"It's a trade secret?"

"Absolutely."

"What about Wholly Grill? Is its know-how also a trade secret?"

"Yes. The highest level of security."

"And without telling me the nitty-gritty, are you personally familiar with how Wholly Grill works?"

"Actually, I'm not," he confided to the jury. "I only understand it in general terms. It's all so technical, you know. You'd have to ask the engineers. But, of course"—he rubbed it in—"you can't, because it's off limits to everyone but them."

Will looked down at his yellow pad as if for help, but there was nothing written on it to guide him. A long uncomfortable silence filled the courtroom.

"So you're telling me Wholly Grill is a trade secret and not even you have access to its core technology?"

"That's right. I wouldn't know what to make of it anyway. After all"—he smiled with feigned modesty—"I'm just a marketing guy."

"If they are trade secrets—and not even you have access—does the company take appropriate steps to ensure that only authorized personnel see them?"

"Objection, Your Honor." Crushjoy, until now indifferent to this exercise, was growing impatient. "The trade-secret status has been verified. We're wasting the court's time now."

The judge's demeanor showed he agreed. Before Will could finally be cut off, he explained. "Your Honor, the law recites that in order to qualify as a trade secret, the information must be 'the subject of efforts that are reasonable under the circumstances to maintain its secrecy.' As part of the verification we've been allowed, I have a few questions to make a record of that." Will gave a hunch of his shoulders to signal he was about done.

"All right, but make it brief, Mr. Swanson," the judge said. "You may answer the question, Mr. Newman."

Art Newman didn't need any coaxing. "As with all our technology, ThinkSoft has the most advanced state-of-the-art security system in Silicon Valley. This breach of security," he added, nodding at the file placed before him, "could only have happened as the result of an inside job by a high-ranking official." He cast a contemptuous glance at Joon before returning his ever-so-certain gaze at Will. He seemed to be enjoying the predicament of the attorney from the enemy camp, pointlessly spinning his wheels. At the same time Art Newman was able to pitch his company's technology to a live TV audience.

"But you have thousands of employees, don't you?"

"Yes, but only authorized employees have access to secure areas," he answered, in a tone that underscored he was stating the obvious.

"But with all those employees, how do you know who is authorized and who is unauthorized personnel?" Will asked, scratching his head.

"Quite simply," he answered with a supercilious smile. "Everyone, including me, must wear a ThinkSoft photo ID." He spoke slowly and with exaggerated enunciation as if Will had a severe learning disability. "An employee is either authorized or unauthorized. *ID* stands for *identi-fication*. The ID identifies the employee as authorized or unauthorized."

A scattering of giggles rippled through the courtroom. Art's smile lit up into a full grin at the signal that he had made Will look foolish.

"Oh, I see," Will said. He then turned and nodded to Persi in the back row. Persi rose from her seat, walked forward to counsel table, and stood between where Will was standing and Lenny sat.

"You know Persi Valentino, don't you, Mr. Newman?"

"Certainly," he responded, suddenly cold. "She *was* a technology reporter, but she was fired from that job for spying on us, after becoming employed by us under false pretenses. We've had to sue her for it."

Persi stood for a moment and stared intently back at the witness before returning to her seat. Art Newman shifted in his seat, having taken on a more serious posture.

"Is this one of the security badges you described a moment ago?" Will had taken Persi's badge from her last night, after she pulled it out of her pocket.

"I'm sure it is—and by the way, that should have been turned in." His eyes were fixed uncomfortably on the badge in Will's hand as he spoke.

"It's just a piece of plastic with a name, number, and picture on it. Right?" Will pressed him.

"Of course," he said. "But security has its procedures."

"Perhaps, if you would be kind enough, you could show me how employees are supposed to wear these badges for identification as you explained."

"Is that really necessary?" Art asked, looking up at the judge to intercede for him. Crushjoy didn't object, perhaps thinking it better to let his adversary incite the wrath of the judge.

"Yes, why don't we have a demonstration!" The judge made no effort to conceal the fact that he had heard enough. "The record cannot be clear enough, I suppose." Then he added more biting sarcasm. "I think we've all wondered, for example, for whose benefit does the telephone company provide a return envelope with a little box that says PLACE STAMP HERE. Believe me, Mr. Newman, this line of questioning has been exhausted. But why don't you put the badge on so that even the very inexperienced and easily confused among us can understand its correct placement."

A seemingly chastened Will traversed the well and handed the badge to Art Newman in the witness box. As he handed it to him up close, he noticed the founder and chairman of ThinkSoft had a line of sweat across the top of his forehead and in front of each ear. Will returned to his station.

Art Newman grimaced as if the lapel of his Armani suit were his outer skin being punctured by the ID pin. "There," Art said, with relief so subtle that Will suspected he was the only one who detected it. "Now you know how to wear an ID badge. Am I done now?" he asked, turning to the judge.

"You are clear enough on that subject, aren't you, Mr. Swanson?" The judge strongly intimated that the wrong answer would bring more humiliating remarks from the bench.

"I guess that's all I have then." Will looked up at the judge, then back at the witness. "Except one more question, Mr. Newman, so that an accurate record is made. For the record, would you simply verify that the knowledge file Joon Newman brought in and which is placed before you contains company trade secrets?"

"I wouldn't call it a *knowledge* file." He chuckled nervously. "Joon . . . dreams up things, you know," he offered in a gratuitous aside.

Will followed up. "Without describing to us what's inside the file, would you open it and tell us: Does it contain trade secrets to which not even you should have access? A simple yes or no will suffice."

Art Newman looked up at the judge again. "Go ahead, Mr. Newman," the judge said. "Please go through the motions, and then you are excused."

The witness started to reach for the file and then, just as quickly, recoiled. Will could almost see the distance calculations taking place in Art's head. Joon had estimated that the courthouse was just inside the reach of the E-Serum transmitter at ThinkSoft. Now he sat in the front row perfectly still, no more moved by the unfolding drama than if he were viewing a configuration of pixels on a video screen.

Art dove at the file with the apparent hope of opening it and saying yes as quickly as possible, then ridding himself of it. Indeed, as Art grabbed the file, "Yeh . . . !" was all he could muster with his own free will.

In an instant E-Serum's neuroelectrical surge roared into and up through his face, now flushed red-hot, rising from his neck and quickly reaching the very top of his head, much like when on a scalding grill hot tongues of fire will leap up and lick an excessively greasy slice of pork butt. Total meltdown ensued.

A gaping Art Newman looked up and spouted, "I ordered the Neuro Group to make it addictive! It's really addictive, just like nicotine! That's a secret! That's what this file says! But . . . the biggest secret is, it's all a lie! Ersatz intellectual property! Licenses of nothing!" His eyes were bulging. "Trust me," he screamed at Will. "I know everything! There's fraud! Believe me, my head is full of empty secrets—!"

"Thank you, Mr. Newman. We got that," Will said, interrupting him. "That's enough. Rules don't allow cumulative evidence." Careful not to hold it himself—lest the badge-connected-to-Art-connected-to-file set him off too—Will pulled the file away from the witness and let it drop to the floor.

Courtroom observers gasped. Others let forth long wrenching groans, as if there was such a thing in this trial as too much. The hurly-burly swept through the courtroom and splashed off the walls, compounding the hubbub.

Crushjoy was on his feet. "Your Honor! This is . . . there's been some kind of trick! An ambush!"

The judge peered at Crushjoy, waiting for the explanation. There was none.

"Mr. Newman has been working very hard," Crushjoy finally offered. "We reserve the right to bring in his doctors to explain the ridiculous rantings you just heard about the company's most valuable property rights."

The people in the gallery, already roiled, now began to buzz with an intensity that made plain their vigorous doubts about Crushjoy's explanation.

"It's a head trip, I'm tellin' ya!" a familiar voice shouted from among the people.

"What was that?" the judge asked, evidently so unfamiliar with the language spoken that he didn't recognize it as human speech. After the call from Joon's attorney at four-thirty this morning, Will had forgotten he'd asked Sky to come in.

Will turned and addressed the court. "At this time I request permission to read the full statement from the Neuro Group file."

"But Your Honor"—Crushjoy was still on his feet—"the court order still stands. Even Mr. Newman—addled as he was—verified they were trade secrets."

"No, Your Honor." Will was firm. "The information is *not* protected by any confidentiality. We have adduced testimony from the chairman of the company himself, who told us candidly about the addictive and fraudulent nature of Wholly Grill. *That* breaks a host of federal and state laws, not just regulations but criminal violations! The secret know-how is no more legally protected than are the blueprints for a bank heist."

"The objection is overruled!" the judge agreed, noiselessly rattling an eye at Art Newman. "Mr. Joon Newman's earlier testimony stands admitted, and my order is modified to allow testimony regarding this file."

Will picked the file up from the floor in front of Art Newman, who remained in the witness chair staring dumbly ahead, catatonic. Will took a deep breath and read slowly and solemnly to the jury.

"'The Neuro Group will launch a new line of consumer food products, beginning with a barbecue sauce that electrochemically mimics nicotine and will replicate its addictive characteristics—'"

First one woman gasped "Oh, my God!" in the back of the courtroom, followed by others. Then everyone started talking at once. Reporters ran out of the room.

"Order!" The judge banged the gavel.

"*Objection!*" Crushjoy boomed. "Already this sensationalized and irresponsible testimony is having a devastating impact on my client and, if allowed to continue unchecked, could cost hundreds of millions of dollars in lost sales! We are requesting that the Ninth Circuit Court of Appeals intercede instantly." He raised his hand and signaled his associates. "We are asking for that relief *in real time*." Ordinarily a decision from a quorum of elderly judges in the Court of Appeals was measured in months and years.

Papers spewed out of a laser printer and were handed to a tall male associate in a blue suit. The young attorney, whom Will had read about in *The Legal Institution*, had been a Rhodes scholar and a track star at Stanford. As he finished lacing up his running shoes, the papers were handed to him; he took off in a flash with the packet of information, seeking to set aside the court's rulings *in real time*.

‹ 35 ›

"You weren't shittin' about uh-*thor*-ities, were you?" Sky blurted out. They were out in the hallway during a short break called by the judge. "And that Art Newman dude. I told you he was a pig."

Sky, Persi, and Will had huddled and agreed that Sky should explain how Wholly Grill worked after first reading summary material from Joon's "knowledge file." After spending ten minutes looking over inscrutable depictions of chemical compounds, Sky took the witness stand. His Grateful Dead patch of "skull-with-roses-in-teeth" adorned the left shoulder of his faded lab coat. The skull seemed to be drawing ghoulish delight from staring back at the no-nonsense judge. When sworn in and asked if he would tell the truth, the whole truth, and nothing but the truth, Sky answered with a resounding "Fer sure!"

The judge rejected Crushjoy's objection to further testimony based on the controversial file. Crushjoy then directed his attack on Sky's qualifications. "Your honor, this witness is not a credentialed expert witness worthy of testifying in a federal court."

The judge dismissed the objection. "You can cross-examine on that, Mr. Crushjoy. Proceed, Mr. Swanson."

Will credentialed Sky with a few brief questions. The fact that Sky had been doing nothing but hands-on work in the area of psychotropic drug chemistry in Berkeley since the late sixties probably made him one of the world's foremost experts on such questions, but no one in the courtroom would have reason to believe Sky regarded himself that way. Fond looks from jury members revealed they were lovestruck with his charm and complete lack of pretension.

"So, based upon your review of the files and your experience, would you consider Wholly Grill addictive?" Will asked him.

"*Whoa!* I'll say it is!"

"How does it work chemically?"

Sky went to a grease board upon which Crushjoy had, earlier in the trial, written the words "water, sugar, tomato sauce" and other seemingly harmless ingredients. Sky erased the board and scrawled the chemical composition for nicotine—$C_{10}H_{14}N_2$—and then wrote another formula for cooked Smoke Crystals, explaining in layman's terms how, chemically, they were designed to do the same thing.

"So, the way it works is this!" Sky leaned forward toward the jury, animated by his passion for chemistry. "The Smoke Crystals get chemically tweaked by the laser flames"—he used a flick of his finger to show how simple a tweak was—"and *Presto!* just like that, a perfectly inert barbecue sauce becomes an alkaloid that simulates nicotine. What looked like just some good eats for the fridge turns out to be more like munchies for the brain. So that's what they did. They went after the tobacco freaks—the ones who'd gone cold turkey—because their heads already have a groove that makes them crave this stuff."

The jurors didn't take any notes. They followed effortlessly, amused and engaged by Sky and outraged at ThinkSoft. Lenny let out a big sigh upon hearing Sky's explanation.

Crushjoy rose to cross-examine. "Now Dr.—"

"Sky. Just call me Sky."

"I have not seen your curriculum vitae." He spoke with scarcely concealed condescension. "Do you have any papers to your name, *Dr. Sky?*"

"Well, yeah, I do." Sky spoke with wide-eyed candor, trying to be helpful.

"And learned I'm sure they are. Would you tell us about them?"

Sky looked up at a stern judge, who was definitely an *uh-thor-ity* figure he had sought to avoid. "Are you sure it's cool?" he asked, looking back to Crushjoy.

"Oh, yes, I assure you it is. The court is eager for you to share with us," Crushjoy said. "Kindly describe your papers, giving the names of each."

"Well, these are named Zig Zag," he said, reaching into his pocket and pulling out a pack of the popular rolling papers with the picture on its cover of a goateed pothead. Sky tossed the pack at Crushjoy, landing it on the defense counsel table. "Happy to share 'em, man. Keep 'em. No hassle. I've got more."

The courtroom burst into laughter. Sky remained politely matter-of-fact, not giving the slightest clue he understood the inquiry otherwise.

Crushjoy apparently had never experienced a witness before who did not respond to him like a marionette. He had no idea how to control this one. He rallied with a few inconsequential questions and then announced, "No further questions."

Following Sky's testimony, and over Crushjoy's objections, Will called Joon to the stand again. He knew Crushjoy would eventually argue that there was nothing wrong with selling addictive products—as the tobacco industry had done forever—unless some serious health problem could be demonstrated. Since there was no evidence of that, Will needed to show some other wrongdoing that could not be questioned. To do it he'd have to find a way to ground Joon in reality, even for a few moments, so that the jury could hear an explanation of Wholly Grill's computer technology. He needed to get Joon talking like the engineer he was—albeit dry, serious, and dull—the voice that had flickered on and off the night before.

"Let me read to you from Exhibit A, the shrink-wrap license entitled the Wholly Grill End User License Agreement. It defines the Wholly WORD as the Wholly Grill WAN Optimization of Research and Development. Are you familiar with that?"

SECRETS OF THE WHOLLY GRILL

"Oh, yes. The Sorcerer's secret brew. Voodoo electronics. Incantational code." He was not going anywhere near reality. Whether it was the crowd of people or the cameras or the rules of the game remained a mystery to Will. It was not going to be easy to land this witness.

"Other than the candid inside information Mr. Art Newman Senior shared with us a little while ago, what do you know about the Wholly WORD?"

"I had reason to believe the game was stacked by the Manufacturer," Joon said incongruously, turning to the jury as if to explain his strategy. "That's why I went on a mission. Last night's output yielded a backup copy of the Wholly WORD from the main server." Joon reached into his shirt again and produced the information vessel. The jury leaned forward to see what it was. "This information vessel contains all the secret information and data the Sorcerer has gathered, all the abracadabra—and I have examined it personally."

Art Newman, who had regained his faculties, was plainly rankled at the sight of the backup information vessel. Having exhausted all objections on this subject, Crushjoy glanced at his watch again, perhaps expecting to see his world-class sprinting associate, who'd raced off to the Court of Appeals ten minutes ago, returning any second now with a favorable ruling.

Unable to contain himself any longer, Art Newman uncoiled. "Don't you dare! There will be nothing for you! No company! Nothing you want! Do you hear me? You know the rule! Nothing for you!" he bellowed, unleashing from on high the fury of a jealous god.

Crushjoy managed to pull his client down just as the judge's gavel sounded. "One more outburst like that, Mr. Newman, and you can watch the rest of these proceedings on TV . . . in the U.S. Marshal's detention quarters!" Judge Wetherborne nodded to Joon Newman to answer.

Joon's eyes widened and then blinked rapidly. He peered around: at the judge, at the jury, and the courtroom spectators. He seemed momentarily incapacitated, as though his father's words—reaching over and behind his back—had grabbed the imaginary cable that plugged him in and ripped it out of the wall.

"It's been touted by your father as *the ultimate intellectual property,* " Will embellished for effect. "What exactly makes up the Wholly WORD?"

Joon took a deep breath. "First . . . "—he began to speak slowly and deliberately, but there was a telling quaver in his voice: of rage, of fear, of the unknown—"you have to understand how the Wholly WORD logs you on. That's done with the Wholly WORD credit card software," Joon explained. "The first time the user signs up, he punches in his credit card number and executes a click-on agreement. Each time his grill dials up, the Wholly WORD automatically recognizes his grill, turns it on, and charges the credit card three ninety-five per hour."

Joon cast his eyes down, perhaps in shame that he was associated in some way with the scheme he was about to describe. Lenny, too, lowered his head. The jury had seen his credit card problems. Where he used to run into trouble purchasing more software and "tech-cessories" than he could possibly use, blowups of his new bills had displayed for the jury page upon page of on-line charges to THINKSOFT SANTA TOSTADA CA.

"All right." Will pressed ahead. "So now that we are logged on, can you tell us what the customer is paying for? In other words, what does the Wholly WORD technology do when it remotely controls the laser flames?"

"The Wholly WORD contains a simple switching device," Joon answered, in the plain English that Will had hoped for. Displaying his game-playing digital dexterity, Joon twirled the information vessel in his hand a few times like a drum major. "In other words, all the Wholly WORD does is remotely switch on the user's grill. All the calibrations of the laser flames are done from a tiny computer inside the user's own grill. Instead of paying three ninety-five an hour, times hundreds of hours, all the user needs in his grill is a three-dollar switch from Radio Shack."

"But the user can't install his own switch because, under the terms of Exhibit A—the shrink-wrap license—he's forbidden from making any modifications to the grill. Right?"

"That's right. Abracadabra Exhibit A. Under the spell it casts, he can't even take it apart to *find out* that all he needs is a switch."

Joon shook his head in disgust. The jurors' mouths were curled at the corners as though they had just been told that the bacon Art Newman served them for breakfast was an imitation made from salted smoked rat meat.

"All right, then, is there anything else in the Wholly WORD besides software that takes your credit card and switches on your grill?" Will asked, summarizing Joon's testimony for the benefit of the jury.

A pained Joon dropped his head another notch onto his chest before disclosing the secret. When he leaned forward abruptly, his chin grazed the witness microphone as he spoke. "Nothing."

The loudspeaker screeched with a jarring spasm. His words reverberated in the silent courtroom. Joon instinctively put his hand over his mouth, apparently embarrassed, not just by the clumsy mistake but by the sound of his true voice—set free, for the first time in years, uninsulated by layer upon layer of characters, personas, and avatars.

"There is nothing else," Joon repeated. He sat straighter, this time finding more strength in his own voice.

Will wanted to reach out and shake him into full realization: *You did it! You've reached the highest level! What you've done is unspeakably unselfish and brave. You're a hero beyond your wildest dreams!* But he couldn't do that. They were in the middle of a trial, and right now it was Will who was confined to a role—that of trial attorney and Joon's questioner.

Although the evidence was now in, Will had the urge to reach for something more. "Tell us, please, who is the chief architect behind the Wholly Grill technology?"

"The man I have referred to until now as the Sorcerer," he said grimly. "To be precise, Arthur Newman, Senior. He's my father." It was the first time Engineer and Dreamer had spoken as one.

"I see. Now, do you have any personal knowledge as to the *reasons* your father developed Wholly Grill?"

"Objection." Crushjoy's voice had lost some its robustness, and he was no longer bolting up from his seat. "Calls for speculation. This witness has no personal knowledge of another's thought processes. He's not a mind reader. And it's totally irrelevant."

Crushjoy was right. The question was out-of-bounds by any legal measure, as wide open as the one Will had asked Santa Tostada to divine the night before. Except this time it was to help Joon.

"It's relevant to show intent, Your Honor," Will countered sincerely. He also hadn't forgotten the treatment he'd received from Crushjoy in Judge Lifo's courtroom. "And if anyone is qualified to explain reasons, it is this witness, the chief designer and developer of reasonware itself. We have a right to explore the reasons resident in the mind of the defendant's chief architect behind the Wholly Grill."

The judge lifted his eyebrows in appreciation of Joon's qualifications. Will noticed that the judge glanced at his computer at the side of his bench, which had to be loaded with ThinkSoft reasonware. "Overruled."

Thurston Crushjoy dropped to his seat and threw his MontBlanc pen on the counsel table in disgust.

Joon Newman took off his thick glasses, exposing the vulnerable boy he was. He began speaking, haltingly at first, and from a distant past. "When I was really little, my mother and I . . . we would have fun together. She taught me games. We would play. She would take me to the zoo and to the circus. I loved the animals there. She told me stories: stories about people, animals, and happenings that couldn't be fully explained. . . . "

"Go on," Will said, nodding his encouragement.

"My father . . . he was mean to her. And I was . . . well, *he* thought I had a gift for computers. He only cared about money and having control. He made it more and more difficult for me to be with her . . . to do fun stuff together. He never understood her. She was the most beautiful woman. . . . " Joon's eyes drifted to the back of the courtroom. He was gazing at Persi.

"He made her crazy, and she was taken away. . . . " Joon bit his lip. "I threw myself at computer games to not go crazy myself. I felt that's what she would want. It was about games and stories . . . .

He stopped speaking. It was perfectly quiet in the courtroom.

"But ever since I was little," Joon began again, " my father took more and stronger measures to hold sway over me, to keep me from what I cared for. That's why I call him the Sorcerer . . . in the game I'm forced to play. The spells, you know.

"When I was twelve, he introduced me to cigarettes. At first I thought it was fun, but of course I got hooked. I was competing already on the computer game circuit. He made me do computer programming, which I hated. That's how I invented reasonware. Getting my hands on the cigarettes I craved was connected to how quickly I could do the programming. Then, when I wanted to quit smoking a year ago, my father sent me to a quit-smoking program on a ranch he said he'd heard about. The treatment worked really well. It was easy to quit.

"Well, they served lots of barbecue there. I couldn't get enough of it. It turns out I was one of the first experimental rats when Wholly Grill was still in beta testing; I just didn't know it. I became the first addict of Wholly Grill.

"Then he used it to control me. Before it was finally in the store, he controlled my supply. 'None for you,' he'd say, 'without'—whatever new code he wanted. It wasn't until I heard about this lawsuit that I suspected there was a connection to my own Wholly Grill craving."

He rubbed his temples with both hands and took a deep breath. Not a breath in the courtroom was heard.

"I found out a long time ago that, as far as my father was concerned, I belonged to him. That's when he became the Sorcerer in my eyes, and my entire life became this dangerous game: my object; to survive and escape, but with little hope of a way out. It was always *program, program,* so I could make him rich and powerful. *That's* the whole reason he invented Wholly Grill."

His voice quivered. "All I ever wanted was to do what I love: to play . . . to explore . . . to reach new levels. Instead, I am a stranger to my own childhood. I didn't care about all the rest of this! I'm very tired. I just want to live my life freely."

The young man broke down, burying his head in his hands.

Members of the jury were now sniffling and quietly shedding tears. Will sat down and stared at the floor, out of quiet respect, waiting for the witness to compose himself before announcing he had no further questions. Suddenly there was a loud *honk*!—a man, sodden with tears, blowing his nose. It was Judge Wetherborne.

"We will recess . . . until one-thirty," the judge managed to declare.

Will poured a glass of water at his table and took it to Joon, who was still seated. He patted him on the arm and thanked him quietly before he left the courtroom. Out in the hallway, Persi met Will and wrapped her arms around him. Lenny met the two of them and folded all three of them into a *burrito grande.*

"Super Chill, I thought you'd never get here," Persi playacted. "You were great."

"Are you kidding?" Will protested. "Burying Art Newman was your doing. From initial scoop to Destination Landfill."

"Thank you, thank you, thank you!" Lenny gushed over both of them, tears streaming from his face. "Lady J's smiling down on us! I can feel it!"

As the three of them held one another, Will looked over Persi's shoulder to where he could see a television monitor perched on the desk of a security guard. Edwin was beaming out at his LNTV audience.

"Yes, it was a terrific examination. Simple and clear. He spotlighted his witness, and let him tell the story without getting in the way. Really textbook. I trained him, you know."

After a long recess that extended from ten-thirty through the lunch hour, Judge Wetherborne began the afternoon session by announcing that he was denying ThinkSoft's motions for nonsuit and sanctions against Lenny's attorneys; there was now more than ample evidence to have the jury decide whether Lenny had become addicted to Wholly Grill.

That's when Crushjoy struck back with a vengeance. Taking a page out of his book *Claims Refusal*, he and his associates served a voluminous motion on the judge. The argument was that, although it was possible the jury could decide to award some modest compensation to Lenny Milton, the request to certify a class should be denied, dismissing the class-action portion without further proceedings.

"Mr. Crushjoy does make a valid point, Mr. Ostermyer," the judge said. "Your complaint is on behalf of millions of addicts. We have only seen two. Why should we eat up six more months of court time treating your case like a class action when there's no class?"

"Your honor," Crushjoy persisted. "The suit was filed on behalf of ten million *supposed* addicts. Recall that plaintiff must prove that defendant had an intent to addict and *did* addict members of the class. Are we to believe that all ten million in this alleged class—save for two with an ax to grind—are in complete and silent denial together? A mass conspiracy of silence of staggering proportions? It's preposterous! Swift dismissal of the class is called for."

Following extended arguments on these issues outside the presence of the jury, the judge recessed for the day. Unless Edwin produced another witness on this issue before he rested his case, the judge might grant the newest thermonuclear motion from the Kilgore Crushjoy war machine.

‹ 36 ›

STUDIO ANCHOR: *Good morning. I'm Janet Jones in New York, and this is the Lawsuit Network with day six of the Barbecue Addiction trial, a rare unusual Saturday session. We heard dramatic testimony yesterday from Joon Newman about his own addiction, suffered at the hands of his scheming father. Let's go to Ben Griswold outside the courtroom in San Jose. Tell us, Ben, about the latest move by the defense.*

TRIAL COMMENTATOR: *Mr. Crushjoy, always a brilliant defense strategist, has done the math, Janet. He knows if he can cut the case down to one ten millionth of its size, it would be a huge saving for ThinkSoft, both in dollars and face. Even if another class action were filed, Crushjoy and ThinkSoft know that they would have years to prepare the case and recruit armies of scientists, accountants, and barbecue experts.*

STUDIO ANCHOR: *What will Mr. Ostermyer do?*

TRIAL COMMENTATOR: *Never one to shy away from creating a sensation, Mr. Ostermyer is calling one more witness . . . none other than Snapple Johnson!*

STUDIO ANCHOR: *Snapple Johnson! What can he possibly say that will help Mr. Ostermyer's case?*

TRIAL COMMENTATOR: *We have no idea, Janet. Before his murder case was dismissed with Judge Lifo's infamous ruling, polls showed that 89 percent of Americans believed Johnson was incapable of telling the truth.*

His name has become synonymous with shameless prevarication. He is universally despised for gunning down his wife along with several innocent bystanders and getting away with it. I don't think I am going out on a limb in saying that Mr. Ostermyer is taking a big risk, especially after things went so well for his client yesterday.

Snapple Johnson was indeed a free man, thanks to the QE Deluxe brand of ThinkSoft reasonware and based upon deduction that was so convoluted and backwards that the Honorable Robert J. Lifo did not hesitate in boldly and decisively yielding to the twisted logic, dismissing all charges. Now, Johnson actually seemed to believe in his own infallibility—that he could deny anything and be vindicated by the powerful artificial intelligence software.

"Plaintiff calls Snapple Johnson, formerly known as A. J. 'Big Apple' Johnson, as a witness in these proceedings," Edwin announced.

Sharply dressed in a Versace suit of gray sateen wool, Johnson stepped into the witness box after being sworn in. He was a peculiarly handsome man, combining rugged good looks with a face that conjured up the butt of a thousand jokes. An outcast of the black community from where he came, Johnson managed to maintain an odd assortment of friends and zealous supporters who were mostly white. When Dr. Elizabeth Stone profiled him in her "What's Their Problem Anyway?" column, she observed that Snapple Johnson had actually come to resemble the beverage moniker he'd only recently adopted, "a stout English breakfast tea mixed with apples, raspberries, and overripe bananas, producing a strange and muddled brew."

It was also apparent that—without another bribe from the Apple Growers, who had toxically dumped Johnson's endorsement on a competitor's turf—there was little chance he would be adopting the name Diet Snapple anytime soon. Since retiring from baseball, the former home-run king had gone from a big all-around athlete to a bigger rounder former athlete, especially since taking up the Grill.

"Mr. Johnson," Edwin began, "you were a chain smoker for a couple of years after you retired. Is that right?"

"That's right. I could quit at any time. And that's what I did."

"But didn't you buy your first Wholly Grill at the same time that you quit smoking?"

"I did indeed," he said, with a fond smile. "I'm crazy about my little grill." Abruptly and devoid of cause, a dark cloud spread over his face. "But I am *not* insane!" he snapped. His eyes grew large, unflinchingly intense, and cold as iced tea. Defiantly, he searched the courtroom for would-be doubters. No one could believe what he just said, but everyone looked down or away to avoid seeing his suddenly fierce demeanor.

A moment passed. Johnson seemed calm again. Edwin continued. "Tell the jury how you are spending your time away from baseball."

"When I'm not out on the road on business, I like to hang in my backyard, just kickin' back and firin' up my Grill." Then he added, "And, of course, I'm always looking for my wife's killers."

"Of course," Edwin conceded, with a patronizing nod. "And when you are at home, approximately how many bottles of Wholly Grill sauce do you consume on a given day?"

"I *choose* to knock eight to ten bottles outa here a day. It's a free country. I'm free to do as I please!" he said, glancing around the courtroom for challengers again. "And I freely *choose*."

"Now, Mr. Johnson, as I am sure you are aware, there are people who doubt you—your innocence in the criminal matter, your stature as a role model, your commitment to finding the real killers—and, now, whether you freely choose. Your doubters say that *you* are an addict." Edwin was priming his witness, making sure the engine would roar upon ignition.

A visibly agitated Johnson deftly reached into his inside coat pocket with his right index finger. As most people in the courtroom trained their eyes on Edwin, striding across the room to retrieve an exhibit, Johnson quickly poked his finger in his mouth and rubbed something on his gums.

Edwin held up a bottle of Wholly Grill and continued. "So tell us, Mr. Johnson, what you have to say. Do you consider that you have a problem with the sauce, as it were?" There were some giggles from the gallery. Indeed, Edwin seemed in a particularly good mood after yesterday's advances.

Johnson waited a moment before speaking, both to give his response greater emphasis and to finish massaging his gums with his tongue. "I can quit anytime. The answer is *'abso . . . lutely* not!'"

This was too much. A number of people gasped and guffawed. He was more over-the-top than his impersonators on late-night TV, except he was for real.

"Do you consider that you have ever been an abuser of Wholly Grill?" asked Edwin.

"No! I have *never* abused *anyone* or *anything!*" he shouted, above a cacophony of snorting, chortling, and tittering. Obviously outnumbered, Johnson simply held his head high, pretending to be above his doubters.

"I strongly object to this 'evidence,'" Crushjoy bellowed, rising to address the judge. "It lacks the barest logic. Mr. Ostermyer offers this testimony as proof that there is a class of addicts out there, but his own witness denies any such thing."

"How curious!" Edwin scoffed. "Surely the defendant is not objecting to testimony it believes favors its position." Then he looked reverently at the jurors as he spoke. "The jury will decide what the evidence means."

"Overruled. Proceed, Mr. Ostermyer," the judge said, with a faint grin.

"Mr. Johnson, now tell us truthfully, did you become addicted yourself to Wholly Grill?"

In what appeared to be staging carefully blocked out, Johnson turned so that his body squarely faced the jurors. Except it looked like he couldn't bring himself all the way around. His head remained turned to one side, his eyes fixed on Edwin, as he proclaimed to the jury, "I absolutely one hundred percent categorically deny it!"

Rollicking laughter, volcanic in magnitude, erupted and rolled through the courtroom. Edwin remained as preposterously deadpan as Johnson was self-righteous. That compounded the reaction. People both on and off the jury were laughing so hard—at Snapple Johnson's unwitting parody of himself, at the lawyer's histrionics, and out of their own need to let off steam after a long week of strictly regimented lunacy—that they were leaning way back in their seats, gasping. One such reveler, a fifty-seven-year old alternate juror, employed as an analyst for a major mutual fund, who'd denied any prior knowledge of Wholly Grill in his juror questionnaire, began spewing milk five to eight feet out in a 180-degree arc, a Rain Bird lawn sprinkler gone berserk.

"Mistrial! Move for mistrial!" Crushjoy shouted above the bedlam, thereby causing the mutual fund analyst to abruptly reverse his spigot in the direction of the great defense lawyer. Splattered, white fluid dripping from his impervious jaw, Thurston Crushjoy still managed to remain stoic.

But it was too late for a mistrial. The FBI barged into the courtroom and arrested Art Newman. Judge Wetherborne had been expecting them. The jury was excused so that Art Newman could stand before the judge and promptly enter his plea to a battery of felony charges involving federal truth-in-advertising laws, the Food and Drug Act, mail fraud, and animal cruelty.

Before Art Newman was led off in handcuffs, the U.S. Attorney presented the judge with a proposed warrant to search ThinkSoft headquarters for a list of items that could lead to more incriminating evidence. Judge Wetherborne looked over the warrant carefully; then, on his own initiative, he asked his clerk, Mr. Danning, to retrieve Exhibit A from the trial evidence, the Wholly Grill End User License Agreement. Reading it over—his left eye perceptibly rattling at the exhibit—the judge proceeded to copy ThinkSoft's own words onto the warrant so as to compel public disclosure of the very materials that Lenny Milton had supposedly agreed were trade secrets. Copying in longhand, the judge extended the reach of the search warrant by adding ThinkSoft's hyperlegal gibberish, giving marshals the right to seize anything having to do with "know-how relating to the Information Sauce" or anything else "relating to the Information System or which depends for its creation or operation on the Wholly WORD."

The judge signed the warrant and handed it back to the U.S. Attorney. Crushjoy, standing by Art Newman—his jacket and tie still wet from the events that had abruptly brought the trial to an end objected to the judge's handwritten addition as being too broad and too vague, possibly covering any kind of information in the company's possession. The judge read it over again, considered the objection, and then wrote in more verbiage designed to root out any damning evidence that could be found about ThinkSoft's development and illicit use of the Electronic Truth Serum. With that, he sounded the gavel and retired to his chambers.

Outside the federal building in San Jose, the sun was shining. All proceedings before Judge Wetherborne were adjourned for the day, and his courtroom remained dark and silent. It was still only 10:30 A.M.; out in the open, the morning air was warming, booting up, throughout the Valley. Nearby, in Saint Chip, the bright sun bounced off all the gleaming ThinkSoft buildings, as it always did. On this day, light shined *into* them, too.

Epilogue

The next day, after seeing Snapple Johnson's testimony on the evening news, millions of users went public with their addiction to Wholly Grill. The television image of Snapple Johnson caused them to be "gravely alarmed, maybe repulsed, by the mirror of their own denial," in the words of Dr. Elizabeth Stone in her morning column. So many people offered to testify that Edwin had to set up a witness intake system in the firm lobby, complete with a deli number-dispenser machine. Edwin considered it the key to bringing the trial and the billion-dollar class action to a successful conclusion. By default, management of the system was entrusted to the New Receptionist.

None of the witnesses testified, however. The trial was over. Art Newman's arrest forced him to resign under the company bylaws, resulting in Joon's gaining control of ThinkSoft. Will sat down with Joon and his lawyer, Angela De Nuevo, and promptly worked out a settlement. Joon was eager to wipe his hands of the company's tainted profits. The plug was pulled on the Wholly Grill division, and all the ill-gotten gains were plowed into treatment centers and court-administered payouts to class members. After the agreement was signed, Lenny accepted Joon's invitation to room together, courtesy of ThinkSoft, in a new treatment program at the Betty Ford Center in Rancho Mirage.

When Lenny's payout check arrived, it was formally presented to him at the kickoff party for the newly opened Law Offices of Will Swanson. Among those attending and cheering on the achievement were both Mary Beth and Roderick Swanson, who braved it all the way down from Pacific Heights to be there. From his new office, in the heart of Santa Tostada, Will's favorite cause now was opposing those who would infringe on the rights of others to use ideas and information freely found in the public domain.

While doing time at Lompoc—and since Wholly Grill was no longer a trade secret—Art Newman applied for a patent on "a gender-neutral formula and method for inducing nasal lactation in humans." Its commercial potential is still unclear. He told *Hard Copy* that the side effect in humans had not been discovered during beta testing of Wholly Grill, and he *still* didn't know why it happened. But to apply for a patent, he didn't need to know; the patent laws only required that he disclose *how* to make milk come out of a man's nose—or a woman's, for that matter. Doctors and scientists are still baffled by the etiology of this phenomenon.

The lawsuit against Persi was dismissed within days under Joon's direction. She ended up landing Jake MacAully's job for the *San Jose Mercury News* as the tech reporter assigned solely to hot trends; Jake was drummed out after thoroughly missing the real story of the Wholly Grill. Persi also landed a two-book deal: the first, an exposé of the Wholly Grill case for the general trade, and another on the uses and abuses of shrink-wrap licenses, geared for the software industry, that included a number of fair-minded forms created by Will. Persi's editor told her the publisher was thinking of generating more revenue by packaging her industry book with a shrink-wrap license.

"Oh, don't get me started!" Persi said, vaulting out of her chair.

Exhibit:__A__

WHOLLY GRILL END USER LICENSE AGREEMENT

By breaking the seal and accessing the Wholly Grill Outdoor Cooking Information System ("the Information System"), you agree that you will only use the Information System according to the terms and conditions of this license agreement ("this License Agreement") between you and ThinkSoft Corporation ("the Company"):

1. The Company grants you a nonexclusive worldwide perpetual license, unless sooner terminated as provided herein, to use and operate the Information System, but only as delimited by this License Agreement.

2. You will only use the Information System when connected by the Information System modem to the proprietary outdoor cooking information and control server hosted by the Company, namely, the Wholly WAN (Wide Area Network) Optimization of Research and Development ("the Wholly WORD"). In no event shall the Company be responsible for your inability to connect with the Wholly WORD or for any interruption of service you may experience, including loss or spoliation of meats, fish and other perishables.

3. You agree to use Wholly Grill Outdoor Cooking Information System Barbecue Sauce with Smoke Crystals ("the Information Sauce") and only the Information Sauce in connection with your operation of the Information System and no other sauce or marinade, whether purchased or homemade. Use of any sauce other than the Information Sauce, or use of the Information Sauce on any system other than the Information System, could result in injury or death for which the Company cannot be held responsible.

4. You agree that your operation of the Information System will only be for your personal and private use and enjoyment, such as food preparation in your home. Without limiting the generality of the foregoing, you agree not to make any commercial or for-profit use of the Information System, such rights being expressly reserved to the Company.

5. You agree that all formulations, recipes, testing, studies, manufacturing data and specifications and other know-how relating to the Information System, the Information Sauce, and the Wholly WORD are the intellectual property and trade secrets of the Company, and under no circumstances shall you have the right to inspect or have access

to such trade secrets, even if you bring legal action against the Company. You further agree that you, or anyone acting on your behalf, will not reverse engineer, modify, disassemble, decompile, or take apart (for the purpose of learning the trade secrets) the Information System, the Information Sauce, Wholly Grill Linkin' Buddies, or any other product of the Company relating to the Information System or which depends for its creation or operation on the Wholly WORD.

6. You agree and understand that the Wholly Grill is an outdoor cooking information system and not a barbecue grill. You accept the information "as is" without any warranties or guarantees, including warranties of merchantability or fitness for any particular purpose. The information is provided solely for your personal dining entertainment. If you desire to achieve or avoid any particular result, you should consult a professional barbecuist.

7. In the event of any breach by you of any material term of this License Agreement, the Company reserves the right to terminate this License Agreement immediately and repossess the Information System, no ownership having been transferred to you. The terms of this License Agreement are enforced by the Society of Manufacturers for the Enforcement of Licenses ("SMEL"), including its K-9 Division. You consent to the entry of SMEL personnel and K-9 officers in your home or on your premises for the purpose of enforcing, or ensuring compliance with, the terms of this License Agreement.

8. The Company warrants that the Information System and the Information Sauce will operate in conformity with the User Manual and documentation sold herewith. Other than such warranted use, you agree that the Company shall not be responsible for any misuse of the Information System or the Information Sauce or any damages of any kind or nature, and you assume the risk of any injury or death whatsoever arising from any such nonconforming uses.

WE HOPE YOU ENJOY YOUR WHOLLY GRILL EXPERIENCE. IF YOU HAVE ANY QUESTIONS OR COMMENTS, FEEL FREE TO CALL THE WHOLLY GRILL DIVISION OF THINKSOFT ON ITS TOLL-FREE CUSTOMER SATISFACTION HOTLINE.

Acknowledgments

Platters of the juciest thanks go out to the following people:

Laura Witter, a fellow writer, for her countless readings and smart suggestions; Evelyn Davidson, a reader friend not afraid to tell another friend the truth; David Thoreau, veteran writer and family friend, for his support and guidance; Frank Lauria, novelist and teacher, for his always-sound advice; Liz Trupin-Pulli, my agent, for her keen eye, dedication, and magical powers; and Philip Turner, my editor, for his vision, sense of humor, and guiding hand.

To one and all, my heartfelt gratitude.